PRAISE FOR THE UNTAMED SERIES

"Dyer packs a punch with *Divided*! As we've come to expect from her, the pages are packed with vivid imagery, high tension, and an earnest and willful heroine. Another great read in an intriguing saga."
Tracy Clark, author of The Light Key Trilogy & *Mirage*

"*Divided* is a powerful novel full of disturbing mental manipulation and a powerful protagonist who is determined to pull through. It's highly addictive, and impossible to put down. Best cliffhanger yet!"
S.E. Anderson, author of *Starstruck*

"A fantastic dystopian tale. Highly recommended for fans of strong heroines and intriguing sci-fi worlds."
Pintip Dunn, *New York Times* bestselling author of the Forget Tomorrow series

"A YA Mad Max—thrilling and deep, with richly drawn characters and spot-on pacing. […] Dyer's Untamed series is a must-read for dystopian fans."
T.A. Maclagan, author of *They Call Me Alexandra Gastone*

"Fascinating and intriguing."
A Drop of Ink Reviews

"Dyer is as much a poet as a dystopian scribe."
Marissa Kennerson, author of *The Family*

"Strong writing and well-rounded characters."
Heidi Sinnett, author and librarian

"While Dyer provides all the elements you're looking for in an action-packed dystopian adventure, I also found her message about women and their rights to be very timely. *Fragmented* and Dyer both have layers that are worth exploring."
Kimberly Sabatini, author of *Touching the Surface*

"A kick-butt story with amazing characters and outstanding world building."
Readcommendations

"Highly recommended."
Dr. Jessie Voigts, *WanderingEducators.com*

"Dyer writes with an urgency and a rhythm that compels you to turn the page."
Sue Wyshynski, author of The Butterfly Code series

"*Untamed* is a fantastic dystopian survival story, filled with twists."
The Literature Hub

"As a person who rarely reads fantasy/sci-fi but grew up with it always on the nightstand, Dyer's book reawakened in me a buried love for the genre."
Jen Knox, author of *After the Gazebo*

"Readers who enjoy dystopian novels would enjoy this book."
The Story Sanctuary

ALSO AVAILABLE FROM MADELINE DYER

THE UNTAMED SERIES

UNTAMED
FRAGMENTED
DIVIDED

COMING SOON...
DESTROYED

STANDALONE NOVELS FROM THE UNTAMED WORLD

A DANGEROUS GAME

This book is a work of fiction. Names, characters, places, and incidents either are the product of the author's imagination or are used fictitiously. Any resemblance to actual events, locales, organizations, or persons, living or dead, is entirely coincidental and beyond the intent of either the author or the publisher.

Divided
Copyright © 2017 Madeline Dyer
All rights reserved.

Madeline Dyer asserts the moral right to be identified as the author of this work.

First edition, July 2017
Published by Ineja Press

Edited by Michelle Dunbar
Cover and Interior Design by We Got You Covered Book Design

Print ISBN: 978-0-9957191-4-9
eBook ISBN: 978-0-9957191-5-6

All rights reserved. No part of this book may be reproduced, transmitted, downloaded, distributed, stored in or introduced into any information storage and retrieval systems, in any forms or by any means, whether electronic or mechanical, without the express written permission of the author, except for the purpose of a review which may quote brief passages.

The author can be contacted via email at Madeline@MadelineDyer.co.uk or through her website www.MadelineDyer.co.uk

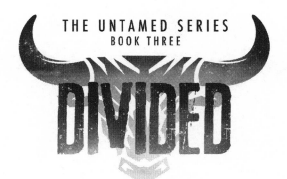

For Tom,

Stay Untamed and follow your dreams!

MADELINE DYER

INEJA PRESS

For Rachel, Alicen, and Rhiannon

ONE

I PLAY DEAD AS THE Enhanced Ones' leader checks on me.

His steps are light as he treads around my body. A second later, something nudges my arm. His foot, probably. I grit my teeth and try not to move. Mustn't move, because then the pain will start. And then he'll know. He'll know he's winning, know that part of me—the tiniest part—wants the augmenters he's holding. I can picture them now, those tiny vials. Pale blue liquids. Pastel oranges. Deep pinks, with the subtlest hint of silver accentuated by the light.

It's been so long since that first concoction wore off... *Too* long. Saliva pools under the left side of my tongue and against my cheek. My chest feels strange, light, as if my lungs are floating away and I need to breathe deeper, stronger, to keep them. Sweat breaks out across my forehead; I feel it, like a shoal of tiny, slimy fish, wriggling and plunging into my soul.

You need them, Seven.

A sour taste fills my mouth.

No.

No.

DIVIDED

No.

I squeeze my already-tight fists harder, clench them as much as I can. Pain leaks through my bruised, aching knuckles. But my fingers are stronger now than before, than after Manning broke them and Jed set them as best as he could. Someone here must've fixed them, or partially fixed them, when I was unconscious, because I know if I unclench my fists, each finger will be straight and perfect again. I shudder, and the scratchy fabric of the strappy top I'm wearing catches on a sore bit on my back. Thinking about the clothes makes something inside me tighten; I had on a white dress when I was caught. Someone changed me when I was unconscious. My new clothes—the top and a pair of dark leggings—feel wrong.

"You're running lean, Shania." Raleigh's voice is brisk, business-like. He's standing over me; I can sense him. "It's been nearly eight hours since Tomas gave you those augmenters. And I was *so* disappointed when Amara told me you forcibly resisted a top-up an hour ago…after all *this* too. Come on. Open your eyes and take them willingly. I'd rather not force them into you like Tomas did."

Three. My brother's name is Three.

My hands start to shake. I try to push them more firmly against my sides, but the movement stirs a stronger angle of the yearning within me. I can smell the augmenters, *smell* them. My stomach tightens. Mustn't take any more. Need to remain in control, need to feel my own emotions, not what Raleigh wants me to feel.

But it felt good…and you were calm earlier, when you arrived here….

Raleigh's clothing rustles as he bends down. A second passes, then his breath brushes the side of my face, too close. Every part of me screams to run away. But I don't move, I won't open my eyes.

"You do understand that I own your soul now, Shania?" Raleigh whispers, and the whisper crawls over me, the words bloated and heavy. "Shall I tell you how this works? Is that a *yes*? Excellent. These Promise Marks on your body—"

He touches my jaw. I shriek. My eyes spring open. Raleigh's face looms over me. I see myself in his eyes: my own fading mirrors blink back at me, and—

My gaze jerks to the augmenters in his hands, so close. They're in a small, wooden rack, and the vials poke upward like spring shoots bringing new life. Bright green. No Calmness this time. My stomach twists. The intensity of the color hurts my eyes.

Don't look at them, Seven. Just get away. You have to get away, save everyone while you can. While you still have the chance.

And I know the voice is right. Raleigh mustn't make me use my powers, mustn't make me end the Untamed.

Raleigh smiles; his lips peel back to reveal perfect teeth that are too big, too white, too bright. "These marks, here," he says, touching my jaw slowly and deliberately, "are the result of your soul being delivered to me. Your soul is connected to your body in life, just as your Seer powers are anchored to your soul. These beautiful Promise Marks are inscribed on your soul *and* all it controls—your body, your Seer powers. My stamp on you. If I have your soul, I can control your body *and* your powers. And I *do* have your soul." He blinks slowly. "Do not underestimate *my* power, Shania. You may be *the special Seer*, but *I* am powerful."

My heart pounds, and I struggle to turn my head away—mustn't look at the augmenters, or his eyes, or me in them—but pain flares across my temples the moment my gaze falls on the opposite wall, red bricks. His touch gets hotter.

"No, I don't want you to look away from me."

His voice creeps through me, and I'm forced to look up at him. More pain dives through me, and there's so much of it. Raleigh smiles, and his fingers curl around my jaw for a long second, then he removes his hand and brushes his fingers off on his jacket.

"I can make you do *anything*." He looks back at me. "I can control your body and your Seer powers *whenever* I want to—they are bound together and to me, and if you resist my control, I'll burn your soul. You'll feel it through your whole body. It will hurt you a lot. Unbearable pain. And you don't want that, do you? Pain is bad. Isn't it, Shania?" The words are loaded.

My breathing speeds up. This is different to the first time the Enhanced had me, a couple of months ago. Then, they wanted to seem nice, because they knew they'd have to let me go so I could become the Seer the augury speaks of, and if I *wanted* to join them again, on my own accord, it would make their job in converting me a second time easier.

Everything at the compound was so pleasant then.

But Raleigh's not wearing pale blue now—none of them have been—and there's no sweet smell of honey in the air. No bed either, no teddy bear. No food. Just a toilet bucket. Because they've got me. Raleigh owns me, he's got what he's always wanted. And for a people supposedly concerned with equality and being happy, Raleigh doesn't seem to care how I'm treated. I'm just an object now. His property. His weapon.

Maybe once he's used me to wipe out the Untamed, he'll treat me nicer, like a person.

But you won't be alive then. You'll die when the war ends.

I try to look behind him, to where the door is, but invisible hands grab my chin, stop me from moving my head.

"My darling butterfly, just accept the fact: you *are* going to save everyone. And that's a *fantastic* thing to do."

My stomach hardens. Converting the Untamed into humanity-less automatons who only feel positive emotions is not *saving* them. And killing the ones we can't convert isn't saving them either.

The Promise Marks over my body burn, along with the memories. I try to ignore the gold splashes, pretend they aren't there, that my dark skin isn't covered with them—but it's impossible. And they keep moving, faster at times, then slower at others. I watched one earlier—a gold mark on my arm that looked a bit like an avenging eagle—watched it swoop down my arm and grow into a bigger blob, before it merged with another, then stretched out to meet the fingers of new splash. My very own lava lamp.

Raleigh clicks his tongue. "Shania, just take the augmenters. The longer you stall, the longer those poor Untamed creatures will suffer. And you know it's right. Deep down. You made your decision the moment you gave yourself to us."

I clench my jaw even tighter, until my gums throb. That's *not* what happened.

My hand goes to my chest, reaching for my mother's pendant—the Seer pendant—but my fingers slap bare skin.

It's not there.

My body tightens. I clench my fists as I sit up, force Raleigh and the augmenters to retreat a few inches. I try not to look at him, or the glass vials.

"Where is it?" My voice is blunt.

"Where's what, Shania?" He smiles in a way that's supposed to be sweet and endearing, a look that, in reality, is anything but.

"My Seer pendant—my mother's pendant."

He snorts, then sets the augmenters at my feet. The glass vials make a *chink-chink* sound against each other in the wooden rack. "Oh, Shania. You won't need that here. No chance of getting lost in the Dream Land. That's another reason why being a Chosen One is *so* much safer."

I grit my teeth, feel sweat drip down the back of my neck. "I *need* it."

"You don't need it, my darling. You need *these*. Look how aggressive you are without them." He takes an augmenter out of the rack, waits for me to grasp it.

I shiver, pull my hands together, clench them, try to stop them shaking. My head pounds.

"Shania, my dear. You're running *far* too lean. Pain and unease are written all over your face. Don't you want those feelings to go? Don't you *want* to be happy?"

I stare at him. He asks the questions, yet it's *him* who's keeping me in a prison cell. Raleigh only wants me to be happy when I've agreed to make his life easier.

He encases my hands with one of his before I have a chance to react. With his other hand, he presses the vial into my palms, then makes my fingers curl around it. It's cold.

My gaze drops to the augmenter. Harlequin green. The ache in my chest gets bigger, stronger, pulls right through me, a ragged cavern widening. I force myself to look away.

"I want my pendant back." My hands shake against the glass vial, and Raleigh holds my fingers around it tighter, exerts pressure. My eyes narrow. "I don't care if it's useless here. I want my pendant back."

I *need* it back.

It's my connection to the Dream Land.

The Dream Land that the Gods and Goddesses banished me from, believing I ignored Seeing dreams... when really it was Jed. It was all him. Raleigh's son. Heat swipes across my neck as I think of him, of what he did.

I *must* get back to the Dream Land. I need the Gods and Goddesses to know what really happened, not what it looked like. If I have my pendant, then somehow I can contact Death, and the other Gods and Goddesses, and this can all get sorted out: they can reverse Raleigh's control over my soul. I just need my pendant.

Raleigh shakes his head, then inclines it slightly. "Only wild Untamed Ones have Seer pendants."

I swallow hard, feel sicker, then jerk my hands from Raleigh's. The augmenter slides away from my touch. I shake my head, catch a glimpse of the door. My eyes linger on it. Raleigh's not controlling where I look now. The door's behind him. Locked—I heard him lock it. I try to think: the key, he's got to have the key on him…his pocket? Can I grab it, run, open the door, get out and—

But you wouldn't get very far, would you? Not when Raleigh can command your soul, your actions, your body, control you…like how he will when he makes you convert or kill the rest of your people who are still out there.

I shake my head again. The gold marks on my arms flash in my peripheral vision. I resisted him before, temporarily. I managed to run away from him for a short time, while out on the mountainside. I hold onto that. I have to believe there's still a way. That I can still fight him.

But I was Untamed then…and now I'm not. Am I? I don't even know. One augmenter is enough to start the conversion—but it finishes with the mind-conversion, when the person completely discards their old life and identity.

I haven't done that, but the tail-end allure of the augmenters is inside me still, and it's a spark that will grow and take over if it's fed.

And I can't fight the augmenters *and* him *and* me.

"Very well," Raleigh says. He unscrews the augmenter's lid and holds up the open vial. With his other hand, he pulls out a radio. "You know, your boyfriend is about to be taken to one of our conversion chambers. These poor Untamed, we're having to queue them up to be saved. But your boyfriend will soon be happy—don't worry, Shania. Mervin is just waiting for my instruction as to the level of his conversion treatment."

My breath catches on my teeth, makes a whistling sound.

Raleigh smiles. "Drink this, and I'll let you see him."

DIVIDED

The augmenter flashes in the light.
Corin.

"Before he's converted?" My head whirls, and ideas of quick plans of escape fill my mind. If we're together, it will be better. We'll have more of a chance then....

But he'll have still had an augmenter or two—they'd have injected him when they caught him. Their first priority is always planting the addiction to their augmenters, because it makes the conversion of our minds easier, if we're already experiencing the positive effects. And no one is really the same after an augmenter, even if they escape before they're completely and fully converted—which can take days for the strongest of Untamed.

Raleigh presses the vial to my lips. Sweetness. Feathers under my nostrils.

Phantom fingers massage my scalp.

"Yes. You can see him before he's converted. See? Don't say I'm not kind to you," Raleigh croons. "Don't call *me* the monster. You can even watch his conversion. Be there for him, welcome him after. But you have to drink this now, Shania. You have to do something for me if I'm going to do something for you."

His fingernail taps the vial, makes it vibrate against my bottom lip. I don't like the feeling of it, but I know Raleigh could just force my mouth open and tip the augmenter up, make me drink it.

But he's not. Not yet. And that seems important. He's still being nice. For the moment.

"Can't he stay Untamed?" I barely say the words, keep my sounds to the smallest of movements for fear of upsetting the vial. I know I sound desperate, and I know Corin will have had at least one augmenter anyway. "You've already got me. Just...just let Corin—and the rest of them—go and—"

Raleigh cuts me off with a crude laugh. "Shania, my dear butterfly. You are caught in the web, aren't you?"

"What?"

Mock-sympathy fills his face. "What sort of person

would I be if I did not save those poor people, but let them continue to suffer?" He shakes his head. "No. I cannot allow that. Suffering must end. Drink this, and I'll let you see your little boyfriend. We will go right away, as soon as you top up again. You're running far too lean, you're not thinking straight. You're letting the darkness of the Untamed life taint your vision. Come on, drink up, and then you can see him and be there when he's converted, make it easier for him."

I eye the closed door again, wonder if I've got time to run—and how fast Raleigh would be in stopping me...either physically or through my soul.

"Don't try anything." His voice is restrained. "The longer I have to hold this augmenter before you drink it, the more painful your little boyfriend's conversion will be."

My ears crackle, and, at first, I'm sure I can't have heard him correctly. He can't have said that because the Enhanced don't like violence or pain or....

But they tortured me. During my conversion at New Kimearo, they tortured me as they tried to convert my mind to their way of thinking. Told me it would stop if I accepted their way of life. I close my eyes for a second, feel ice in my blood.

And they are violent. They kill people. They—

Lies!

"Level two conversion... Level three...." Raleigh whispers. He points at the radio, and a drop of the green liquid splashes onto the floor. My eyes follow it. "They're just waiting for me to instruct them. Don't make me make it more painful than is necessary. Drink that augmenter *willingly*."

I stare at him, my mind frantic.

"Sometimes, you have to be cruel to be kind."

My heart thumps against my chest.

"Level four," Raleigh whispers.

My stomach twists. Corin can't go through a level four conversion. Not when it stays with you, and—

I snatch the augmenter, drink it. The sickliness coats

DIVIDED

the back of my front teeth like a thick syrup. I shudder, feel sick at what I've done.

But I can resist. I've done it before. I'll do it now. And I'll see Corin—and I will make myself think like an Untamed—and he'll be resisting too. I know he will. He's strong.

And somehow, Corin and I *will* escape and purge the augmenters from our bodies.

But you won't be the same. He *won't be the same.*

I inhale sharply, nausea increasing, and—

My mother's face flashes into my mind. For a second, she's here—all I can see.

Then she's gone.

I start to gag, but the feeling passes. I wait for the euphoria to rise, or whatever positive emotion will now control me.

"Good girl." Raleigh smiles. "Level one," he says into the radio.

Level one? I breathe hard, know I should feel relieved. But I don't. I feel cheated. Again. I wipe the back of my hand across my mouth, try to get rid of the saccharine taste of the augmenter.

"Administer another round of Calmness and Tranquility to Corin Eriksen," Raleigh continues. The radio hums, and he pushes his jacket sleeve up, looks at his watch. It's small and silver. "The new augmenter shipment should have arrived five minutes ago. Give him a blend before moving him to the conversion chamber as he'll be running lean again, and we don't want trouble in the corridors."

Oh Gods. No. No. No. My heart pounds. Corin *won't* be running lean…and neither will I… Escaping will be harder. And what if I'm wrong, assuming that he *can* resist? What if he can't? It happens sometimes… The weaker Untamed can't resist augmenters, and, after just one taste, the visit to a conversion chamber is practically unnecessary—though most often still done. And it won't just be one augmenter in his system… They'll have been filling him with them as much as they can, trying to make the conversion easier for them.

But Corin's not weak. He *will* fight. I know that, and I hold onto it.

Raleigh turns back to me and smiles as he presses a button on the radio. It stops humming. "It was always going to be a level one, Shania. The Enhanced don't believe in unnecessary violence, or unnecessary pain, suffering. We're good people. We're—"

I retch with no warning. Coughing and spluttering, I fall forward, end up on my hands and knees. A string of saliva flies from my mouth, hits the opposite wall.

Raleigh jumps back. "What are you doing? You can't vomit an augmenter, especially not Loyalty."

Loyalty? I feel like I've been slapped. He's increasing my loyalty to the Enhanced…making me….

Unless it increases my *natural* loyalty—to the Untamed?

I shake my head, try to clear it so I can think properly. My throat burns from the augmenter, doesn't feel nice at all.

"Come on." Raleigh pulls me up, then marches me out of the room and into the corridor.

My head feels strange, my limbs heavier. The Promise Marks on my back burn and make my top feel like it's scorching metal. I look at Raleigh, see the way his face pinches together. He's controlling my soul right now. I can see the effort it's taking him, and I understand why he wants me to at least take the augmenters willingly—to save him some energy. And knowing this, understanding what it's costing him, is important, I know that—can I use it against him? Resist his control so much that, overall, it weakens him? Then I could escape and….

To the left, I see a new door. I try to resist Raleigh's control, step toward it, put every ounce of my energy into moving to it. But I march straight past.

Raleigh chuckles.

The room he takes me to is clinical. Bright light, one

DIVIDED

window, white walls, a ceramic floor. A counter with various instruments on it. I see a scalpel; it reminds me of a nightmare I had, one where Raleigh carved my eyes out. Or tried to. The details seem foggy now. A part of me wonders whether he's still using my eyes, using that tracker he previously put on me to see everything I see. But he doesn't need that now, does he? Not now he's got me.

"He'll be here in a minute," Raleigh says. "I'm sure he will be *delighted* to see you. My men say he's been shouting for you a lot... Come and sit down."

He pulls me to a hard, wooden chair, presses me into it. I can't do a thing.

On the other side of the room, there's a door and a bed. A hospital-style bed, only it has restraining straps as well. I cringe as I imagine Corin lying there, with mirror eyes, strapped in, yelling, fighting as they convert him, as they try to destroy the last seeds of the Untamed within him, so they can never grow again. They tortured me. Said I was too strong, that I needed it.

But what's a level one conversion? A milder torture?

Two Enhanced men appear in the room and walk over, until they're standing either side of me. Neither looks me in the eye.

My breathing gets a little shallower as I try to watch both of them at the same time.

"Bring him in," Raleigh says loudly, and the men turn to look at the door as it opens. Two more Enhanced enter, and between them, fighting and struggling, is a man in dark jeans, scuffed shoes, and a disheveled button-up shirt that's too bright a blue for him to have chosen it himself.

Corin.

A hardness, like iron, settles in my stomach. And I look at him, want him to be a clone. They can't *really* have Corin. Not my Corin.

But then Corin shouts, and I know. I just *know*. It's him. No Enhanced would swear like that—or describe in such gruesome detail exactly what he's going to do to Raleigh and the Enhanced. It's him all right. Corin. They've got him too, and—

I jolt.

His eyes. *Untamed*—his eyes are Untamed.

No…no mirrors?

Those beautiful dark brown eyes.

My eyes widen, and I stare, try to see him better. The mirrors? Have they faded? But there'd still be signs, wouldn't there?

Unless he hasn't had any? Wasn't given any augmenters when the Zharat were captured…eight hours ago… My mind whirls. And the more I look at him, the more I'm sure he hasn't had any, that he managed to avoid them completely. But how?

Corin shouts, his face reddening as he tries to twist around. Then he sees me.

His Untamed eyes meet mine—my mirror eyes—and I feel a bolt of something in my chest. He stops struggling, stares at me, and the men lead him forward. He doesn't resist. Why isn't he resisting? He needs to fight, not stand still, staring at me.

"Why hasn't he been given augmenters?" Raleigh demands, his voice cold. He points at Corin.

"Because I'm never joining you," Corin snarls.

Raleigh growls and points to one of the Enhanced. "I *said* administer them before leading him here, before—"

"There were none left in the stock cupboard on the fourth floor," the Enhanced says. "One of those Zharat women was proving problematic—you know, the blond one who bit Ian and Amara. She needed *eight* vials of Calmness and four of Tranquility before we could restrain her. I strongly suggest her conversion is next, Raleigh, because her fire is burning through our augmenters. We cannot waste our supplies like this."

Raleigh mutters something under his breath, then looks at Corin. "Stand him there." He points to a pale yellow circle on the floor. "We'll do it all in one go.

DIVIDED

First taste and the conversion."

"Sev," Corin yells, twisting against the Enhanced holding him. "Fight him! Fight this. You did it before, we can—"

"No talking," Raleigh says, and then he leans closer to me, his head next to mine. I shudder, and—

Raleigh's tongue swipes down the left side of my face.

My body stiffens into stone. I feel sick. Something inside me moves.

Corin swears loudly, and, in my peripheral vision, I see him struggling with the Enhanced men again, kicking and punching.

"Don't talk to her, Corin," Raleigh says, his voice loud, but he's looking at me. He's so close I can see the slight line that goes around each iris, separating it from the sclera. But it's all just a mirror still, as if a pencil line has been drawn on. "If you talk to her, I'll do that again." He pauses, and his lips twitch. "I'll do more than that."

More than that.

I try not to react, but I start shaking, feel sick, horrible. Am I part of Corin's conversion? Getting him to agree to become Enhanced if he thinks he's saving me from Raleigh?

Raleigh steps back, away from me. I let out a shaky breath, watch him walk to Corin. Raleigh plucks something from the counter on his way. An augmenter.

My breath catches in my throat, and then my eyes are directed to the counter. And I see them. I see all the augmenters. Twenty of them. Orange, blue, yellow, green, black. And I lean forward, expecting to feel a strong pull.

But I don't. It's not like before. It's nothing like before. If anything, I feel *sicker* than before. And I'm not supposed to feel sick, not when I look at augmenters, not when I've got them in my system. I'm supposed to only feel good stuff.

Oh Gods.

Raleigh places his hand on Corin's shoulder, and Corin tries to get away, but the Enhanced men hold him. Raleigh turns, looks at me. In his other hand is the vial, the augmenter. It's black, unfamiliar.

Raleigh grins.

My breathing quickens. Oh Gods. I need to get out. I can't watch this. Can't... Oh Gods. No. No. No.

I gulp, feel myself sweating.

Corin's eyes are on the vial. "Get that away from me." But his voice is quieter. I can almost hear his heart rate jumping, getting faster, faster. He looks at me. "Sev, help me. Fight him. Fight the augmenters, fight them! We can get out of this."

"You can't." Raleigh smiles, and he steps away from Corin, nears me.

For a second, I'm sure he's going to lick me again, and I try to move, but my legs burn, held in place against the legs of the chair by Raleigh's command. Sweat breaks out across my face, around my neck, down my spine. I try to swallow, but can't. I can't do anything. Saliva trickles down my throat, my eyes water.

I try to move, but invisible hands squeeze me, hold me in place. I try again—but Raleigh's too strong.

"Oh, Corin, it doesn't look like she wants to help you," Raleigh says, then lets out a small laugh.

"No!" I scream. "He's got me—Corin, Raleigh's got control of me, my soul, my body. I can't—"

"What?" Corin's head turns toward Raleigh, and then the Enhanced around him move, and I can't see him.

"It's Raleigh!" I yell. "It's—"

Pain lashes around my neck, like a whip. I shriek, head falling forward. My chin hits my chest, hard, winds me. I cry out, and I'm trying to move, trying to move forward, but I can't. The hands are stopping me, invisible hands. I can't move my arms, my legs. I'm just...suspended here, and—

"Corin!"

DIVIDED

"Run!" he yells, twisting around. His eyes meet mine for the briefest of seconds, then he punches the Enhanced next to him. The man falls like a doll, and then Corin's going for the next one.

Raleigh shouts something, and I start to stand, start to move—but pain lashes through me, winds me. I fall back against the chair, miss what Corin does next, and then an Enhanced man flies toward me. I see myself in his eye-mirrors, and—

"Run, Sev!"

And my head jolts up, and I see him, Corin. Standing there, free.

Then Corin runs.

And, at first, I think he's just going to the right because Raleigh's on his other side, and I'm sure he's going to circle back. That he's going to come for me.

But he doesn't.

He looks back, just for a second. His Untamed eyes meet mine—my Enhanced ones, my mirrors. His lips tighten, press together. A slight line appears between his eyebrows as he frowns—as he thinks. Just for a split second though. But I know that look.

The bridge between us shatters.

Corin runs, sprints out of the open doorway.

I try to follow, but I can't.

He's gone. Left me.

And I know—just *know*—I won't see Corin again.

TWO

"AFTER HIM!" RALEIGH'S FACE CONTORTS as he shouts, and then he's running too, racing toward the door, leaving the room, rapidly followed by some of his men.

I drag air into my lungs, try to move, but there's something holding my body on the chair—the control Raleigh has on me. Even though he's gone.

I shout at the two Enhanced men who are still here—one's on the floor still, but the other's standing, pulling a radio out of his belt.

"Put the compound in lockdown now." His words are fast. "One escaped Untamed. Male. Twenty years old. Five foot eleven. Headed out of Room 124C, down the corridor toward Zone E, second floor. I repeat, put the compound on lockdown. One escaped Untamed. Male. Twenty years old...."

The man with the radio glances at me, then sprints out the door, still yelling. A second later, red light fills the room and a siren blares. I try to move again, but my arms—they're not mine. My body it's...numb? I can't feel it, not like I should.

I stare at my fingers. Try to move them. Can't.

DIVIDED

I curse Raleigh in the most colorful language I know.

The other Enhanced pulls himself up. He rubs his arm, grimaces for a second. Pain? He shouldn't be able to feel pain. He looks at me, smiles.

"You're ours now."

My chest tightens. My mouth dries immediately. Oh Gods. Raleigh's strong. So strong. He's not even here—he'll be chasing after Corin—yet he's got full control of my body. I try to fight against it—against him—again, and energy buzzes through my body, but it's contained, can't escape. I can't do it. Can't move.

And Corin's out there. Running through the corridors? Or is he outside now? How much time has passed?

I try to turn to the window, but my head won't move, and more pain cements itself into my neck. I breathe hard, then wrench my neck as I force my head to the left. Pain whips around me, jars me, but, for a second, I think I see a glimpse of a pale sand-colored building, shabby, with dirty marks on it, and trees behind. But then it's gone, and I'm staring at the white wall next to the open doorway.

My breaths come quicker, deeper bursts that leave me panting and dizzy. White spots hover in front of my eyes, and I will Corin to make it out. He has to get out of here. He'll be safe out there.

He'll remain Untamed out there.

My heart's beating too fast, then I taste slime at the back of my mouth. I try to bring my hand up to my mouth, but the effort is futile. My stomach twists. I gag, feel everything in my body moving. I look down; my dark leggings seem to be shimmering.

"Shania?"

Through bleary eyes, I see a figure pushing through the red, pulsing air. The siren gets louder.

"Shania?"

And then his arms are around me, holding me up on the chair. *Three's* arms. He's here. And it's all right, because my brother's here—we're still together. Safe.

And he's concerned about me. He's on our side still?

No. He called me *Shania*.

But he called me *Seven* before? Didn't he? I blink hard, try to remember...only what? Hours ago...was it hours ago? When I saw him again for the first time since he was converted... He did say *Seven*, didn't he?

"What's happening?" Three's voice is crisp, authoritative—his usual tone? I can't tell. "Are you okay?"

I manage to shake my head, despite the pain—and then another wave of nausea hits. My body jolts, and I'm sick all over him.

Three shoves me to the side, but I don't fall off the chair, just bounce back and sway—Raleigh won't let me fall? Is he even aware of me, of what's going on now? Or has he just commanded my soul—my body—to make me sit. Can I only sit here?

"He said that would happen if you try and resist." Three stares at the vomit dripping from his sleeve in long gray strings. "You mustn't fight Raleigh, Shania. He's saving us all. Being a Chosen One is right. It's good."

He smiles, exuberant, and the artificial light catches the metal plate under his left eye. I focus on it for a moment, on him, then I look at his eyes. His *mirror* eyes. A sour taste fills my mouth, and I stare at the mirrors, barely register my own reflection in them, only seeing what he's become. What he is now. My hands tremble.

"You must need a top-up," Three says. A slight frown follows as he assesses me. "You're running far too lean. All this anxiety—it's radiating from you. Why didn't you tell Raleigh how you felt?" He moves his hand toward his pocket. "Here, this will make you feel better."

"No!" I manage to get the word out, but it's weak. Insubstantial. Like it's floating by, a cloud that dissipates, shredding my word into a million flakes that can never be put back together.

DIVIDED

"No?" Three studies me. "Of course you need one—especially when the wildness is still in you." Then he laughs, and it's a laugh so unlike my brother's that I go cold.

He's not the same man. He's Enhanced.

He's not my brother anymore?

And it's your fault. You didn't rescue him.

I flinch, force that thought—the guilt—away.

Three produces a syringe of pale blue liquid and an encased needle from his pocket. I try to turn my head, but I can't do anything except watch as he pulls the casing off the needle with a loud click. He attaches the needle to the vial with expertise, then holds up the augmenter.

Calmness.

Somewhere, deep down in my body, there's a yearning for it. A distant memory stirs, trying to break free. My breathing quickens again.

No.

I can't. Mustn't. Got to stay Untamed.

But what's the point? Raleigh's got you now. They've got you. You're theirs.

"You'll feel a lot better," Three says, moving toward me. He takes hold of my arm gently, tenderly. As if he's still my brother, as if he doesn't want to hurt me. "I'm going to put it here."

He taps the top of my left shoulder. Not my bad one, but I still wince. He notices. Of course he does. He's my brother—and he's Enhanced; he wants everything to be perfect, for no one to hurt or suffer. Maybe he'll give me a better room than the cell Raleigh allocated to me.

"You'll feel better after this, I promise," Three says, and I stare at his metal cheek, wonder why he's not had it completely fixed. The Enhanced certainly have the technology to do it. Three inclines his head slightly. "You're only feeling scared and uncomfortable because the Untamed part within you hasn't shrunk or disappeared yet." He shakes his head in a way which reminds me far too much of Raleigh. "There's a war going on inside you, dividing you. Making you hurt. But as soon as the Untamed part has gone, you'll feel better. You'll be one of us properly. And I've heard Raleigh's plans. We'll save everyone, thanks to you."

I can't do anything as he pierces my flesh with the needle, as he injects the Calmness. I just stare at Three, my brother, bathed in flaring red. Coldness radiates through my shoulder, and I imagine the liquid simultaneously diving down the veins in my arms and across my chest, spreading, spreading, spreading....

"They'll catch Eriksen. Don't worry." Three gives me a smile that I think is supposed to be sympathetic and encouraging. "I understand how scary it must be for you. But it's just the unknown and the fighting within you. We'll make you better—Raleigh's promised that. And we'll be safe. All of us, together. You, me, Eriksen, and Esther."

"Esther?" My voice is a hushed whisper, but I'm glad I manage it. It takes effort, but I *can* speak. My voice is something Raleigh can't seem to control. Not like my soul, my body. Because my voice is still me. *Completely* mine.

Three nods. I think he blushes. I wait for him to say something, but he doesn't. But still—the blushing. His old feelings are still there; does that mean the Untamed part is too? I look into his eyes, and I try to see past the mirrors, try to see something deeper, something more...genuine.

"How is Esther?" I watch him carefully, need to see emotion from him. Real, true emotion. Not whatever artificial ones he's been filled with.

Three smiles. "She is being saved now."

"Saved? Converted?"

He nods. "She looked beautiful earlier—even though she was wild, unkempt, and full of raging emotions... She tried to stab one of our men, but she still looked beautiful. And she will look even more beautiful once all that Untamed darkness within her has been destroyed."

"What conversion level?" Speaking's getting easier. Raleigh's letting me? Or am I getting stronger?

Three continues to smile. "Level one. They're being gentle with her. I checked. Matt said she's doing well. She can probably be released into society in a week, once she's been monitored for any lingering Untamed thoughts."

The siren seems softer now, yet at the same time, I know it hasn't changed. It's still blaring, I'm just more used to it…less upset by it…

Calmer.

My eyes widen. The augmenter—no.

I try to concentrate, try to breathe. Try to think clearly, but my head's now too hot, like everything in me is heating up into a mass of molten metal that just needs to be ignored. The augmenter, it has to be.

Heavy footsteps pound down the corridor outside. A man's coming, and I just know it's Raleigh. The siren stops and the red light disappears as he enters the room.

Raleigh's nostrils flare, and his upper lip curls. "He got out the far gates." He spits the words like they're missiles. "The Untamed parasite in him is strong, poisoning him."

My mouth dries as I stare at him. I feel something strange in my chest, all fluttery. "Corin got away?"

Raleigh nods, and then he and Three are speaking fast. I try to pick out their words, but I can't—it's like there are too many things going on, and I can only concentrate on one. Only have the effort to concentrate on one.

The one thing that's the most important.

He got away.

Corin got away.

And he left you.

I tense. But that's good, I tell myself. Corin's not here—not going to become Enhanced. And I need to focus on that. And maybe if he's out there, he'll find a way to get me out. And Esther. We don't give up on our people…not the ones who've been taken to a compound…we always make arrangements to save them.

But Corin hasn't got a rescue team working with him. It's only him.

Him on his own…out there. In danger. No food, no water, no shelter…and anything could happen. My gut clenches. If he was here, he'd be safer….

No.

I mentally shake myself, but everything's getting foggy.

"Not to worry," Raleigh says, stepping closer. "My men *will* find Corin. He won't be suffering out there for long. And," he adds, turning to me, "if my team can't locate him—you will." His gaze bores into me, even though it's just the mirrors.

"Me?" A metallic taste spreads across my mouth.

Raleigh nods, a sly smile taking over his face. "*You're* the key to the Untamed. You've got to have some sort of Seer power in you that means we can find all the resisters and save them. And I intend to find out what that Seer power of yours is very soon." His teeth get whiter. "The day isn't over yet."

Back in my cell, my dreams are strange.

At first, I'm sure I'm in the Dream Land—and hope surges within me. The Gods and Goddesses, they've realized it was a mistake—that I shouldn't have been banished because it wasn't my fault—and they're going to help me. Because, before, Death said he'd be watching me—and he's still watching me now, even though I've been banished?

I lift my arm up, and I see the gold Promise Marks

there. But it's okay because the Gods and Goddesses, they'll get rid of them, and they'll break Raleigh's control over my soul. He won't be my soul-commander then. I'll be free, and I can get away, get out of this prison, get all the Untamed out, and we can win.

I look around the Dream Land. The desert landscape; soft, warm colors that welcome me. My eyes search every rock, every boulder, for a figure hiding.

"Death!" I scream, then I use his proper name: "Waskabe!"

But he doesn't answer, doesn't appear. And so I shout his name again. And again.

But there's only silence.

And so I run, my feet kicking up plumes of dust around me. Specks of sand stick to my legs—bare legs. I'm wearing shorts. My own shorts, a pair I had at Nbutai. And I keep running, trying to find them, trying to find Death and those Goddesses with the long white dresses, and—

I need them!

But they're not here.

No one's here.

This isn't the Dream Land, Seven.

I don't know who says the words, but I turn, skid to a halt. Small, sharp stones lift up and attach themselves to my lower legs in a gritty mesh that constricts around each limb. I try to pull the stones off, but my fingers curl before I can use them, and I'm dragging my clenched hands across my legs, cutting my skin on the sharp edges of the gravel casing.

A chilling breeze wraps around me, and I look up. The sky is moody—darkening, angry—and there's no bison.

This is the land of nightmares. Run, Seven.

And so I run—got to get away, need to get away—and I don't know why, but I know that I must. So I keep running, but my legs are heavy; the stone layers become chains that wrap around my ankles and pull me backward.

I'm yelling and crying. I taste the salt of my tears, and I force myself to move.

They're behind me. Who? I don't know. But I know they're there. Just the feeling of them being there, and my overwhelming urge to run.

Can't look at them. Mustn't look at them. Mustn't let them catch me.

I keep going. My breathing gets labored. I'm running all wrong, the chains are jangling, and I can't keep up this speed. My thighs burn. Lactic acid.

The wind picks up, and the wind is full of knives. Knives that slide in between the links of the stone chains around my legs and tear at my skin, cut me. My skin rips like paper, and I'm drenched in blood.

I scream louder, try to keep going. But the chains get hotter. They burn me, and the air gets wetter. Steam. The Fire Mountain. The volcano…gases.

"Save my baby!" a woman cries, and I turn, but I can't see her. There's no one here. Just the desert and the steam and—

Kyla's in front of me. The little Zharat girl, with Manning's axe in her head, splitting her skull open… and her eyes are empty, staring at me.

"You killed me."

Her small hands reach for me. I step backward quickly, but her fingers get longer, longer. So much longer. They're everywhere!

I scream and turn, but the desert sand is sticky. It holds me in place, and I can't—

"Sev."

My head jerks to the left.

Corin.

I'm reflected in his eyes, a permanent part of him. And he shouldn't have mirror eyes, and I don't know what he's doing here—this place is dangerous. So dangerous. He shouldn't be here. He's unprotected.

"You traitor." Corin spits the words at me. "You've joined them, after everything they've done—"

"Corin, I couldn't—I—they've got my soul!" But the

DIVIDED

wind picks up, and I don't think he's heard.

He just stands there, mirror eyes narrowed. I try to reach him, force my legs to move, but they're heavier now. Stone again? My muscles strain, but I get a step forward.

"Corin, no, you don't understand!"

"You didn't try." He shakes his head, digs his hands deep into his pockets. "You didn't even *try*, Sev." His voice changes slightly. "No true Untamed Seer lets innocent people be converted without at least trying. But you ignored the warning. You let this conversion attack happen."

I stare at him... No. *No*. He's—they're not his words! That's what Death said—before, when...when I was being banished from the Dream Land.

"Corin...." I raise my hands in the surrender gesture, and I don't even know why I'm doing it. I try to stop my hands, but I can't. Someone's lifting them up. I can feel their fingers around my wrists.

Corin points at me, and smoke erupts from his hands and dives toward me. "You are a traitor." He punctuates each word with a snarl, and his mirrors flash. But they can't be his eyes. He's not Enhanced. "I do not take kindly to traitors."

I try to turn away. *Death does not take kindly to traitors*.

"Look at me," Corin snarls.

Oh Gods. But it's not him. It's a nightmare. That's all it is. Corin's not Enhanced and Corin's not Death. But Death's smoke wraps around me, clogs my nostrils, burns my throat...just like how the Loyalty did.

"Prove it, Sev."

"What?" My shoulders sag. I'm shrinking. Corin's getting bigger.

He takes a step toward me, and his elbows flash a deep purple. "Make sure the Untamed win the war." He pauses, and when he speaks again he has Death's voice, low and throaty. But sharp. So sharp. "It is your choice," he says. "The winner—the surviving side—it is your choice. It is written in the augury: *the Seventh*

One, born of Light, holds the strongest Seer powers. Her side will win the War of Humanity. The rest will be destroyed, and Death will call the Seventh One back to him at the end of the war." He looks at me pointedly. *"That* is the only way this war will end. You are the Seventh One, born of Light. Prove you're Untamed and make sure the Enhanced do not survive."

But I don't know how my side will win, how I will do it. I don't know….

I start yelling, just words—don't even know what I'm saying.

Corin coughs. "You know what to do," he snarls. "Give me one less reason to hate you when I have your soul at the war's end."

And then—then he's gone, and the fuchsia fire appears out of nowhere.

I don't see it in time.

It slams into my body.

I fall.

Traitor, a voice screams. *Be gone and never return.*

I gasp as jolts run through my body. I'm lying on the ground. In blood. Steam is everywhere, but not as much as there was in the cave. I hear cries. Bright light. All around me. Above. The sky. I'm outside. I'm outside and…I'm on my own.

No. I'm not.

My *dead fiancé* is here.

I stare at him, clench my fists, feel my heart pound. My jaw clenches.

"Do not say anything," Jed says, and his words catch in his thick accent for a second before they fly free.

Jed leans closer, and the steam gets thicker around us, binds us together. His face looks more like Raleigh's now… His father. I feel sick. Start to gag.

"Touch me, S'ven…touch me now."

I stare at him in shock, and the scenery around us changes. The desert disappears, and huge stone walls shoot up around us. The steam vanishes, and I can see the walls. Volcanic rock. I look around.

"It is our wedding night." Jed smiles and holds his hand out to me. I stare at his hand, his Promise Marks have gone. Or they're hiding. "Come on, I am waiting. We are perfectly alone, if that is what you are worried about."

I stare at him, can't stop looking at him. It looks like him. Looks exactly like him…but….

"But—but you're dead… He…."

And why am I even talking to him? He's dead *and* he's the one who got me into this mess. And this is a dream—I know it's a dream. A nightmare. Not true.

Jed laughs. "I am not dead, S'ven. That is not a nice thing to say to your husband. Especially when it is our wedding night. And we want to have the *perfect* time." He pauses, and I look around. "Come on. I will show you what to do. Do not worry, I will look after you. I am very gentle."

There's a bed behind us; then we are on it. So quickly, just like that. I lie on my back, and he leans over me, a knee either side of my hips. He bends down, until his lips brush against my neck.

"Arch your back," he whispers.

I do it without hesitation: before he's finished saying the words, I'm doing it. I haven't got a choice. I'm being controlled. No. No. *No*. Anger flares through me.

I feel Jed's hand close over mine, and then he's moving my hand, moving it onto his body, onto his chest, then over the taut muscles of his stomach. Jed grunts as he kisses my neck.

The world darkens.

"Use your Seer powers," Jed says. "You cannot be controlled *all* the time. You will not be helpless."

I wake with a start.

Raleigh leers over me. "I said it is time to use your Seer powers, Shania. There's no time like the present."

THREE

I AM TIED TO A chair by a thick rope that coils around my torso and makes me think of the kavalah snake spirits. Another rope binds my legs. But my arms are free. That's good. Except Raleigh's not letting me move them.

Raleigh stands in front of me, with a small Enhanced girl with long blond hair.

I look around. Not my cell. He's moved me. My head pounds. I shake it, then test the strength of the rope around me. I can move half an inch, within the coils, at the most.

"Have you found Corin?" I look around again. "What's happening?"

Raleigh clears his throat. "This is Elia Jackson." He places his hands on the girl's shoulders.

"Where is Corin? Is he okay?" I grit my teeth, and a huge part of me hopes that Raleigh doesn't know—because that means Corin's still out there.

But if he's out there, he's suffering...like you are.

No. I shake my head, breathing hard. Being Untamed isn't suffering.

Oh Gods. I've got to get away. I can feel the pull of

DIVIDED

the augmenters in me—the desire for more. But I'm still fighting it for now—I'm not *completely* one of them—yet I know I haven't got long.

I swear under my breath.

Raleigh points at the girl. "She will be helping us today—and I've got many more participants for when your powers are developed enough."

I take a deep breath and try to believe that that's a good sign. If Corin was here, Raleigh would delight in telling me, I'm sure.

"Come on, Shania. Say hello to Elia."

I stare at the girl. She's about eight years old. Or maybe a bit older. She just looks so young because she's small. Her mirror eyes are on me, but there's something different about them. She's not looking at me—not looking at anything. I glance back up at Raleigh. He's looking at me, glaring right at me—the intensity of the mirrors on me says that. But she... No, she's just blank.

A horrible taste flares in my mouth. Saliva pools on my tongue, and I lean over, spit it out.

"You won't get rid of the augmenters that way," Raleigh says. "I injected them straight into your blood when you were asleep. A huge dose. Loyalty, Calmness, Obedience, and Compliance, ready for our session."

"Session?"

He smiles. "Yes. Before we work out *how* you're going to use your powers to save everyone, I need to know exactly what you can do, what your powers are, what stage you're already at."

I breathe deeply, press my lips firmly together. It's too hot in here.

"Shania? Come on, my dear butterfly. Let me in. We're going to do great things together." He pauses. "Let's just think of this as a getting-to-know-each-other session."

"Getting to know each other?"

"Yes. Each Seer's powers are slightly different. I need

to know what you've already unlocked, and then I can teach you, guide you, help you develop your abilities until you're ready. So, Shania. What can you do?"

I try to move my foot. My bare foot. Imagine myself kicking him. "Nothing."

For a second, irritation crosses his face. "This isn't helping. It's wasting time. Just tell me what you've already unlocked yourself."

Pain sears behind my eyes.

"*Tell* me, Shania."

"Nothing. It's the truth." I hold his gaze—or what I think is his gaze—for as long as I can, trying to block out the fiery serpents' tongues, but they push through, push into my brain. I imagine them slinking and slithering into the gray matter, digging deeper, burning everything within their reach. "And it's going to stay that way. You're *not* using me."

You don't want to save everyone? That's very selfish, isn't it?

I squirm, feel more sweat line my forehead. No, I insist to myself, to those thoughts. It's not selfish. Not at all. Because the Enhanced are bad. They're wrong.

The corners of Raleigh's lips tug upward. He shakes his head. "You forget that I have your soul. With your soul, I can control you. I can control your body—*and* your Seer powers. Now, it's a lot easier if you work with me. It will be less painful for you. But I can get direct access to your Seer powers myself, if I need to. Come on, Shania, I know you've got powers. And I'm being nice here, offering you a less painful way. Because we *are* going to do this."

"No."

He bites on his bottom lip slowly. "I think you need some more Loyalty."

I snort and meet his eyes, see my own mirrors in his. I look Enhanced, but there's still some Untamed in me—and I concentrate on that. I have to. I have to keep it alive. "So your control over my soul isn't strong enough on its own," I say. "You need me drugged to

DIVIDED

do this. And you think *you're* powerful."

Raleigh bends down, until his head is level with mine. "Oh, my powers are plenty strong enough. But the Untamed part of you is clearly still controlling you, and you're suffering. I'm trying to make this easier for you, kinder. I really am, poor girl. The Untamed within you means you can't see me for what I am."

"I can see you fine," I spit out through gritted teeth.

He reaches into his pocket and produces a green vial.

My mouth dries, and I inhale sharply.

Don't look at it.

But what's the point? They're already in me... I know that, yet I don't feel calm or obedient or loyal. It's not like before. I'm fighting it—really fighting it—and I'm fighting the pull better this time than ever before.

But there are only so many augmenters I can fight, I know that.

"No," I whisper. "I don't want that."

"*Of course* you want it. And you need augmenters. They're what make this world bearable."

My chest shudders. "No."

He flicks the lid off and grabs my face with his other hand. His fingers try to hold my chin still.

"No!" I kick out, but the ropes don't give me much room, and—

I feel the vial against my lips—the coldness of the glass—swiftly followed by the sweetness of the Loyalty.

Heat floods my body; for a second, I can't move, can't—

"You'll work with me now, Shania. Won't you?" Raleigh pulls back from me, straightens up, smiles. His teeth are too white. Yet...beautiful... *No.*

Yes.

"Shania? We can work together now—save you from suffering, yes?"

I struggle to keep my lips together, but there's

something building inside me, trying to push its way out.

"Shania?"

Whatever it is tickles my throat, and my eyes water. *Say yes. You want to help everyone.*

And I do... I want to... I need to be faithful... These people are good, they're helping...and Raleigh's going to show me how to help, how to....

Think of the bison!

"Shania?"

"Yes." The word is a squeak, but it comes from me. Sweat drips down my back, cold and savage.

"Good," Raleigh says, smiles brightly. "Now, what powers have you already accessed?"

"I... I haven't."

"You haven't? No, Shania. You must've. Come on, push that Untamed part of you away. It's making you lie to me, and lying is an evil trait. Just tell me what powers you've accessed. Give me something to work with—to work with you on. Working together is better than me controlling you, I promise."

I shake my head, eyes still watering. "I haven't got any Seer powers. There's nothing for you to use."

"Oh, you've got powers all right." Raleigh sighs. "We'll start with the basics then, before we move onto the more advanced abilities—like how you're going to find all the Untamed. Yes? Good." He rubs his hands together. "There's one power *every* Seer has. It's a defense power, and I *know* you've got it, so don't pretend you haven't. But I need to check that you can do it adequately, efficiently, and quickly—you should be able to, you've been a Seer for long enough. It's perhaps the most important power." Raleigh turns and points at Elia Jackson. "Kill her."

My head tingles, and all the muscles in my face slacken. "*What?*"

The girl doesn't react. She just stands there, as if she hasn't heard, hasn't understood.

Raleigh gives me a vexatious look. "Those wild men

DIVIDED

will want to kill you, Shania, when they realize whose side you're on. And this girl is expendable. She knows what greatness her death would bring us, don't you, Elia? Yes. Good girl."

My eyes widen. "No one is *expendable*. And...and you don't believe in violence."

I feel stupid as I say the last words. I know it's not true—but it's what I was taught. It was drummed into me from a young age.

Raleigh smiles, but there's a warning within it. "Elia realizes you need to practice on real people, and she's honored to be your first test subject."

He reaches down and ruffles her hair. She doesn't react, and, though I can't see any detail in her eyes, I'm sure they're unfocussed...still.

"It makes sense to practice your killing power first," Raleigh continues. "Killing is, after all, the best method of defense in case the Untamed you attempt to convert try to fight or kill you. You can zap their life away. Now, show me what you can do. Don't make me force you to do it—because that would hurt you. See? I don't want you to suffer, Shania. But you *will* do it."

I stare at him, feel my shoulders tighten. No. This can't be real. Can't be. I shake my head. "I'm not killing anyone."

He stretches his hand out toward me, and a bulb of bright white light grows from his palm. "You won't *need* to kill anyone with it after this. Not unless it's necessary," Raleigh says. "*You* control the strength of it." The globe of light gets bigger. "But I need to know that you can protect yourself to the highest degree should you need to. Self-preservation is important for you. And Elia is a *willing* participant."

I point at the girl. She's still just standing there. But I know now there's something wrong. It's like she's not here. She seems empty.

"No," I tell Raleigh. "I'm not hurting her."

"She's given her consent."

"That doesn't mean anything—she doesn't understand, she's not even speaking." I fold my arms, keep my eyes on the white light cradled in Raleigh's hand. "And I'm not doing it—I can't anyway, so don't torture me. I haven't got that power."

"*Every* Seer has that power."

"Not me." I flex my fingers against my arms and try to look around for something that might help me. But my eyes just fall on the girl. Would she?

Raleigh lets the white light die as he leans toward me, until there's less than an inch between our faces and he is all I can see. "*Of course* you have this power. Shania, I understand that you don't *want* to kill anyone. None of us do, but sometimes we need to. For the greater good."

I resist rolling my eyes. "But I can't do it."

"You can. All that's stopping you is your negative attitude."

"I haven't got any Seer powers." I keep my words firm. "I never have. I'm not like you—or Jed. I saw him do that power, and guess what, Raleigh? I even *tried* to use it. I tried to use it against Jed, but I couldn't. I *haven't* got that power."

Raleigh exhales hard, and his sour breath washes over my face. "Well then, I'd better help you unlock it. You *need* this power. Self-preservation is of the utmost importance."

I glance back at Elia. "I'm not killing her—or anyone." Least of all any Untamed. His plans are useless. He's *not* using me, not for killing or converting.

"Of course you'll kill people." Raleigh laughs as he steps away. "You're a Seer of Death. So what's it going to be? Are you going to work with me and try to find this power? Or are we going to do this the hard way? Because the more control I have to use, if you resist, the more painful it will be for you."

"You already said that." My voice is sulky.

"And you haven't given me an answer."

I look at the girl. "I'm not killing anyone," I repeat.

DIVIDED

"Very well." Raleigh steps around behind me, then his fingertips touch my head. He flattens his fingers against the side of my face, applies a little pressure against my temples. I squish my face up, try to get away, but I can't because of the rope and him and—

Sharp pain digs into my skull.

I inhale quickly, gasping.

"I can quite easily make you do this," Raleigh says. "So, let's unlock your first power and kill this girl. I'll show you how easy it is."

"Get off me!" I try to move, try to kick out, but it's useless.

"None of that, Shania. Or do I need to give you even *more* Loyalty?"

I call him the rudest word I know, and I keep shouting it. His fingers dig into my head, his nails sharp—I scream.

Hot white pain flashes into my eyes, my vision blurs. Everything starts swimming.

"Come on, Shania, tell me. Where do you keep your Seer powers? I know they're in here."

"No!" I shout, my word dragging on and on, on and on.

Sweat drips into my eyes, burns. I twist around, manage to move. I fight the rope, turn my head, see Raleigh for a second, see the maliciousness in his expression.

"Come on, Shania. Hurt me. You want to hurt me! You want to kill me with the power in you," he yells. "Or I'll keep hurting you. Fight me!"

I screech. No! Can't! Mustn't! It's what he wants. Because I know if I do somehow manage to hurt him with my abilities, he's going to control the power—redirect it to the girl.

My breath comes in short, sharp bursts. Too rapid. He's going to make me. He's got control of me. I can't stop him. Only the Gods and Goddesses can break the connection between us.

I scream again, but this time I scream Waskabe's

name. I force myself to look upward, imagine the Dream Land, hope that Death *is* still watching, that he's seeing this...and even though the Gods and Goddesses see fragments and distorted versions, I hope they'll see the pain...that they'll see the truth when they didn't before...that maybe this pain will take me straight into the Dream Land, somehow....

"You won't get anywhere near there," Raleigh snarls. "It's no use. No Enhanced Seer can break into the Dream Land."

Enhanced Seer.

Rage fills me, drips through every part of me. I am *not* an Enhanced Seer.

Raleigh's pain digs deeper, tunneling into every part of my brain, then down through the sinews of my body.

"Fight me, Shania! Use your powers to fight me. Come *on*—search for your powers and break the seal."

I scream. He's shaking. I'm shaking.

Give him what he wants!

No!

My neck stiffens.

But it's what you want really. Surrender completely, and you won't hurt anymore... And you're hurting now so much... And it can stop... It can all go away if you—

No.

"Very well, Shania." Raleigh's breath is torrid against the back of my neck. "Very well, indeed."

Something stabs me in the back.

I shriek, try to move, but can't. The dagger—must be a dagger... It moves, waggles, side to side. I shriek even louder, redness fills my vision. For a second, I see the girl in front of me. She hasn't moved, hasn't reacted. She's just...there. Not even my screams have changed her.

And then—at first, I don't feel anything. Not anything different... But then there's something in my head, moving—like a mouse digging and—

He's close to my powers—I know he is. Oh Gods!

DIVIDED

And I don't know how I know—I've never used these Seer powers before…only used my intuition, my access to the Dream Land…but….

"Run!" I yell at Elia, but my vision's jumping about and blurring, and I can't see her properly. She's just a smear of color that dances before me.

"Come *on*, Shania. Show me where your powers are," Raleigh growls. Each word is drilled in with another movement of the dagger in my back—and an echoed movement of the mouse in my head, digging harder, faster. "Reach for your powers."

I gasp, try to breathe. Need to breathe. I try to pull away from him, but the movement flares up more pain and—

Raleigh laughs. "I'm enjoying this, you know. But only because I know pain is the gateway—it will help you, help us all, in the end."

My stomach twists, and the—

Protect yourself! Use your Seer powers! Fight him!
No!

Heat rushes to my hands. My fingers are on fire, burning hotter and hotter. A jolt of electricity flies through me. My skin, no—it's going to peel off, lift away in great rugged sections, going to—

Raleigh laughs. And then my hands rise—no, they're pulled up. I can barely see, but I can see my hands. They're shaking.

"Come on!" Raleigh yells.

His own hands burn the side of my face. I try to twist away, got to get away. I feel something in my neck click and move, and then I'm covered in foul-smelling sweat, drenched.

The pain intensifies. I'm screaming. My throat's raw.

Give in! End the pain! Go along with it, do what he wants!

No. Don't. Prove who you are. No Untamed Seer would give in or willingly allow him to do this. Fight him! Get control back.

But I can't—the voice doesn't understand. I can't

get control back...only the Gods and Goddesses can destroy the Promise Marks—destroy Raleigh's control over my soul—and they've destroyed my contact with them because I didn't save the Zharat, or my brother—because I didn't try and—

"Shania!"

The mouse digs deeper.

Something clicks inside me.

No.

I lunge forward, diving through the maze of dots, my head exploding and—

I projectile vomit everywhere.

My insides heave, raw.

When I've finished, I look up through bleary eyes, exhaustion pulling at every part of me.

Raleigh moves. He's in front of me. There's a strange look on his face, then he tilts his head to the side. He's annoyed.

Annoyed that I'm resisting him and his control, still resisting the augmenters. But I'm doing it—somehow, I'm doing it. I'm stopping him from getting my powers.

"I think we'll have a break," Raleigh says, his words slow and careful. Yet there's something else in them too. Something calculating and cold. "You must be tired...and you're not in the best condition... No. You need to rest... But I'm close. Made great progress, we have. I can feel your powers already—they're strong. You're strong, Shania. And I'll reach them soon. But the Untamed in you is too strong, too potent." He indicates around us with his fingers. "We'll resume *this* when you're in better condition. When we can work together—better for both of us."

He shakes his head.

"I'll book you in for another conversion process. Something a little stronger than waterboarding this time."

FOUR

RALEIGH TAKES ME STRAIGHT TO my cell, controlling my body. I expect him to give me more augmenters, but he doesn't. And that's good, I remind myself. I need to be myself. Have to be.

But how can you be yourself when augmenters are already in your system? When you'll have another conversion soon?

A conversion.

Oh Gods.

The cloth over my face gets tighter. It presses against my nose, trying to force it down. I can feel their hands all over my body, pushing me onto the platform with cold fingers. I know better now than to resist. But they don't believe me. They aren't taking chances, they say....

The water slams against me.

My body's crushed deeper into the platform.

My throat constricts. I taste bile. I turn, trying to pull away. More water hits me.

I breathe deeply and look at the ceiling. I'm lying down. I don't remember lying down. My tongue feels fuzzy—no, my whole mouth does.

"Rest," Raleigh says. "Try to let the evilness escape from your body. Don't hold onto it. It is bad, and you need to accept that. If you do, it will make the conversion easier." He crouches down, and I see myself in his eyes. I look pathetic. "I don't want you to suffer."

I flinch as he places a cool hand against my sweaty, clammy forehead. His fingers are like metal bars, pressing into me, marking me, branding me like an animal.

"We'll do this. We'll save everyone, I promise."

Those words ring in my head as I listen to his footsteps disappearing down the corridor outside. I wait until it's silent out there—or about as silent as it can be because something's clicking continuously—before I force myself to stand. I haven't got long. No idea how soon he's going to come for me again, how soon I'm going to be strapped to a bed, tortured. The thought makes my stomach turn, and what little contents is still inside sloshes about.

Moving is harder than expected, but my legs just about take my weight, though they wobble. I look around the cell again. The metal bucket for toilet needs. No window. Just the door—the only exit. I try the handle, but it's locked. I rattle it harder, listening for a telltale click or change in the pressure of the handle as I move it, in case there's a weak spot.

There isn't.

Breathing hard and slightly dizzy, I turn and look at the walls. Red brick and cement. From top to bottom. One air vent sits at the top of the far wall. I stride toward it, pull myself onto my tiptoes, so my forehead's an inch from the vent. Cool air hits my skin; it's an outside wall. And just knowing that makes me feel better. I'm at the edge of the building—one wall separates me from freedom.

Visions of me running out there, through desert sand and dust, fill my head. How far could I get before Raleigh realizes and exerts control over my soul? Would a larger distance between us make it harder for him to command my movements?

DIVIDED

I try to move the air vent. But the metal bars are firm, not going to give. So I turn my attention to the filler around the metal grid, run my fingers over the bumps and lumps, try not to see the gold splashes on my skin. They're stationary now.

But seeing them makes me think of Raleigh. Is he watching what I'm doing now? He's still got my eyes, hasn't he? Or does he automatically know what I'm doing given that he commands my soul?

Except he's not controlling me *now*.

Because he thinks I'm safe in here? That he can rest? That he doesn't need to exert control and use up his energy when I'm imprisoned?

I try to pull chunks of filler out, but the only bits I get off are small, tiny crumbs. I curse as one of my nails bends right back, pushing sharp pain into the soft, fleshy underside, and snaps. A line of red appears. My eyes water, and I breathe deeply, but it only makes my head hurt more. I press my thumb over my broken nail. Tears pierce my eyes, and then Elia's face flashes in front of me.

I jump, wrap my arms around myself, squeeze tightly. I'm shaking, shaking so much. My knees knock against each other.

Oh Gods. I need to stay calm—mustn't think about what Raleigh tried to get me to do…what he'll make me do next time. Because I know he will succeed.

Or maybe I'll do it willingly, if they've fully converted me by then.

The thought makes me freeze.

No.

That can't happen.

It *can't*. I need to concentrate, concentrate on being Untamed. Have to.

My brow furrows. The wall. The vent. There's got to be a way out of here. Has to be. I just need to get out and join Corin. It's safety in numbers, and together we're stronger.

But there isn't an obvious way out. I test every brick

FIVE

"BEING UNTAMED IS BAD. IT is wrong. And it is evil."

There are three men in here now, with me. In my cell. Three Enhanced men, and they keep saying those words over and over again. I'm not sure how much time has passed since I saw the blue-eyed Seer. Could've been hours, or maybe even a day. No one's fed me still, and my stomach feels strange and swollen. The smell from my toilet bucket isn't helping.

These Enhanced haven't tied me up, and they haven't made any move to do so. They're standing by the locked door, and I'm sitting against the opposite wall.

"Do you agree?" one now asks me. They all look the same.

I shake my head, and my stomach rumbles. But I feel stronger—stronger in myself. I'm resisting the augmenters. And I'm doing it well. There's no pull for them within me. Nothing.

I don't want them.

Because I need to be Untamed.

And I *will* be Untamed.

I clap a hand to my mouth, try to breathe.

Air.

I need fresh air.

My legs shake as I stand, and it takes me too long to reach that tiny air vent. But the weak breeze against my forehead doesn't help much. I try to lift my head higher, and the back of my neck creaks. I wince as fresh pain grips me, as waves of fogginess try to take me.

But through it all, I think of one thing: hope.

There's a Seer out there, and she contacted me... when she was cooking?

But next time—next time I *won't* lose the connection. I'll make her help me, make her contact the Gods and Goddesses for me, get these Promise Marks removed and—

But the Enhanced are going to win.

I shake my head, don't know where that thought came from.

"Not so long as there's hope," I whisper back at the nothingness around me.

Not so long as there's hope.

And there's always got to be hope.

DIVIDED

opening my eyes. "We can't eat that."

Pain flashes through my head, makes me gasp. My eyes—I can't open them, can't... Oh Gods, what is—

A young woman, right in front of me. Sparkling, blue Untamed eyes set in the whitest skin I've ever seen. Shoulder-length reddish-blond hair that curls slightly in the humid air—because it is so humid. The air is thick and alive, and mosquitoes buzz and—

My body jolts—something scrapes, and my eyes spring open, freed. I inhale hard, feel pain in my lungs. I jump up, look left, right—look for the woman, that Untamed woman—but she's not here.

It's just my cell. Brick walls.

My heart pounds. I'm still here, and the air is—

The air is clear. A little sweeter than before? Air freshener? But there are no smells of food. No cooking. No burning.

Yet I smelled it. I did.

And I saw a woman—a woman who wasn't here.

I try to picture her, hold her in my mind. Red-blond hair. Blue eyes. But that's all that comes to me. No face...no distinguishing features...no idea what her nose was like or....

I touch my head gingerly, wince at the pain. My vision blurs as I stare at the walls; the bricks are dancing.

My eyes widen...that woman...was she a Seer? Someone trying to help me? Someone who knows I'm in trouble, knows how important I am?

I reach for my Seer pendant, but my fingers touch bare skin. Emptiness grabs me, and my vision gets smaller.

A Seer? Trying to help me? Trying to contact me?

I'm not alone... It's not the—

I press my lips together—they're buzzing slightly, make me feel off. Off and sick. I try not to think of how I vomited earlier, but now that putrid odor is all I can smell. I look down at my clothes, see the stains on me. Feel sicker than ever and—

that I can reach, convinced that one might just move back—shift a few inches—if I press hard enough. But no secret exit reveals itself.

I sit on the ground, my back against the far wall, so my eyes are on the door. I take several deep breaths, but everything's swimming inside my head—like I'm not getting enough oxygen, and everything's fuzzy.

My skin starts to burn—a thousand pins driving into my flesh—and I wince, lean back, my head against the bricks. My eyes get heavier, so I close them, block out everything. At first, the telltale signs of panic start to take over: the fear of not being able to see, the way energy jumps into my fingers, how my toes start to buzz.

And the aroma of roasting meat wafts over me. Lamb.

Instantly, I relax a little.

See? It's good here.

My lips move a little, and I wet them, feel saliva pool in my mouth. The Enhanced haven't fed me yet, not given me any food in all the time I've been here... How long has it been? Those bad dreams I had, were they in the night or the day? I can't tell, everything's merging together, but my stomach groans for food. So it must be time to eat—and they're cooking for me. For all the Untamed.

I hear sizzling—sizzling of fat in a pan—and the sound distracts me, makes me forget what I was thinking. Because all I can think of now is food. It's what I need. I'm so hungry.

I breathe in deeper—immediately able to breathe more easily—and my body shakes with the anticipation of food. Meat and vegetables. Potatoes. Maybe even cake for desert.

Burning meat.

No! It's burning! And I see it in the pan—a slab of meat, with smoke rising from it and—

My body jolts, and I—

"It's too charred," a voice says, stops me from

I will not make it easy for Raleigh to use me to end my people. No. A slight smile tugs at my lips.

My stomach moans.

One of the men steps closer to me. "You can't have any food until you agree, until the Untamed part of you has left. Food just feeds the badness within you. Come on, Shania. You have to try."

So, starvation—that's the torture method this time.

"And you can't have any water. Not until you are pure once more. Water will make the evil parasite grow bigger. And we need it to shrivel up and die."

Dehydration too.

"Nor can you sleep again, Shania, not until you've been saved. Sleeping fuels the badness in you, and we can only let you sleep once you have accepted that being Untamed is bad *and* once you have purged it from your system—once you are truly a Chosen One again. After that, you may have food and water."

The first man smiles again. "We will crush the badness in you, and you will expel it."

The balls of my cheeks plump up a bit, and I bite my bottom lip quickly. I want to laugh—the urge is there as I look up at them.

"It will work," one of the Enhanced says. "Because we won't leave here until you've surrendered to us fully, until you are pure."

"And when you're so tired that you're hazy, when you're so hungry that you will try to eat the augmenters we give you—eat them like they are food—and when you're so dehydrated that you're dizzy for our lifestyle, you'll agree because you'll understand then. You'll accept that there is badness in you and only then will you start to get better."

"Repeat after me: being Untamed is bad. It is wrong. And it is evil."

"No." I shake my head. "Being *Enhanced* is bad. It is wrong. And it is evil." I don't even know why I'm saying the words, why I'm not just staying quiet.

"No, being a *Chosen One* is good. You'll soon see it,

DIVIDED

you'll understand it clearly when you realize it is the Untamed within you that is denying you of your basic human rights."

I shake my head again as I stand. "That's *you* denying me basic human rights, not *the Untamed within me*."

I hold their gaze—all of them, collectively—for as long as I can. We stand like this for a while, and the man on the left continues the mantra that I'm supposed to agree to.

My chest tightens. This is easy; compared to the waterboarding, this is a piece of cake.

Cake.

My stomach rumbles. Shouldn't have thought of that.

But this is still easy. I could go for days, couldn't I? Without sleeping, eating, drinking....

You'll need water though. Else you'll die.

But they won't let me die. Raleigh won't. If I refuse long enough, until I'm in a bad condition, they'll have to stop this. And I just need to contact that Seer with the blue eyes, get her to help, and then the Gods and Goddesses can sort everything. I'll get my soul back, and I'll escape.

I fold my arms. "You won't win. I'm not one of you."

"Everyone can be a Chosen One. And you shall be. You poor creature, you cannot see that this is a disease you are suffering from."

A *disease*.

I feel a sense of darkness rise within me, sharp and pulsing. Then I spit at them, sudden, quick.

Two of the men flinch.

"And you like being violent like that, do you? Can you not see that violence is wrong? It is bad. It is the monster within you."

My lips twitch, and I'm tempted to shower them with more of my saliva. "Spitting isn't violent." I ball my hands into tight fists, unsure of where my sudden confidence is coming from. "You want me to show you what *is* violent?"

I take a step forward.

"Don't," one says, his voice low, even, measured. "You're running lean. Jeremy, top her up."

The man nearest to me pulls two vials out of his lab coat pocket. Two dark blue augmenters.

No.

My mouth dries.

He steps nearer.

"I'm not having them," I say.

"You have no choice. Augmenters are a staple of a good life. And, Shania, my dear, you need to learn how to live a good life."

I keep my fists steady, by my side. "What are they?"

"Just Tiredness, for now," the man says, holding up the dark blue vial in his left hand. "We can add in Hunger later if we need to weaken you a little more. Are you ready?"

I stare at him, then my gaze crosses to the other two. They all smile at me. My mouth dries even more. Tiredness? Hunger? But I thought their augmenters only gave good emotions…did good things…not….

"You can't give me those—they're not positive attributes." But my voice is too high, my confidence is seeping.

"Oh, they can be positive. There are times when someone needs to sleep so they can rest. Tiredness fixes insomnia and even anxiety in those who are prone to worry at night. It prevents broken and disturbed sleep, encouraging natural, restorative rest. Tiredness is a powerful augmenter, and it fixes many, many things. And Hunger is needed for appetite stimulation at times, to save someone who is sick and needs energy."

I try to keep my breathing even.

"And these augmenters will help fix you." Smiles, all around.

"I'm still not going to agree."

"We'll see."

The men all come at me at once. I yawp and kick out—glad that my body is mine, that Raleigh's not

DIVIDED

making this even harder for me and easier for them—but there are three of them. Hands clamp over me. A fist in my hair, my head yanked back, pain at my scalp.

"Open wide."

One of them forces my mouth open. Cold glass against my bottom lip. I try to step back, try to twist my head away, but the dark blue augmenter fills my mouth. Fingers press my lips together.

"Swallow."

I hold the liquid in my mouth. I managed to resist the augmenters before that were in me—that are still in me—but the more there are, the less *me* I'll be.

Fingers stroke my throat. The liquid moves over my tongue, and I feel a knee-jerk reaction building up.

I turn my head, start to swallow, and gag as the liquid burns. I spray it out—as much as I can—coughing, but some trickles down my throat, makes me gag again.

One of the Enhanced backhands me to the floor, and I cough, on all fours. My eyes water, I see a flash of color and—

"Get the other one in her!"

I scramble forward, choking, trying to get away, but the arms of another Enhanced spring around me. My head's yanked up. Fingers pry at my face. I don't even see the second vial of Tiredness. The first I'm aware of how close it is, is when I'm swallowing it, when all the muscles in my throat are screaming.

Almost immediately, my eyelids get heavier, my vision slightly blurry. Exhaustion pulls at my body, and my stomach feels strange—empty, hollow.

I try to take a deep breath. My eyes follow one of the men as he walks about. He takes a radio out of his belt.

"Turn it up," he says. Then he looks at me. "Repeat after me. Being Untamed is bad. It is wrong. It is evil."

I shake my head. The air around me starts to feel thick with warmth, warmth that scratches my skin. I look around for the source, but I can't see anything. It's...it's just air...the air's heating up and growing bristles.

The men exchange weak smiles.

"Say the words."

Do it.

"No."

My movements get slower, and my head feels... hazy. Everything's hazy. It's happening so quickly... too quickly... I claw at my face, rub at my eyes. Blink several times. But they sting, my eyes just sting, and the lids are too heavy.

"Come on, Shania. Those were the highest grade of augmenters. And it *is* hot in here. We know you *need* to sleep now. Acknowledge the badness within you, and we will let you sleep."

My head feels like it's going to explode as I shake it again. How can the augmenters work that quickly? Even if they're of the highest grade....

I force myself to stand. Start pacing. The Enhanced stand together now, forming a human wall in front of the door. Blocking me in.

My muscles burn. My head buzzes. My eyes sting. My throat feels strange. I blink again, feel my eyes watering. I yawn, the movement hurts my jaw...and something else too...what it is, I'm not sure because....

"No, you can't sleep, Shania. Not yet."

Arms pull at me, and I realize I'm lying down. Confusion fills me. The heat rises, surges over me. My mouth dries. My lips feel like they're about to crack.

"You have to acknowledge the badness within you. You have to drive it out *before* you sleep. Your sleep mustn't refuel the parasite. Come on, Shania."

I'm pulled up, and the light in the cell is too bright. It's like a knife, tearing at my eyes. I try to put an arm over my eyes, try to shield them, but the Enhanced don't let me. Pain sprinkles across my head. They yank my arm back, start shouting about how bad the Untamed are, how bad I am—but they can save me if I help them save myself first. If I just take the first step toward it on my own.

More exhaustion washes over me. The air gets hotter

still. I'm sweating, sweating too much. They're not—must have taken augmenters to prevent them from feeling the heat…but the sweat's pouring off me… I'm losing water.

Water.

My eyes widen.

Shit.

Dehydration—but they won't let it get to a dangerous level, will they?

My heart pounds, and then my arms feel strange, as if each bone inside them divides into two, three, four, peeling into layers and floating inside me, catching each other with the slightest movement of my body, sending ripples of enervation and pain through me.

"You can have a drink once you surrender. As soon as you surrender, we will get you water. And you can sleep too."

Just agree with what they want! Pretend!

No….

I shake myself. I can resist this. I can…can't I?

I have to.

Corin.

Suddenly, I see him in front of me. His eyes wide and Untamed. Those beautiful dark brown eyes, warm like the evening sun, but strong and penetrating like fire. And he sees me—sees my mirror eyes. He glares at me; his bottom lip pushes out slightly as his eyebrows knit together. The look in his eyes changes: gets sharper.

"Fight them," he says, and his words zoom toward me, like darts tailing ribbons, and the colorful threads wrap around me, tighter and tighter, tighter and tighter.

And my head feels strange. Too…too foggy inside… like I'm slipping….

"Fight them," Corin says.

Still slipping…still and….

"I will," I say to him, but then he disappears—his image shimmers, and then he's gone.

Gone....

"Excellent," one of the Enhanced says. "Repeat after me—"

"No! Not that!" The volume of my words surprises me, drills through me. My head pounds more, harder and harder. Palpitations fill me. My heart's going to....

Sweat...too much and...my mouth's too dry. And I'm....

Everything becomes a blur. I need to sleep...but I can't. They won't...and I can't... I look up and see shapes on the walls. The bricks are moving, changing, forming big circles and squares of darker colors. Patterns.

I try to lift my arm, but I've got no energy. It's just all...gone....

"Being Untamed is bad, isn't it?"

"Concentrate on what you're feeling now, Shania. The discomfort, the pain—that's what being Untamed is."

"The evil inside you is making you feel this way."

"Expel it."

I look at them through my blurry eyes. "No...."

Just do it. You're too tired. And Raleigh's still got you. Whether you're Untamed or not, he's going to make you save everyone. It won't change the outcome.

No...no...no... There's still...still something.

"Hope," I say. And I see a set of blue eyes before me. Like blue crystals.

Whose eyes are they? Can't think...my head...too....

"Join us, Shania, join us and we'll let you have some water and let you sleep. And you need water—you haven't drunk any in ages... And you're weakening fast...so little energy, no fuel. And you need it, don't you? You are hungry. So, Shania, will you join us? We'll feed you when you join us. Imagine that: food, water, *and* sleep."

Yes.

"No...."

I think they smile as they look at each other.

DIVIDED

"Give her two more vials of Tiredness and one of Hunger. And turn the temperature up again. That's sure to weaken her."

My mother stands in the cell over me. I'm sitting up, but barely. She wobbles in my blurry vision, and I know she can't be here. Not really.

No, it's because I'm tired. I'm seeing things.

But she looks real as she crouches down. She's wearing a spicy perfume, and its scent washes over me. Hints of cinnamon and cardamom and pepper and something woody.

"My baby," she whispers, and her beautiful black hair falls in a curtain around her face, obscures her mirror eyes from me. "Don't take the augmenters. They are full of badness."

I try to frown, but my head hurts too much.

"Seven, do you hear me? Don't take them." She moves her head, and her hair moves, reveals her mirrors again, as if it's a game.

"I won't," I whisper, and my voice cracks. Everything in my mouth cracks. Too dry and—and it's still so hot in here. Yet she's not sweating. It's just me.

My mother looks at me. "I've seen how it ends, and it ends in fire."

And she touches my hand and—

A woman falls in flames. She screams, and long, dark hair whips around in front of her face, obscures her features. Orange tongues rise around her. They eat her.

Her scream goes on and on, cuts the night.

And then it's over.

I flinch as the vision disappears, as my mother yanks the images back into her own head.

I look at her, my eyes wide. "What was that?"

"It ends in fire for you," my mother whispers again, but it's just her voice. For when I look around, when I search for her again, she's not here.

There's no one here. Not even the Enhanced…when did they go?

It's just me.

Tired and thirsty and hungry and weak—

So tired.

SIX

"WELL, AREN'T YOU A STRONG one? Resisting for so long."

I look up at the man hovering over me as he gradually slides into focus. Raleigh. His lips peel back as he smiles, but the movement reminds me of skinning a bird. Like how Marouska—the real Marouska—used to do back at Nbutai. She'd pull the skin off with long tugs. Sometimes, she'd throw the skin for the dogs, and they'd all go mad for it.

"But you saw sense in the end, and I'm glad."

Saw sense?

I... I... I agreed with them? Flashes come back to me, but it seems so long ago... The men shouting. Mirror eyes glinting. Me screaming, trying to sleep—them not letting me. I swallow with difficulty; my throat's sore, and there's a dull pain behind my eyes.

But I didn't agree.

I wouldn't agree.

I *wouldn't*!

Everything about Raleigh's body language says that he's surveying me carefully, his gaze covering every part of me. It's then that I see what he's holding out to me. Food. Behind him, two Enhanced stand by the door. It's partially open; for a second, I entertain the idea of running for it, trying to dodge the guards.

But I wouldn't get far. Raleigh would ensure that.

No. I've got to be careful. Wait until the Gods and Goddesses have forgiven me, so that when I'm out there I get the warnings again. And wait until I'm in contact with the blue-eyed Seer again?

My body jolts. I'm still Untamed. I must be. I'm thinking about rebelling. About escape.

I'm Untamed.

And they don't know? They think they've broken me?

The smell of chicken stew wafts over me, and I sit up and take the bowl and spoon from Raleigh, nervous. Does he know? Or did they stop that torture session because I wasn't complying and I was getting *too* weak, dangerously weak? No, he said I *saw sense in the end*.

"Where's my mother?" I ask, remembering that... that dream? That hallucination?

"She's still posted at New Kimearo."

"I—I want to see her."

"You can't. Not yet."

Not yet... So in the future, I will? I look up at Raleigh, but something makes me seal my lips.

A moment later, he hands me a bread roll, getting it from his pocket, still watching me. The roll is furry, covered in tiny hairs, makes me feel like I'm holding a tiny animal. I put it down on the floor quickly. Raleigh sits down opposite, crossing his long legs out on the floor in front of him so his toes touch my feet. I draw my knees closer to my body, yank my feet toward me.

Raleigh snorts. "Eat."

I look down at the food. The bowl is warm in my hands, but the stew doesn't smell strong anymore—not like it should. Not like that burning lamb did. I swallow hard. My stomach churns as I stir the stew with the spoon. There's oil on the surface of it.

DIVIDED

"You have to eat, Shania. And I know you're hungry."

But he's wrong. I don't feel hungry. Not now. Did I before—after the Hunger? I can't remember. It's all just...like it's not there. Gone. And I can't remember. My mind protecting myself?

"I want to see Esther," I say. "Is she all right?"

"You'll see your friend as soon as you're good for me. It can be a reward." His mirrors flash, and I look away as he turns more toward me—don't want to see my own eyes, in his. "Eat up."

The spoon hits a lump as I continue stirring. My gut clenches.

"I'm not hungry."

"You *need* to keep your strength up, Shania. You need to be strong now—strong enough to keep the Untamed evil away, because it may try to come back." *It's already back. It never left.* "Not eating won't solve anything." There's something about his tone that reminds me of Jed, and my insides curl a little. Raleigh smiles.

"I don't like chicken." It's a lie, but just the fact that I'm able to say it makes me feel better. Proves I'm definitely still Untamed, because, if the augmenters were working, I wouldn't be able to lie. Would I? Not when lying's bad.

So why aren't they working?

"Nonsense," Raleigh says. "You love chicken. It is good for you."

I bite my lip. The augmenters—I *still* don't feel the pull of them. Not like before. All I feel is...*sick*. My stomach churns.

Raleigh leans forward, looks at me carefully. His eyes narrow a little, and he inhales sharply, stares at me for several long moments. "Your powers are stronger. I can feel them now, even without getting in your head. I can *feel* your Seer powers." He nods, rubs his hands together. "That last session with me must've helped. Partially unlocked your abilities. They're closer to the surface. And getting rid of the Untamed evil has helped, because you know it's the right thing to do really, don't you?"

His grin makes me feel sicker.

"If you're not going to eat, you'd better come with me."

He takes the bowl of stew from me, with the spoon in it, and I watch him set them on the floor. And then—then my Promise Marks burn, and I'm getting up, following him to the door.

No.

I speed up, let him take my arm as we walk, as we get out of the cell, as we go down the corridor.

I try to pull my arm back—feel my pulse quicken—but I can't.

Raleigh chuckles.

And I know—I know what he's going to make me do even before we get to the room. Even before a guard brings Elia Jackson back, and two more Enhanced stand by the door. Even before Raleigh sits me down on a stool, and—

His hands clamp around my head.

"No!" I try to get away from him, pour every ounce of energy into getting away from him, but I can't—can't do anything, can't….

"Still refusing?" Raleigh's voice is like a cold worm. "Well, I suppose there will be some residual evil in you. Come on, Shania. I'll guide you again. And then next time—when you're *completely better* you'll be able to do it yourself."

Next time? My heart palpitates.

He lifts my head up, makes me look at the girl. She looks just as gormless as before, her expression unfocussed, just blank.

"Concentrate on her. Don't look away."

Pain lassoes around my eyeballs, and I can't look away. He makes sure of that. Can't blink.

"Now. You're going to give me access to your powers, Shania. Aren't you?" Raleigh croons, but his

DIVIDED

voice is distant and—

Something crashes into my back. Something hard and—I scream as I realize it's his body, and then he lifts me up—by my head—so my buckling legs are on the stool's top, and he presses me against him. His grip on my skull tightens—his fingers are like nails, digging in, deeper and deeper.

I feel something wet around my temples, wetness, sliding down.

Something inside me clicks.

"Yes..." Raleigh mutters. "Oh, yes."

Scorching pain, inside my head. A flash, behind my eyes, and—

No.

My breathing speeds up. I think of the blue-eyed Seer. I'm not on my own. It's not me against Raleigh. It's me and her—whomever she is—against Raleigh. And Raleigh doesn't know that. I've got the element of surprise.

And I try to get to her, try to contact her; I need her help, but....

"Lift your arm," Raleigh whispers, and I don't know why he says the words aloud, when he makes me do it, when my left arm rises because it's what he wants.

My fingers tingle, and I start to curl my fingers, make a fist.

"No," Raleigh whispers.

My fingers uncurl. My palm is flat, facing away from me. Facing toward the girl.

"Run!" I bite the word out, try to aim it at the girl, but I haven't got enough volume, and she's not listening to me, and—

I howl as the pain gets sharper. As white light flickers from *my* hand. Blinding.

No.

No.

No.

"Yes, I *knew* you felt stronger." Raleigh's smiling. I can't see his face, but I know he's smiling. Smiling as if this is the most brilliant thing to have happened to him in his life.

I try to lower my arm, but the pain in my head gets harder.

Need to stop him. Need to....

"And again," Raleigh whispers.

Slugs. No, maggots. His voice reminds me of maggots. Maggots festering in a wound, crawling round and round in raw flesh, their creamy bodies swollen and pulsating.

I feel the energy slithering down my arm this time. Through my veins, my tendons, to my palm, and I try to stop it—I really do, but I—

My scream cuts my ears as white light bulbs from my hand, shoots forward, and hits Elia squarely in my chest. For a moment, she doesn't do anything. But then she falls, hits the floor with a small gasp.

Raleigh lets go of me, physically and mentally, and I fall forward, smash into the floor. My head pounds, darkness, darkness, darkness, and red and blood and pain and....

I start choking, feel bile burn as it rises. I throw up noisily, projectile vomiting an awful lot of liquid and slimy green stuff. Acid burns my tongue, makes my eyes water. My arms flail, and then my foot hits one of the stool's legs, and it scrapes across the floor. Raleigh shakes his head in mock-sympathy. He crouches over Elia's body, two fingers against her neck. His lips twitch—in disgust? Then he points at my pile of vomit.

"It's a pity there's still an Untamed seed inside you. All that pain—those negative emotions—could've been avoided, if you'd just tried harder. But I know what will help."

He's back at my side—moving too quickly—and clasps my arms.

"André, pass me those scissors."

One of the Enhanced by the door moves to the side of room and retrieves the implement from a cupboard I hadn't realized was there—it's almost as if it just

DIVIDED

appeared. Then he hands it to Raleigh.

I stare at the sharp points of the scissors as Raleigh holds them in front of me. Two sharp points. Like life and death.

"It's the way you're seeing yourself," Raleigh says. He moves the scissors so they point at my face. "Look at you." And he gestures for me to lift my head. I do, because the points of the scissors get too close.

I see myself in his eyes. Wild, matted hair, plastered to the side of my face by sweat. Torn clothes—different ones to before…no leggings now. Dark jeans. And a murky colored shirt. When were they changed? I can't remember…hadn't even noticed. Oh Gods. I look dirty. And my teeth—they're *dirty*. I taste the dirtiness on them.

"You need to start again. A new image," Raleigh says. "It's what's holding you back still. You need to separate yourself from your Untamed image. A *clean* start."

He lifts the scissors, and, before I have a chance to process what he means, he cuts off a lock of my hair. I watch it fall to the floor, like a feather. A black feather. Death's feather.

Then I cry out, twist around, my hands going to my head. "No!"

Raleigh seizes a fistful of my hair, pulls it hard. I struggle, try to fight him, but I'm weak after everything, and he knows that. I move my left hand, feel the cold metal against it before Raleigh directs my hands to go down. The scissors snatch more of my hair.

Snip snip snip.

I try to hit him again, try to kick him—try to do something—but I can't. Can't because—

Pain.

Oh Gods!

He laughs.

"Yes, this will work well. It's exactly what you need. And, wow—don't you look different? It changes the shape of your face completely. And now the Untamed evil that was in you won't recognize you any longer. It will *want* to get away from you."

My head pounds. Fine hairs stick to my skin. I blink as fast as I can, try to get them away from my eyes.

"Yes," Raleigh says, still cutting my hair off in uneven chunks. "You're not its host any longer. The Untamed part doesn't even know you."

My breathing speeds up. It doesn't work like that. I'm still Untamed. Cutting my hair won't change a thing. But seeing my locks fall around me, feeling the cold metal of the scissors against my scalp, does something to me. Sadness fills me. And I feel stupid. It's just hair. I'm being vain, like Five.

But it's me, it's *my* hair. It's part of me.

And then it's gone. And I look at my head, in Raleigh's eyes. My hair, what's left of it, hacked into uneven chunks, some an inch long, other sections cut almost to the scalp.

"And congratulations," Raleigh says, handing the scissors to one of the other Enhanced. He points back at Elia Jackson's body. "You've used your Seer powers to kill your first victim." He smiles widely. "And we're not going to fight anymore, are we? Not now we're on the same side. And once you're completely pure, once those last bad tendrils have died and left you, you'll understand."

I stare at Elia's body, feel everything inside me move and shift and burn.

The girl I killed.

No, the girl *Raleigh* killed.

But me...it was me.

Killed with my power.

Dead.

A *child*.

Eight years old.

A child...like Kyla.

I look up, see Raleigh beaming at me. "We can probably move onto seeking and conversion powers in a day or so. You're strong. We could wipe out all the

DIVIDED

Untamed within a week."

SEVEN

I FEEL SICK, AND I try to run—where, I don't know—but I only get three steps before I collapse and choke on bile and stomach acid and saliva—too much saliva—and I choke on it for so long, my eyes streaming, my throat burning raw.

I lose track of time as I throw up continuously—covering myself and everything around me in vomit—but, at some point, Raleigh and the Enhanced men disappear. They take Elia's body with them, then three women come and take me to another room. They strip my clothes off and hold me up under a cold shower. But there are mirrors in here too, and I stare at the marks on my skin, somehow emphasized by the water and my convulsing body as I heave. The small dark punctures—the kavalah spirit scars—they mark me. And the huge gold welts—the Promise Marks. They're everywhere: my legs, my arms, my face… Not even the fetid soaps and lotions the women drench me with as they try to get rid of the smell of my vomit can mask them.

Raleigh said they were *his* marks on me. I don't want any part of Raleigh on me.

DIVIDED

I need to get the marks off.

I grab a brush from one of the women. She seems surprised, but lets me take it. It's got hard bristles, but they're not hard enough, and I use what little energy I have to scrub at my side, where a gold mark is. I keep scrubbing at it, even when my fingers ache and there's so much pain everywhere. I feel the burn of the friction, the sharpness of the bristles, and the women start shouting at me, then hands claw the brush back.

I stare at my skin, my head's all floaty, doesn't feel right. Red oozes out, around my waist, and I wipe it away with my fingers, smear it to the side, down my thigh. But the gold mark is still there. Not moving now. But it's alive. I know that.

Oh Gods.

It's true. Only the Gods and Goddesses can get them off me…and they won't… They think I'm a traitor. They won't let me in the Dream Land in case I…in case I kill them… They think I'm an Enhanced Seer… They've banished me. They can't see the truth.

But the blue-eyed Seer knows. Somehow, she knows.

"You think she's got it too?" one of the women says to the others as they dress me in a pair of blue overalls that are far too big. They roll up the sleeves and the legs. The waist is baggy but it's a one-piece suit.

"No. Raleigh said this was shock. And the purging of the last bit of the…."

I lose their voices as my head starts to swim. My body flushes hot and then cold. Then hot once more.

I throw up again, but there's now a bucket next to me, and I manage to get most of it in it. A woman next to me grunts, then takes it away. Her skin is as dark as mine, but her hair is a luminous silver. Like the moon. I stare at her in awe.

Then I'm back in the first room. The room Raleigh first took me to. My cell.

I lie down. Someone's put a mattress here.

Sleep.

But I can't sleep. It's too hot in here, far too hot.

Within minutes, the mattress is soaked with sweat. I stink badly, still, and the smell engulfs me. Stuff shifts in my stomach again—don't know how there's anything left—and I force myself to sit up, look for the bucket.

It's back, and I grab it. But everything moves—the walls, everything, and I can't—

I cry out, see my mother in front of me. She watches me, shakes her head softly.

"Mum!"

I hold my arms out toward her, and then I'm a little girl again—I'm five years old—and she holds me, and I stare at her red-rimmed eyes and her swollen face. Swollen with tears, days and days of crying because Four and Six were taken by the fever only days before the enemy attacked and killed Two, and Corin and Esther's parents, and we're all tired. We've been walking for days, scared, trying to find a new place to set up village because we had to leave Kyzik.

"She's delirious again," my mother says, but she's not talking to me.

There's someone else here. A shadow at the back of my room. A girl.

Elia steps forward, her long hair flopping forward, only her hair's darker now. And her face changes, and her skin and—and now she looks like Kyla, Nyesha's daughter.

She *is* her.

I gulp. Then she's Elia again.

Don't worry, she says. *You freed me. Death was what I wanted. Thank you.*

Oh Gods.

I seize the bucket; part of me wonders why I'm being sick so much. It's like when we got that virus before... we all had it, except for Rahn and—

Another wave of nausea rises, and all thoughts are pushed from my mind.

When I've finished, I turn back. But there's no one here now. My legs are wobbly, shaking as I walk around my room. I check all the corners for them, the people. They're here, somewhere, hiding. Got to be. But the corners get bigger and bigger, stretching farther and farther back, and I can't reach them and—

My *throat*.

Fire.

It's burning.

I grasp at my neck, but it hurts my fingers.

I stare at them, see the deep cuts across my fingers and the palms of my hands.

The white light.

I feel sick, see Elia's body as I shut my eyes.

"I'm sorry," I whisper.

And everyone's gone. It's just me. Just me.

And the darkness... The darkness is growing... bigger and bigger.

It comes toward me in waves. Huge waves that crash over my head, that pull me down, that drown me.

"Seven?"

The voice is urgent... Urgent and fast... Trying to pull me out of the...out of the water. Water?

I groan as I'm thrown onto the bank, as I taste sand and grit and feel rough abrasions all over me. Waves of exhaustion try to hold me down.

"Seven? Are you awake?"

Esther's words start to fade, get dimmer because of the buzzing in my ears that's taking over everything.

I sit up slowly. Every single part of me aches. I breathe hard, heavily, try to focus on something, but my eyes are blurry. I bring a hand up, touch my head. Pain rebounds through my temples, and I wince, freeze until it settles. Then my vision clears.

I see the cage I'm in. And the rows of cages, the metal bars. A person in each one…and Esther, she's in the cage next to me.

Fading mirrors dance in her eyes. For a second, I can only stare.

I move closer to her, slowly, dragging myself. My legs…they feel different. I touch my forehead, my hand shaking. My blue overalls rustle.

I look around at the cells—the cages, the people in them. Then back at Esther. She's got overalls on too. We all have. I stare at her, at the rashes that have spread down both sides of her face.

"What…?" I shake my head as I look back and forth. Oh Gods. I feel awful. My head, it's heavy, achy and… I look at Esther. "We're locked up?"

She nods, squints at me. "Your rash is *gold*?"

"What?"

"You're covered in a gold rash." She lifts her own arm, rolls back the sleeve of her overalls, and against her creamy skin I see thousands of tiny red dots. "Most of us have got rashes…but yours is gold."

My stomach twists. I try not to look at them, the marks, and concentrate on my surroundings instead. "What is this? These cages…" I frown, can't remember coming here.

"Quarantine," a weak voice says.

I turn, wince as my sore muscles protest. A Zharat woman. I recognize her distantly. My eyes focus almost too much until she's *too* sharp, *too* in focus. Nausea rises, and I bring a hand to my mouth.

"We're all sick," she says. "They've sectioned us off to protect themselves."

Sick?

I look around, head spinning. I start counting. Five…ten…fifteen…twenty….

"There are one hundred and forty-eight of us, across the different quarantine bays." Esther's voice is raspy. "Including you." She sighs. "They got us. When we were trying to escape, when the volcano exploded."

DIVIDED

"It didn't explode," a Zharat man says. "It was a steam release."

"Right into our living chambers," the woman who spoke first says. "The Gods were angry with us. Forced us out of our home."

The Zharat all start talking now, and I lose track of their words, just can't focus. Can't concentrate. Their words are like butterflies soaring over me, twirling round and round, weaving invisible threads around me, pulling them tighter and tighter. A mesh of words.

Esther shifts her weight on her side of the bars. When she looks at me, the circles under her eyes seem even bigger. Her bottom lip wobbles. "Corin's left us."

Her eyes darken. The fading mirrors look strange in them. She's running lean—but she's not acting like she is…is she? There's no desperation. No jumpiness. No obvious anxiety. I don't understand. This can't be real. A dream? A nightmare?

I pull my hand back, fold my arms. My chest feels strange. Hollow. And my stomach—sick. This has to be a nightmare. The augmenters wouldn't let me feel sick. They shouldn't.

"Seven, didn't you know?" Esther looks at me carefully. "Corin's escaped."

I nod. "I knew."

Her eyes widen a little. "And you're okay with that? Being left here? He didn't even try and get me out. I didn't even *see* him. Not after they caught us, brought us here, and—"

"But he's safe now," I say. Or at least he is until Raleigh's men find him.

Or until I'm forced to locate him.

I breathe deeply, try to steady myself, my thoughts. It's not going to happen. It won't get that far. I'll escape. I will. I'll do something.

"He's safe, and *we're* not." Esther says darkly, then looks at me with a different light in her eyes. "What's going on? Your eyes…."

"What?" My heart rate shoots up, and I lean against

the bars to steady myself.

"They're darkening. The mirrors are fading." Esther frowns again.

"So are yours."

She presses her lips together for a second. "Why are they letting us be Untamed again? I don't understand... I thought augmenters were supposed to be addictive. But I don't feel... Do you?" She winces, as if she doesn't like asking the question.

My eyes narrow. I should feel happy, I know that. Or if not happy, something positive. Calm? But I don't. I'm shaking. I feel jittery. Like I've got withdrawal symptoms—yet Esther hasn't, and her mirrors are fading too....

This isn't real. It can't be. The Enhanced wouldn't let us become Untamed again...this is... I look around. The cages. A manifestation of my mind? My soul trying to separate the Untamed part of me, locking it away where Raleigh can't get to it, can't destroy it. A prison where I'm trapping my memories of Esther and the Zharat, trying to keep them Untamed too....

But they've all got partial-mirrors....

So Raleigh's been here? Got them...*partly*. My head pounds.

"Seven? Do you feel it? Do you want augmenters?" Esther's voice wavers, and I look across at her, see her pale. She clutches her stomach, breathing deeply. Behind her, there's a bucket.

My own stomach churns, and I shake my head when she looks back at me. No, I don't want augmenters.

Yes, you do. Don't lie to yourself.

But I can lie...and it's not lying. Is it?

My gaze returns to Esther just as she starts coughing, and then she leans forward, away from me. But I see the frown on her face, the same frown that Corin has.

Corin.

I picture him. Rugged, handsome. I know I should feel a pull. I should feel something. But I don't—because this isn't real. Because I can't feel properly in here, locked away....

Or because the augmenters won't let me feel love for him, excitement...because Raleigh's controlling me, choosing what I do, what I feel.

No, that's not right. That's not—

I freeze as I see *him*.

The hairs on the back of my neck stand up. "Oh Gods."

I try to lift my hands up, to protect myself, but they shake and—

It's *him*.

He's here too.

Alive.

Not dead. And—

Oh Gods.

Jed.

My breath catches on my teeth, my ribs squeeze together. No. No. *No*. But—but it is, it is, oh Gods. And he's in my cage, and he's moving closer, and he's bending over me, and his lips are by my ear.

"You do not feel anything for him anymore, because you are my wife, S'ven. You are mine," he whispers.

I scream, and Esther turns back, still coughing, her face red, and the Zharat are looking at me and—

And he's gone—Jed's gone and—

"What the hell?" My words are shaky. I point at thin air. "Did you see him? He was there...and now he's... Jed was *here*."

Esther shakes her head. Her skin looks sallow under the crimson splodges and rashes. "We're all seeing things. People. My mum was here and...."

Her mother. She's seeing someone she wants to see. I'm not. I don't want to see Jed. But my mind's playing tricks. Why him? Why's it making me think Jed—of all people—is here?

Oh Gods. It's Raleigh. It's down to him, has to be, he's playing with me. I'm a toy, and he's....

"Stop it!" I yell out, know he's watching, somehow, somewhere. Or is he here?

I struggle to stand, to move, looking around. I grab the bars as dizziness pulls at me, use them to support myself. Then I shake them. I need to get out. I won't be played with.

I won't.

"Seven?"

I turn back to Esther—Esther with her nearly-Untamed eyes. No. This can't be real. She was being converted earlier...was it earlier? Or yesterday? A day ago? I don't know how much time has passed since I've been here. A couple of days, surely? But none of this can really be happening.

Esther exhales. "Are you okay? What's going on?"

"That," says a new voice, "is exactly what I'd like to know."

Raleigh. I look up. He *is* here. He's playing with me. I see the big boiler suit he's wearing and the safety visor in front of his face, and a strange feeling—like thick, tarry bubbles—passes over me. He looks ridiculous. This is my dream, and I've made him look like that... because I don't want to see him. Because the suit creates a barrier, and now he can't get to me.

"Right," Raleigh says, directing his word at me as he stops outside my cage. "Tell me what you've done."

I frown, try to keep looking at him, but my eyes are tired, so tired. And I don't understand. This is my... imagination. *Mine.* So, I'm in charge.

No, Raleigh's in charge of you.

I shudder, try to push that thought away, but it keeps bouncing back, like it's on elastic.

"I didn't think it could be you at first, when it started, but clearly I was wrong. And I want to know how you've done it." Raleigh's voice gets louder, and it's echoing. Is he saying the words in real life, and they're filtering through to my...to whatever this place is? Am I *inside* my head, my imagination?

"Shania!" Raleigh shouts, and the decibels of his voice make me grimace. Too loud...my ears....

"Why... What?" I wince and blink harder as the

DIVIDED

pounding grows.

Esther's looking at me strangely. The shadows under her eyes are growing again; they're getting bigger as I watch. I take a shaky breath. Why've I painted her like this, in my safe cage? My world... It should be... she should look beautiful—just like Three said she is.

"How have you done it?" Raleigh barks, jolting my gaze away from Esther and back toward him.

I want to tell him to shut up—his tone is making my headache worse—but then I see myself reflected in his visor, and I lean forward, try to see my eyes in it. I squint, need to see them, that's important...I think.

"Undo it now," Raleigh hisses. "You can't win against me, Shania. I still command your soul, your body, your powers, and I still have your eyes."

My eyelids promptly feel heavier. I rub at them, but I just get the sand in them. Sand... No, there's no sand here. My safe place for the Untamed doesn't have sand? I look down. The floor is smooth. Marble? Yes. It's marble. I like marble.

"Shania! All my new Chosen Ones are getting ill," Raleigh says. "This has never happened before, and I know you were resisting. And you know what else I know? That you're a powerful Seer." He presses his visor against the metal bars. "Thought you'd be clever, did you? Thought you'd make them all unwell— thought you'd kill them right away to *save* them from me, from even having the chance of becoming Chosen Ones?" He shakes his head. "I didn't think you would be so selfish."

Killing them? Saving them from Raleigh?

Sweat runs down my spine, sticking my overalls to my damp skin. It's too hot in here. Far too hot...like in that conversion and...and my chest, it's too tight... My mind races, races over Raleigh's words, the ones he's just said, and then I look at Esther and the others again. They're coughing, wheezing. And the dark shadows under everyone's eyes look bigger. The Zharat woman in the cage opposite me is just lying on the floor, her chest barely rising and falling.

And I've done this? My safe place isn't safe....

I'm a Seer of Death, and these people are dying.

Except they're not here. No one is. It's my... imagination. Yes. Just my imagination. I nod, then wrap my arms around me. My ears start to burn, and I step back, away from Raleigh, away from his reflective visor because all I can see in it are the ill people around me. They're everywhere, reflected and real and—

Raleigh growls and snaps his gloved-fingers in front of my face. "And you. You're ill too, Shania. Tell me how you're doing it. *Tell me*. Is it contagious? Will my people get it? Are you already targeting them?"

My people... His words seem important...because he's not including me. I'm not one of them. A smile graces my lips, and using those muscles feels strange.

"Shania, *I'm* talking to you. Are you targeting my people?"

He doesn't know. But he should...if he's commanding my soul, shouldn't he know whether I'm doing it or not? But he doesn't. He really thinks... thinks I can hide stuff from him. And I *have* been hiding stuff; he doesn't know about my contact with the blue-eyed Seer.

Raleigh yanks open my cell door and marches in. Before I can do anything, he grabs me, shakes me hard. Something clicks in my head, and then the pain....

I wail.

"Seven!" Esther's voice...and she's shouting at Raleigh.

But I can't...pain...my head....

Heat...in my hands...and I know what's happening... But not if I'm doing it or if it's him or... I try to lift them, try to lift my hands... I manage it... The white light grows from my fingers, flickers dimly...not like before...but Raleigh's there and—

"I don't think so," Raleigh spits, then he slaps me hard.

I lose my grip on my powers as he propels my body

DIVIDED

backward. My head hits the wall. Hard. I grunt, see stars flash around me. And it hurts. It hurts—why does it hurt? This isn't real so it shouldn't....

But it does.

It hurts.

It's *real*.

Oh Gods.

"How *dare* you use that against me."

I try to open my heavy eyes, try to see Raleigh.

He's above me, looking down at me, and someone's shouting at him. No, several people are.

"This won't work, Shania," Raleigh snarls. "You can't beat me. I *will* convert your people—them being ill won't stop me. In fact, we're already re-mind-converting several in the other quarantine bays. You're just causing unnecessary suffering—proof of the evil that you are."

The words make me feel strange. I start to go dizzy. A second later, a door bangs, and I realize Raleigh's left...left so quickly. Too quickly. That's not right....

"You're doing this?" Esther stares at me. "To save us all?" There's a strange warmth in her eyes now. Warmth I don't deserve.

I shake my head. "I don't know... My powers...."

My eyes widen and—oh Gods.

Elia Jackson.

I swallow with difficulty, as if my throat is too small. It feels like a bad dream, like it didn't happen. Yet, I know. I *know*.

"I killed her." I look at Esther. "He made me." My breathing gets quicker. "He's going to... Conversion powers, he said."

"You're not making any sense." Esther shakes her head, and I see most of the Zharat—the ones who are still able to move a little—are looking at me now. Faces against bars.

I press my lips together. They feel strange. I bite down on my bottom lip. It hurts. This is still real. Very real.

I try to keep the wobble out of my breath as I realize just how much I've *not* told anyone, how much I need to tell Esther: how I met Death—the God—and the augury, how important I am. What Jed did, how I was tricked, how the Gods and Goddesses banished me from the Dream Land. How Raleigh now has my soul, and how he made me kill that girl. How he's going to make me convert all the Untamed—and kill the ones I can't.

How the Untamed are going to lose the war because of me.

Oh Gods.

But there's the blue-eyed Seer too.

I look around at the Zharat—at the people who don't believe females can be Seers—and I'm glad they're in cages. No one can hurt me when I'm in a cage. Only Raleigh.

I look at Esther.

"I need to tell you something."

EIGHT

THE MAJORITY OF THE ZHARAT threaten me with death, for being a fraudulent Seer, for angering the Gods, for getting them into this mess.

Esther just stares at me. She's taking it a lot better than I expected, especially given *how much* I've kept from her. Something tells me that if Corin was here, he'd make more of a fuss.

"Jed," Esther says. "It was him? *He* did this...after the volcano...."

I nod. I don't want to go into all this. Just hearing Esther say Jed's name makes me feel colder. Guilty. That's how I feel, and I don't understand. It's not my fault.

The look in Esther's eyes changes, makes her look more like herself. Not the semi-Enhanced Esther.

"But there's a Seer out there who's going to help?"

I nod again.

Is she? You don't even know who she is.

But she's Untamed—that's all that matters.

"And Corin's out there," I say.

"So he might find these other Untamed out there—was the Seer Zharat?"

"No. She was female."

"What else?"

"Really clear blue eyes."

"She far away?"

I shrug, and the movement pulls at my bad shoulder, makes the pain flare up, reminds me of the rest of my aches. I wince. "I don't know."

Esther bows her head a little. "So, Corin might find others. And he knows where *this* compound is, and that Seer's been in contact with you—so they could come. A rescue party *could* come."

"And you've got us all together in here," a new voice says. I recognize her immediately, and a grin spreads across my face. *Clare.* A few cages down. Don't know how I didn't see her before. "That would make a rescue easier, if they did come for us. And we're resisting augmenters—because of you."

I nod, though I feel strange—like I'm taking credit for something someone else did. Yet it can't be a coincidence that we're all ill and not feeling the pull of the augmenters. Unless we were all exposed to something in the Fire Mountain, and it's only just come out now? And it's that which is interfering with the augmenters?

"There's still hope," Esther says, and she says the words firmly. "You just need to stop Raleigh using your Seer powers and making you hurt people."

"And for that I need the Gods and Goddesses back on my side and full control of my own soul," I whisper.

Esther leans forward. "And that Seer you saw—I bet she can help. You've just got to find out who she is and contact her." She looks at me expectantly, as if I can contact the mysterious Seer right away.

"I don't know how."

I think of my father's words: *the moment you think you've lost, then you have.* And he's right. Even now, when he's gone, he's right.

I breathe deeply. "I don't know how—*yet*."

Would Raleigh realize I'm contacting another Seer

DIVIDED

for help? He didn't seem to notice before—but it was just a fleeting image of the Seer. But if I did get in contact and talk with her for a long time, would he feel it? And he's still got my eyes; if he was looking, would he see her? Or does he only see what's literally in front of my physical body? Either way, I don't like it, and I frown. There's got to be a way I can reverse the control Raleigh has over me *and* get my eyes back. There has to be. I shake my head as I think. I've got to get into the Dream Land—but how? The benevolent spirits aid the Gods and Goddesses as they summon Seers—and they wouldn't ever summon an Enhanced Seer. I need the help of another Seer for that.

Another Seer.

I stand and look down the length of the cages, my knees protesting. "Are there any Seers here? Zharat Seers?"

"I'm a Seer," a male voice says. "A *proper* Seer. Active for the moment, 'less you're taintin' me with your darkness."

I breathe deeply, try to think. But this Zharat Seer won't have access to the Dream Land. He can't get there because the male Zharat Seers kill the female Zharat Seers, which is just as much treason as converting. I shake my head. What we need is for the Gods and Goddesses to make someone here a Seer. But they wouldn't do that—not when we've all been caught and have augmenters in us...even though we're not feeling the effects and our mirrors are fading.

"We ain't escapin' from 'ere," the male Seer says. "Look at us, we're weak. We're locked up. We're in a bloody Enhanced compound for the Gods' sake. And there ain't no rescue team comin' for us."

I press my lips together. "Did any of the Zharat get away? How many got out of the steam eruption *without* the Enhanced getting them?"

"Some."

"So they can help us too...."

"So long as the volcano's anger didn't get them

after," Clare says. "There was some magma surfacing too. But they're not goin' to come here. Or know the way... We traveled for a long time to get here."

I breathe deeply. I can't remember the journey. I was unconscious then? "How long?"

Esther frowns. "It was about a four-hour journey, I think."

"Four hours?" I try not to grimace. "That's... doable."

"Four hours in vehicles that flew," another Zharat man says.

"Planes." I shake my head. "So we're probably not in the Noir Lands." I press my lips together, then curse under my breath. "Okay. But there's still got to be a way. Something we can do. Something active we can do now."

The blue-eyed Seer. She's the only option. I've *got* to contact her.

But how? Using Seer powers? Then I go cold. Did I subconsciously use them earlier, when I saw her the first time? Was that how my powers were stronger... strong enough for Raleigh to kill Elia Jackson with them?

My stomach twists.

Breathe, Seven. Just breathe.

"But Raleigh can control you," Esther says. "You can't get away from him. He won't let you. *And* we've got nothing to fight them with."

"I've got a knife," Clare says.

We all look at her in surprise.

A *knife*. I bare my teeth slightly as a thought weaves toward me.

"Give it to me." I glance down at the gold marks on my arms again—they're just visible, peeking out from under the rolled-up sleeves of my overalls where they have retreated...as if they know what I've just thought of. I look back up. "Pass it along."

"Yeah, stab yourself with it, you fraud," a Zharat man says.

DIVIDED

But they pass the knife along, and Esther pushes it through my bars a moment later. I take it and run the blade lightly over the fleshy pad of my thumb, ignoring the way my head starts to feel heavier. The knife's edge is sharp. It won't need much pressure exerted.

"What are you doing?" Esther asks, starts to stand up on the other side of the bars.

I take a deep breath, work out which bit would be the best to do. Because it might work.

The gold marks on the back of my hands wink back at me.

I press my lips together.

"Have you seen something?" Esther asks. "Sev? You know what to do—what we can do?"

"Of course she hasn't *seen* anything! She's not a real Seer!"

Claire lets out a frustrated sound. "For the Gods' sake! She's real, but the Gods have blocked her. Weren't you listenin' to a word she said? No more Seeing dreams for us—because of you."

"Not us—Jed."

"He was one of *you*, one of the men."

I glance at Clare briefly. Her own sister was killed by the Zharat for being a 'fraud', and she's been against the misogyny the whole time I've known her.

I take a deep breath and return my attention to the knife. It's crude, and I wonder if it's a Zharat knife. Maybe Clare didn't get searched thoroughly, or she hid it somehow? Didn't one of the Enhanced say a blond Zharat woman had bitten someone? I look at Clare again, then press my lips together, trying not to smile.

I push my left sleeve higher up, exposing most of my arm and the marks. My breath shakes as I stare at the gold patterns. They seem brighter in here, because of the artificial lighting.

But it's them, the marks—*they're* the problem. Scrubbing them off didn't work—because the women stopped me, they knew what I was trying to do and Raleigh must've warned them before—warned them all—that I mustn't do anything to the marks. But now I've got a knife. And there are no Enhanced to stop me now.

"Seven?" Esther's tone is sharp. "What are you doing?"

I try to stop my right hand shaking. I hold the knife in it, over the gold mark on the underside of my left arm. It's near my Zharat mark, the scar one of the tribesman made when I was welcomed into their community.

I touch the tip of the blade to my arm and wince.

Then I press harder.

"Seven! You're hurting yourself!"

I try to ignore Esther's voice, need silence. The thin line of red around the gold gets a little stronger. I need to get the knife under the Promise Mark, the blade level—need to scrape it off. One quick movement. That would be best.

For a second, my vision blurs, and I think of Raleigh. Is he aware of what I'm doing, watching through my eyes? And a part of me wants him to know, to know how serious I am.

Or maybe he'll feel the pain too—my soul is bound to him, after all. Maybe I'll be hurting him. I smile. Yes. He needs to hurt.

The pain—could it be enough to make Death notice me, for him to realize, take me to the Dream Land as well? Get rid of the Promise Marks—get my soul back—*and* get the Gods and Goddesses to trust me again? To prove to them whom I am.

I take a deep breath. I nod.

Then I go for it.

"Seven!" Esther screams.

I look up, see her throw herself at the bars between us. She dents them with her weight, then forces her hand through, reaching for me.

And—and I've got the knife half under the gold

mark. Half of it is loose. But Esther distracted me. Shit. I stare at the knife peeking out from under the mark—and the flap of gold skin that's moving, shedding blood. The muscles in my throat constrict, start burning. My stomach twists, feels slimy, and my breathing's too fast.

"Give me the knife." Esther's voice is low, like a crouching cat, ready to pounce.

Tears prick the corners of my eyes, and I try to breathe through the pain, through the waves.

But my blood's everywhere now. It's covering my arm, dripping on the floor. I can't see what I'm doing. I wipe my other sleeve across my arm, try to clear it. The gold mark, it's still there, still attached on the left side. And it has to go. If it goes—if *all* of them go—it will be all right. Everything will be okay.

I pull the blade out. White sparks flit in front of my eyes. I wait for them to clear, blinking several times, then move the blade. I scrape it across my arm, from the other direction, biting sharply on my lip.

My skin flays off.

Esther screams at me, and the Zharat shout. But I'm quiet. Strangely quiet. And I—I stare at the mess on the floor: the Promise Mark among the blood. *My* blood. Something whirs inside my head.

My stomach tightens and twists.

"Seven! *No*! Give me—look at me—"

I straighten up a little, shaky, lightheaded, breathless.

My vision dims; for a second, I'm sure I must be getting to the Dream Land. But more seconds go by, and nothing else happens—nothing more than the searing pain. It's in waves, but the waves are getting stronger and closer together, harder and harder. They're crashing into me, trying to take me. Yet, at the same time, it doesn't feel like pain. It's not *hurting*. Nothing in me is hurting. Not really. Not my head, my throat, my hands, my joints—nothing.

"Death?" I call out. The Dream Land? But I know I'm not…haven't made it that far, haven't….

It's not enough. Another wave crashes. All the Promise Marks need to come off. I look for the next gold mark, and....

The metal bars hit the side of my face, and my body jolts as I move, try to work out what just happened. My hand shoots out and the floor meets it. Pain rebounds through my wrist. Then Esther grabs me—her arms through the bars—holds me to her, the metal between us.

I blink, woozy.

"Seven? Seven...." Her voice fogs my ears, and I can't breathe. The pain. The *pain*.

I try to get away from her. I've still got the knife, and I grip it tighter.

"I need to get the others off...the Promise Marks," I tell her, but my words are sandwiched between sharp bursts of breath and pain, and I don't think she hears me.

But I have to do it. And the Gods and Goddesses, they need to know I'm serious—need to understand... and they must be watching me, they *must* be—Death said before that he was always watching me.

But that's not right, is it? He didn't see what really happened....

What didn't he see? I peer around me. My vision sparkles.

"She's blacking out!" Clare yells, her voice feral.

I jolt my head up, feel Esther's hands trying to hold me up.

I sink closer to the floor, my back to Esther, the knife still in my hands. I smile at it, feel strange....

"Seven, give me the knife."

Esther's right behind me, and her arms are reaching around my body, straining against the bars, as she becomes my walls. But she can't reach the knife because I hold it out of her reach. It's the only way, and she doesn't understand.

"Just give it to me," she hisses.

I stare at the knife, the way the blood drips from the

blade. I can get the other marks off, soon, as soon as I can breathe properly again...just got to wait....

Just got to....

"Seven, please don't...just give me the knife."

"Come on, Seven. You're lettin' them win, you're...."

"I'm not," I whisper back, but I can't use my energy on speaking...not when I need to....

Something bangs next to me, and I flinch, eyes springing open. Light and—

Enhanced men. Everywhere. Shit. My chest tightens.

Do it now. While you've still got the knife. Get them all off!

The room's quiet—but a trolley squeaks...and other stuff...other stuff happens, but I can't follow it. Can't....

I see augmenters...somewhere...hear a voice telling someone to drink up, that he's running lean and—and...and my head hurts too much, and the knife shakes. And there's so much blood. More blood than I remember... So much blood.

"Move her out of here!"

And maybe I lose consciousness because, the next thing I know, I'm not in the quarantine bay. I'm in a clinical-looking room, lying on a white bed, and someone's bandaging my arm with something that smells strongly of antiseptic.

And then—then I'm not.

I'm back in....

"That's not true," Esther shouts, and I look up, see her face and—and my vision's bad, slightly doubled, but my eyes feel different. I look down at my arm, at the tattoos covering it, and the hair—a *man's* arm hair—and I stare at it all, stare at me, but it's not me. I'm not....

Snap.

Cold air against my face, the wind. Cold and fresh, crisp, with dots and sand that are like salt. Salt grains against my skin, and—

"Shania."

The name jolts through me, and I gasp, look up. Colors swirl, and I'm in the clinical-looking room again.

"Shania." Raleigh walks up to my bed, shakes his head. He's wearing that protective suit again, and he's got my knife—Clare's knife—in his hands. "Why did you do that?"

I stare at him, groggy. They've given me something. Another augmenter? But no, I don't feel calm or good. There are no positive emotions, and I don't understand now. I don't understand at all. I should feel better if I'm Enhanced.

"The Promise Marks..." My words slur. "Need to get them off...so you can't... The Gods and Goddesses, Death and...."

"Oh, Shania. The Promise Marks are *spiritual* marks. They have a physical appearance, yes, but they can't be got rid of by physical means."

Only a powerful God can undo them.

The thought flashes at me, and I grimace. I knew that, didn't I? Part of me knew, had heard it before...but I struggle to think where. And I *need* the blue-eyed Seer's help to get the Gods and Goddesses. I wish I didn't, because I need to do this myself—sort it out *myself*. It's when other people get involved that things go wrong. It's when I'm not in control that bad stuff happens.

Raleigh's hand snakes out toward me, and I'm too exhausted even to try and stop him from stroking my face. But he's still wearing gloves. Worried about contagion? That illness? Was that...that was real....

My head pounds.

"You can't reverse this, Shania. Accept it. Your body and powers are mine, and we *are* going to do these great things for humanity—whether you agree or not."

NINE

SOME TIME LATER, THE BOILER suits take me back to the quarantine bay. They've already filled me up with new augmenters—ones they say will block out the pain, make me feel better, calmer, more like myself. I don't know whether that's a good thing or not—I can't think, not properly. Everything's just….

Better. There, you feel better now.

And I do feel something—a strange numbness starts to take over my body as the augmenters spread throughout my system, blocking out the bad stuff.

My shoulders relax, and I start to hum. Hum a soft tune.

What? You never hum?
But humming is nice, isn't it?

I get back in my cage without hesitation, unsure whether it's my decision or Raleigh's, wherever he is. But getting back in the cage is good. A cage means safety. Means no one can hurt me. I breathe deeply. Safety. It's what I've always wanted.

Corin was your cage before.

There are Enhanced guards in here now, and one tells me that everyone has been thoroughly searched.

He doesn't say anything about me causing the sickness in everyone, even though I know immediately that the Zharat and Esther are much, much worse.

I stare around at them, my eyes widening as far as they can when I realize just how much worse everyone is. Sallow skin, lusterless. Several of them look queasy, and, within a few minutes, two women and three men are sick. The Enhanced guards switch their buckets as quickly as their protective suits will allow them.

"Seven...."

I turn to Esther, see her sweat-lined face and the huge dark circles under her eyes. She looks like she wants to say more to me, but either she can't or she doesn't know what to say. I see her gaze drop to my arm. My bandage is very white, no sign of blood seeping through.

Blood.

I cut myself. Alarm filters through me. I inflicted pain. On myself.

Pain is bad, very bad, isn't it?

My head pounds, and I lift my arms up, want to wrap them around myself—need security, comfort—but it'll hurt. And the voice inside me is right: pain *is* bad.

"Are you really doing this? Making us sick?" a voice calls out to me.

I shake my head. "No."

But then a lump forms in my throat, and my heartbeat goes all sluggish, heavy. What if it *is* me? What if I'm doing this subconsciously? What if I kill them? It's violence...and violence is bad and—

I groan.

The augmenter.

I'm thinking like one of them.

But you're hurting these people!

No.

I'm not.

Am I?

Oh Gods. What if I *do* end up killing all the

DIVIDED

Untamed…not just the ones here…and I fulfill the augury that way?

I sit down slowly, lean against the bars. They are cool and refreshing against my sweaty skin. Esther is on the other side of the bars, and she reaches through to hold my hand. After a moment's hesitation, I let her. I stare at my hand in hers, and I don't feel anything. Nothing now. Like the emotions have just flown away, left me. Left me empty and alone, in a room full of people.

My stomach rolls, a sour taste spreads across my mouth.

Bad.
Bad.
Bad.

The word echoes through me.

And Esther and I just sit here. People are coughing. Someone's sick; I stare at the vomit, the stringiness of it. And the color. Clear but iridescent. My eyes narrow. And—and I'm fascinated.

Someone sneezes.

An hour or so later, the rash returns to Esther's face, and then she's sick. My stomach twists as my own nausea flares. The Zharat start screaming, moaning. A man calls for his mother, begs her not to leave him. Others join in, reaching through the bars with thin arms that shake. They scream more and more. They're still screaming when trolleys of food are brought in. But the smell of food makes my stomach turn. I hold my breath, trying not to inhale anything.

No one eats any food, and the guards scowl. One tries to force-feed Clare, and she snarls and bites him. He yells something about infections and safety. And everything's just a…a fog. A wash of things. And, inside my head, it feels too hot. Like the air's thick, muggy with artificial heat that clogs every part of me.

My ears click; I hear my breathing louder. Strained. Wheezing. I turn onto my side, my back aching, but the floor is now too cold, and it chills my body through in seconds. I reach for a blanket, sure I can feel one over me, but there's nothing. My jaw slackens after I grimace. I feel my eyelids get heavier still. Too heavy…can't….

Voices.

They filter into my empty thoughts, and I don't know how long it's been.

But then Raleigh's here. And he's unlocking my cell, dragging me out.

He leans over me, and he's not wearing his suit. His protective suit. Why isn't he wearing his protective suit?

Raleigh smiles. "Let me show you something."

TEN

"SHE SHOULDN'T BE OUT HERE—it's too risky."

Several Enhanced Ones eye me warily as Raleigh leads me outside, into a courtyard. These Enhanced have their protective suits on, and it makes it harder for me to see who they are. Not that I'd recognize them anyway.

"She's feeling better," Raleigh says, his grip on my arm tightening. "And she is seeking redemption. Aren't you, Shania?"

I nod, because he makes me. And I try to ignore the nausea welling up in me, and how weak my legs are, how Raleigh's power over me is the only thing that holds me up.

Another Enhanced shakes her head. "We're all going to get sick now you've brought her out here. She'll be targeting us too now. You shouldn't have brought her outside until you know the parasite is dead and gone."

Raleigh doesn't say anything, just presses his lips into a fine line. A second later, a sliver of pain squeezes around my stomach. I don't know whether he's responsible for it or not, but he continues leading me forward.

My head pounds as we walk. I try to think, try to remember.

Something in my chest twists hard, and I gasp. Raleigh looks down at me, then makes me walk quicker.

The courtyard seems to go on and on, forever. But at last we reach the end, and then he's leading me down steps. The steps go on and on too, and my body's sagging, and Raleigh's using more power to keep me upright.

"You'll want to see this," he says, and he's smiling. "Don't worry. I understand that the evil isn't really a part of *you*, Shania. Not the real you. And we will make sure the evil has completely gone before we begin the next session, when we examine your true Seer powers of conversion and defense—Seer powers that *aren't* controlled by the Untamed evil."

His words make me feel strange. How can he believe that, when I know *Seer powers of conversion and defense* include using my powers to kill—how can he believe that isn't evil?

"Here we are," Raleigh says as we get to the bottom of the steps.

There's a low arched doorway, guarded by an Enhanced, and Raleigh leads me through it. The room beyond is small, and there are candles in it, and—

I go cold as I see who lies on the plinth at the back of the room.

My body locks up. I can't move.

I turn to Raleigh, try to shake my head, but he's smiling.

"He is here, awaiting the drawings and measurements for the statue construction."

I blink at him, feel my eyelashes get heavier. Blood rushes to my ears. A statue?

"Of course," Raleigh says, and I must've said the words aloud. He prods me forward, makes me look at Jed's body. "We don't bother with death rituals—after all, the New World is nothing but a wild, Untamed construction, and death itself is final, there is nothing beyond for anyone to be scared of—and I am having a statue made of my son as he gave you to us, ensuring the fate of the Chosen Ones. So we will worship his memory in much the same way we will worship yours when you seal the fate of this world, guaranteeing evil will not continue."

The room goes cold. Everything goes cold. I start shaking. I try to turn away, don't want to look at the body—don't want to see it at all, not when I thought I saw him earlier—but I can't...can't look away....

And I look at it. At him. His mouth is slightly open, and his lips look strange. There's a strange waxy surface over his skin, and the dull yellow light above him makes him look even less real.

But it's him.

It's Jed.

His body.

His dead body. Looking...*dead*. My heart speeds up, but it feels too heavy. That image, that apparition I saw—my mind playing tricks—it wasn't... I squirm. It was only as real as that nightmare I had where—

And this is real.

His body, here. His skin is only marred by the kavalah spirit bites and his tattoos. No gold splashes—his Promise Marks must have disappeared after death. I try to think back to when he was killed. The gold splashes didn't vanish immediately, did they? My shoulders tighten. I didn't hang around for long.

I ran.

But they're gone now, the marks. He just looks—

Touch me, S'ven.

The words spring up around me—his voice—and I turn sharply, my head pounding. I start to choke. I can't breathe. My throat—it's closing.

"Ah, young love." Raleigh makes a guttural sound at the back of his throat.

I start screaming. The body—it shouldn't be here... Raleigh's wrong. The New World *is* real. The Spirit

Releasing Words...they should've been said...they should've been said immediately...but they weren't... they still haven't been said.

Oh Gods.

But the body—and Jed's eyes are open, they're on me—how didn't I notice before?—he's watching me... and he's still here. He shouldn't be... No, not he—*it*. It shouldn't be here.

And what about him? His soul and—

And Raleigh's making me look at him, at the man who did all this. The man who made me a Dream Land exile, who bound me to my enemy.

"Tell me what you feel." Raleigh's words are low.

My heart thumps, and my hands are clammy and sweaty. The ground beneath my feet feels too soft, springy.

"Tell me, Shania," Raleigh says. And his hand is still on my arm. "Look, you're shaking. There are droplets of sweat forming on your brow. You're leaning toward me for support; I'm the only reason you're not on the ground. What is it you feel? Overwhelming grief that threatens to destroy you? Fear of death itself? Horror at a natural part of life?"

"Natural?" The word escapes me, but it doesn't sound like my voice. And to my right, Jed's dead body watches me.

Natural. Natural. Natural.

No!

"Death is the natural end of life—and yet the darkness in you is conditioning you to feel horror at a natural event." Raleigh shakes his head softly. "It is controlling you."

But Jed's death wasn't natural. It was murder. He was *murdered* by his father. By the man who's touching me, holding me up.

Revulsion spreads across me in waves. I try to wrench myself away from Raleigh's grip, but he won't let me. I can't move. Oh Gods.

I scream. A short, sharp scream.

DIVIDED

"Do you see what the darkness, the evil in you, is doing? How horrible it's making you feel," Raleigh purrs. "And those are not nice feelings filling you, are they? And it is this darkness that is fighting the augmenters—fighting what you have chosen to feel. It is going *against* your will, Shania. It is disobeying you, and it is tricking you, making you feel that it *is* your choice to feel this pain. But it *is not*. And it's those bad emotions that are taking control, that are making you think that viewing Jed's body isn't a happy occasion to celebrate, but a torture. Can't you see it, Shania? These emotions are twisting the truth, getting you on their side so you can fuel them—they're tricking you, controlling you, rendering you weak, useless, pathetic. They're making you *want* to be upset, to feel pain. And that isn't right, is it? Manipulating you like that, and doing it so secretly. And you can feel them, can't you, if you search for them? Those small tendrils of darkness... Feel them now, Shania, feel the darkness getting stronger, growing. And think how bad you feel now, when there are only a few tendrils left. And imagine how much worse you'll feel again, if you let the darkness grow. And if they grow again, they'll infect your mind once more—you won't be able to see or think rationally. You won't see the darkness as a separate part, and you'll think it is you, because that's what the evil wants you to think."

At last, Raleigh allows me to turn away from Jed's body, and I look at him. His animated face. The slight stubble on his jawline. The way my disheveled appearance fills his eyes.

"But *you* know those tendrils are bad now," Raleigh croons. "*You* know it. And that is why you screamed, so I am proud of you. That scream was *you*. That was you fighting against the negativity the parasite is trying to breed in you. Recognition is an important step." His lips get thinner as they stretch into a wide grin. "So, now, I shall make it so that you see *this* as the happy occasion that it is. I shall help you see clearly.

"Few Chosen Ones are worthy enough to view a great man's body. But you are. I can see the worthiness in you, Shania, despite the evil. Zahlia begged for access, but she is not worthy enough. But you *really* are. And now you shall understand and appreciate it on your own, without the darkness trying to evoke fear and loss within you. You shall compare the two viewings, and you will see the evil for what it is, and you *will* renounce it."

Raleigh grabs me, and, before I can even register what's happening, I'm swallowing an augmenter. It slips down my throat like sand, catching and burning.

A few seconds pass, and then the knot inside me unravels a little.

I try to back away, make it a few steps before Raleigh's hands catch me around the shoulders. I flinch.

He stares into my eyes, but all I can see is my Enhanced face in his, and I start to feel...not sick exactly, but....

"Now, isn't that better?" he says, and he makes me look at the body. "Now you do not feel those bad feelings, do you? No. Now you feel calm, and you feel strong. Death does not affect you. And we all need to be strong, don't we? Isn't it wonderful—being able to stand over the body of a man you loved and feel not sadness and pain and fear, but strength and happiness and relief, because you know he is free and not suffering any longer, that another small part of the world is right?"

Right? The word burns through me, but I can't think. I look at Jed's body, and I don't feel scared anymore. But I don't feel calm or strong—not like Raleigh said I do. I feel...nothing. No goodness. No badness. Not even any sickness.

And isn't it good to not feel the bad?

"Being able to face death with courage and intrepidity is important. We cannot have those emotions clouding us, changing our actions, making us weak and useless in times when we must be strong. Look, Shania, death is not something to be feared, is it? Do you feel fear now?"

I shake my head. He makes me. But, for the first time, it feels like it might also be my choice. Like it's both of us. Like we're working together.

Somewhere deep inside me, something cries a long, drawn-out cry.

"And you do not fear your death now, do you, Shania?" Raleigh whispers. "Not when you know that your death will end the evil in this world, not when you know that you'll ensure that everyone has the perfect life. Not when I can promise you that you will feel no pain, and your name will go down in history. You'll be the savior."

No pain. He can make a deal with the God of Death? But Enhanced Seers can't contact the Gods and Goddesses….

"And you want to be strong, don't you?" Raleigh says. "You want to be the best you can be—it's what everyone wants. It's a natural human desire—a need. And it's essential for survival. And soon, very soon, you will be better, now that you have chosen to walk the path to redemption. I understand it is and has been difficult—and that is not your fault. When you came here, there was such an immense amount of evil controlling you, and it will take a while to drain completely from your soul and body." He pauses. "But you are on the way there now. And that is wonderful, is it not, to know that nothing—not even the death of a loved one—can break you? That you are strong and perfect. Invincible."

He lifts a finger to my face, pushes my chin up so that I shut my mouth. I hadn't realized it was open. I stare at him, my head feeling heavier. Inside my chest, I feel a strange jittery rhythm, and I concentrate on it as it gets smoother, like an engine starting up.

"And now you can see it properly, can't you? You thought I was being cruel showing you Jed's body, did you not? But I wasn't the one being cruel. That was *you* being cruel. Do you see how the darkness in you twisted things? It made you think I was bad, because it knew that you were. You were the one inflicting cruelty on your friends, making them ill. Can you see that, my dear butterfly? Can you see the truth behind the picture the darkness paints?"

He makes me nod.

"And the Chosen should not want to inflict cruelty on one another. It is bad. And you don't want to hurt your friends, do you?"

I shake my head. I think he makes me. But I'm not sure. I'm slipping. Slipping again.

Raleigh smiles. "You mustn't worry. For this—this has awoken you, has it not? This has taught you that. And you mustn't feed the darkness, must you? No, my dear. You mustn't. And you'll stop the sickness, won't you? You'll make your friends better?"

"I want them to be better," I whisper.

"Good girl," he says, and he strokes my head. "What a good girl. What a brave girl. And now your bravery will be rewarded with feelings of only goodness and joy. It may take time to get the last echoes of evil out of you, but we will do it, I promise you, Shania. Darkness cannot live in you when you've renounced it." He strokes my uneven hair. "See, it's leaving already—now you have seen it for what it really is—and it will not return, because you, my darling butterfly, you are stronger than it is. You'll feel better soon, and you'll be with your friends. You'll be rehabilitated together, shown how to live true and prosperous lives, because you are Chosen Ones, and soon you will feel only beauty and wonder and happiness."

Raleigh makes me drink three more augmenters, then he takes me straight back to the quarantine bay.

"Keep an eye on them," he tells one of his guards. "They'll start improving now. But it may be a while until they're back to full health; there's a lot of evil Shania needs to draw out of herself, as well as

DIVIDED

removing her evil substance that has been infecting them. But she will help them now that she has decided upon the right side and begun to squash the evil. I've broken the darkness within her, and she will not let it repair itself now. She has proven she's in control."

Then Raleigh tells me that he's being kind, letting me rest and see my friends, that seeing them—and how they're suffering—will help me fight the evil, and seeing the pain will help me heal them all sooner, take away the evil sickness that the Untamed part of me planted in them. Because now I will be shocked. I will be horrified.

But—

Something clashes through me like a thousand weights being dropped on my soul.

He's wrong.

There's no evil inside me.

It is him.

He's the evil.

Pure evil.

Evil. The word burns through me, makes me feel sick.

And then I am sick, sick into the bucket in my cell.

For several seconds after, all I can do is concentrate on breathing. Even though with every breath I take, I smell the putrid bile in the bucket. No one takes it away.

I turn to my left, look for Esther.

But the cell is empty.

"Where...where's Esther?"

No one answers, so I repeat my question again.

At last, a Zharat man looks at me. "She got sicker. Worse than...us. They took her."

"Took her?" My heart drops. "Took her where?"

But he glares at me, then turns away.

I touch my forehead slowly. My head feels hot.

Clare lies on her side, her back to her barred door. I try to watch her, try to see the movement of her breaths—something. But I can't, and—

No. No. No.

Time passes.

I look at the others. One of the Zharat men is sitting up, and he shakes his head at me. His eyes look more Untamed than they should be—the mirrors are only ghosts.

"I'm not doing this," I say. I hold up my hands toward him as they start to tingle.

"I know."

My body jolts. "You know? Tell them!"

"You are not *directly* doing this. But it is your fault," he croaks. "Upsetting the Gods... Your fault. This is their punishment. We must die because a fraud has tainted us. You have tainted us. Still, death is better than being an Enhanced."

I try to ignore him. I look back at the two Enhanced Ones at the other end of the room. Then I look at my hands as they start itching. A rash appears, so quickly.

More time passes, and the rash spreads. Quickly now. I'm on fire.

"It's not me," I call out. "It's *not* me—it's..." I break off, coughing; green phlegm flies from my mouth. "You have to get help... It's something else... Leaving us here, you're killing us... Proper help...we need... they're dying...you're supposed to save us."

But they don't listen.

No one listens.

And no one else comes to listen.

There's no one here.

This is what evil feels like.

ELEVEN

SHE'S NOT HERE. SHE'S NOT here. She's not here.
"Poison!" my mother hollers.

And I look for her, try to fight the heaviness that's everywhere, that's….

I blink, but it slips away, the feeling—whatever it was and—

My mother. *Poison. Poison. Poison.* The word thrums through me.

And we're moving… moving fast. Air's rushing past me, fills my ears, makes them pop.

I cry out, and a voice tells me it'll be okay, but those words are a lie, I know that… I've always known that and….

The floor is damp. No, more than damp. It's wet. Wet…and it smells bad. My nostrils curl.

I try to speak, but my lips won't move. They feel heavy, too heavy. I move my tongue, but the energy to do it is too… The thought slips away, replaced by death. My death. I'm dying.

We're all dying.

I see a skull as I close my eyes. It's grinning at me, and its grin is garish, and it won't leave me alone. It chases me, chases me until I'm running, and things are crashing into me. Fine wires spring around my body, bind me to a table.

And the blue-eyed Seer is here, and I'm trying to shout to her but my tongue's swollen, and my lips! I can't open them, and—

And I'm naked and people are laughing at me. Raleigh's laughing at me, and he's hauling me about, showing me to everyone, all the Enhanced.

"It's happening too quickly... The symptoms are accelerating and increasing...."

Sweating. I'm sweating. Sweating so much and—and it's pouring off me. I'm leaving a river behind as Raleigh drags me along and—

And I blink, try to blink through the sweaty fog, because there's something important about my death...something....

"Shania."

Raleigh's voice is here now—some time later? I'm not sure—but he speaks now, and his voice is different. And he speaks a lot. I wish he'd shut up, let me....

"Shania, don't let the evil take over again... Beat it, fight it, draw it out, and trample it. Come on, Shania—we made great progress before. You were doing so well. Don't undo it."

Warm hands shake me, and I open my eyes. A bright light hovers above me. And something's humming. I'm... Something soft...beneath me...a bed. But trying to work out anything else is too...too exhausting and....

Remember! You have to remember!

But I can't, and the world slips into more voices and sounds, and I don't know whether I'm awake or asleep.

"Now?"

"Yes."

"Get it ready."

"There's availability for a full scan of the...."

"... No."

DIVIDED

People are running. I hear their footsteps, fast and heavy. Like a countdown to….

Someone shouts.

"Raleigh, Shania is barely responsive. Brain activity is unusually low—our records indicate that active use of Seer powers always causes an increase in these levels. How can she be controlling this?"

"Scan her again. This must be a Seer power. She is doing it. She has to be. She and I are the only Seers here whose powers are strong enough to do this."

And I'm moving, sliding. Something flashes above me. A green light in the darkness.

Time swallows everything up, swallows me up.

I'm falling.

More voices. A softer one, and a heavier one. And Raleigh's.

"No, I don't care about the others. It's *her* I want. We need her alive. Her death like this isn't going to—"

"Scanner's ready."

"Do her first. If she's not doing this then…."

And then I'm moving. My bed's moving. I watch as a series of bright lights run past me on the ceiling. Each one winks at me as the bed wheels me into darkness. Complete darkness.

Then a red light flashes. I whimper as it dives at me, as it gets me. My eyes—it burns my eyes. Redness, everywhere, and….

Something's burning me. My fingers…my hands… I try to move, try to stop the burning, but it's spreading up my arm…goes over the Zharat mark on the inside of my elbow, prickles my skin, like it's injecting poison, more poison, and….

And then there's…movement…voices…mumbled and dark and laughing and playing…and we're at the….

I'm standing between my mother and my father, in the big house—the one we use to hold supplies in. Their hands are on my shoulders, and I turn, see them both beaming. Their smiles make me smile, and I can't help but smile widely.

Everyone's smiling.

"Isn't she a darling?"

"Have you thought of a name yet?"

"She's a fighter, look at those kickin' legs."

The chattering is loud, and there's music playing. Three finally got the machine to work then. He's been working on the CD player for months, ever since our father found it in a skip, during a raid. Three will be pleased he's fixed it. I smile and look for him, twisting my head, but everyone's here, all together. All for the baby. And it's hard to see.

"Here, Seven, come and look at this."

Five appears at my side, then steers me away from our parents, to the side of the room, where Keelie, four years older than me at fourteen, holds a huge bag. She grins from ear to ear and pulls out a small pot of fine powder and a handful of small cosmetic tubes.

"Elf found it all!" she yells, and then she clutches my arm, plasters some sort of thick paste around my eyes.

I squirm backward, but there's nowhere to go and—

"You don't want to look pretty?" Five asks. That's when I notice she's covered in glittery stuff. It's even in her hair. "You won't get a boyfriend unless you look pretty…" She turns around, then points at Finn. "See, *he* won't like you."

My eyes travel to Finn. He's not paying any attention to us—he mainly looks bored—but behind him is Corin, and he's watching us, a look of disdain on his face.

The music changes abruptly, and Five and Keelie start scream-dancing, waving their hands in the air. I take the opportunity to move back toward my mother. She's still where I left her, though my father's gone now.

I squeeze through people. My mother sees me and reaches for me, smiling. And then—

Then the light in her eyes changes. She falls. Motionless.

DIVIDED

And I try to reach her, try to—

But everyone's dancing and then…then when I reach her it's a minute later, and she's awake now and—

"Enhanced!" My mother's call is loud and shrill.

The moment I hear the word, concrete fills my legs. My lungs turn to stone. Adrenaline pumps through my veins, trying to paralyze me, yet urging me to run as fast as I can. A rushing sound fills my ears. Too much sound, like someone screwing up a paper bag in my eardrums. I can't get away from it.

But everyone's trying—everyone's moving, but there's nowhere to go because—

"They're at the back door!"

"They're waiting out front too!"

"Smash the windows!"

Movement, to my left, and then there's a tinkling sound and—

Mirrors flash from the other side of the window, and someone screams.

Rahn's father flies across the room. I see his eyes: too white and sunken back into his face. Then he hits something and—

More people bellow. Hands reach for me. And—

"Get out!"

The air gets thicker, heavier. I try to move, don't understand… My throat tickles, and then I'm coughing, bending over. Everyone's coughing, spluttering.

Someone pulls a gun out near me, and the barrel catches my shoulder as they whirl it round.

"Esther!"

"Clear the front door!"

My father appears, pushes me behind him, and then—

Then the gunshots go off.

"Get out!"

The heat soars. I see flames—flames in the house. The house is on fire. For a second, I can't move. Can't do anything but stare at the flames.

They've set our house on fire.

People are screaming. The Untamed are screaming all around me. And the baby, Kayden and Faya's baby is crying and screaming, and no one's—

"The windows!"

More glass breaks, and the fire hisses. Heat squashes around my body, and I try to turn, but there's smoke in here too, and it's scratching my throat, my head, everything.

"Get out the windows!"

"No, not the door! They're waiting out there!"

Flames lick toward me. Their pattern is mesmerizing. So mesmerizing. Oranges and reds and deep blues, among the smoke.

Someone screams, and I turn, my body jolting. The movement makes me cough...can't stop coughing.

The room is... I'm... Pain in my lungs.

"Where's Faya?"

"She's still in there, with the—"

"Seven's in there too, and—"

Distant shouts fill my ears.

My breath catches in my throat. The fire's in front of me, cutting me off. But it doesn't look real. Can't be a real fire...not when the Enhanced are out there, they wouldn't set our house alight on purpose. A mistake. They can't be trying to flush us out. They're not violent, they're—

Hands grab me from behind, and I shriek. I twist, see Kayden, red hair shining. See the sweat on his skin as he pulls me with him. But I only see him for a second, because then the smoke is there. Dense, black smoke. Smoke that tries to cut me off and—

Kayden stabs an Enhanced One with a knife.

And there's someone else in here, another Untamed person because more gunshots are going off and—

I trip, pain twisting through my ankle. And the carpet is burning...fumes and...something hisses against my skin. I cry out, trying to move, but there's nowhere to go, just a wall.

DIVIDED

My body hunkers, fear grasps me. I try to look, try to see someone, and—

"Faya!"

A hand pulls me up, and then—

Then the window, appearing through the smoke, and—

I soar toward it, catapulted, glide through the gap and—

Behind me, the walls collapse. Sparks fly out, hit me. So many sparks...my skin... I scream. Pain, too much pain, and....

"Keep her alive. Do everything you can. *She* must survive. I'm not losing her...."

"Yes, sir. I'll need to do another round of bloods and...."

More people... They're moving too quickly, I can't keep up. So many faces, with their mirrors, and voices. Voices, shouting and shouting. Panic. But they weren't in the burning house...so why are they here, breaking into my memory?

The smell of coffee washes over me, and I gasp. Open my eyes. But everything's blurry, too blurry. Can only see shapes and colors. Reds and grays. Pale blues that stretch on and on, forever.

"Are you sure it's them that are causing this? Why aren't *we*...."

"The signs were there before. It's to do with *this* group. I don't understand. But Esther Eriksen collapsed after the very first..."

"So it wasn't the Tranquility and Sleepiness that...."

"No. We thought the grade must've been too high, but...."

An alarm goes off. *Bleep. Bleep. Bleep.* People move. More people, rushing past.

"... I want a full team of scientists down here. We need to know why this has happened, why these individuals are reacting and why it's so bad now. I want the medical...."

Bleep. Bleep. Bleep.

"… Get onto the Section, see if there are any similar reports and…."

Something hot passes over me. Another light. Too bright.

A radio crackles.

"We've lost two in bay six. Severe anaphylactic reactions. Both stopped breathing within three minutes of tonight's third administration of…."

And then Raleigh's here, right in front of me. But he's not looking at me. He's looking at someone else, a woman. She's standing on the other side of my bed, and papers are passed over me. She's beautiful, with perfect skin and glossy, black hair. She's pale, but she also looks like Jed, the parts of him that don't look like his father.

Raleigh swears loudly, then looks down at me. His fingers reach for my face and touch my chin roughly. He looks into my eyes, before asking the woman for my temperature. She tells him, and he grunts, shaking his head.

Then he nods at her. "All of them. We'll have to."

The beautiful woman's lips quiver as she tucks her hair behind her ears. "But then we wouldn't be saving them… We'd be letting them live with their fear and violent thoughts."

Raleigh leans over me, until his face is an inch from the beautiful woman's. "Zahlia, we have no choice! If we don't, we'll lose them all." He gestures around us, and my vision starts to blur again. "It's too dangerous at the moment. We've lost some already. Antihistamines aren't working, and we've got eight more in a critical condition since we topped up those in bay one."

He pauses for a long time. When he speaks again, his voice is low and controlled.

"No, I am *not* risking Shania's life. We have to stop until we know *why* our augmenters are killing these Untamed."

TWELVE

I DREAM OF THE SKY, and I'm outside, and the sky is a soft blue, edged in gray clouds—the kind that are heavy and dense, yet won't give up their water—and I'm running, feet throwing up sand.

I keep running, weaving around clumps of grasses, but my rhythm's bad; I'm not breathing properly and—

I stumble over a ridge. Long, flaxen-colored grass brushes my legs, but there's something sharp in it too. Thorns. Pain and—

I glance down, my hand batting at my right knee and—

The legs aren't mine. The skin's the wrong color. It's too pale, but sections are reddened with sunburn and—

I freeze. Only the body doesn't freeze.

The body keeps running. *I* keep on running, twisting to the left, turning my head back for a second. A glimpse of more land—dry and dusty, with clumps of grass and a few stilted trees. I cough and—

This isn't my body.

I breathe in deeply, aware that somewhere else, my

own short, sharp breaths are audible. But not here, not when—

But it's a dream. And I'm dreaming I'm free because I desire it most and—

A Seeing dream?

I try to look high at the sky, but my head—no, the *person's* head—isn't tilting that far up now. All I can see are the sparse trees with their flattened tops, the bumpy horizon in the distance, small beige mounds rising out of the plateau into the lowest murky clouds.

The person—me—coughs again. Deep and throaty. A man. He wipes a hand over the back of his mouth, and I see his hand—thick fingers, hardened skin over the knuckles—but only for a second, then he's pumping his arms.

I'm pumping my arms, because I'm in his body, and it feels like *I* must be moving, but I'm not. I'm not in control. I'm just here. Trapped.

Oh Gods.

My stomach tightens. Don't know if it's his or mine. But I'm—

He's Untamed.

The thought flies at me. I'm in an Untamed man's body.

I'm—

He coughs again, and I go cold. How didn't I notice? That cough? That sound—that tone.

It's him.

I'm him.

He's out here, free.

And I'm in *Corin's* body.

THIRTEEN

WHEN I OPEN MY EYES, I know two things. One: I'm myself, I'm Untamed. Two: I had the weirdest dream *ever*. It's like no dream I've had before. Seeing dreams I remember with clarity, and little details of those don't make sense. Nightmares haunt me after I wake up, even if it's just the impressions of them that are left. And normal dreams often die the moment I open my eyes.

Yet this one... A strange feeling builds inside me. *Corin*.

I breathe his name. Remember the sensation of me running—running with his body.

Is Corin coming back for me?

My mind races and my shoulders feel strange, too tense, like the muscles are too hard. Do I want him to come back for me—to risk him getting caught again? I don't know. My heart cries an emphatic *yes*, but my head says *no*.

He's safer out there.

I stare at the big light above me. The lightshade is ornate, and I blink into the brightness, pick out the swirls there. I'm in a different room. I turn my head, see pale yellow walls. Then I take a deep breath and sit up. Metal jangles again metal, and I flinch, look down, see the manacle around my wrist and the chain attaching it to an iron unit on the wall, a few feet along from me.

Locked up, restrained, because I'm Untamed.

A smile breaks across my lips as if a switch has been flicked and new life has bolted into me. Tears well up as I close my eyes for a second—as it *really* sinks in.

Untamed.

Untamed.

Untamed.

I blink as words echo through my mind: *poison* and *augmenters* and *fluids* and *scans*. I see Raleigh with his head in his hands, next to me, and then him shaking his head. The distant memories of people shouting fill me. And then me—lying on something cool, feeling weak, someone stroking my forehead gently and....

I flinch. How much time has passed? I don't feel weak now. I flex my fingers slowly. I feel strong, better. *Untamed*. And the augmenters were making us sick?

I slouch, let my head fall back against the wall, and my lips buzz with energy, with the need to smile. I'm Untamed, and now it's possible—it's got to be; the Enhanced aren't going to win now. Somehow, I'm going to escape.

Because I'm Untamed. And Corin's still out there, and we're going to find each other.

And they're letting us be Untamed and—

"This doesn't change anything."

Raleigh stands in the doorway to my new room, to the right. I hadn't noticed him—or the door—and, suddenly, I feel stupid, too preoccupied with my Untamed state and my dream of Corin to take in my surroundings. Oh Gods, if my father knew....

I take a deep breath and look at Raleigh as confidently as I can.

"This does not mean you are winning." Raleigh crosses the distance between us, quickly and efficiently.

DIVIDED

"And this—" He points at my eyes, my Untamed eyes. "This is only temporary. As soon as my labs know why you were all reacting to our augmenters, we can resolve the issue and quell the darkness once more. Do not worry, you won't be Untamed for long. I will not keep you like this, for long. It would not be fair, would it?"

He touches the chain, the part high up on the wall, makes it jangle more, sending ripples of movement to my left wrist. The chain is about six feet long; the length means I can move about if I want, and that makes me smile.

"But you must still fight for *us* even when you're one of them," Raleigh says. "Fight for the Chosen Ones. Do not let the Untamed evil have a big part of you again. Keep it locked up. I'm sure you can do it, even on your own without the augmenters, you're strong, my darling. I know you can do it, and it will make it all the easier for you, when we have suitable augmenters, if you haven't regressed back to your truly wild state. Just think of the happiness our lifestyle offers…never having to feel negative emotions, never being in pain, never—"

I lift my arm up, test the full weight of the chain, and the clanging metal cuts him off. I stand, slowly, carefully. Raleigh steps back a little, but only an inch or so. Momentarily, I see my Untamed eyes reflected in his as he moves his head a little. It makes me feel giddy, seeing them, seeing my eyes. Giddy, but good. Things aren't as bad anymore. They're really not.

"Where are the others?" My voice is light, bubbly.

"The ones who survived are each in solitary confinement."

"What?"

I start to shake. Anxiety floods me. Waves and waves of it. And it feels worse—more horrible than ever before…because the augmenters were working then, even though they were making us sick? Or did that cancel them out? But the Zharat—they weren't calm, weren't free of negative emotions. They shouted at me to stab myself—a negative command. Or maybe their anger *was* curbed slightly?

I swallow hard. Augmenters are supposed to be so good they're addictive. But I'm not yearning for augmenters. Just the thought of one makes me feel sick. Has the sickness conditioned me not to like them? The opposite of what they're supposed to do....

And they've killed people, the augmenters have killed people?

Raleigh presses his lips together for a moment. "It's too risky to keep you together. Being around other Untamed would cause the parasites in each of you to strengthen. You would cultivate plans of evil together. No, each of you will only see myself and my men. Do not look so alarmed, Shania. You will be allowed out as soon as we have this augmenter problem fixed and you are all Chosen Ones properly—once you can all be happy and productive members of society. I truly am sorry for this delay. It has never happened before."

I stare at him. "Who... Who's still..." I can't speak, my words are too thick. I get sudden images of Esther and Clare—*dead*—flashing through my mind. "Is... Are...."

The corners of Raleigh's lips lift up. "Like I said, this doesn't change anything. I still have command over your soul, and I can still control your body." He nods, and I clap—I just do it, and I know it's him, proving to me what he's saying. The chain clatters in laughter. A second passes, and then pain forks through me. Raleigh smiles. "We will have our second session later today."

"Session?"

I go cold. I blink and see Elia's body. Everything in me slackens.

No. No. *No*.

"I'm not wasting time." Raleigh edges closer, closer than before, and my eyes have trouble adjusting to the sudden proximity. "And you still need to learn more about your powers. You just have to make sure the darkness *isn't* fueling them. You're so strong, my darling. You can do it."

My heart beats a little faster. I was Untamed before… wasn't I…when he made me kill Elia Jackson… I was still Untamed in my mind then—the augmenters weren't working and I was resisting…and me being Untamed didn't stop him. And he's got my soul. I can't fight him. Not even now. He can still control me…but can I resist better now? Being physically Untamed as well as psychologically has got to count for something… It *has* to. But I need to be careful too, I know that. And I don't know for sure if being physically Untamed will help. I don't know anything. Not really.

I lift my gaze, need to appear strong. "But there's no point… If we can't have augmenters, you can't convert us, whatever my powers are…and…."

"Oh, Shania. So naive." Amusement dances on Raleigh's lips. "My men are working on the augmenters now, and they will create a safe composition for you once we've isolated the ingredient you're all reacting to. By the time the labs have the *modified* augmenters ready for you, you and I will have worked out your conversion powers, and you will be able to rescue the remaining Untamed with no problems. We are still going to save everyone. We cannot let a little problem like this stop us."

My fingers click as I squeeze my hands into tight fists. I shake my head. "No… I'm not doing—"

Sudden pain snaps through my head, and I flinch.

Raleigh laughs. "I still control your soul, and I can still inflict great pain on you if you do not co-operate. Don't think that just because you're Untamed again, you have an advantage. You don't. It's the darkness in you, Shania. Remember, it manipulates you. You *will* still do as I say because I will help you to be good. And you need to understand that I'm doing this because it is the right thing to do. It's a pity the parasite is still active in you, that it's going to try and mar your way of thinking. But you can fight it. And you will."

My breathing gets shallower as I stare at him.

He bows his head slightly, so the new angle means his mirrors are directly in front of my eyes again, closer and steadier this time, only inches away. And I see my Untamed eyes, see them perfectly, *properly*, and I stare at them, feel the same giddiness, the wonder. At me. At him.

"Should the evil in you even attempt anything, your Untamed friends would suffer."

Raleigh leans toward me more, going slightly to my left. I stiffen, eyes widening, heart pounding. His lips move toward my ear, and I freeze.

"So, let's just make that clear now, shall we?" he whispers, and his words catch my breath in my throat. "I have no qualms in hurting Untamed creatures if it means *you* obey. It will be for the greater good." There's something about his whisper, something dangerous in it, that crawls under my skin. "But if you force me to hurt your friends, then you would watch it—via video link, of course. And they would know—your friends—they'd know the pain they are experiencing is because of you." Raleigh smiles as he pulls back and straightens up. He moves away from me. "They'd know they're suffering because you let the evil in you take hold, because you are trying to make my job harder and make everyone hurt."

I stare at him, my body shaking, and the chain rattles like a bad omen.

His smile gets wider. His teeth almost seem to glow. "Like I said, you being temporarily Untamed doesn't change a thing. You are still on our side, under my control, and you *will* ensure that the Chosen Ones are the only survivors of this war. Got it? Good. I'll be back later for our session."

He leaves, and the light goes out, plunging me into darkness. His words ring in my head. I try to ignore what he's said...pretend that it didn't happen, that

DIVIDED

there is still a way out of here—because I'm Untamed now, but the thought of Esther or Clare—or both of them—being dead won't leave me.

What if it was them who didn't make it?

No. Raleigh would've told me. He'd be happy to rub it in... He'd... Oh Gods.

At least Corin's not here.

"Raleigh!" I shout, and my voice breaks. But I keep shouting. If I make enough noise, he'll come back.

And I bellow his name, over and over. But there's nothing.

I scream until I'm shaking, until I can feel sweat dripping down my back, until my throat is even more swollen.

Raleigh doesn't come running back.

No one does.

Solitary confinement, until the next session? Can I wait that long to find out which Untamed died?

I blink, but I may as well have my eyes shut. It's too dark in here now.

For a second, I imagine all sorts of horrible things in here with me. Rats and skunks and scorpions. I think I feel something brush against my foot, and I yank it toward me quickly, stand on trembling legs. My breathing is loud—too loud.

And I'm trapped here...until later... I shudder and see Elia Jackson lying on the floor, strangely illuminated in the darkness. I freeze, shake my head, and she disappears. *No.* I can't. No, I need to get out.

I go to first to the iron unit on the wall and try to see if there's a way to detach my chain from it. There isn't, so I search the room as best as I can, still fettered.

The length of the chain allows me to move some distance, and I nearly reach all the walls. I feel my way around them. Rough stone, not the crumbly kind. Just hard and cold. Painted yellow, I remember. I search for gaps with my hands, but there are none. And the walls are solid. There's no air vent in this cell.

The doorway—that's my best bet at escape. But the

door is metal, fits the frame snugly. No light shows around the edge. I throw my weight against the door, but it doesn't budge. I push my right hand against each corner, trying to see if there are any weaknesses, but there's nothing.

There's no way out of here.

Of course there wouldn't be. This is a prison. And I imagine the other Untamed in similar rooms, in the dark, scared. Those little Zharat children...are there Untamed children here?

All of us trapped, imprisoned, because we're Untamed.

If you were Enhanced, you wouldn't be locked up in here....

But there's no point in thinking like that, because we can't be converted—and just the thought of conversion, of the augmenters, makes me feel sick again. I frown. I don't understand. It doesn't make sense. It is *too* convenient. The augmenters didn't make me ill before...why would they now? What's different? Me—no, *all* of us Untamed—or the augmenters?

Yet I know I shouldn't be thinking too much about why it's happened. I don't know how long this will last, how soon they'll be pumping us full of augmenters again.

And I'm Untamed now.

And I need to escape, need to get my soul back from Raleigh. Need to undo as much of this mess as possible.

I sit down slowly. Through my overalls, the stone floor is cold against my legs; I shiver. The Dream Land. I need to get there. I touch my left arm slowly. The bandages are still there... The area's still painful. That didn't work, that didn't get me back into the Dream Land.

I take a deep breath and close my eyes. Then I try to reach the Dream Land.

I imagine a silver ladder, and I climb it. My hands get sore, and my muscles start protesting.

DIVIDED

I keep climbing it, imagining the Gods and Goddesses at the top.

But then the ladder changes angle, and I'm crawling along it, over nothingness and—

The door creaks open, and the sound jolts me back to reality—not that I was far away.

The light flickers on again; brightness that makes me blink, narrow my eyes, and—

"Three?"

I stare at him as he shuts the door. His brow wobbles as he looks around. Then I see what's in his right hand.

My mother's pendant. *My* pendant. The light catches the crystal, makes my breathing sound funny. My fingers get hotter as I stare at it. I want to touch it. It sounds silly, but the pendant is calling to me.

I look at Three carefully. I look at his eyes. Look for anything that isn't the mirrors, that isn't me staring back into them. But there's nothing else, just me and the distrust on my face as I look at my Enhanced brother.

But he can't be. Not fully. Not if... It's *my* pendant.

"Take it." Three pushes it into my hands, and my heart jumps.

I clutch at it, sweaty skin against cold, precious stone. A slightly sharp edge presses into the pad of my thumb, then slides away as I turn it over. It's just the crystal. The piece of sinew has gone, and I examine the exposed hole. It is tiny, a lot smaller than I remembered.

Three starts to turn away, but I grab him, somehow keeping a hold on the pendant. I've got it back. Three got it back. For me. My legs wobble and my head feels strange.

But you won't get into the Dream Land, let alone get stuck there.

"Why?" My word is loaded, but it's important. Because this is it—this is where I find out for sure. This is the revelation.

And I look at my brother, really look at him. Again,

I try to see if there's anything Untamed left in Three's eyes, begging for there to be a glimmer of something. Because it has to be that—that he's on my side. He's given my pendant back to me, so he has to believe that I need the Seer warnings about the Enhanced One's plans and that I need to be able to act on them without getting stuck in the Dream Land—that I need to be able to escape from this compound and make sure the Untamed win. He doesn't want me getting stuck in the Dream Land, ruining the Untamed's chances of winning. Three mustn't be up to date, mustn't know about the banishment—Raleigh mustn't have told him. But it doesn't matter. It's the gesture—symbolic of whom he still is.

"Put it away. Keep it on you, but hide it." Three's voice is brisk and so unlike him. Doesn't sound like him at all. Yet he presses his hands together, rubbing them in the way he used to at Nbutai when he was nervous.

Nervous.

"Why?" I repeat my question. I need the confirmation, the assurance that I'm right.

Three looks toward the door quickly, then back at me. He touches his metal cheek gingerly. "Because Raleigh doesn't know. He can't know, can't see you with it. You've got to hide it."

"No. *Why give it back?*" I take as deep a breath as I can manage. My brother is normally blunt about things. He says what he means. But his actions have always spoken louder than his words. "You're still you, aren't you? Still Untamed." Saying the words makes me feel strange, but better. "*You're* still in there."

Three's nostrils wrinkle, and he takes a sudden step back. "No."

I shake my head, soften my voice. "You are—it's okay... It's only me here."

He looks up toward the ceiling—for cameras? Microphones? Am I being monitored? My mouth dries.

DIVIDED

"I'm a Chosen One," Three says.

"No!" I reach for him, but he doesn't let me touch him again. "It's okay—"

"My *name* is Tomas."

I'm shaking. My hand with the crystal is shaking. I lift it up and see my brother's eyes go to it.

"This... *You* gave this back to me, Three. No Enhanced would do that. You did that to help me, didn't you? To prove whom you are. It's okay, you can trust me."

He breathes noisily, then cracks his knuckles—something he's never done before. The sound makes me flinch.

"You're wrong. I didn't give it back to you because I'm Untamed. I'm a Chosen One," he says, and he says the words strongly. *So* strongly. My eyes narrow. "I gave it to you because a Sarr Seer should have it. Mum says it's always been in our family, our line. All the Sarr Seers. It gets smaller each time there's a generation with more than one Seer. Mum cut part of it off for Two." His eyes appear to darken, even though they're mirrors. "And Mum gave it to Esther to pass onto you when she joined the Chosen Ones. She left it behind for *you*. She says you must have it. Keep it, Shania. Hide it from them. Don't let Raleigh take it from you again."

I open my mouth, then stop. I stare at him. The pendant flashes hot in my hand.

Three shakes his head quickly, then looks around. "I must go."

And...and he walks off. I feel too strange, too shocked, to do anything. So I watch him leave, and I turn the pendant over and over in my palm. Then I stare at it and wonder how many Sarr hands have touched it. All my mother's ancestors? All the magic from her line? For some reason, I'm reminded of the time when I was little and thought that Sarr was my father's name and how annoyed my mother had been that I'd thought that. She'd shouted at me, and

I hadn't understood why. But she said the Sarrs had to continue.

I take a deep breath. The pendant is cold.

Keep it, Shania. Hide it from them. Don't let Raleigh take it from you again.

I nod quickly, then place it in my bra. The surface is smooth, except for the slightly sharp edge, and I angle it carefully. It's cold, and the coldness of it makes me shiver. It makes me tingle—because I know now. I know there's a part of my brother that he's hiding, hiding beneath the one-way mirror, waiting....

He won't admit it, for fear of being caught, but he's shown it.

And I've seen it.

A weight lifts away from me.

I've still got my brother.

He's still in there.

Three can resist too.

FOURTEEN

THE MOMENT AN ENHANCED ONE enters my cell, I turn my body away from him, to hide the pendant from him, even though it's already concealed.

He takes a key out his pocket, moves to the manacle around my wrist.

"It is time."

I stiffen, watch him carefully. I vaguely recognize him, but nothing more than that.

The man tells me he has a gun and that he'll shoot me if I try anything.

His words repeat themselves in my mind as he leads me through corridors. We pass a window at the top of some steps, and I get a brief glimpse of the outside world: sandy ground, a few sparse trees to the left and a denser group to the right, a newly-painted white building opposite, and—

And the sky. Soft, edged in gray cloud. Looks exactly the same as in my dream, when I became Corin.

I feel my expression slacken. That was just a dream. Just my head messing with me.

Wasn't it?

Unless....

"Where are we?" I try to linger at the window, but my legs don't let me. Raleigh's not in sight, yet he's controlling me. And it feels just as strong a control as when I had augmenters in my system.

"The Second Region of New Kitembu," the Enhanced says.

"The Second Region?"

"That's where our conversion compound is. Here."

I grimace. "No. Why's it the *Second* Region of New Kitembu? Why not just New Kitembu?" Other cities and towns I've been in didn't have long names.

"The city of New Kitembu is big." He nods, and I'm surprised when he launches into a detailed explanation, almost as if he's a guide. "This region contains the conversion compounds, middle-housing, and factories. The First Region has the top-housing and the majority of the shops. The Third Region contains the farms, but that's farther north than we are. The First and Second Regions are pretty much side by side. The Fifth Region is a little way away, beyond the farms, up where Mount Etu rises. The land there is higher in altitude, and we use it to test the performance-enhancing augmenters when creating or developing new formulas."

"What about the Fourth Region?" I ask.

"The Fourth Region no longer exists." His voice is blunt. "Nor does the Sixth Region."

"Why?" I ask.

The man steers me left sharply, without any warning, his fingers digging into my arm. We pass two other Enhanced Ones, and they watch me warily. They almost seem nervous, except that can't be right—it's a negative emotion.

The Enhanced man waits until we've walked down the next corridor and ascended a flight of stairs before answering my question. "The living conditions were not sanitary enough for human living, and the residents were evacuated and dispersed among the newly-built towns farther south."

DIVIDED

I frown. "They weren't sanitary enough?"

"Slums," he says. "The kind of places that breed wild thoughts...the places the Untamed would like to occupy if they could...breed more of their badness. In the old days, many humans lived like that, but we know that it is not right. Everyone is entitled to security, comfort, and safety. The Fourth and Sixth Regions were demolished. That land is being cultivated for future crop yields." He pauses. "Raleigh has mentioned that he'll be moving you back to New Kimearo soon though."

"New Kimearo?" I raise my eyebrows.

"Raleigh may be the leader of our section, but he is not the leader of New Kitembu. He's brought many of his men with him, but Zahlia will not host him for much longer. Divorce is rare in our society, but their separation was, of course, amicable. We do not want any trouble to arise, so the sooner he leaves, the better. And, I'm sure Raleigh would much rather have the glory of winning the war from his own town, else the place of the war's end will go down in history as New Kitembu and Zahlia will be credited in part when she had little to do with it."

"So why did he bring me here?" I ask.

"New Kitembu is nearest to the Noir Lands, but it's also the city where new technology is developed as Zahlia has the top engineers and scientists. We believe Raleigh wishes to utilize our resources and then take you away so the final act of the war's closure is done on his own territory."

I mull over his words, and, a few minutes later, we get to the room. Another new room. Bigger than others I've been in, and there's no furniture in it. Another chain is attached to the opposite wall, and the Enhanced leads me over to it, forces my hand into the new manacle, locks it. Then he lets me go.

I try to pull my arm away, but the manacle's too tight.

Behind me, Raleigh laughs.

I turn and—

I don't know how I didn't see the screen before. Or her.

Esther.

Of course it's Esther. And just seeing her—though she's on a screen, not here—makes my heart squeeze. She's alive.

The picture is sharp. She's chained to a wall, and she looks awful. Dull eyes, dull hair. Her skin is closer to gray than any other color, and she crosses her hands in front of her stomach as she looks at me. She can see me? Is it a two-way connection?

"Esther!" I cry.

"She can't hear you, but she knows you're here," Raleigh says, his voice low. He takes a Luger out from behind his back. "I've set this up so you can *see* one of your Untamed friends. My team is with her, and if you don't co-operate, I will instruct them to hurt her. So you know what to do, don't you, for the greater good, yes? She can be our insurance. If you try anything or let the darkness take over, I'll hurt her. She'll know it's your fault, because my team have briefed her— and she's putting her trust in you. Trusting you *not* to hurt her, Shania. But if you do, you'll watch it." He chuckles. "A rather effective method of controlling your evil tendrils, don't you think? If you so much as *try* anything, she will suffer. In fact, let's have a demonstration." He says those last words loudly, looking at the screen.

Before I even register Raleigh's words, an Enhanced man appears next to Esther, in the screen, and hits her.

I gasp. "Esther!"

"I told you not to communicate." Raleigh whirls around, moving quickly, glares at me.

I clamp my mouth shut, but I'm breathing heavily. Shaking. Furious. Sweat's already forming over my body.

Esther whimpers.

"So," Raleigh says, a malignant smile unfurling.

DIVIDED

"Now we can get down to business. You weren't very quick at killing last time, were you? All that resistance. But that'll change now, won't it?" He smiles, proud. "I should've done this before, this insurance."

Killing.

Elia.

No.

My eyes widen, my chest tightens.

I stare at him and move back, against the wall. This one is smooth. My breath comes in fast, short bursts, and, for some reason, I look around for the Enhanced man who brought me here, as if he will help me. But he's not here now, and I didn't notice when he left.

"Now," Raleigh says. He puts his firearm down, a few feet away—out of my reach. "Given your Untamed state, I suggest the easiest way to do this is that you allow me to take full control—because I know you won't do it willingly as you're already letting the darkness grow stronger. So, give me access—*full* access—to test on the subject and if you resist or try to stop me, I'll have *her* hurt." He steps back, points at Esther. Her face is even grayer now. Raleigh just smiles, then pulls a radio from his pocket. "Bring the subject in."

The door opens, and two Enhanced women step through. In between them is a small child with curly blond hair and a cute, button nose. He's Enhanced—his tiny eye-mirrors blink at me, and then he smiles. A sweet, innocent smile.

My stomach knots, and, a second later, I imagine him lying in front of me—dead. I shake that image away, breathing heavily.

Then I turn on Raleigh. I'm shaking.

"I don't want to kill him." My voice is laden with venom, and I shake my head again.

But every Enhanced One deserves to die. You know that.

Not children. I shake my head.

They're still part of the disease. They're the ones who'll grow up to hunt your people down.

Raleigh raises his eyebrows. "You don't *want* to?" He laughs. "How wonderful—you're averse to violence. Maybe the Untamed part isn't as strong as it was. That's really good! But, Shania, you don't have a choice. I have to make sure you can protect yourself, and you gave up any choice you had when you signed yourself over to me."

"I didn't sign myself over, and you said it was just that one time I had to…" I gulp. "With Elia. That I wouldn't have to do it again."

"Did I say that?" Raleigh's voice crawls through the air, as if it's got a hundred little caterpillar legs. "Or did I say that I need to know you can defend yourself adequately? And so far, you haven't shown *adequate* skill. You were too slow before. And time can cost you everything. I assure you, this session is necessary. Kill him quickly, Shania. The quicker it is, the nicer it'll be for him, and the more satisfied I will be that you can defend yourself *adequately, efficiently,* and *quickly.* And there is a part of you that wants to be nice, isn't there? Just concentrate on that. Don't let the darkness get stronger. Try to help yourself, please."

I spit at him.

At first, Raleigh doesn't move. I just watch my spit on his face. How, at first, it clings to the end of his nose, and it reminds me of the shiny marbles I used to have when I was little. Then the weight of my saliva gets too much, and it drips off. My eyes follow it to the floor, then I look back up at Raleigh.

He tilts his head to the side. His neck clicks, and his upper lip curls. "You should not have done that." His voice is low and coiled, concealing venom, like a Gaboon viper slowly moving its tail, getting ready to strike.

Then he lunges at me, but Esther screams.

Raleigh stops, and I twist around, try to see past Raleigh to the screen and—

He grabs my arms, turns me back to face him. I try to fight him, try to move, but pain welds my muscles

DIVIDED

together. Esther screams louder.

"We are going to use your Seer powers now, Shania," Raleigh snarls. "Any resistance and my team will hurt your dear friend more."

Rushing sounds fill my ears, then Raleigh's hands are on my head.

"Open up to me—let me in." His fingers dig into my temples, pressing and pulsing, and then his nails, and sharp pain.

Stuff moves inside my head, and—

Pain, my forehead. And Raleigh….

I sense him…inside my head…looking for the…and…but….

No. No. *No.*

I feel my chest rise and fall too quickly, and I try to get away from Raleigh, try to move my hands up, try to pull his hands from my head, but I can't, and—

"Do it!" Raleigh yells, and then Esther shrieks, and my gaze jerks up.

Her body convulses as she starts to fall, but the chain stops her, and she screams again.

"Come on, Shania. I told you what would happen if you tried to stop me." Raleigh's voice is low, and his words slither through me. "I told you I would hurt her. You do not want that, do you? And young David here knows it's a *great* honor to die at your hand—for the greater good."

For the greater good. He keeps saying that, and every time the cliché makes me feel sick.

"No!" My word goes on and on forever.

More pain radiates through me, through my head—a pick-axe of pain—and I gasp. My vision blurs, but I grit my teeth, force myself to keep breathing. Breathing evenly. Stay in control. Have to—

Raleigh shouts something and then Esther screams louder, and she's screaming, screaming, screaming, and I don't know what to do. There's nothing I can do—nothing right… What if my resistance *kills* Esther? But I can't let Raleigh use my powers to kill another child. I *can't*.

"I'll get my way," Raleigh shouts. "I *always* get what I want, Shania. You know that. I got *you*, didn't I?"

My vision blurs. My head turns a little—don't know which of us does it—and I see the women who brought the child in. Their faces swim past me.

"You can't resist me for long!" Raleigh shouts, and his fingers dig deeper into my flesh.

Blood—I feel it, sliding down my face. And then my hands are warming up—*no*!

I blink and see Elia lying in front of me, and then the Enhanced boy.

Dead.

More blood on my hands.

"No!" I cry, that can't happen—can't!

"Stop it, Seven!" Esther shrieks, but her voice sounds strange.

But I can't—she doesn't understand, and Raleigh laughs, low in my ear. But the sound is strained, and he's having trouble—I know he is. I'm resisting him too much—I *can* resist him more when I'm Untamed and—

Heat runs down my arms. My body jolts. I look to my left, see the boy watching me. So young. But he's not watching in horror. He's watching like he's interested, like I'm entertainment for him. Not like I'm going to kill him.

I clench my hands into tight fists, they're getting hotter. And I can't let that happen—can't let the next bit happen, but—

But Raleigh's getting my power, he's directing it to my hands... The white light—no!

"Don't block me out, Shania. I am in control, you're just hurting your friend. Look at her, look at the agony you are cruelly inflicting on the woman you say is your friend. But calling her a friend is a lie! No friend would hurt another like this! Do you see what the darkness is doing to you?"

I gasp, and I see Esther: my eyes zoom in on her,

as if I'm a robot, and I see the sweat running down her face, and how she's crumpling up, pulling on the chain.

"Stop!" she screams. "I'm pregnant!"

FIFTEEN

EVERYTHING STOPS.

Raleigh holds onto my Seer powers, and the pain in my head doesn't lessen. His hands are still on me. I'm very aware of the contact as I push my way through the layers and layers of thick, tangible pain, as I stare at the screen, at Esther.

"What?"

My head pounds. Pregnant? She's *pregnant*?

"Turn the two-way sound on," Raleigh says, and he taps his fingers against my head. Hard.

Two-Way Sound On flashes onto the screen—voice activated.

"Now, listen," Raleigh says, and he lets go of me with one hand, points at Esther. "Lying is bad. Very bad. And although your physical state is Untamed, you should at least try not to let the parasite take over. You need to be virtuous and honest."

David starts laughing, and the sound is nearly enough to drown out Esther's heavy breathing. I stare at her. The image on the screen zooms in, until her face fills it. She's looking down, and her bottom lip trembles as her nostrils flare. Then she looks right at

DIVIDED

the screen...at me, straight into my eyes.

"I'm not lying."

David stops laughing and starts frowning.

"Esther Eriksen, you *are* lying." Raleigh's voice is cold, and he removes his other hand from my head. I breathe deeply, try to move, but he's still controlling me. The pain's still there. In front of me, Raleigh snarls. "You are lying because *that* would've shown up on the scans."

"It did," one of the Enhanced women says, and David runs toward her. "I gave that file to you to review before."

Raleigh curses, then lets go of my mind and withdraws his control over me. The pain disappears. I gasp as my vision separates into two—but only for a second. It slides back, and a new type of pain burns in my chest.

I turn on Raleigh, chain rattling, fire in my hands. In my bra, I feel a flash of heat from my Seer pendant. Raleigh turns and his eyes widen and he screams and—

And I shoot white lights from my palms. Two channels that flow together, create a huge bolt that flies out. It hits Raleigh. His body jolts backward, and he falls, hits the floor hard, one arm crossed under his body. For a second, his feet tremble. Then he's still.

I inhale sharply, freeze.

My eyes widen. He's dead? I did it—killed him.

Just like that....

A loud *thwack* sounds, and I flinch, look up, my movements jerky.

Esther howls.

I whirl around, see her fall. See the heavy, wooden bat the Enhanced man on the screen is holding.

I try to run forward, but the chain yanks me back, and pain wracks my shoulder. My vision blurs for a second, then I see Raleigh stirring on the floor. Not dead. Shit.

Kill him.

I lift my arm again, my fingers tingling, and—

The door flies open. Movement, people rushing in and—

Something hits me hard.

I fly back; my head hits something. Darkness and white light and—

Pain tunnels down my spine, makes me look up, see the gun above me. The gun aimed at me, at my legs.

I don't know who's holding it, but the fingers around the handle move and—

I roll to the left just as the person pulls the trigger. The sound makes me flinch, and I cover my head, hear the bullet hit metal—a loud clang. Open my eyes, see Raleigh scrambling up, fury in his eyes, and—

Not dead. Shit.

Another gunshot. So close, so—

Raleigh falls again, coughing, spluttering. An alarm pierces the air.

I freeze, then scrabble backward, try to stand, try to make sense of it, try to—

"Seven!"

I look up and see Clare. Just Clare, smiling, with a gun, standing in front of me. Clare, *here,* and there are other people shouting not far away—and the Enhanced women? They're not here.

It's *Clare.*

"Come on!" she yells. "Soraya's getting Esther! Miles has disarmed the guards out there, and—come on!"

I start to race forward, but the chain and manacle yanks me back by my arm. Pain flies through my chest at the sudden change of direction, and I stumble. I pull on the chain, and the unit on the wall moves a little. Seems looser.

"Come on!" Clare yells again, then she sees what's wrong.

She raises her gun.

My mouth dries.

She shoots, and I scream, throw myself down and

DIVIDED

to the left—

The bullet hits metal. Fragments fly. The chain hits the back of my head as it falls—it's still attached to my wrist, but not to the wall. I cry out, see dark spots for a moment.

"Run!" Clare shouts, racing toward the door. And she disappears.

I turn, see Raleigh. Raleigh who's injured, blood pouring out of him. I look up, see the screen for a moment: Esther and Soraya are huddled on the floor, Soraya's arm around Esther, and two Zharat men fight Raleigh's team, and—

Get out! Go!

Red light fills the room, the siren blares in my ears. Adrenaline gushes through me.

I gasp as my vision blurs, and then there's pain and—

Shit! No!

But I step forward, the chain clanking. And my legs work, they obey me. Raleigh's not as strong—he's injured, and I'm strong. I'm Untamed. I throw the pain away from me, feel something wet sliding down the side of my face and—

"No!" Raleigh yells.

I don't look at him. I run for the open doorway, trailing the chain, try to lift it up, try to hold it because I can run easier then, but the length is long—too long—and it's dragging, can't help it.

I make it out into the corridor before the next surge of pain sets in. Raleigh's screaming at me, and every time he screams the pain gets stronger, sharper. And my head—where the chain hit me...so much pain. But I keep going. Clare went this way. I need to find her—she'll be going to Esther. Or the other Zharat.

We're escaping. Oh Gods!

We've got the upper hand. We're Untamed *and* we're no longer sick.

We're escaping.

But Clare's not here. I don't know where's she's

gone. The corridor's empty.

My arms flail, and I grasp at the wall as my vision fuzzes. *Raleigh*. Shit. For a second, I can't breathe. My insides squeeze together, and there's so much pain that I can't think, can't do anything.

"Come back!"

His yell is a roar that crawls through every nerve, that tries to make me turn back—and my feet start moving, and—

No.

I grit my teeth; sweat pours down my back. I make myself stand still.

The moment the pain lessens, I force myself onward. But the chain's weighing me down, snaking along the floor, trying to drag me back.

Somehow, I keep going, and I try to look around—because where are they? Where are the Enhanced? They're not here…why not?

Raleigh's screams get quieter, more distant, but the siren gets louder. My head pounds. My legs shake harder and harder. I curse myself. Got to keep going. Got to get out of here. Raleigh's weak. I'm Untamed. I can resist. And, somehow, I get more energy. I force my legs not to shake as much, I make my body obey me, and then I'm running down the corridor, heart thumping. My Seer pendant thumps with it.

The corridor branches into two. I take the left one, but there's no sign of an exit. I keep running, flinching away from people that aren't there.

I curse, try to look around, try to see some signs somewhere—but there's nothing.

"Clare?" My voice sounds weak, not like me at all.

But there's no one here, no one to answer. And I don't know which way to go, how to get out of here. The alarm laughs at me.

My legs start to burn—*no!*

I skid on the smooth floor. There's a doorway ahead. I reach it, hands straining. My fingers curl like claws. It takes me too long to get the door open, and my head and heart pound. Pound deeper and deeper. But then I yank it open, find myself in another corridor—a narrower one—and I keep running, my bare feet slapping against the cold floor. The light above flickers—and then the room fills with red. The walls start to close in. For a second, I pause, start to turn, and—

"Stop!"

He's to my right. I see him in the doorway—the one I've just come through. My brother. Twenty feet away. My Seer pendant flashes hot. He'll help me!

The door to my left—the one I was heading for—clicks loudly, then I hear footsteps. Shit. Enhanced. I snake my head around and look. My stomach hardens as five Enhanced step through the doorway.

I run back, run for my brother. My pendant gets hotter still. Run as fast as I can toward him; he'll know what to do. He'll—

My brother steps out of the way, beyond the doorframe, leaves the way free for me, so all I can see is the corridor on the other side and walls, and I run faster, hear the Enhanced behind me. My arms stretch out, I reach for the doorframe, ready to grab it, to propel myself through, and—

The door slams shut.

I crash into it. My head hits it hard. I jolt, dazed and—

"Three!" I yell, and my hands go for the handle, and I'm rattling it, and the chain's rattling—everything's rattling—and I'm trying and trying, but the door won't open and the handle won't move far enough.

Locked?

Or being held still on the other side....

My gut squeezes. No. Three wouldn't. He proved to me who he was!

He wouldn't!

"Don't fight us, Shania." The door muffles his voice. But it's his. Undeniably his.

No. No. No.

He wouldn't.
But he is.
Cold hands land on my shoulders, and I yell, whirl around, spit at them, kick them. See glimpses of myself in their eyes—bleeding red—and—
My head pounds. There are too many. So many and—
I'm not going to get away.
"Seize her!"

SIXTEEN

"STOP STRUGGLING."

The Enhanced haul me away from the doorway, still kicking and screaming, and then it opens. My brother steps through it. He shoves his gun—a Glock—into my face; the metal is cold as it connects with my cheekbone. I wince, but I do as the Enhanced say and still myself.

"I may not kill you with this, but I can still inflict serious injury."

I stare at him, and it's like time is standing still. Three...my *brother*. It's his voice, but not his words. Can't be. And I try to see him—see my *brother*—but all I see is myself reflected in his eyes, from the portals of his cold, half-metal face. So unfamiliar, yet close.

"Give me your hands."

I twist my head around, try to see—there's got to be a way out, an escape. My heart pounds.

"Give me your hands."

But the Enhanced don't wait for me to obey my brother; they're already holding my body, and they seize my arms roughly. I scream as I see metal cuffs, and they click them over my wrists, and then wrap the dangling chain around my arms. I try to wrench my hands back to me, away from them, but it's no use. They're too strong, and I'm outnumbered—even when Raleigh's not controlling me.

They drag me through the doorway, back the way I've come. My heart pounds, and I try to think. Need to think.

"Walk properly." The words are deep and snarled into my ear.

I obey, my heart pounding, and I look at them all. Try to think of a plan.

Fight them.

I have to fight them. I know that. But which one? The man nearest me is the smallest. Yes, him. I wait a moment—all their eyes are on me, and they look wary, even though I'm walking like they want.

Then I kick out. My foot connects with the shorter one's shin, and he yells.

I spin around, the chain around my arm slowing me, but a hand slaps my face. Hard. My cheekbone stings, and I fall back against another, but I step to the side and—and my foot hits something, throws me off balance, and I turn and—

Something smacks into my stomach.

The momentum throws me back, and I lose my footing. The back of my head hits the wall. I cry out as sharp twinges grab my neck, and I see more dark spots and—

"Shit!"

"Shania?"

I try to mumble, but pain lassoes around my left eye, and then there's something hard against my face, and it's moving, and something's catching against me, and....

Silence.

But....

No....

My head's too....

And my arm...it's too heavy....

DIVIDED

"Shit. Shit."

I feel hands on me—Three's hands?—but I can't see, can't...my vision's too dark and wavy and... And I don't want Three's hands on me! The traitor! He gave my pendant back to fool me! Made me trust him and....

"Pick her up. Come on."

I'm lifted up, vaguely aware of it and—and something's humming inside me. Humming strongly. A tune. A—

"Will she be okay?"

"She's the powerful Seer. A knock on the head ain't going to affect her."

A pause. A pause that stretches on and on forever. My ears crackle, tears cover my eyes. and pain...pain behind my eyes and—

Why, Three? *Why*?

"They should've all been exterminated," one of them says, his voice foggy. "They're too much of a risk—how soon will it be before more attempt an escape?"

"Not exterminated, not Shania." Three's voice...but he sounds...he's singing? I think he's singing...like, no, he doesn't sing. "She's too important."

My stomach tightens, and the smell of benachin, and then chipsi mayai, washes over me. My stomach rumbles, and then it's all I can concentrate on, and everything else is just background stuff, not important—like the words, the conversation they're having.

"The Section doesn't like Raleigh's methods though—he's too fixated on violence. He's moving away from what the Chosen lifestyle is all about."

"And he's had two escapes now."

I see a light on the ceiling, but it's winking at me. I stare at it, feel strange. But it's lighting the way, and we're going to get food and—

"Zahlia never had any when she was the sole commander of New Kitembu."

"Zahlia never caught a whole tribe of Untamed though.

Raleigh's still got many in his custody. Quite a few survived the allergic reactions."

The chipsi mayai aroma gets stronger. And then I hear the sizzling as the potatoes are fried, and—and oil's spitting out. I can hear it, and my ears crackle with it. Something slides around in my stomach.

"But Raleigh caused harm to a pregnant woman."
Esther.

My eyes snap open. Hadn't realized I'd shut them. I blink, groggy, and—

"She shouldn't be pregnant though," another voice says and—

Someone's carrying me. I'm in someone's arms. The metal chain is clinking. How long? Fear chugs through me.

"She hasn't been approved for population growth. And she's Untamed, spreading that evil...."

"Raleigh's still going to be reprimanded though—she's still pregnant, and he had her injured. Outrageous!"

My head pounds and my chest—there's pain, and they keep talking. I'm not sure if I miss the next words or not. Because there's a gap. A gap when I'm just floating. Floating—and my head, it hurts. I hit it and—

"Raleigh won't stand for that." That's Three's voice, and I try to latch onto it, try to dig my nails into it.

But just then the delicious smells get stronger and stronger, and my mouth is watering, but I feel sick, and the alarm's still going off. I listen for more of their conversation. But they're quiet.

And we're at my cell.

The air's cooler. Easier to think...even though my head's pounding and—

Clare. Esther.

I flinch as their names flash through me, as I remember.

"Did they escape?" My words are mumbled, my voice sticky.

"Our teams will find them," an Enhanced tells me,

his voice glassy. "Those poor creatures don't have a clue where they are..." His lips keep moving, but, for a moment, it's like the sound's been turned off. Then his voice is back. "We'll find them, and we will bring them back to civilization and safety—"

"Raleigh's in surgery," a new one says, running up to the group. "He was shot by that vile woman, but Dr. Andy is as excellent as always. Our master will be back in no time."

The Enhanced take the metal cuffs off me, then unlock the first manacle and unwind the chain from my arm, before locking my door, shutting me in on my own. I wait a few moments, listening, trying to get my head to stop pounding. Don't think they've moved away—I haven't heard any footsteps yet.

A moment later, I hear the steps. I count them, to be sure—though the numbers are heavy, and they keep running into each other and echoing, trying to confuse me. I shake my head, try to get my ears to stop ringing—and they're suddenly ringing so loudly. I place my hands over my ears. They feel too warm. Oh Gods, I haven't done something serious to my head, have I? I breathe out slowly. I need my wits about me. I need to escape.

Escape. Yes.

When the Enhanced have definitely gone, I try the door handle, but it won't move. On wobbly legs, I pace round and round my cell, breathing deeply, then I have to sit down as my head, it's too... I rub at it, at the back, and wince as pain flares up. My eyes smart, and, through my blurry vision, I see the iron unit on the wall with the big ring; at least I'm no longer chained up.

I tell myself to think. Got to think. Need to think. But there's fog in my head, and it's churning round and round, trying to confuse me.

Esther and the others. Did...did they get out?

Nausea wells up in me suddenly, and I freeze, hold my breath. Wait for it to pass. Wait for minutes and minutes. Sweat lines the back of my neck, then drips down my back, sticking my overalls to me. I breathe deeply, go to run a hand through my hair, then stop when my fingers touch the short strands. My shoulders sag, and the movement sends chilling pains down my spine.

I flex my neck carefully and take another deep breath. I *need* to think. Need to get out. Need to escape.

But my head's still fuzzy—so fuzzy…and I know there's no escape from this room. No… I need a…a window. A window equals hope. But I can't see a window…and even if I could, what happens when I'm outside?

I groan. That Enhanced man earlier told me about the different regions…didn't he? Knowledge of the outside? I frown, and the words come back to me, but they're so slow, as if they're caught in thick honey that's trying to drag them back, stop me from seeing their shapes.

I touch the side of my head, tentatively. Then the back of it. Everywhere feels raw, tender. Like everything's trying to stop me from thinking about escape. But I need to.

I try to think harder. There must be a way out into the wilderness nearby—Corin got away. If he was in the city, they'd find him… No, he'd have gone for the wilderness—it's what all the Untamed do. I swallow hard, think of that time when I thought I was him. When he coughed, but it was me.

Only that didn't happen. It was a dream.

But then the flash of an image enters my mind. Me, looking down, seeing tattoos on a man's arm, a man's hairy arm… Oh Gods.

But it can't have been real! Hallucinations…they were both when I was sick…weren't they? When I was sick from the augmenters? Yes, that dream where I was Corin…that was when I was becoming Untamed again…the end of the hallucinations,

I stare up at the brick wall as adrenaline slams its

way around my body, like it's a comet bouncing off rocks, destroying rocks, and shards of rock are flying about, puncturing me. I bare my teeth, grimace, shake my head. There's too much stuff in my head, in my body…just zooming round and round. Each one wanting attention.

And time seems to pass slowly, but quickly too. Or maybe it's not passing, I don't know.

I think of my traitorous brother, and I feel sicker, but my thoughts are a little clearer now. My pendant's still hot against my skin. Or maybe it's cooled and is now heating up again—I'm not sure. I breathe deeply, and darkness washes over me. I was wrong when I thought he was on my side because he gave my pendant back to me. He's not.

But why did he give it back? I exhale hard. So I don't get stuck in the Dream Land and prevent the Enhanced from winning the war?

I flinch, breathe deeply. More pain in my head, but it's like a worm, not a snake.

Or maybe he did just give it back because it's mine, because it's always been in our family, and our mother left it for me.

I scratch at my face, shake my head.

And Esther's *pregnant*. I blink several times. Manning's name tastes bad as I think it, and my hands squeeze into tight fists. My knuckles click, and then something in my head keeps clicking. Clicking with names.

Corin, Esther, the Zharat.

And they're out there.

And I'm in here.

And I didn't escape because of my brother.

Instead, I'm concussed or something. I groan again, put my head in my hands, feel weak, vulnerable, small.

Anger takes over me.

I didn't escape because of Three.

He stopped me.

I shake my head, hard. Feel like screaming.
Next time, he won't stop me.
No one will.

SEVENTEEN

SOME TIME LATER—I'VE NO idea how long has passed, but my grogginess has mainly worn off—a single pair of steps returns to my door. I hear the bolt slide back, and I get ready—need to get out, have to join them.

The door creaks open, and I run—

Run straight into Three.

He shouts something and shoves me back, locking the door, all in one fluid movement. My nostrils flare, my lips flatten. *Traitor. Traitor. Traitor.* But I force myself to push the waves of anger away—need to be calm, in control—and stay surprisingly light on the balls of my feet. I can't let my emotions dictate my actions. He's just an Enhanced One.

"What do you want?" My question comes out as a snarl, and I see the shock on his face. His reaction makes me feel good.

"The drones have found them," he says.

"What?" My eyes widen, and I stare at them, in his mirrors. "Drones?"

"Yes, Shania." Three folds his arms slowly. "The Chosen Ones use thermal imaging to scan the lands as relatively few spirits inhabit these regions when it's not the Turning, so few spirits can interfere with the imaging. But the drones pick up on extra heat levels indicative of humans out there. And anyone not at a compound will be Untamed." Suddenly, his arms spring away from his chest and he gesticulates wildly. "Gods, the technology here is *phenomenal*. You've no idea! They've got assemblers...and the height of medical equipment. And their *radios*—no foxholes here, they've got multi-way devices that can send and receive across huge distances. Like the ones we used to have—only better. And the *computers*! Raleigh says I can meet his head technician when we're back at New Kimearo, and I can start training in IT management."

The excitement in his voice is tangible—so strong, I could reach out and hold it—and it makes me look at my brother carefully, at the way his right cheek is plumping up as he smiles and how his shoulders bounce with energy. It's that excitement that makes him *seem* Untamed.

But I know better. It's just an act. Has to be. If he was Untamed, he would've let me escape, no matter what.

And he didn't.

And now he's trying to trick me again; this display of enthusiasm over their technology—this synthetic emotion—is to try and fool me, to make me trust him again.

I stare at him, coldly, feel my body lock up. I'm not stupid.

"They're assembling a team to collect the escaped Untamed now," Three says, his voice returning to a more monotonous tone.

His face is a plain of expressionlessness once more, and I immediately feel more justified in my anger at him—because it proves he's really just an artificial shell of who he once was. He's been *converted*. And I hate that I need to feel justified to feel as I do about him, an Enhanced One. As if our familial status should override my feelings about what he's become—even if

DIVIDED

it wasn't his choice.

And it wasn't.

I thought he was dead, that he couldn't have survived the gunshots to his face and abdomen. Even when Esther told me he was alive, I refused to believe her. I didn't go after him, didn't even try and rescue him when the Enhanced were converting him. Even when the Dream Land warned me—because I didn't *see* the bison, didn't realize it *was* a warning. My fault. I let him become like this. The tips of my anger turn inward, and then it's a torrent of red-hot pain rushing at me. The guilt I've been ignoring, pushing away, suppressing; it's an angry storm inside me.

"I'm going out as part of the team," Three says. "I came to let you know."

"To let me know?" I keep my voice low, blunt, and touch the base of my neck, rub it. Need to stay in control, mustn't show weakness...or my guilt. "Why?"

"So you don't need to worry," he says. "They'll be safe again soon. I'm going to bring her back. Bring Esther back. *My* Esther."

I tug on my earlobe, still watching him. My fingers find a scabby bit of skin, and I pick at it, wonder if it's one of the old kavalah spirit scars. Three smiles softly—thinking about Esther? *His* Esther?

"She's pregnant." And I watch him carefully for a reaction—something genuine. And I don't really know why I'm still searching. Because I know what he is, *who* he is.

But you don't want to believe it.

I grit my teeth. I don't. But I have to. Have to accept reality. He's one of them now.

Three nods. "I know. I scanned her when she came in."

"And you didn't tell Raleigh?" My fingers move to the edge of my jaw, and I find another imperfection there. My nails savagely gauge it out, as if they've got a life of their own. As if it's not me...as if it's Raleigh doing it? No. That's not right. He wouldn't do that.

This is just me.

"I wrote it on her records," Three says quickly. "It's not my fault that he didn't read them. Or the later reports. But it will cause trouble with the Section, his negligence."

My hand drops to my side. "What's the Section?" The Enhanced have mentioned it before, and information is important. I straighten up.

"The circle of leaders," Three says, "from across the world. All the Enhanced. They make up a governing body. Raleigh's power outweighs the rest of them as his lands are the biggest and the wildest. Most dangerous. He governs this continent, delegates leaders of the other compounds within his kingdom. But—" Three pauses. "Raleigh's the leader with the biggest Untamed population within his lands. Because the spirits are bigger here, in this section, more problematic. They make it harder and—" His eyes widen, and he presses his lips together.

"Three?" I frown. "What is it?"

"*Tomas!*" he shouts. "*That* is my name. And—and I have to go." His voice is strange, so unlike him, so cold. "We leave in twelve minutes, and I have to get Esther back."

He's too quick with the door for me to attempt an escape. I hear him slide the bolt across on the other side.

Twelve minutes. How long will it take to get them?

Oh Gods. Drones. I shake my head. If they've got drones and can scan the lands for body heat, why hasn't Corin been found? I shake my head slightly. Maybe they don't know where to look.

Or maybe they've already got him... Maybe they haven't told me in case we try and find each other, start a rebellion... Keeping me in the dark does seem like a logical thing for the Enhanced to do. Yet I can't help but think that Raleigh would gloat about finding Corin.

But now they're going to get Esther and the others

who escaped.

They know where they are.

And they're going to bring them back.

Shit. Why didn't I get away too? I clench my fists—if I'd been faster, if I'd escaped too and was with them, I could fight the Enhanced with my Seer powers. I could save my people.

But I can't. Because I'm not there. Because I wasn't fast enough.

Me, not fast enough? I'm the fastest runner the Untamed have.

But I've *got* to stop them from catching Esther and Clare and the others, got to stop my brother—but he's not my brother. Not anymore. I can't afford to see him as my brother.

Can't you?

No! I want to scream, and I push the thought away. My brother has gone. It's only *Tomas* who's here. And I need to treat him as just another Enhanced, not my brother. I can't waste my emotions, my feelings, on him—or let him dictate what I feel, how I feel. It's exhausting. He's *just* an Enhanced.

I press my lips together. And now I've been concentrating on him, when I should've been concentrating on the Untamed, on Esther and Clare and whoever else got away.

But I can't help her, can't help any of them. Not from in here. I'm trapped. Shit.

No! There's got to be something I can do! Got to be!

I look around at the walls again. And the painted stone blocks start laughing at me.

I stare at them, and they're stepping closer, dragging the walls with them.

Pins and needles fill my legs and I'm trying to keep standing, but I—

Scrape. Scrape. Scrape.

What the hell? I touch my head.

But the walls are still moving and—

I'm hallucinating? That damage to my head?

No.

No.

No.

I look up, but then Esther's *here*—right in front of me. But—but she's... My eyes widen.

Her distended stomach watches me—distended much more than it should be—and there's a door *in* her stomach, and it's opening and—

I take a step back, eyes widening, breathing fast.

"Help me, Seven!" she shouts.

And then there's an Enhanced in here too, and he's reaching for her stomach, and the door's opening wider—and oh Gods, I don't want to see—but something's appearing. A tiny hand reaches out and—

What the hell? Heat whirls around me, and I stare at her. But it can't be her. It can't. I know that and—

"Don't let them have my baby too!" Esther screeches, and she kicks out at the Enhanced, screaming and screaming, and there's fire—fire everywhere.

It ends in fire for you.

I shrink back, heart pounding, feel my sweat dripping everywhere. I try to move, try to make sense of it all. But I can't. This just...it can't be real. Hallucinating. My head. It's—

The flames lick toward me; the roar of the fire fills my ears. But under it, there's a pulsing, a steady pulsing I can hear and—

"Seven, help me!"

Esther's voice rattles me, but it puts the fire out, and—

What the hell is going on?

My shoulders tighten, and my breath bursts in and out.

"Seven!"

Snap.

Esther disappears and something prickly washes over me. A flash of red in front of me, and—

And everything...changes.

The walls shoot toward me, and something hisses. A

DIVIDED

door—the door—hurtles at me and—

I scream as I turn, hunker down, cry out, but my tongue's tangled and—

Fine dust hits me. I try to move, try to turn, but there's darkness—darkness and—where's the door? The walls and—

Pressure fills my chest, my head, my whole body. A flash of white light, and my hands burn, my arms burn, everything burns, and colors swirl around me and—

My body folds in on itself, and I try to lift my arms up, need to protect my head, my back, my neck, and—

Cold air whistles toward me.

I stay as I am, cowering. I listen.

Silence.

Slowly, I lift my head up an inch, so I can see a little and—

My eyes widen.

There are metal pans in front of me, with the remains of food in them. They're on a thick, woven mat. I stare at them, feel a strange creeping sensation fall over me.

My neck cricks as I lift my head higher, as I take in all the things around me. A kettle with a big black handle like an arching snake. Brightly colored fabrics, and a few furs and tanned hides. Woven baskets, and a baby's crib made from fine pieces of wood all twisted together and—

I'm wearing gloves. I see my hands in them, see my fur sleeves, covered in a white dusting that's melting. My eyes widen.

I turn and—

I am in a hut.

A hut.

I'm in a hut.

Not my cell. It's—

Gone.

No. It's a…not a hut. It's a…it's like a tent. A chum. Fabric walls. I stare at them for a second, then turn and see the rest of the…the hides that are stretched over the poles and—and bones? I turn and look around me. There is a small hearth in the middle, but it looks cold. I look up. The hides stop about six inches from the top of the wooden frame above me, and I can see the poles bound together, and broken fragments of a white sky. There's a fold-up chair to my right, and I grab onto its back, feel dizzy. My knees shake and—

And I see myself in a mirror. A shard of mirror, propped on a box on the other side of the tent, against one of the wooden poles that make up the chum's structure.

Adrenaline tingles through me, and I look at the girl in the mirror.

Look at her round, pink face, and the rosiness in her cheeks. Her eyes are two dark beads that look nearly black in this light. She looks shocked as she stares at me. Her fur-lined hood encases her head, and—

And the door behind her is open. The world is white out there.

I shake my head, confused—and the girl in the mirror shakes her head and—

I swear, feel my heart rate rocket.

No. No. *No.*

And then I'm moving toward the mirror, then away from it, looking around the hut, panicking, my head pounding, trying to see her—the girl—trying to see where she is and—

I crash into the side of the chum, feel the stretched hide give a little with my weight, and then I'm thrown back. I pause, breathing hard. Look up into the mirror again.

My breath hitches in my throat.

I'm in someone else's body.

My lips start to move, but no sound comes out.

Shit. Shit. Shit.

Someone else's body... What the f—

I swear loudly.

It's like that dream but...but this is real. That was real? With Corin?

DIVIDED

Oh Gods.

My chest rises and falls too quickly. Can't breathe, can't gulp in enough air, can't—

And that Zharat man's body... I was in him too... and....

And you got out of them both.

Oh Gods.

I turn again, feel how much smaller this body is than my own. I breathe in deeply; this girl's throat is rawer than mine. I sniff loudly, then shake myself hard. With Corin and the Zharat—if this *was* what happened—it lasted, what, seconds? And they weren't hallucinations? Weren't because I was sick from the augmenters?

I squeeze my eyes tightly shut. I tell myself that when I open them, it'll be okay. That this is just a glitch, and it won't last. That I'll be back in my cell—and I've never wanted to be there so much as I do right now.

But before I even open my eyes again, I know nothing's changed. The air here smells different.

Somehow, I've been swapping bodies.

And, this time, I'm trapped.

EIGHTEEN

I STAND STOCK-STILL AND WAIT for whatever wrongness has happened to correct itself. I keep waiting, giving the Gods and Goddesses and spirits more time. Because they have to…this is a bad spirit? Messing with me? Forcing me into another person's body?

Like…like what Raleigh did with me? When he had my eyes? Was this what was happening to him?

Oh Gods. My stomach twists, and I feel sick. This is…this is invasion—and I'm doing it. I'm like Raleigh. The waves inside me build up, stronger and stronger, rocking faster and faster. Anger at Raleigh's violation of privacy pulls through me…and *I'm* doing it. I'm doing it to a girl I don't even know.

I'm just as bad as him.

Oh Gods.

Except I didn't mean to. *I* didn't do this! When Raleigh did it, it was intentional.

I bring a shaky hand up to my forehead, feel my shoulders curl forward. And I wait. I start counting, because my mother always said that when you're nervous, you should count. Count the seconds,

DIVIDED

because then you know that you're surviving—that you're alive and...and I get to twenty, and then tears hover in my eyes. The girl's eyes.

And this body—this...it...it's real. It feels like a body I'm *really* in. Not a fleeting image, a dream, a weird hallucination like before. This is different, stronger.

And I know it's real.

My Seer powers tell me it's very real.

I feel something digging in, right round my waist. The girl's waist. A belt? I look down, stare at the fur coat, adorned with leather. The different shades of orange and brown and beige.

The door of the chum is still open, and the air blowing in is cold and carries white flakes with it. Snow. A strange sense of wonder floats through me. I look at the sleeves of the coat I'm wearing. But the white specks that were on it have gone. The fur is wet, and I lift my arm to my face, wipe the fur against my cheek and—

I jump when I feel it, feel the coldness, like I hadn't expected to and—

Four chairs. There are four chairs in here. Four people live here. People other than this girl I've become and—

What if I'm permanently her now?

I push that thought away and get to the door quickly, but my body feels strange—heavier. I look at the world outside. Flat. White. Gray. Stubby trees, stilted growth. The fur of the hood tickles my forehead. I stare at the sky. Slightly blue. But mainly gray-white, especially up high. Looks thick, heavy, like it's going to fall down.

Outside, everything is calm. So calm. The ground is covered in a white blanket.

Then I lift my hand—her hand. I stare at her gloves. Purple. Some kind of thick wool.

I'm moving. *I'm* controlling her. I'm in charge. My head tingles. It's not like it was with Corin—if that *was* real...was *this*...he was in charge then....

And I'm controlling this girl, I'm moving her limbs. But where is she—her soul? Is she still in here too? Scared? Confused? Have I squashed her?

"It's all right," I try to tell her, but my words come out in a high-pitched, shaky tone. Her voice. I nearly jump.

Oh Gods.

It's all right. My words float back to me. But it's not all right! Panic rises in me, and I try to squash it down, but then I'm running, running outside, and there's a hammering in my chest. I run through the snow, turning, and I see another hut, and—and big animals. Like…like big, stocky antelopes, but furry and with chunkier heads and huge antlers that aren't straight, but are like trees. The animals watch me. Ten of them. They don't run. They're used to people?

My vision blurs a little, then I see there are more of them behind the first lot. I narrow my eyes, counting more and more. A whole herd of these animals?

Pain pushes on the back of my neck. It's bitter out here—and I'm acutely aware of just how cold I am. My feet are like blocks of ice in the thick boots—and the boots are so small. I stare at them, fascinated by them even more than the animals that aren't running away. This girl's feet are *tiny*. Then I stretch up, stretch my arms out. I'm small. No, the *girl's* small.

I turn and look around. I'm thinking too hard. I take in my surroundings. One more chum. Made like the other one: hides stretched over wooden poles, making a circular shape. A little smoke rises from the top of the second chum.

Behind, the land is white. Snow.

The Frozen Lands.

It has to be. But I never thought they existed. Not really. Not when all I knew for years and years was the desert and sand and dust and rocks.

And now I'm in the Frozen Lands.

I'm in *someone else's body* in the Frozen Lands.

Oh Gods. I'm far, far away. This—isn't the same

DIVIDED

continent. This is....

I shake my head slowly, bewildered, feel all the muscles in my face slacken.

Behind all the whiteness, the sky looks like it's starting to darken. I try to think what the time is. Late afternoon? Is it the same time here? I pause, hold my breath, don't know why. It gets darker earlier the farther north you are. I know that. And the Frozen Lands are in the north and—

"Viktoriya!"

The voice roars out, and, startled, I see two women standing at the entrance of the other chum. One of them is a foot taller than the other, and both are bundled up against the cold weather. Like I am. Except they're not wearing gloves.

They start shouting at me—it must be at me.

I hurry toward them—they're Untamed! They'll help me.

My heart pounds, laughing at me. But what do I say? Will they know what's happened?

"What are you doin'?" the tallest one yells at me.

I squint as I stare at her.

Her eyes are younger than the other one. She takes in my appearance; for a second, her eyes widen, and she knows. I'm sure.

"Thank the Gods!" I cry, but the voice doesn't sound like me, and it feels like another kick to the gut. "You've got to help me!"

She grabs a fistful of my fur coat and pulls me into the other chum. I stumble, smell smoke, and—

I look to the corner, see a fire burning in the grate. Its flames entrance me.

"What are you doin'? Huh? Viktoriya? Thought you would go out after them, did you?"

"You *can't* go after them, Viktoriya," the other woman says—the rounder, shorter one. She grips my arm, like an eagle catching its prey, and I flinch, stare at her.

"Girl? Spirit got your tongue?"

I look at the two of them. They push their hoods back. Both have the same eyes—maybe mother and daughter?

"I—I'm a Seer..." I struggle to get my words out. "I'm... I just... I need your help—"

The two women burst out laughing.

The younger one flicks her head from side to side, freeing long black plaits of hair. "Hear that, Dominika?"

"Aye, I heard that all right," Dominika says. "I told you she weren't right—right from the day she was born, I told you. And right from—"

I step closer, feeling stronger now. "No, you have to listen. I just found myself in this body—I'm a Seer. This is... I don't know what the hell is going on. But I—"

"Ha, Marina, look at her." Dominika snorts loudly. "Look at the lass, believing she's—"

"What's that?"

The low rumbling voice jolts through me, and I look up, see a man partially hidden behind the small stove in the center of the chum. Don't know how I didn't notice him before. I crane my neck. He's old. Very old. Hunched over in his seat, his gnarled and twisted body is nearly completely hidden by the many furs draped over and wrapped around him. His face is pink—ruddy—as if blood vessels have broken in several places, but his eyebrows are strangely vigorous. Dark and black—like his eyes. His nose is long, wide, and the skin around his mouth looks chapped, bitten by frost. A few wiry-looking hairs have sprouted from his chin, and they stick out at strange angles.

"Nothin', Taras. Just Viktoriya bein' silly," Marina says, and she turns back, glares at me. "Just her lookin' for attention. As if we haven't already got enough to worry about." She turns toward the closed door, then pulls her parka closer. "There're not comin' back, are they? I told them not to go lookin' for them! I told them we'd got away—and we can't wait much longer, we've got to move the reindeer on to the woods—there's nothing here for them to eat and—"

"They'll be back," Dominika says. "Your husband is strong."

I stare at them, my eyes getting wider and wider. My vision gazes over.

"But Vasily saw the mirror men—"

"And your husband speared fourteen before, did he not? Vasily saw only *two* mirror men. He can take them out easily. And his brothers are with him."

"But so are the children. And it's been too long. They should be back by now."

I try again, interrupting Dominika. I lift my gloved hands up, stare at them. "Look, I'm not Viktoriya—my name's Seven. I'm a Seer, caught by the Enhanced—but we reacted to augmenters and we're still Untamed. But they've got us all trapped and...and you can help?" I stare at them. Can they help? No. This is... we're too far away. "I just...found myself in this girl's body and—"

It sounds ridiculous. My chest stutters.

The old man, Taras, watches me eagerly.

Dominika and Marina look at me sternly. The older woman shakes her head, then smacks her lips.

"Get her out of here. The evil spirits be gettin' her."

Marina nods. "Viktoriya always was weak in the mind."

She speaks as if I'm not here—as if Viktoriya isn't here... But is she? If I'm in Viktoriya's body, is Viktoriya in mine, back at New Kitembu? My head pounds. Is she scared? Alone? And—and what if the Enhanced come back for me when she's there and—oh Gods!

Marina picks up a wooden spoon and points it at me. "Effects of that Turning she was left out in as a babe. Go on, child. Get back to our chum. I'll be there shortly."

Pain shoots up the inside of my leg as I shift my weight.

"No. You have to listen—you have to believe me. I—I need your help. I don't understand this!"

"*Get out.* You think we haven't got enough to worry about with Vasily and the others out there after the mirror men? You think you can make up some stories, make this about you?"

I shake my head. "No. Look, please listen. I'm Seven Sarr. I've been captured and—"

"Get out!"

And I retreat out into the white land outside, feel something break in my chest, feel my tears make tracks down my face.

What if I'm here forever now? Millions of miles away from Corin and—and what if he goes back to New Kitembu? What if he rescues the girl who's in my body and falls in love with her?

I stare numbly into the snow.

"Oi!"

The shout is gruff, and I jump and turn to see Taras—the old man—striding after me. He moves surprisingly quickly, and it only takes a few seconds until he's by my side.

He's short—very short, like Dominika.

Then he walks past me, beckons me back with gnarled fingers. He hasn't got gloves on.

"Child, I believe you. First proper time, eh, leaping bodies? Come on. This way. We haven't got long."

NINETEEN

TARAS LEADS ME AWAY, AROUND the herd of animals—reindeer, that was what one of the women called them—and then I see another chum, one I hadn't noticed before. A smaller one. Its hides are white, and it nearly blends in with the landscape, except for the exposed dark wooden frame right at the top.

He points at it. "We'll go in there."

I nod and take in the surroundings again. Snow and a few more snow-covered trees in this area. And the land isn't as flat as I thought it was, spilling down into a shallow valley to the right. I see a frozen lake.

"What's going on?" I ask, turning back to the old man.

He shakes his head. "No more talking until we're inside, child. Spirits are out here, listening. And you never can tell with spirits whether they're helping or not. Poor souls, but they've made it hard for us. Brought the snow much earlier than it should be."

We walk across the compacted snow to the hut. Coldness seeps into my feet—into Viktoriya's feet, and, again, I wonder where she is and whether it's permanent. My hands tremble.

Taras holds open the hide door of the hut for me. I step inside. The air is sharp, strangely fresh, but warm. Taras lights a candle, then sets it on a stand in the middle of the hut. It's one room. Wash-pans in one corner, two chairs in the other, and—

And bones fill this hut.

They're everywhere. Little fragments, carved into figures. I see little whales and walruses. Is there ivory too? I squint and see some pieces shaped as the same furry beasts outside.

"This is the Tareskl Peninsula," Taras says. "Farthest north you can get on the mainland, where, in a few moon cycles, we'll have only darkness. And *this* is the Divine Chum."

I look at him carefully. The farthest north you can get? But instead, I say, "Divine?"

"For praying to the Gods and Goddesses." He gestures for me to sit down, and he takes the nearest chair. "Now we are here, we can talk Seer business."

"You're a Seer?" I sit down hurriedly, and as soon as I've said the words, I know that he is. Now, I can feel it. Don't know how I didn't realize before. But detecting Seers seems to be erratic—for me, at least. Maybe for others? I didn't realize Jed or Raleigh were Seers when I first met them.

Taras nods; his eyes are haunted. And they bore into me. Not just into Viktoriya's eyes—but into mine. Into my soul.

"You—you can see *me*? You know I'm not Viktoriya?"

"Of course. You speak differently—different syntax, way of holding yourself. She slouches, you don't." His eyes are sad. "And what is your message, child? What danger is Viktoriya in?"

I stare at him. "I—I… What?"

"Viktoriya—and my group—we are in danger. Tell me, child. Tell me what you're been shown."

I stare back at him. "You think I've seen something?"

"You must've. Marta's stories say so."

"What?" I look around. "Who's Marta?"

DIVIDED

"The first Keeper of Lore. Now, tell me the message. You've flattened Viktoriya so you cannot tell her. Tell *me*."

"Flattened?"

"Yes, child." He sounds exasperated. "Different levels of dominance. Rather than co-existing and communicating, or hiding in the body undetected, you have completely dominated and flattened your host: my granddaughter. She's in sleeping mode. You've taken control."

My eyes widen. I open my mouth, but I just...I stare at him. "There are two of us in this body? She's...she's still in here?"

The light in his eyes changes. "You don't know, do you, child? You're new. But there's no doubt you're one of them. A powerful Seer who can walk into the mind of the one she's closest to. You're a body-sharer, child."

I stare at him.

He leans forward, looks at me intently. "A people-leaper, a message-giver, a Seer-traveler. You must've heard one of those names? No? It's an old Seer power for delivering messages." Taras's eyes flash. "It's written in the ancient stories, and I'm the current Keeper of Lore. You body-share to protect a loved one, to help them. To warn them. I can sense your powers and you're learning; but the lore says the first strong and *complete* soul transferal is always for a reason, and it's *that* reason—perhaps the knowledge of an attack—that feeds your powers, that makes sure you're strong enough to pass on the message to the one you love. So what is it? Why is my granddaughter in danger? Tell me, have the Enhanced found my group, child? Have our missing men compromised our location? Have they been caught? Is Marina right? Is that your message?"

"No—no, I don't know." I shake my head, feel flustered, too hot. Strangely hot. The fur on the hood rubs against my face—Viktoriya's face—makes me feel itchy.

A body-sharer?

I look back down at Viktoriya's gloved hands, at her arms, her legs, everything bundled up.

"Why've you come here? Think. Come on, girl. Talk. There has to be a reason, especially for the first strong connection—the time when your Seer powers have been forced to strengthen, forced to become strong so you can protect your loved one."

My loved one…?

But what about Corin?

And now I'm *Viktoriya*.

This…this is absurd.

"Come on, child. The warning—"

"There's no warning." I shake my head.

"There must be. I do not have the power myself, but I know Marta's stories. Body-sharing is for the transferal of warnings to the one who you are the closest to, should they be in a different location to you. That is what the stories say. A body-sharer forges a connection with their most treasured person—or sometimes two people—to keep them safe when they're apart. That is why it is valuable to be the loved one of a Seer who has the body-sharing power. Extra protection."

The one I'm the closest to?

And I've connected with a girl I've never met before?

But I'm connected to Corin as well?

And that Zharat man too….

Taras looks at me carefully. "You and my granddaughter? How do you know her?"

My lips feel strange. "I don't."

"But you've connected with her—something that requires a great emotional bond."

A great emotional bond?

I shake my head again. "No…it's… I didn't even know you were all out here, let alone know her. I've never met any of you."

Taras's brow furrows. "No warning? And you

do not know your host? Then perhaps she has not become important to you yet—but she will. The body-sharing connection proves her worth to you—you connect to one or two whom are the most precious to you. Perhaps she will be your *only* host. And you do not even know her yet?"

I frown. "One or two? No. She's...this has happened before. But in flashes. Little bits. Not like this. With other Untamed."

"How many?"

I squint. "This is the third...maybe the fourth," I say, thinking of the time I saw the blue-eyed Seer too. Was that body-sharing too?

"Three or four hosts." His eyes narrow. "But that's unheard of in Marta's stories..." He rubs his chin. "Unless you were testing...looking for the right host..." Then he shakes his head. "No...the first few times are when your powers are just emerging and are unstable, flighty—it's you adjusting, getting ready for the first *proper* sharing. And then a sudden fear or dream of danger is said to prompt the first major body-share, and the Seer uses all their energy and risks dominating their host in their overexertion...which must be what's happening here. But it's *always* the same person in the tests as it is for the first connection, always the same host. Always a message too, life and death... Marta's stories say that a powerful body-sharer can sometimes forge a new connection later on, but only years after the first, once the first connection is strong enough to support itself." He blinks rapidly. "But you say you've got multiple connections already, before this current journey? Child, you need to tell me everything."

And I do. It pours out of me, like a tap's been turned. About who I am, the augury, how I must've body-shared before, how the Enhanced have got me, and how they've got drones going out after Esther and the Zharat.

When I finish, Taras is silent for a long time. He

stares at me, and his eyes take on a distant look.

Then he leans forward. "You're... Three or four hosts..." He shakes his head. "That's power. And you say you're the one the augury speaks of... The only one who can save us? You *must* be powerful then... powerful enough for three or four bonds. Maybe more...who knows? And with my granddaughter, a girl you've never met... This is... You're no ordinary body-sharer, Seven Sarr. And you've definitely got no message for me?"

I shake my head. "You're not in danger, not that I know. It's Esther and...."

I go cold. *She's* in danger. I saw her—that strange vision—with the child coming out of her stomach, and an Enhanced One there.

A sudden fear or dream of danger.

"You can help me," I cry. "That must be why I came here...why my Seer powers led me here—to find you, another Seer. You can save Esther and the Zharat!"

The look in his eyes deepens. "But I cannot. I'm a Seer, girl, yes. But if you've been with the Zharat, in warm lands, and you're still there—then you're far to the south of here. I cannot astral travel, not like the body-sharers. I'm stuck in my body. You've come to the wrong Seer."

I stare at him. I've come to *the wrong Seer*?

He tugs on one of his chin-hairs. "But perhaps you came to me because you could feel this power was about to strengthen—that you were about to have your first proper episode—and you needed someone to explain your powers to you. And you found me, because your powers knew that I am the Keeper of Lore, that I know the old stories, and not because you had a message for me. You're different. But it's you, child. *You* chose to come here. You needed the knowledge, to know about the power. Nothing controls your Seer powers apart from you."

Apart from me...and Raleigh.

I grit my teeth.

DIVIDED

Then I go cold. Will Raleigh know I can do this? Body-share with other Untamed...even find them, using my power? Ones I don't even know exist... My breathing gets faster. Is this how he's going to find them all—through me?

My head pounds, and I feel sick. Oh Gods. If Raleigh's looking through my eyes now, then he could know—because I don't *know* his vision is only limited to my physical body. And he could know about these people in the Frozen Lands and—

And the blue-eyed Seer—if that was body-sharing too, then she doesn't know I need help. My chest tightens. She's not going to contact the Gods and Goddesses for me and—

"You can contact the Gods and Goddesses!" I shout at Taras, and my volume surprises us both. "That's why I've come to you! I can't get in the Dream Land, because of what happened... And I'm covered in Promise Marks—my real body. I need to stop Raleigh controlling me too—else I can't do anything, can't escape, not when he's going to control me as soon as he—"

"Contact the Gods and Goddesses?" Taras gives me an odd look. "No Seers can contact the Divine Ones, child. Not at our own will."

My lips burr with the cold. "But you *must* be able to."

Taras shakes his head. "We each see our Divine One only twice, child. Once at the beginning, after they've gifted us. And once at the end, when our souls leave our bodies for good, when we hope to reach the New World. That's the only way. We can't summon them, and they can't walk in the mortal world."

"No—you go to the Dream Land to see them," I say. I shake my head. "We *can* see them, not just when we die and... I've seen Death—the God of Death, Waskabe—twice already. No, three times."

I grimace as I recall the last meeting: my banishment.

Taras shifts his weight. "My time is drawing to a

close, child. I am old. But I am not done yet. When the Goddess of Morning Song arrives for me, I will tell her your message. The lore says she is close to Death."

My mouth slackens. I want to ask how soon that will be, but I know I can't.

"I cannot guarantee she will listen. Few will trust a Seer they believe to be a traitor." Taras wrings his hands together.

"But you believe me?" My voice rises an octave.

Taras nods. "Yes, child. I believe you. I can feel it radiating from you. But you need to concentrate on what you can do *now*. Your body-sharing powers are different, and so you must see if you can find Seers closer to where you are. Maybe they can help your friends? Using your powers should be easier now... That's your best chance." He rubs his chin, and all those sparse wiry hairs flick back and forth, remind me of something, but I can't think what. "But you are the sky, child. Do you realize what this means, if your powers are beyond the scope for a usual body-sharer? You could be the thing we have in common. You've connected my group with yours. And I'll bet you can form a few more connections; the power in you must be strong, for the augury speaks of you... Make a web, child. Start close to home, spread your wings. See if you can connect to others. Unite some of our groups. Unite the Untamed. Give us hope."

Unite the Untamed.

I nod, breathe out, shakily.

"Now, child, you—"

Coldness burns me, and I scream, twisting around and—

I'm in my cell, sprawled on the floor. Breathing hard and—

I'm back. So quickly.

I look at my hands, dark with gold splashes.

No longer Viktoriya.

Relief floods me. But my head burns, and I can still see Taras in front of me. Those haunted eyes. And part of me can't believe I did it. That I've just been to the Frozen Lands.

But I know what I need to do now.

Unite the Untamed.

And it's in my power. I'll do that—and Taras will get my soul back, won't he? But only when he dies....

Something bristles along my back, and I look up. How long has it been? Have I still got time to contact another Seer? A Zharat Seer out there? Or someone else close by? Someone who can save Esther and the others?

Time is like a clock. Tick. Tock.
Unite the Untamed.
Before it is too late.

TWENTY

FIND SEERS CLOSER TO WHERE you are.

My shoulders tighten as I repeat Taras's words over and over in my head.

And I know Taras is right, but I don't know if there's time now—no, there won't be. I was with Taras's group for more than twelve minutes, so the Enhanced will have already left—they'll be out there now, homing in on Esther's location. And time works the same with this body-sharing, doesn't it?

Pain and exhaustion hover in front of me, within easy grasp. And I know it's a test—that I mustn't succumb to them.

"Need to find a Seer," I mutter, and my voice surprises me. Somehow, I'd expected it to be different. To still be Viktoriya's, but it's not. It's my own and….

Oh Gods! The Frozen Lands! I was in the Frozen Lands.

I take a deep breath, and Esther fills my mind again. But it's not like before—that…that hallucination—my fear, *her fear*, of her baby growing up Enhanced…it's just her. As I remember her. And a part of me knows it's too late to save them—twelve minutes…unless

DIVIDED

they've evaded capture.

I sit up a little straighter. They're Untamed. There's a group of them. They *could* get away. But they need help. And I have to get help to them.

I lean my head against the brick wall, and I try to do it again—to body-share. Taras said it would be easier now, but I don't know what to do, how to start it. Tingles run across my scalp; trying to connect with a Zharat Seer who evaded capture is the obvious choice. I close my eyes and think of the Zharat back in the Fire Mountain. Picture the men with their tattoos. Picture Jed. My gut squeezes.

Stop it. Concentrate.

I try again, and I remember the men, but no specific men come to mind—not for Seers. Just faceless men with bison tattoos. The one at our welcoming ceremonies had the bison tattoo on his forehead, but I can't remember his features. Can't—I rub my eyes, tired. And I know I need to sleep. It calls to me. But I can't. Mustn't.

It's like the sleep deprivation…the torture….

No.

Stay strong.

Have to stay strong.

I try again, force myself to relax. Try to remember what it felt like, what body-sharing felt like in my head. How that power felt. A vague sensation comes to me: my mind divided from my body, planted in another. An egg taken from its nest, given to vultures, and—

No, not vultures.

My eyelids get heavier. Corin. Corin's out there. He'll be in the area. The same area as Esther and the Zharat who escaped, and I can contact him. Make sure he finds them, then they can work together and make sure the Enhanced don't get them back.

I don't know why I didn't think of it before, and a strange feeling fills me as I try again, try to connect. And I've done it before with Corin…that dream…the dream that wasn't a dream...that was real when I was sick and coming off the augmenters and—

Waves of darkness touch my eyes, try to push them shut, try to—

No. Corin. Corin. *Corin.*

I grit my teeth, and my jaw throbs. Connect to Corin, have to—

Sleep falls on me like a blanket. And Elia Jackson's dead body fills my dreams.

"You'll be pleased to know Esther is safe once more."

Raleigh's voice—loud, abrasive, and grating—drags me from my sleep, and I jump, look up, see him. For a second, I'm confused. Hundreds of images flash through my mind. Of furry beasts and tan leather. Of white ground and gray skies. Of a man with a weathered face. Of a golden door, closing with a loud snap, and—

I jump. The door?

Then I look at Raleigh, realize what he just said.

Esther is safe once more.

They've got her, got them all again....

My eyes narrow as I take in Raleigh's appearance. He looks perfect, not as if he was shot earlier. Or yesterday? I blink. Is it the next morning now? Oh Gods. I don't know. A creeping sensation encases me as I wonder how long he's been here. Watching me sleep? I swallow fast as I sit up—does he know? Does he know what I can do? What I was trying to do until I gave in, until I slept, until I condemned Esther and the others to their fate.

Raleigh smiles, looks happier than should be humanly possible. "And I think it's time to resume your session."

DIVIDED

"Resume?" My eyes widen, and I think of David—that little Enhanced boy. I shake my head, a bitter taste filling my mouth. "I'm not doing it." I glare at him, feel my pent-up frustration rise to the surface.

"Nonsense," Raleigh says. "You mustn't resist, mustn't feed the Untamed part of you. But don't worry, we'll be making huge progress in the labs soon. We'll have augmenters for you shortly, ones that work perfectly. And after that—one final mind-conversion for you will do it. I'm sure."

Those words do not make me feel any better.

"Come on."

Raleigh commands my soul, so I follow him. I must look like an obedient little girl, but, inside, I buzz with energy. Energy that doesn't feel right. Energy that fizzles away before I can really understand it.

All too soon, we're back in the room—the same one as before—and David is here too. He smiles at me, but he doesn't stop smiling. Just permanently smiles—at anyone, at anything—and it's eerie.

I glance at the screen. It's turned off. Raleigh mustn't be using that tactic again. I let go of the breath I was holding. Esther's safe from me—for now.

Safe.
David won't be safe.
Elia's not safe.
Elia's dead.

I taste badness and rust behind my teeth, nearly gag. That wasn't my fault. It was Raleigh. He made me do it.

But they were *my* Seer powers.

Raleigh's hands are cold against my head as he stands behind me and tries to latch onto my powers. He doesn't talk this time, doesn't even acknowledge David. I squirm and try to get away—Raleigh can't know what I can do, and he can't make me kill another child. But, immediately, I have visions of him finding out and controlling me, of him sending me back to Viktoriya's body, of him making me bring her and the whole group to their nearest compound. Or making me kill them.

Just like I killed Elia.

I look straight ahead, see David smiling, imagine David dead as well. Or if Raleigh finds out about my body-sharing, maybe he won't make me kill David too?

My stomach twists. Raleigh presses his hands harder against my face. A ring on his finger digs in painfully. I try to move my head, try to free some of the tension in my neck, but I can't. I look at my legs. I'm neither tied up nor fettered—but when I try to move my feet, I can't feel them and—

I feel Raleigh in my head. His presence. His power. Feel him move through the layers and layers of *me* and—

He inhales sharply, and I freeze, feel like I've been kicked in the gut.

No.

No.

No.

Heat surges into Raleigh's left hand. His pointer finger moves and presses against my left eye. Sharp pain. I gasp. Shit. He knows. I wait. Keep waiting.

He makes a clicking sound in his throat after a moment. Then he lets go of my head and moves forward, into my view.

"What have you been doing?" He says the words delicately, but there's force behind them too. "Shania?"

An acrid taste fills the back of my mouth. I try to look away from him, but he snaps my gaze to him, and pain rebounds through my skull.

"Your powers are exhausted." Raleigh's voice is full of darkness. "They feel weak. They need to regenerate. *Why* do they need to regenerate, Shania? Answer me. What have you been doing?"

I meet his mirror eyes, see myself in them—and I glare at him, at myself. But inside there's a voice screaming in me: *He doesn't know! Doesn't know about*

DIVIDED

the body-sharing! He's got my soul, my eyes, but he doesn't know! And I'm trying not to smile, so I glare harder, concentrate on it because he can't know and—

And I've got an advantage. Something he doesn't know about. And it's going to stay that way.

"Nothing," I say.

David repeats my words, it's eerie. I try not to look at him.

Raleigh straightens up and folds his arms carefully. Then he kneels in front of me, so our eyes are at the same level. "Lying is bad, Shania."

I grit my teeth, try not to shake. "I haven't been doing anything. I've been in my cell the whole time, alone. Your men took me there. You can ask them."

He makes a noise close to a snarl, then lifts his hands up. I wince as he touches my face, but I can't turn my head—he makes sure of that. His fingertips run lightly over my skin, following the contours of my face. I want to bite his fingers as they cross over my lips, but I can't open my mouth—he's prepared.

"Your powers are burned out." His tongue moves like a snake as he speaks. "Don't worry, it'll be a temporary thing. They'll heal and replenish their energy in no time." His hand moves to my left ear; he gives it a sharp tug. "Must be because your powers are newly awoken, and I took too much yesterday and didn't check afterward how much you had left. I remember when I was younger, my powers would run out quickly. Only for a while though. Now I have a near infinite source." He smiles his creepy smile. "Not to worry. I'll let your powers have some time to renew. We don't want to burn you out. Not with all the greatness we will do together. But now, there are… other things we can do." He licks his front teeth very obviously and intentionally. A short laugh follows. "Come with me."

My vision blurs for a second.

Other things. The words turn over and over in my mind as he makes me get up, as he commands me to follow him from the room. I try to resist, try to look back at David, but his hold is strong, and—

There are other things we can do.

My mouth dries.

Fight!

Fight!

Fight!

But my body's locking up, and I can't.

"This is my office," Raleigh says, when we reach a new room. "My *personal* office. Sit down."

He directs me to a chair in front of the table. It's a soft chair, makes me feel like I'm sinking. He laughs softly as he walks behind me. I try to turn, but I can't move. I hear rustling sounds, then he leans over me, places a large metal sheet on the table. I smell his breath: liquor and…chocolate.

"Turn on," he says, and a screen appears on the metal. Raleigh, still leaning over me, taps on it in several places until he's satisfied. "Have a look, Shania."

I stare at it.

It's a map of the world. The diagram is divided into seven parts by thick black lines, each expanse labeled. Every land mass has been color-coded. Nearly everything is yellow, but in the areas marked as Section Three and Section Five there are some areas blocked out in lime green, with a few pale blue dots too.

I lean in closer. The land to the far western side of Section One also has some blue dots—and some green ones. As do parts of Section Four, though the dots of both colors there are much smaller.

"Those are the regions of the world. Section Three is where we are." Raleigh indicates the middle bottom section, and I stare at it. "Yellow masses indicate areas that we—the Chosen Ones—have saved. And green is where the spirits are most active. Blue is where we believe there are remaining Untamed settlements or lone individuals living—and, unsurprisingly, they go

DIVIDED

where there the spirits are most prominent. Or perhaps it is the spirits who gather around the Untamed. Both are wild creatures." He points at a predominantly green and blue area in the bottom half of the main land mass in Section Three, then he moves to my side so he's no longer leaning over me. "Those are the Noir Lands. This map hasn't been updated, it would seem, not since we caught many Zharat. We can reduce the blue part quite a bit, now that those Untamed are no longer there… They can count as Chosen Ones, for the purposes of this map now; they'll be saved soon."

He taps on the map, and the blue area reduces in size until it's only a few dots. He looks at me.

"There are still some there, but you'll find them. Just like you'll find them all. Save all the poor Untamed, make the Chosen Ones victorious."

I stare at the map, my pulse quickening. The blue dots represent the Untamed, the ones still out there. I lean in closer. There are still a few in this section then—Raleigh's section. People like me. Out there. My eyes narrow as I search for where Nbutai is. But this whole section is vast and straddles areas either side of the equator. My eyes narrow as I look at the other parts of the map. Section Five shows some Untamed, as does Section One. And Section Four. Which one of those blue dots is for Taras and his group? And then I see a blue dot high at the top of Section Five, near the border to Section Six. The land around the blue dot is white. Ice. Snow. That's got to be it.

But then I frown. Other areas can have snow. Even the mountains near the equator get snow, if they're high enough.

"As you can see," Raleigh says, "my section—Section Three—houses the largest number of Untamed. Because my section is also where the most spirits are, and they make the land dangerous. We have lost many of our sacred men venturing into those areas." But now he smiles, radiant. "But with you on our side, with you luring the Untamed out and bringing them to us, that won't happen."

I stare at him, my eyes widening. No. No. *No*. He can't know about my body-sharing...he just, *can't*.

"You think I'm going to *lure them out*?" My voice wobbles. I shake my head. "No. I'm not."

"I don't *think*—I *know*." Raleigh smiles brightly. "So, Shania, we need to work out how this might work. I could direct you to physically go to each place and round up the Untamed and bring them to us—I can even give you some mirror-destroying drinks so they trust you more, as you'll definitely be a Chosen One by then... But it would be time consuming, would it not? And very tiring. Lots of travel. No." He taps my head—actually *taps* my head. "You must have a conversion power in here...something that can be used across a wide area. It's the only logical explanation. Something that makes you special, makes you the key to one race's survival."

"I haven't got any special powers. Not at all." I wince; I spoke too quickly, too forcefully.

Raleigh laughs. "We don't know what you've got. Every Seer is different. Even though we share some powers—like we all have the white light for defense—a Seer has multiple other powers too, and the combination is nearly always different. *I* can put trackers on another person's senses, for example. Most often, I get their vision, sometimes their hearing." His lips twitch a little. "I also possess a degree of natural healing power, and even without the augmenters, my strength could be called superhuman at times. And that's just touching the surface. Your mother can project a spiritual form of herself in front of another, usually a Seer, only for a minute or two at the most though. Body projection can be very difficult."

My eyes widen. When I was traveling with Three, Rahn, Corin, Esther, and Marouska, the second time I secretly consumed part of an augmenter was because I was stressed and upset as my pendant had been stolen. And I saw my mother then. She...she was disappointed, upset, annoyed that I'd taken the Calmness, gone against everything she'd told me. I'd thought it was my imagination, but it was...it was her? Body projection?

And I saw her again, here...when I was tired, and the Enhanced were torturing me with Tiredness and—

And the moving image she showed me, it flashes into my mind again:

A woman falls in flames. She screams, and long, dark hair whips around in front of her face, obscures her features. Orange tongues rise around her. They eat her.

Her scream goes on and on, cuts the night.

And then it's over.

My eyes narrow. That was really *her*?

Raleigh's still talking, and I look up at him, strangely startled.

"It's possible you can project too, though I doubt that would be the conversion power that would save us, given that projection usually only occurs in front of another Seer, and the projection itself does not have a physical form."

But she did. My mother touched my hand, gave me the vision. She had a physical form. Raleigh's wrong.

"So," Raleigh continues, "we've got to work out what *you* can do, what it is about you that makes you so important. Why *you're* the key to the Untamed."

Unite the Untamed.

I try not to think about Taras. But I know—just *know*—the body-sharing is *part* of the reason I'm the key. Or *the* reason. It's obvious. I just don't know why, or what I'll actually *do* to end the war in favor of the Untamed—uniting us can't be enough. We—or rather *I*—have to do something when we're united. But how can I know what that is when I couldn't even contact any Zharat Seers or Corin earlier...because I was worn out? And I don't know how to control it.

Not yet anyway. I press my lips together firmly.

"It should be easier to do this once your Seer powers have renewed themselves," Raleigh says. "Be easier to detect the individual energies then. I'll have a probe around in them, then. See if we recognize any energy types. Yes. We can do that tomorrow, you should be strong enough by then, and it'll work better—get us more accurate readings—if your energy levels are strong. But we do need to get a move on, Shania. Understand? The other section leaders expect me to have a plan ready for the next meeting as well as an estimated date for the end of the War of Humanity. The end of the Untamed."

The end of the Untamed.

I try not to look at him.

"Now, study this map, Shania. I want you to memorize it, learn the names of all the identified areas where Untamed beings still live."

He touches the map and thousands and thousands of words appear on it. Names of towns, cities, rivers, forests.

Raleigh makes me stand up, makes me step closer to it. My neck aches horribly as I look down at it.

Raleigh laughs softly.

I look at the map—because I have no choice—but I search for New Kitembu. Need to know where we are, what's around us. At last, I spot it, and, for a moment, my chest feels cold. We're so far from the Noir Lands... and so far from New Kimearo, the nearest Enhanced settlement to Nbutai. I don't think I've ever been so far east.

I glance over the rest of the map, at the huge masses of yellow that make up at least ninety-five percent of the color-coding. Green is the next biggest collective area—the spirits. The Untamed really are just a splattering.

"How many Untamed are there?" I ask.

Raleigh points at the map. "We estimate between three and five hundred, worldwide. The number was bigger before, thanks to the Zharat, but many perished during the volcanic steam eruption. Such a shame... But three to five hundred is nothing. Not when there are just over seven billion Chosen Ones. And with you, we will find the poor wild ones, and save them, make them feel better, make the world better."

My eyes widen. Three to five hundred of us against billions of them? My hands tremble. Even if I hadn't been captured and my soul bound into Raleigh's command, how could we—even including the Zharat's number—have overcome *billions* of Enhanced?

Unite the Untamed.

Taras's words drive through me again.

"Come on, Shania," Raleigh says. "Memorize the regions believed to house Untamed. I'll be testing you on the co-ordinates later."

I fail the co-ordinate test two hours later, as planned. I need Raleigh to underestimate my intelligence, my abilities—if that's possible—and I know I can use it to my advantage.

"You've got to do better than this," Raleigh says. He's kneeling at the opposite side of the table now. "I know you're a clever girl—I know you can do it. You are a Seer. But you're letting the Untamed evil in you stop you—because the Untamed part of you is misguided, and it thinks you must not know this information, that you must not help save everyone. But you must. It is your duty. It is what you are meant to do."

Meant to do.

No free will.

He's sorted that.

"I'm tired," I say. "I can't think properly." I pause, then look at him carefully. "How do you expect me to remember a bunch of numbers if I can't get a good night's sleep? Have *you* tried sleeping in a cell? And these overalls aren't exactly comfortable. The seams are really rough."

"You desire something more comfortable? You want to live a luxurious life?"

"I don't want to be kept like a prisoner." I press my lips together. What I want is a room with a window. A window offers escape.

"But, Shania, my dear. You *are* a prisoner. The Untamed evil is *keeping* you prisoner. And I'm sorry that I'm forced to keep you in this state, but my men are working on the augmenters, and soon—I promise, soon, you'll be able to feel better. For now, you need to be strong."

I snort. "And *you're* supposed to be kind."

The look on Raleigh's face changes in an instant. "I *am* kind."

"You were kinder at New Kimearo," I say. "I had a nice bed there. And a teddy bear. I wasn't kept locked up in a dungeon."

"I was able to save you *quickly* there. Shania, don't concentrate on the negatives—it's what the Untamed entity wants you to do. Instead, show it how strong you are."

I shrug. Then I choose my next words carefully. "Then give me an incentive. Give me a nice room. With a window. I don't like being cooped up. And my powers would regenerate quicker, wouldn't they, if you at least tried to keep me happy, rather than treating me like I'm evil? You said before that the Untamed part of me was a parasite. Yet you're not just punishing the parasite by locking me up, you're punishing *me*. You're turning me against you. You're making me more likely to side with the evil, to let it grow."

Raleigh is quiet for a long time. Then he sits up straighter and folds his hands carefully on the table. "You won't resist as much, if I provide you with a *nice* room?"

"Of course not," I say as sweetly as I can.

DIVIDED

Raleigh grunts.

A moment later, he takes me back to my cell, only exerting the smallest bit of control on me—just to guide me really. But I don't fight him.

Not yet.

Timing is important.

I smile at Raleigh as he leaves. And I get the desired satisfaction when I see how much my behavior has unnerved him.

I don't know how long I've got until Raleigh comes back—either tomorrow, ready for our next session... or before that with a room-change? Have I really got through to him? And if he does give me a window, I've got more of a chance of escaping.

What if the window is barred?

Then I'll break the bars. Raleigh said he had superhuman strength. I stare at my hands. There's a chance I do too.

But there's one thing I *do* know for sure: I body-shared and used a significant amount of Seer energy yesterday. So much so that Raleigh couldn't find my powers, couldn't use them, and so, instead, he gave me the location of every Untamed out there instead. And, despite what he thinks, my memory is fine. I know where they are, and when I get a new room with a window, I can escape and find them.

My smile gets wider.

I couldn't have imagined things would go any better.

TWENTY-ONE

KNOWING I NEED TO BODY-SHARE, and that I need to use up my powers so Raleigh can't exploit them, doesn't mean it's any easier for me to actually body-share. Especially when I don't know what I'm doing. Taras seemed to think it would be easier for me now, but it's not.

My mother's pendant feels strangely heavy as I hold it up in front of me, twirling it between my thumb and forefinger. I free up my mind, empty it.

I don't know what the chances of slipping back into Viktoriya's body are—so far, it's never been the same person twice, yet I've only done it less than a handful of times. And none of those were *me* actively wanting to do it. Still, I concentrate on how Viktoriya's body felt smaller, but stockier, denser than mine. The way the fur on her hood tickled against my—her—forehead. I picture her reflection again, then think of Taras.

Then I expand the image and the features of the Untamed person in my mind change. Feeling strangely in a dream, I morph the face into Rahn's, then switch the eyes for Keelie's. Elf materializes for a second, then he's gone and I'm looking at Finn. Then Keelie. Then

DIVIDED

the other Untamed who I know. Who I knew. The ones who are dead.

At the same time, I picture the map. I zoom in on places, see place names. I try to find the Untamed living in these places, pull the face of one back up, and let its features change so it's no longer Bea, Keelie's sister, but a man who looks more like Taras—but not quite.

More features change, and then I'm zooming along the map, drinking in place names.

And then I see my mother in my mind's eye. But she's not Untamed. She's Enhanced.

I open my eyes, stare at the pendant.

It's not working.

Or maybe I'm trying too hard, letting my imagination take over, rather than my powers.

I get up and pace about. My powers are probably still burned out. How long will they take to renew? I swallow uneasily. What if they only renew just before Raleigh's next session tomorrow and I haven't had time—or been able—to use them up before then? And how quickly do they renew? Is it gradual regeneration—or will it just suddenly flood me, like a switch has been pressed?

I grit my teeth and focus on the stone wall ahead. I will not be the Enhanced Ones' weapon. I will not. I squeeze my hands into tight fists and—

Footsteps. Outside my room, the corridor.

I freeze.

Raleigh? Coming back already?

But he said tomorrow....

My breathing speeds up. What if he's changed his mind? Or knows, somehow, that I can body-share?

The footsteps get closer. *Closer*. Heavy footsteps—heavy enough to be a man. To be Raleigh, to be—

The man who walks through the door—walks straight *through* the closed door—is not Raleigh.

I freeze, then jolt back. Ice fills my body, my soul. My throat constricts, gets tighter, tighter, until I can't breathe...can't....

The man stops a foot away from me, watches me. And I stare at him—at *him*. At the tattoos and the....

No... My breaths quicken, my heart pounds.

It can't be. Just can't....

But it...it is.

It's him.

It's *Jed*.

"Wha—" I start to say, lifting my arms up, but my voice is breathy, and my head feels light. I take a step back, try to swallow, but my throat's blocked, too thick. "Stay back! Get away from me!"

I hold my hands up, but all I see are the gold flashes on me.

I shake my head.

Jed takes a step toward me.

"Stay away from me!" I yell.

The look in his eyes—his Untamed eyes—changes. Gets deeper somehow, tries to draw me in...into the darkness inside them.

"S'ven."

He says my name. But there's something different about his tone. It's more of a hiss.

I flinch, twist my head, look around. Half expect him to be behind me as well—two of him. But he's not. He's just in front of me. One of him.

What the hell?

I stare at Jed. He's dead. Dead. I saw him die. I saw his body.

Yet he's here.

Like he was in the quarantine cell....

My heart speeds up. I'm panting. Delirious again? No. I can't be—can I?

And he looks real. So real as he inclines his head slightly, as he strides toward me.

"Stay back!" I yell, and it's all I can say.

He stops, freezes. "S'ven, I am sorry."

I flinch at his words. If you can call them words. He's—he's not real...*can't* be real. I clench my hands

DIVIDED

together. A hallucination. Has to be…he's….

"You're dead." And I don't know why I say the words out loud, as if he's here to hear them, because he *can't* be here. It's just my mind…I'm talking to myself.

Unless he's traveled from the New World, like Five did… No. That's…somehow, this feels different.

"Please." Jed steps closer, and I throw myself backward. "You are not safe here."

"You think?" And I don't know why I'm still speaking. Why I'm interacting…because he's not here. Can't be here. Can he? And he doesn't care…not about me….

Madness. I'm going mad. I really am…and…and what if I never body-shared? What if it was me making stuff up, making me feel better, allowing me to escape temporarily?

Oh Gods.

My heart pounds. The muscles in my legs tense. And it's too hot in here. Far too hot.

And now Jed is standing in front of me. I shake my head, try to quiet my pounding heart. He can't be real, he can't be, can't—

Jed walked *through* the door. No, didn't walk—*glided*. Glided straight through it. He can't be real. Yet he's speaking to me. We're having a *conversation*.

"S'ven, *listen*," Jed says, and his voice does that weird thing again, where the words are more like a hiss, like a release of air being expelled quickly. "I cannot stay in this place long."

Stay in this place? Then I freeze.

He's on his way to the New World? He has to be… but…but—but he died nearly a week ago—or was it longer? My sense of time's mixed up. Still, it doesn't take that long…does it, to reach the New World? Not after the Spirit Releasing Words are said.

I flinch.

The Spirit Releasing Words weren't said….

They *weren't* said.

He won't get there.

And it's been....

Too late. The words flash into my mind.

My eyes widen.

Shit. He's...he's trapped? The biggest fear of the Untamed—after the Enhanced—is to be trapped between worlds and—

And he's...alive? No. He can't be....

Jed moves closer. There's a vicious look in his eyes. "I need you to know that I am sorry, S'ven."

"Sorry?" I bite the word out.

"Shania?"

I jump, turn, find Three stepping into the room. I nearly scream with relief, feel my heart slam into my chest. And I know I shouldn't feel relief—he's just an Enhanced, not my brother. Except he is, he is my brother. I *can't* think of him as *Tomas*.

Not when he's Three. And he's here. My brother. And I'm scared. And so many times when I was younger and scared, he reassured me.

"Who are you talking to?" Three tilts his head slightly.

I turn back. Jed's gone.

Like he was never here.

Except he was.

Wasn't he?

That *was* Jed. Trapped?

That happened.

Didn't it?

TWENTY-TWO

LATE NEXT MORNING, RALEIGH COLLECTS me. I stayed up most of the night, scared. Waiting for Jed to come back, and trying to body-share, without success. I can't tell whether my powers have returned properly yet—but maybe *I* can't feel that? Or maybe I'm too scared, distracted—because of Jed.

Because he was here.

Or maybe he wasn't.

Maybe I imagined it.

Maybe I really did imagine everything with Taras....

"Today, we're going to see what powers you have." Raleigh holds open the door to a new room, and I want to ask him about Jed's body. Whether it's still in that underground place. Whether he's seen him. Because, if Jed was here, wouldn't he want to hurt Raleigh—or speak with him at the very least? Haunt him? His own father *murdered* him.

But Raleigh doesn't give me a chance to ask anything, he just encourages me to walk into the room.

I step in first and stop short when I see what's in the center. "What's that?"

I point at the machine. It looks like a highly glorified

chair, yet there are loads and loads of wires around it. So many. And little stickers on the end, and metal things. Three would love to examine a chair like this.

Raleigh beams. "My team have just finished calibrating it to your DNA and the results from your previous brain scans. Beautiful, isn't it?"

Beautiful is not a word I'd use. I watch it dubiously. It's the only thing in the room—right in the center—except for a cabinet on the far side, by the opposite wall.

Raleigh crosses over to the cabinet and pulls the top drawer open. I watch as he fishes inside, then picks out a heavy volume bound in red leather.

"I have a vast list here," Raleigh says, and he opens the book to what appears to be a random page.

He shows it to me, walking back toward me, and my eyes scan over it once the book is near enough. The pages are split into columns. Several are filled with numbers, others have words. Raleigh moves the book out of my line of vision before I can read the words.

"A repertoire of all recorded Seer powers and their energy frequencies." He beams, then points at the machine behind him. There's a small monitor, sticking up from a rod on the headrest, and it flashes twice, illuminating the display in a sickly blue light. Raleigh clears his throat. "This one will pick up your brain waves and record the frequencies exhibited as I probe through your powers. We'll see which frequencies show up—even in the tiniest traces—and cross-reference them to the numbers recorded in this book. Any similarities—reoccurring patterns—in any of your readings that match any parts in these lists could indicate something about your abilities. Code A4124 shows up a lot in Seers who had some sort of psychic voice. See, Mr. Arnold Winters." He points at a line near the bottom of the right-hand page. "He could send words straight to another Seer, and when he used that power his energy reading was 8242A4124C. And A4124 shows up within the codes of others who

DIVIDED

also have levels of psychic voice. Make sense? Good. Sit down."

I try not to, but he makes me. My legs take me to the chair, the strange contraption. The moment I sit in it, the wires snap around my stomach, trapping my arms to my sides.

I cry out, try to twist, and—

Pain circles my core.

"None of that, Shania," Raleigh says, and he picks up a remote and types something in. The machine starts humming. "What I'm really hoping is that codes GS352 and GS342 show up on your energy readings. They're related to compulsion and radar. If you can find and persuade the Untamed to join us so easily, it would be perfect. If you can do it through a psychic voice, even better. You could save everyone from the comfort of a compound as soon as you've learned how to use the powers. You could bring everyone to us, no bloodshed. Perfect. Now, just relax."

He makes me lower my shoulders and rest my head against the headrest and—

The machine grabs my head, stretches my neck up. I cry out.

Needles drive into my scalp.

Or, at least, that's what it feels like.

"Don't move," Raleigh whispers, his voice tense.

I can't see him now, can only see the top section of the wall on the far side of the room because of the way the machine has grabbed my head. But, a moment later, Raleigh moves back into my line of vision. I get the feeling he's looking into my eyes, into my soul.

And I think of Elia.

Murderer. Murderer. Murderer.

I stiffen.

"Relax." His voice is a croon, reminds me of a panther cub.

He lifts his hands up, and his fingers get nearer and nearer to my face.

I grimace, make the mistake of moving my head

slightly to the left—to avoid his fingers—and the needles drive deeper.

I gasp, shudder, feel something building up in my chest.

"Stay still."

Raleigh's fingers flex in a way that reminds me of claws, and he presses an arched hand over each of my temples, so only his fingertips and the edges of his nails touch my skin. Ten searing hot points. His palms are too close, and I can't focus on them; trying makes my eyes go funny.

"Now, open the way into your mind, Shania." He moves one hand away, and I see him glance above me—at the screen?—before returning his gaze to me. "Are you ready?"

I don't say anything. Don't know why he's even asking me. As if he thinks we're working together.

And then the pain starts.

The same as before.

Always this painful when he's….

"Don't fight me, Shania. It's only painful if you fight me…if you don't give yourself freely. Come on, you know what to do." His breathing is labored. "Let me find them…."

I wince, try to keep breathing. Something moves in my head, as if a sheet of metal's being scraped over another and then wrenched back with force.

A creaking, grating sound pulls through me.

The humming of the machine builds, gets louder, pulses through me.

"I can't reach them, Shania—don't resist me."

Click. Click. Click.

"Come on, Shania. Let me find them—don't try and block me. Let me feed your energy into the machine. Let me—what the *hell*?"

The needles jerk out of my head, and I fall, my top half collapsing forward over the wires that hold my lower torso up. Something hits me in the lower back, and I grunt, try to move my head, try to turn, but my muscles won't work—no energy...or Raleigh?

My breath bursts from me, and I'm shaking, shaking so hard, and I can feel sweat plastering me. Nausea lashes through me. I try to move my arms, but the wires are still so strong.

"Shania." Raleigh's voice is like a coiled snake above me.

My gaze jerks up, and my vision wavers.

"Look at that." Raleigh points above my head, at the screen.

He makes me twist around, turning my head too far, and I'm sure it's going to snap away from my neck for a moment. Pain worms its way behind my right ear, and I see the screen. It flashes blue, illuminates words, then alternates between a black screen and flashing words.

But I see the words.

No Seer Energies Detected.

No Seer energies?

I stare at it, waiting for the words to change—but they don't. They stay the same. My stomach flutters, and my interior feels too warm, too hot, like I'm burning up. The sweat against my skin is too sticky and—

Raleigh slaps me.

I cry out, the side of my head hits the headrest, and heaviness slams into my chest. My eyes smart.

"You're blocking them," Raleigh says. "I don't know how, but you are. You shouldn't be able to. But it won't be tolerated. Do you understand me?"

I shake my head. "I—I'm not. Not blocking them!"

Raleigh's eyes seem to darken. "All I can feel in you is a weak residual energy—the shadow of your powers left behind, and it's getting weaker, disappearing. Now, it can't be exhaustion, as I thought before, as this machine would detect *active* Seer energies in the residue, and your powers would be regenerating. Yet you have no active energy now, and the shadow is diminishing. And I know that's not true. *You're* the one the augury speaks of. So, tell me how you've done it. Because, according to this, you're no longer a Seer."

TWENTY-THREE

I'M NO LONGER A SEER?

For a long moment—one that stretches on and on—Raleigh and I stare at each other. The chair's torso wires unclick, freeing me.

I stand up slowly, feeling like I need to. My chest tightens.

You're no longer a Seer.

No. I shake my head. That can't be right. I'm the Seer the augury speaks off. I'm the important Seer.

Of course I'm still a Seer. I have to be!

"You're *obviously* still a Seer." Raleigh advances toward me. "So, how *dare* you block your powers. *I* own your soul, your body, your powers."

"No. You don't own any part of me." I tense, glare at him—and he lets me. It feels like an achievement.

"I *command* you. You can't beat me at this, Shania. You can't hide your powers from me forever."

Raleigh grabs my arm, pulls me to him in one swift motion. I freeze, try to ignore the way he's breathing over me, how hot his breaths are.

I swallow hard. "If *you* command it all, then you should know I'm not blocking my powers. Whatever has happened, I haven't done anything." My muscles tighten even further, and I look down at his hand, still on my arm. His grip reminds me of a vulture. "Maybe you just can't find my powers—maybe you're not as strong as you think you are. Maybe you're not strong enough to control me—not after you unlocked my Seer powers and made *me* more powerful. Maybe I'm too strong for you."

But...but I couldn't body-share when I tried. Earlier. I couldn't. Oh Gods. My powers...what if they've... My eyebrows furrow. No, I *must* still be a Seer...if I wasn't, Raleigh wouldn't need a machine to tell him— he'd feel it...wouldn't he?

Except Seers can't always sense other Seers... I didn't realize Jed was a Seer until the fight for me. Or was that because he was inactive until then? But then I didn't sense Taras either...

I frown. Am I *inactive*? Is this what being inactive means? No active powers? I try to remember what Jed said about being inactive, but my head's getting fuzzy and—

Jed.

My mind races. I saw Jed. And he said he was sorry. Because he gave me to his father and didn't realize how important I was?

And now he's taken my powers? As a way of fixing things?

"Don't underestimate me," Raleigh growls.

I yank my arm back from him, take a step back.

Raleigh smiles, and—

And then—then I step up to him, undo what I've just done, and I'm closer than before.

No.

My body presses against him. I feel every part of him. So close.

I try to pull away, but I can't.

No.

No.

No.

DIVIDED

Raleigh stretches up—the muscles in his torso move against mine. One of his hands goes to the small of my back. I try to pull away, but he exerts his control harder. The smell of liquor engulfs me, gets stronger. Tingles radiates through my chest, and my stomach rolls. Pain seeps into my neck as I try again to move.

Then Raleigh presses his lips against my forehead.

Everything inside me curls up.

I try to hold my breath, to not breathe him in, his smell—the liquor, the sweat, the faint fragrance that clings to him. I try not to feel anything—but I can feel him, his warm lips against my skin. I swallow, but the muscles in my throat feel too big.

"Yes," Raleigh whispers against my forehead. "I still control you. Remember that. And whatever you've done with your Seer powers, I'll find them."

"I haven't *done* anything." I move my head a fraction, and my lips are close to his ear. "Maybe I really am no longer a Seer. Maybe the Gods and Goddesses have taken my powers away so they can't be used against us."

Or Jed has.

I sound a lot more confident than I feel.

And it has to be Jed—doesn't it? It would explain why Raleigh didn't detect the absence of powers before...as then they really were just needing to regenerate. But now they've gone.

"Nonsense," Raleigh mutters.

I feel his body react against mine. Nausea wells up inside me.

My eyes narrow. "Maybe I'm no use to you now. Maybe the augury has changed."

"Auguries don't change."

"Then where are my Seer powers, Raleigh? Where are they?" I manage to pull my head back from his, but it takes every ounce of energy I have, and pain reverberates through me. "Because I can assure you *I* haven't done anything. This isn't my doing. And I can assure you I'm not lying because lying is bad, isn't it?"

My words are loaded.

Raleigh purses his lips as his mirrors absorb me. "Not your doing?" He tilts his head to one side, and I can't tell whether he believes me or not. "They'll still be in you, Shania. Buried deeply, sealed away, hidden." His voice smolders. "And I'll find them. I don't believe you're not a Seer anymore."

"Your machine said so. It couldn't detect them," I whisper, and the words pour from me before I'm even sure I'm going to say them, sure that I'm going to go down that line. "I'm empty. I can *feel* it, Raleigh. I'm no longer a Seer."

I wait for him to contradict me—to say he can still feel that I *am* a Seer, because part of me wants to hear it—and a thousand voices start screaming inside me. I want to shake, to cry, to panic. No longer a Seer? Can I feel that I'm still a Seer?

And…and I… I don't know.

But if I'm not it solves everything… I'll have no conversion powers.

But it can't be as easy as this.

"Seer powers *cannot* be taken away," Raleigh says. "The Gods and Goddesses can only block our access to the Dream Land. Tell me, Shania. Do you really think that they'd let me have my powers when they do not like the Chosen Ones? They are misguided, like the Untamed. But if they could take them away, they would. No. Your powers are still there. But something has blocked them. That's why the chair couldn't detect any. They're blocked. But only temporarily… But not your doing?" A strange look passes over his face, and then I see his knuckles pale as he clenches his fists. "*Weak Untamed,*" he mutters, then he points at me. "Come with me."

I have no choice, because he makes me.

Raleigh takes me back to his office, sits me down in the same plush blue chair. He sits in a matching one that wasn't there before. He stares at me for a long time. A long, long time. And he doesn't exert any

DIVIDED

control over me, because I'm free to turn my head, to take in the furnishings of the room—there are lots of paintings here now. All new ones that have been put up since the last time I was here. With a jolt, I realize they're all of Jed.

Jed.

And he looks just how he did last night. I shudder.

"I know what's happened," Raleigh says slowly.

"What?" I keep my voice as even as I can.

"Grief. Grief is stopping your powers." He nods at the nearest painting of Jed. "A delayed reaction, possibly brought on by seeing Jed's body before, but still delayed, perhaps because of the recent sickness. But now this grief must be blocking your Seer powers." His lips press together for a long moment. "And you are letting it. Shania, grief is a negative emotion. I know if you were able to tolerate our life-juices, you'd be free of it in an instant. But you must work hard to overcome this grief. Grieving is selfish."

"Selfish?" I stare at him. All around the room, many Jeds watch me. I feel strange. Why's Raleigh put the paintings up now?

"Yes. It is selfish. You're letting your grief block your powers. The new augmenters will be ready soon, and if you're still grieving then, you'll be letting everyone suffer when they could be saved. So, let's talk." He leans back in his chair.

"Talk?"

"Talking is a good therapy. Expressing yourself—how you feel, how much you miss your lover—it'll help you accept the fact he's gone. Help you get over your grief."

"My lover?" I stare at him, shocked. "I'm not grieving for Jed. I never even liked him."

He tuts. "Well, that's harsh. He was your betrothed. No, Shania. You *must* be hurting. Hurting so much that you've hidden it away, that you don't even know yourself. And being in this Untamed state once more has made it build up so much worse. There's so much pain and negativity inside you. I will have a word with my lab technicians—see if anything can be done to speed up the creation of new augmenters. They must've isolated the reactive ingredient by now. So, come on, talk."

Raleigh stares at me expectantly and grips his chin between his thumb and forefinger.

"Talk about Jed?" I fold my arms.

He nods.

"Talk about your son? The one you murdered?" And I don't know why I put so much of a load into my voice, why it feels like I'm trying to get a reaction from him. What do I expect to see? A moment of remorse? Genuine emotion? That's almost laughable.

"Yes," Raleigh says. "Tell me about him."

I shudder. "I don't want to talk about Jed."

"But you need to. Your soul needs you to cleanse it. Get rid of your grief, Shania. Open up to me."

"No. I tell you what *would* help. A better room, with a window. A proper bed. Lack of sleep makes grief worse. Lack of sleep makes everything worse." And as soon as I've said the words, I think of Jed. How he was sleep-deprived because he was sending kavalah spirits to me as I slept, making them block my Seeing dreams. I continue quickly. "And I want to have fresh air when I can sleep. A window that opens."

"Not this again, Shania."

I raise my eyebrows. "Have you sorted one out? A nice new room?"

"I am in the process of doing it."

He is? I lean forward. "I'll tell you what else would help me cope with my *grief*. Going outside."

"You're *not* going outside."

"I want to run. I'm a runner. I need to run."

He smiles softly. "I'm not falling for that."

"Exercise helps. It produces endorphins. It'll make me feel better. Make my powers come back." I smile slightly. "And that's what you want, isn't it?"

Raleigh leans back in his chair, and the way he sits—

the angle—shows off the powerful nature of his body. For a moment, I feel intimidated, weak.

"You think you're so clever, don't you?" A smile graces his lips.

"How about you let me see my friends?" I continue, but my voice is getting higher now. "*That* will cheer me up."

"I can't allow that," Raleigh says. "Not while you're Untamed. I am sorry. No. We'll have to stick to talking, talk the grief out of you, try to loosen the hold the Untamed parasite has on you. But I will find you a new room. I promise. And perhaps you should see Dr. Andy. He specializes in old-fashioned medicine, pre-augmenters. He did the facial surgery on your brother. But he also has knowledge on anti-depressants."

I sit up straight. "I'm not depressed."

"I want him to assess you—now, in fact. Perhaps traditional medicine will help. You need your Seer powers back as soon as possible."

Dr. Andy is a strange-looking man. Ironically, he obviously uses augmenters to change his appearance; no one's nose is that small when their ears are *so* big. He even looks like he's having trouble breathing through his pinprick nostrils.

He sits me down on a hard, wooden stool, then walks around me, slowly. Each step is deliberate and planned—as if he's worked out his movements prior to our meeting.

Suddenly, he turns. "You are staying, aren't you?" he barks out—in a very low-pitched voice—to the two Enhanced who brought me here, under Raleigh's directions. "I don't want to be alone with one so inclined to violence as…as…" He looks at me. "As

Shania in her wild Seven mindset."

I snort. *Of course* the other Enhanced are staying. Raleigh gave them strict instructions.

I watch Dr. Andy as he circles me twice more. Each step sounds like a slow countdown.

"How are you feeling?" The tip of his nose goes ever so slightly pink.

"Fine."

He takes a step back and tilts his face up. "You're not feeling at all violent?"

"Should I be?" My tone is sardonic.

"Untamed creatures are *writhing* with negative emotions. Their biggest desire is to injure and kill one another."

"Not one another," I say. And I can't help myself. "Just *you*."

He sucks in his breath, but, just when he's about to look *worried*, his face relaxes and he smiles. A sudden transformation. Eerie.

"Raleigh has informed me you are deep in the stages of grief. Would you like to tell me about it in your own words?"

"No." I swing my legs back and forth, look toward the door. It's open—apparently it stays like that as doctors' rooms need to look inviting. One of the Enhanced, on the way here, told the other that he was thinking of dropping into Dr. Mara's surgery to request stronger augmenters. Thinks he needs grade three in Calmness, rather than grade two.

I wonder how fast Dr. Andy and the other Enhanced in here are at running.

"Talking about grief—expressing yourself, your true feelings…even if they are bad and Untamed, is the first way to overcome it. To make you feel better. And you don't want to be feeling all this negativity, do you?"

"I'm not feeling *any* negativity." My eye is still on the door. I try to remember the way we came, but there were lots of twists and turns. There was also a security

DIVIDED

door, and I tried to see the number the Enhanced typed in, but he deliberately blocked it from my view. If I ran, I'd probably only get as far as that door. And then Raleigh would punish me.

"Denial won't help you," Dr. Andy says. "It'll just make you feel worse in the long-term."

One of the Enhanced by the door clears his throat. "There isn't going to be a long-term though. The lab'll have suitable augmenters done soon. Dr. Treena said they've almost got a new prototype done. They just need to test it."

Test it? The muscles in my face slacken.

Dr. Andy smiles. "And our job, my…my dear, is to make sure you are as comfortable as possible—as happy as possible—until we can truly save you. Letting you suffer as you are, without us even trying our non-conventional methods would simply not be fair. Not fair at all. So, please, do tell me how you're feeling. Be *honest*. Even if you are falling into the dark river of tears, talking will help. I will pull you out of the water, drag you to the side, dry you in the sun myself, if I have to."

My lips twitch, and I bite on my bottom one, try to keep a straight face.

"Inadvertent and inappropriate reactions—such as laughing—are perfectly common when you are grieving, when there are so many negative emotions inside you. Now, my dear, I'm going to set up regular counseling sessions for you. If there is no improvement, I can prescribe tablets to help with your mood—until the augmenters can kiss you better."

I clench my fists. "My mood is fine."

"No, it's not. Look at the anger—that detestable emotion—in your voice."

I grit my teeth for a second. "Maybe I'm angry because I'm being kept here, a prisoner."

"You are misguided because of the Untamed darkness spreading its web in you, creating new tentacles, and infecting you deeper and deeper, until the very core of your soul is blackened and wizened from so much evil."

I don't say anything more. Just watch him as he walks to the side of the room and speaks into a phone.

"Yes. I want to run some tests. Check Shania's blood levels. And a few scans. Ensure that her dopamine and serotonin levels are as they should be." He turns back to me. "Don't worry, my dear. We will save you fully, very soon."

Raleigh collects me after Dr. Andy has finished.

"Did he give you anti-depressants?" It's the first question Raleigh asks.

"No."

Raleigh glares at me. "But you are depressed because of your grief. It is blocking your Seer powers."

I can't help but smile.

"This way." Raleigh steers me to the left. We're not going back to my cell.

We walk quietly, quickly. Going to my new room?

Then I look at Raleigh. "How far along *are* your men with developing the new augmenters…for us?" My fingers twitch.

"Close."

"How close? How long?" I start to slow as I look at him.

Raleigh shrugs. "A few days. Possibly less."

A few days? My chest tightens. It could all be over. In a few days, I could be Enhanced again—and this time I wouldn't be able to resist the augmenters as well, would I? I only could before as I was being conditioned against them.

But next time….

"It'll be very soon." Raleigh smiles. "And then we

DIVIDED

can catch up on this unfortunate delay."

He stops in front of a doorway, a few minutes later.

"I have a surprise for you, Shania." Raleigh beams at me as he takes out a golden key, unlocks the door. My excitement builds. Raleigh's beam gets brighter. "Something to help you feel better. A new room *and* a new companion. He's in there waiting for you. This will cheer you up."

He?

Every muscle in my body tenses.

Corin.

I push the door open.

Something hits me in the chest. I stumble back, fall against Raleigh, end up on the floor and—

The dog jumps on me, licking my face, my arms, my neck, wagging his tail.

And I—

I don't know what to do.

It's—it's my terrier.

TWENTY-FOUR

I STARE UP AT MY dog—his nose inches from mine—and hug him tightly.

It's him.

It's really him. His tail wags so fast, slapping me, but I don't care.

The terrier lifts his head, looks over my shoulder. A warning growl emanates as he looks at Raleigh.

"He's not very friendly to any of us," Raleigh says.

"He wouldn't be. You're all Enhanced." I look up. "How'd you find him? Where?"

"Do you remember Rosemary Webber at New Kimearo?"

I hold my dog tighter. "I think so." She was one of the Enhanced who was present during my conversion—my first conversion. She gave me cake, I think. And she named me *Shania*.

"Rosemary was out with a surveying team, and she found the dog wandering alone. She told your mother. Your mother seemed to think it was your terrier, and a quick visit confirmed it. She requested that the dog was brought to you, and arrangements were made yesterday, as it happens. The animal arrived not long

DIVIDED

ago."

"My mother?" I sit up straighter. The terrier moves in my arms, curls his head around, so he's nestled into my chest. "Is she here too? Did she come with my dog?"

Raleigh shakes my head. "Your mother is still at New Kimearo. But she will be here shortly, as soon as she's finished her work. And then we shall *all* go back to my domain."

She's coming here?

"Work? What work?"

Raleigh smiles, shows off those perfect teeth of his. "Don't worry yourself over things that don't concern you. Concentrate on yourself, on getting over your grief. And—" He gestures at my terrier. "Teach him to be nice. I haven't forgotten how his teeth sunk into my flesh before. Should he do that again, there will be consequences."

The terrier barks—short and sharp—and I hug him closer as I sit up more, lean against the doorway.

"Come on, Shania. You have to go *into* your room now. I have to make sure you are safe."

I get up, my overalls rustling, still holding the dog, and step into my new room, look around.

A simple bed in one corner, with a bookcase next to it. Books. *Entertainment*.

I've got an en suite. The door is on the far side of the room, and it's open. Through the doorway, I can see a bath. I run in there, the dog at my legs, and turn the hot tap on and off several times, feel the jets of hot water.

But there's no window in either room.

Raleigh snorts. "It always amazes me when you Untamed are so surprised by modern conveniences."

"I'm not surprised," I say, turning the tap off.

"I'll leave you in your excitement—and with your new companion. Hopefully this will pull you out of your grief and make your Seer powers accessible to you. And to me."

I watch him leave. He shuts the door firmly, and then I hear a key in the lock. I wait until his footsteps have died away, then I check the handle. It doesn't move. I evaluate the door. Thick, sturdy. Made of a solid sheet of oak. Not one I can kick down.

The terrier yips.

I look down, see his large eyes. His tail's still wagging, from side to side, so fast, creating a draught. I bend down and hug him again, bury my face in his fur. His coat smells strangely sweet. Someone's washed him.

"Bet you didn't like that, eh?"

The terrier nuzzles into me more, then he reaches up, licks my face and my neck again.

And, for the first time since arriving here, I feel better.

I've got my dog back.

The rest of the day, I try to body-share, on and off. My dog watches me. He's lying on the bed, and I'm sitting on the floor.

But nothing happens, no matter how hard I try. I start to get jittery. Have my Seer powers *really* gone? It can't be grief...can't be. Not over Jed anyway. But I don't understand. They can't just disappear.

So it has to be Jed. He has to have taken my powers.

The terrier whines.

I look at him. He needs a name. Really needs a name. Back at Nbutai—and before—we never named our dogs because we used the packs for hunting small game. And the dogs we used frequently changed, as they got older, as some had puppies, as some died. And even though the dogs had favorite people, and *we* all had favorite dogs, they weren't pets, not really.

DIVIDED

Even our dog, who lived with my family for years, wasn't supposed to be a pet, even though he wasn't as good at hunting as the others and we all hugged him whenever we could.

But the moment he was in the truck that I drove away, he became a pet. A proper one. He became *my* pet, *my* dog. And I tried to name him before, but I never succeeded. *Dog* suits him. But it sounds uncivilized.

He wags his tail, then scratches behind his right ear.

I try to body-share again, then give up. I'm tired. And hungry. Before I go to bed, I have a quick meal of dried biscuits and fruit. Earlier, I found several items of food in the cupboard in the corner of my room, including some pouches of dog food. The terrier wolfs down his food, from a small plate that was under one of the pouches.

I finish my meal, go to the en suite and clean my teeth—something I relish—then take a shower from the unit over the bath. The hot water feels amazing, but, as I stare at the pale blue tiled walls, I can't help but wonder whether it's really happened—whether my Seer powers have really gone. They can't have, can they?

And I keep thinking about it all night, as I curl up in bed with the terrier. He croons softly, and I listen to his regular breathing. But I can't sleep.

I notice a small digital clock on the bottom shelf. I move it to the top. Then I look at the books.

I've never really read a book before, but I know how to read. My parents taught me. They taught all of us children, back at Kyzik and our homes before that. And it's important; being able to read signs when you're raiding a town or city is vital.

The first book I pick up is *Poems to Free the Mind* by A Chosen Seer. Odes and ballads about many beautiful, victorious cities, where people can only feel happiness, and how wonderful it all is.

I put the book down quickly, and curl back up with my dog.

My dog.

I still can't believe it.

But as I lie there with him, not really thinking about anything, my eyelids start to feel heavier. I breathe deeper, and then I'm dragged into the world of the sleeping.

Elia is waiting for me. She offers me her hand.

I take it.

I tell Elia how sorry I am.

But she won't listen.

And so I tell her again as she stares up at me with big doleful eyes—eyes that change and become my terrier's.

But Elia never listens, no matter how hard I try to tell her.

It's like she can't....

Can't.

TWENTY-FIVE

THE NEXT DAY, RALEIGH KNOCKS on my door twice before coming in. I'm still in bed, and I drag the duvet over me quickly, covering my bare shoulders as I sit up. I slept in my underwear, and my overalls are on the floor. My Seer pendant has fallen onto the sheets, and I shift my weight, cover it quickly.

My dog's next to me on the bed, and he watches the Enhanced One suspiciously.

"And how are you today?" Raleigh asks, smiling.

"I slept a bit better," I say slowly.

He continues smiling, and it unnerves me. He folds his arms slowly. "I have a fun day planned for you."

I stare at him, waiting. "A fun day?"

"Yes. I've not been treating you very kindly. After all, it's not your fault I cannot save you yet. And perhaps my previous treatment of you is fueling the Untamed parasite, contributing to your grief. So, I am changing my ways." He smiles. "You wanted to run."

I sit up straighter. "We're going outside?"

Hope surges through me, and I've got visions of me outside, running. Running through sand and desert and trees, with my dog next to me. Free at last.

"We're going to the leisure center," Raleigh says. "It has a great gym. Now, get ready. We'll bring your dog too."

Raleigh shuts the door, and I grab my pendant and get ready quickly, trying to fathom him out. He's being too nice. There's got to be a catch. But the gym, it could have windows in it. Or an emergency exit? It could have something. Or maybe we'll pass near where Esther and the others are being kept. If I can break them out….

And maybe the fun day is for them as well, and we'll see each other. We could group together, get out, escape—but escape *properly*. Find some way to get out of here fast. Maybe Corin, on the outside, will have thought of something, have something in place so we can just go. Go and be free. And maybe when I'm out there, away from all the badness here, my Seer powers will return?

But, on the way to the leisure center, Raleigh tells me it's just me who's to have the fun day.

"But that's not fair," I counter. "The other Untamed aren't choosing to be allergic to the augmenters either, to be unable to be saved."

"But the Zharat have ten times the amount of evil that you have, my darling butterfly. With you, it is the parasite. With them, it is their nature too. They are ruthless, violent people. I was so disappointed when my son joined them."

My mood darkens.

"But you didn't exactly give him a choice about who he was going to join, did you?" I glance down at the dog, check he's still with us as we weave through corridors. "Jed told me you abandoned him and his sisters, Raleigh. They were just children—barely more than babies. And you didn't take them with you."

Raleigh is quiet for a moment. "Zahlia didn't want them with us."

"Zahlia?" I frown.

"Their mother," Raleigh says, his tone dismissive.

DIVIDED

"And she was right. We had a long way to travel to reach a city, and the spirits were not kind to us. The children were too little. They would've died had they been with us."

"Jed died anyway. You killed him. Don't pretend you care about them."

He shrugs. "My girls are still out there, and they will be saved when you save everyone. For once, the Untamed evil is doing a good thing in keeping them alive until the time is right for them to become Chosen Ones."

Until the time's right? I stare at him. But the Enhanced always want to save everyone there and then, as soon as possible. No, there's something he's not telling me. Lying? A bad trait. Or just withholding information?

"My girls, my beautiful girls will soon be with us," Raleigh says, his voice soft, and the way he says *my girls* makes me shiver, makes me realize I don't know who Jed's sisters are. Were they at the Zharat cave when I was? Why didn't I know them? Why wasn't I introduced to them?

I think of Jeena, Jed's daughter, Raleigh's granddaughter. I wonder what happened to her. Is she here too, imprisoned? Or is she one of the Zharat who escaped? Or one of the ones who was killed in the steam eruption? My stomach clenches, and I try not to think about it.

"Here we are," Raleigh says a few minutes later.

We step through a doorway into a room that is most definitely not a leisure center.

"A kitchen?" I say.

"You haven't had breakfast."

"You didn't care about that before. I've barely been fed here."

Raleigh doesn't say anything, just goes to the cooker where a pan of steaming porridge sits. He takes two dishes out of a cupboard nearby and then ladles the creamy mixture in. So we're going to be eating together. And this is...this is weird.

"And what would your dear dog like? Sirloin steak? A pack of gourmet chicken and turkey mix?"

"Ordinary dog food is fine," I say, exhaling quickly as I look around for any knives.

The terrier whines at me, as if he knows I've chosen the less than luxury version. But I don't want him getting used to gourmet food, not when very soon I plan to be out there, in the wilds again. Don't want the dog becoming a fussy eater—he'll need to eat what we can find.

"Do you like the porridge?" Raleigh asks as we eat at a small table at the side of the kitchen. Again, there's no window in here. He's being careful of that. And there's also nothing I can use as a weapon either. The dishes are plastic and the spoons are wooden.

I nod, and I remember how Marouska used to make it. My father said hers was the best uji he'd ever tasted. "So are we going to the gym after this?"

"Not so soon after eating, Shania! We don't want to make ourselves sick. No, I've got a surprise first."

A surprise. I stare down at the remaining porridge in my bowl. It's going lumpy.

"Don't look so worried," Raleigh says. "You'll like what I've got planned for you. You'll like it a lot."

We go to a room with an enormous screen. His private cinema, he calls it. And then he corrects himself. It's Zahlia's, he says. But he outranks her, and, when he's in her city, he's in charge.

He shows me a film. A romantic comedy. I don't like it, nor do I like how close Raleigh sits next to me, or that we're the only ones in there, when there are hundreds of seats. My dog's in with us though. And that makes me feel better.

Finally, hours later, Raleigh gives me a neon orange tank top and black shorts to change into, and then we reach the leisure center. There are no windows in the gym.

He sets me up on a running machine, and then I just

DIVIDED

start running. He's making me run—I know that—but part of me enjoys it anyway. I run for half an hour, and then I try out different machines. I like the rowing machine and the lift platform—though I find I'm weaker than I thought, and Raleigh makes me stop. When I see the sign for the pool, I'm glad he doesn't suggest swimming. I shudder, remember the black lake.

I want to shower, but apparently that's not on the schedule.

We eat again.

And then an Enhanced girl about my age comes over, introduces herself as Stacey. She says they've set up a clothes shop for me in the next room, and she'll help me pick out some new outfits as my gym clothes will need washing and I needn't wear my overalls all the time. She says it like it was my choice to wear the overalls in the first place. I glance at Raleigh, and he nods.

Feeling strange, I go with the girl. Raleigh doesn't come, but I feel him exerting power over my soul, my body, making sure I can't run off.

"You've got a great figure already," Stacey says, smiling as we reach the clothes room—again, no windows. "You won't need many physical alteration processes when you are finally able to become a Chosen One."

I nod vaguely, then smile.

Stacey's calmer around me than the other Enhanced I've passed in the corridors today. The others seemed wary about me being Untamed. But not Stacey. I wonder how many augmenters she's been given, how many it took to override her—her fear? But fear is negative, and the Enhanced shouldn't feel it.

But Dr. Andy was definitely scared when I saw him. Worried I'd harm him because I'm evil. Maybe he was running lean. Maybe the daily augmenters aren't enough to overcome their fear of us, to make them happy around us. Maybe they run lean quicker when

I'm around….

Stacey picks out a long dress for me, and then some ridiculously high heels, and a couple of scarves. I choose the simplest of the clothes on offer—the ones easiest for escaping in: shirts, shorts, jeans that don't restrict movement. Keep the choices practical.

"You can have more than one posh dress," Stacey says. "Raleigh won't mind."

To please her, I slide a navy blue chiffon dress off a hanger. She's still talking—saying she can book me in for waxing treatments, if I want them—but then I see some tennis shoes, and her words float away. My chest feels lighter as I run my fingers over the shoes. I examine the soles. Sturdy. Stacey's face drops when I pick the tennis shoes over a second pair of heels.

I'm delivered back to Raleigh, and the last stop in the day is that chair-machine again. Raleigh checks my Seer status.

It's still the same.

But he's not angry. He just smiles, and the expression looks so fake on him that I shudder. "Don't worry, Shania. Your grief must be healing now. Soon, your powers will come back. Soon. I promise."

TWENTY-SIX

TWO MORE DAYS OF RALEIGH being kind, of him giving me 'fun' days, follow that first one. Two more days of him acting strangely, of me feeling nervous. Two more days of other Enhanced Ones trying to be my friends—those who are brave enough to mix with *me*, the wild girl, or given enough augmenters so they don't fear me—and two more days of Raleigh testing me at regular intervals and still finding that I'm not a Seer. Two more days of me looking around the compound, going to new places, and creating a mental map of the layout. Two more days of me searching for windows or any weapons. Two more days of me eating well and building my strength.

Two more days in which I wait for Jed to come back and own up to what he's done. Two more days in which he doesn't.

And I don't like it.

Raleigh drops me back at my room at the end of this third 'fun' day, and I curl up with the dog.

"What's going on?" I whisper to him. "And when are they going to fix the augmenters?"

The terrier looks at me, his eyes big and wide. I'd

thought the new augmenters would be ready by now—so does that mean the new lot didn't pass the testing? I tried to ask Raleigh, but he just said he didn't know. And I was sure that was a lie. It had to be. He's the leader. Of course he'd know.

It makes me uneasy, and it's no surprise to me when, that night, my dreams are waiting for me.

There's a girl running, ahead of me, down corridors. She wears a pale blue pinafore—the exact same shade as my en suite's tiles—and golden sandals. Every few minutes she looks back at me, checks that I'm still following, but no matter how fast or hard I run, I can't catch up. She stays just that little bit ahead of me.

"Come on!" the girl cries. A sing-song voice. It's a game. "Come on, don't be slow! We've got to run."

We pass no one else as we run. No doors. No windows. It's just a corridor. A long, rectangular tube that stretches on and on.

My breathing gets harder. An hour I've been running now, chasing her.

"Stop!" I call after her. "Please."

But she doesn't stop, and then she's gone. Disappeared.

I can't see her ahead. It's too dark or she's not there.

My skin crawls. A tingling at first, but then it gets sharper, harder. I look down. See the gold Promise Marks on my forearms…see them moving. Like insects crawling about. My stomach tightens, my throat dries.

The floor tilts. I throw my arms out, try to catch myself, but the floor's soft as it comes up, as it—

It wraps around me, a cocoon that gets tighter and tighter.

Squeeze!

My breath bursts from me. And, when I try to drag the next gulp of air in, the floor presses against my mouth. Stiff fibers, and then they're inside my mouth, rubbing at my tongue, my teeth—abrasive, horrible.

I scream, but the scream gets stuck, and I try to fight the fabric around me.

DIVIDED

I hear footsteps, a soft murmur—from outside, outside my web.

My nails tear at the fabric; something warm touches my head.

Light.

Sunlight.

I'm *outside*.

Automatically, I look up at the sky. Blue. Not a cloud in sight.

No bison.

Of course, there wouldn't be. Even in my dreams I can remember.

The land is flat, the color somewhere between dusty orange and blush pink. There are buildings. Concrete buildings, huge blocks piling up around me.

I jump back, out of the way of one, and—

The ground shakes.

"Sev! Wake up!"

I whirl around, see him—*Corin*.

He's here.

It's him.

Then he's got my hand, and we're running. Running fast. Faster than either of us should physically be able to go. We're like lightning, weaving between the buildings, the electricity poles, the—

We're out in the open, the soft desert.

Corin's hand burns stronger. My head turns toward him.

His eyes are mirrors.

Mirrors.

I go cold, try to pull my hand from his, but he holds on tighter.

"We have to be together," he says. "I told you we'd always be together, Sev."

A cage. A cage around me.

Run!

"Come on, this way! Show me the way!"

The way?

"The way to—"

Stop it!
A flash of white light. My head pounds, and I'm—
I'm falling.
Plummeting down, down, down.
No....
I try to—
See the ground coming up at me.
Empty!
See the ground getting closer....
Where are they?
The ground stops. Everything stops. I stop.
I'm suspended in the air.
In darkness.
Nothing but nothingness for company.
You're doing it, aren't you?
The darkness is my friend.
Minutes pass.
How are you doing it?
The darkness is soft.
A blanket, but not like the carpet that squeezed me.
A blanket of thoughts, comforting me.
HOW ARE YOU DOING IT?
I jolt awake—properly awake and—
Something's over my mouth, something....
I scream into the thing—the hand—try to move, kick out.
Bright light and—
Needles in my head, diving deeper and deeper.
I try to twist, try to—
What the—
My Seer powers?
The chair. I'm in the chair.
And Raleigh stands in front of me. A wicked look plasters his face. "This isn't good enough, Shania."

TWENTY-SEVEN

"YOUR POWERS ARE *STILL* BLOCKED." Raleigh shakes his head, his earlier kindness gone. Now, there's something dark and dangerous in his voice, his face, his manner. "This isn't right, Shania. No, no, *no*. Your conscious mind is…" He wipes the back of his hand across his mouth. "It's your grief. *Has* to be. But you're not even *trying* to get over it. And with all I've done for you as well, getting your dog back and the fun days—and you've looked so peaceful in your sleep! No—this is just selfish, holding onto your grief, using it as a shield."

I twist around as much as the chair with the wires will allow—at least the needles are no longer in my head. I'm still in my room. The new room. But the chair's here—that machine.

The dog? Where is he?

How has this… *Raleigh*. Oh Gods.

"You're being *selfish*." Raleigh steps closer, stoops a little, until his face is directly in front of mine. "You shouldn't be able to hold onto grief this long, this strongly." He shakes his head. "Get over it *now* and get your powers back. I know you can do it."

I force my neck to turn, manage to look to my left. See a shape on the floor, see—

It's the terrier. My terrier. Just lying there.

My heart jolts.

"What have you done to him?" My voice is high, and my words tumble out.

I flinch, try to move, but the chair holds me in place.

"Raleigh—what have you done?"

"He's just sleeping."

"He's not sleeping!" Somehow, I get an arm free and point at my dog. "He doesn't sleep through *anything*!" I yell.

And especially not Raleigh doing this to me. The terrier should be barking and growling and attacking Raleigh—he hates him, hates the Enhanced.

"You drugged him?" The realization dawns on me, and I think hard. How? The food—the last meal?

And I didn't wake up either—not when Raleigh came in, brought the chair in here, moved me out of the bed and into the chair....

"You drugged me too?"

"Easier that way," he says. "And I wanted to be sure that it really is grief. And not you actively blocking me."

How are you doing it? The words echo through me, but they're in his voice...spoken earlier, when I was dreaming...they invaded my dream.

I swallow awkwardly, though I don't know why—because my lack of powers isn't anything I'm doing.

"And you're satisfied that it's not me? That I haven't got control of it?" I ask. Because he has to be, if he probed and is still blaming my grief. Didn't find what he was looking for?

"Your mind was the same unconscious." He cracks his knuckles—it's the same thing Three did before, and my stomach hardens. "It would appear you're not in control of it. But you're *letting* the darkness win, Shania. You're not fighting the grief. You're letting it take hold."

DIVIDED

I look at my dog, limp on the floor. I remember how safe I felt, curled up with him before I went to sleep. How, for the last few days, I've finally been able to relax and sleep soundly at night—because my dog is my guard, my best friend. And he's on my side.

My terrier being here made me feel safe. And Raleigh knows that—oh, I'll bet anything he knows that.

He played me.

"And now you need to get over your grief, Shania. You need to fight the evil in you that's making you upset, not let it grow at this extortionate rate, and you need to get access to your powers again." There's something so dark and dangerous in Raleigh's voice that my blood runs cold.

I stare at him. "I can't. There isn't any grief for me to get over. I told you before." I keep my voice neutral, then point at the screen. "When are you going to accept that the machine is right? That what you're finding is right? I am no longer a Seer."

And, for a moment, I consider telling him about Jed. How Jed must've taken my powers.

Only Jed is dead. And Raleigh would think I was going mad—that the Untamed evil has a stronger hold on me than even he'd thought.

And maybe it has.

"That is nonsense," Raleigh says. "That is wrong. *You* are a Seer. You're the one who will save us all." Then he moves back, takes something out of his belt.

A small pistol.

No.

My body jolts. My eyes widen.

He can't.

He can.

"If you don't overcome your grief this instant, I will kill your dog."

I gasp.

Raleigh points the gun over the unmoving body of my dog. Then he smiles—and it's the smile that really gets to me. It's the smile that makes the dam inside me break.

It's the smile that spurs me.

And I break out the chair—don't know how I do it. I just do. Wires snap under the pressure, the strength I somehow exert—Seer strength? But no. It's just me. It's me when he's threatened my dog.

I fly at Raleigh, hands going for his throat.

He yells, we stumble back, and I reach for the gun. My fingers brush the metal, and I try to grab the handle, try to—

It goes off.

A hole bringing darkness and—

Sparks fly over me, and glass. Sharp and—

"No!" Raleigh shouts, and then he's pushing me back, shoving me.

I fall, twist around. My left hand hits something soft and squidgy.

Then movement to my right—

A growl and a flurry of movement. Fur against my hands and then—

"You *will* overcome your grief." Raleigh jumps on me, kicks my dog away. The terrier yelps, and I screech at Raleigh, whack my head on the floor as I try to get away.

Raleigh seizes my arm, and I spit into his face.

"Overcome your grief now—get your powers back this instant!"

"I'm not doing anything!"

He grabs my chin, and his fingers are like clamps. Clamps with talons on the end. He presses my head into the floor, pushes down on my jaw. Sharp pain and—

"Shania, fight this evil in you."

The evil in you.

A huge wave of anger flares in me. "I'm not evil," I cry. "The Untamed are not evil!"

"Don't protect the parasite."

A surge of pain hits my head. Sharp and hard. And then he's inside my mind, searching again. Digging,

DIVIDED

digging, digging. His talons get longer—magnificent claws—scratching away, deeper and deeper, pushing aside everything and—

"*What* are you doing to my daughter?"

The new voice startles Raleigh because he pulls back, lets go of my head, and—

My vision comes back—I hadn't realized it was gone but—

But when I look again, when I can see... I can't breathe. No, it can't be.

He can't be....

"Dad?"

My father is here. *Right here.* In the room and—and he doesn't look any different, he's still....

He's dead. Because of me. I left him in Nbutai.

He's....

My father's eyes narrow as he looks at me and Raleigh. Raleigh stands up swiftly, brushes his hands down his suit. Then he glares at me. I sit up slowly, dizziness tugging at my edges. Raleigh can see him?

He's...he's here...but....

And then my father's eyes—they turn into mirrors as I watch. He's here *and* Enhanced? My father....

What the hell?

I look around. Expect to see Elia—another person who's dead because of me. But she's not here.

"What were you doing to my daughter?" My father's voice is slow, crisp.

"This Untamed creature is not your daughter, Paul," Raleigh says. "Shania is your daughter. And, at the moment, *Shania* is not in control. Seven is."

It's the first time Raleigh's said my name—my proper name—in a long time, or maybe the only time, and the way he says my name, like it's the most disgusting thing ever, makes me feel sick.

"I'm glad you could make it, Paul. And early too." Raleigh gives me a dismissive glance. "Maybe your presence will help Shania beat the evil and overcome the selfish grief she is feeling. Perhaps a father can do what no one else can."

My father raises his eyebrows. "Perhaps. But then, as I'm sure my wife would point out if she were here, grief is not selfish. It is natural. Negative, but natural." Then he looks at me. "Are you okay?"

I stare at him. "What's going on?"

My father turns to Raleigh. "I think you need to leave. Seven and I need to talk."

"She is called *Shania*."

"You just said that it is Seven in control." Something in my father's eyes flashes again. "Perhaps you had better make your mind up."

I stare at my father, amazed.

Raleigh grunts something and leaves. He locks the door after him.

The dog, awake now, rushes over to me, and I check him over. When, at last, I'm satisfied that he's not seriously hurt, I look up at the man in the room with me. My father.

Except it can't be.

Oh, it *really* can't be.

I look at my terrier, in my arms. He's not relaxed, not with this man in here. His hackles are raised. But he's like that with any Enhanced. Why would my father be any different? But I feel the earlier enthusiasm—the excitement—drain away.

"Is it really you?" I drink in his appearance as I stand, shakily.

My father looks the same. But different, besides the eyes. Different in a way that I can't put my finger on.

"It's me." His voice is soft. "And you're still Untamed?"

I nod. The terrier jumps down from my arms.

"Good." My father breathes deeply.

"Good?" I shake my head. "How—how can you think that if you're one of them? Dad, I don't understand."

He steps forward and hugs me. "I told you I'd always be here for you, Seven."

DIVIDED

I tilt my head to one side. "You're...so you're resisting?"

"No. I'm not your mother. It is only Katya and yourself who can resist at times. You know that."

Resist.

The word tastes odd, makes me feel strange. Like it's a lie. I can't resist. I was going to join them, all those months ago.

But I didn't.

But would I recently, if the augmenters hadn't made me ill? Was that all that was stopping me? Because briefly, I did feel it—didn't I? The pull of the augmenters, the serene tranquility the Calmness planted within me....

"I haven't got the Sarr blood," my father says.

I frown and think of my brother. "But Three has? So...so he *can* resist?"

"He is no Seer."

My stomach feels too light. "But he has the blood... same as me...."

But he can't resist. He's one of them—I know that. Why am I torturing myself, still hoping? A lump forms in my throat.

My father takes a step back, looks around the room, cranes his neck. "Where's Corin?"

"He escaped—didn't you...didn't you hear?" Then I frown again. Should he have?

"Hear from whom? I'm not here."

"What?" I stare at him.

The look in his eyes—even though I can't see any expression in them, just myself reflected—seems to get fiercer.

"You need to stay with him, Seven. Stay with Corin—you know that."

"But he's not in this compound. He got out."

My father shakes his head. "Then find him. You have to stick together, you two."

The tingle starts at the base of my spine. Then it grows and grows, stronger and stronger. "Dad, why...

why are you here? Are you going to help me escape?"

"You're going to do that by yourself," my father says. "But I have a message from your mother: have a bath, and dream."

"From Mum? What? Dream?"

"Dream, my girl," he says, but he's speaking in my mother's voice. "You know what you need to do."

I shake my head, stare at him. Still him. Still my Dad. But her voice? This is...this isn't right. "I don't understand—I can't contact the Dream Land, I was exiled."

"Dream for your powers. You've left them for too long, left them behind, lost them. Dream and find them again. They are yours. They will be waiting for you." He pushes me gently toward the en suite, and then his eyes are Untamed again. "Find them, Seven. Find them and save us all—"

"But if I have them, Raleigh will—"

"You're strong, Seven. Don't underestimate the strength in you. The strength in the Sarr line. Now, go and dream in the water. It's what your mother wants—and you know you need to do it. You know that, deep down, don't you? I'll keep watch. Go."

Go.

I trip as I walk and turn, look back at my father and—

He disappears—vanishes into the air and—and....

And *Raleigh's* there. Right where he was.

It's him.

Him all along and...? What the hell?

"Where'd he go?" I stare at him. "My father? He was right there."

Raleigh gives me a strange look. "Your father is dead, Shania. An unfortunate death in the conversion mission at Nbutai."

"No." I shake my head. "He was here—he was talking to me. You talked to him!"

Raleigh's eyes narrow, and then I feel him take over my mind, exerting what control he has, ripping through my mind, searching, searching. And then—

My breaths wash through me as he leaves my mind.

I take a step back, feel something like lead drop through my body. Nausea washes over me.

"This is very selfish behavior, Shania. But I'll be kind again, give you until the morning." Blood drips from his lip and—and I look down at my hands. There's blood on me. His blood? Mine?

We've been fighting?

Fighting all that time and—

The dog.

Where's my dog?

I look around, but he's not here. I can't see him. Panic rises within me. I don't understand. This is… Is the terrier hiding?

Raleigh points at me. "If you've not got over your grief by tomorrow morning then I *will* take drastic measures. We have to save everyone, Shania. And we will. I will find a way."

He leaves, dragging the chair-machine out with surprising ease, and locks the door.

And I—I'm going mad? But no. I shake my head. My father *was* here. I know he was. I spoke to him. And Raleigh *had* left. It was just me and my father.

But *was* it him? Didn't he seem…different? Unreal?

A hallucination. Seeing him and our whole conversation? *Am* I going mad?

And I haven't got my Seer powers…so it can't have been me contacting him like how I've contacted those other Untamed. No. That was different anyway. I shake my head. It wasn't me or my powers.

But Raleigh and my father talked—unless I imagined that too?

I press my lips together, feel sick. My skin's sticky, and I'm too hot. Dirty. I need a bath.

A bath.

Have a bath, and dream.

My mother's request? No. It doesn't make sense.

My head pounds.

I search for the terrier again.

He's not here.

Definitely not.

Oh Gods.

What is happening? I hallucinated seeing my father? My father telling me my mother wants me to have a bath to get my powers back? I snort, breathe deeper. Maybe part of me thinks I can get my powers back if I have a bath.

Is that what you want? So Raleigh can use them? Use you?

No.

I clench my jaw. He's not going to use me. I'm strong. And I need to be a Seer again. My powers are an advantage.

And a bath *does* seem like a good idea.

I run the water quickly. I'm shaking as I strip my clothes off—one of my new outfits. At the last second, just when I'm about to put the Seer pendant on the side, I look around. I grab my top and go to the hem, rip a thin length of fabric off—it comes away surprisingly easily. Then I thread it through the pendant's hole and tie it around my neck.

I step into the bath.

The water is hot. Steam rises.

I stand in it first, wincing at the heat. Too much really. But the heat feels good. So hot. Scalding my skin. I grit my teeth, watch my arms gooseflesh strangely in the steam.

And then I sit down, splash hot water over me.

I shudder, gasp, lift my head up higher. Pain darts down my back.

Have a bath and dream.

Water touches my pendant.

Dream.

Dream.

Dream.

My lips are moving, muttering the word over and over—or at least I think it's that word…but I can't tell

DIVIDED

because the world is hazy and—

Click.

Inside me.

And I know it's my powers. My Seer powers are finding me again. Lost, but found. So easily?

I jolt, turn, and—

Fur brushes my face, tickly, prickly, but soft. Cold air washes over me. A jarring sensation in my head. The hot water running over me.

A strange feeling takes hold.

Let go of your own body, Seven.

I stiffen. My father's voice?

But he's not here this time.

I wasn't here last time. And he says the words, but I say them too.

They're my words. I'm saying them. Me. And something clicks into place inside me, a sense of knowing, of certainty—and deep down, a part of me realizes it, can see it clearly now.

But at Nbutai, my ideas that I dared to voice were constantly shouted down by Rahn and Corin. It eroded my confidence, my belief in my own ideas and knowledge.

I'd thought that I was confident enough to trust myself now.

But maybe not.

Because it's easier, sometimes, to have someone else tell you what you to do, to tell you your own idea, because then if it goes wrong, you won't be told off.

And I wanted someone who loves me to tell me what to I needed to do. Someone I miss.

It was all me—the only explanation. My father wasn't there.

Just my subconscious.

It feels like bricks falling on me, knowing it wasn't real, but, at the same time, it makes part of me stronger. I have the answer, the information. Why didn't I trust myself to know?

But I close my eyes and imagine my father. Indulge

myself.

Now go, he says. *Find your powers, get them back, and keep them close. Find them and—*

A splintering shriek.

Coldness.

A flurry of snow against my face and—

"Run!" Dominika yells into the darkness.

TWENTY-EIGHT

SNOW BATTERS DOWN IN LARGE clumps, laced with ice and sharpness. White fills my vision: it's everywhere. Yet it's dark as well. Moonlight. I see a ghostly lone tree up ahead, weighed down under snow, pushed to the side, wind-beaten, and—

"Run! The spirits are active!"

My head pounds, and I can't breathe. I feel sick. I try to run faster, try to catch the others, those who are ahead, disappearing into the white world of the Frozen Lands, but I can't—this body's too—

Something shoves into me.

Not into Viktoriya's body. Into me. Me inside her and—

What are you doing? Get out!

Her voice. I just know.

I freeze. *Viktoriya?* And I know how to say the word—how to say it into her mind.

What? She sounds angry.

You heard me?

Of course I heard you—you've not made me sleep this time. Grandfather told me what happened! That you'd come back, told me what it would feel like—

"Run, Vik—"

My head—Viktoriya's head—jolts upward, and I don't know which of us does it. Maybe we both do and—

A shriek cuts the air. Snow flurries up in front, dancing. And the spirits are here. Flashes of silver—like huge snowflakes made of metal, but it's metal that twists and changes.

Viktoriya starts running before I'm aware of her decision, and I feel like I'm being shaken about inside her... This is like with Corin that time when he was in control...that dream. The dream that wasn't a dream.

A spirit brushes my hand, Viktoriya's hand.

We shriek. Coldness, icy pins diving through the thick gloves, and—

"Run!"

I can't run fast enough. Help me, Seer!

I try to run too, try to run with her. But her legs are clumsy, and her body feels heavy. Slow and disproportionate. Thicker limbs. Pain surges through me.

And I get her legs—control of her legs—make her go faster. Don't know how I do. I just manage it and—

And I'm exactly like Raleigh. He controls my body, and I know what that feels like. And I'm doing the same to Viktoriya, exploiting her, controlling her.

I freeze.

Don't stop! Viktoriya's voice. Loud and deafening in my mind. *Help me. Help me!*

I take hold of her body—all of it, as much as I can—and I don't know how I know what to do, *exactly* what to do, but I know. And I pour my energy into it, into her, feel our efforts mix. We work together. We run. We run as fast as we can. And I'm fast, the fastest.

We pump our legs, share everything. Our feet slam the ground, the compacted snow. Frost and icy bitterness drive over us, showers us. A flash of gold.

We dive to the ground. Snow invades our mouth, numbs our teeth. Pain in our head and—

DIVIDED

A hand grabs our left arm.

I jolt, feel myself momentarily separate from Viktoriya who doesn't flinch at the contact. I look up, slide back into her, see the face. Taras.

"That way!" he yells, and his eyes! They've got a golden light in them now, no longer dark, and that light bores into us—into me. Straight into me. He knows I'm here.

A streak of orange flits across the sky. Rusty sparks fall down. A cackle of laughter.

"Get inside!"

Viktoriya and I are one again, and our head jolts up. We see the chums, through vision that blurs with the biting, dark air. Taras surges forward with surprising speed—fueled by something? Seer powers? And then a white light flashes from his hand, aimed at the spirits and—

The spirits scream. More of them.

Here.

Our heart pounds, harder, harder. Adrenaline floods our system. Our blood burns and—

We see the others. Marina and Dominika, the men—men who weren't there during my last visit—and—

A spirit erupts from the ground.

We scream, jerk back. A branch or something flies out, and we duck.

More white light.

Shit.

A spirit, sharp teeth—flesh and—

I push our hand forward, reach for my powers. Something clicks around me, a deafening click, and I stumble. Viktoriya rights my error, and I turn, feel jarred, feel…feel the surge of energy as my own white light bursts out of Viktoriya's hand. I feel her surprise as it springs forward, hits the spirit, and—

A flash of lightening. A shriek.

I hunker down, feel Viktoriya shaking. Feel her thoughts, her feelings—her fear at angering the spirit.

"Get inside!"

The chums—abruptly so close.

We trip, and then Viktoriya's got more control than me and—

Something's squeezing me. A flash of pain. Movement in my head. Things are shifting inside me, compressing, stretching, slotting into place and—

I feel them, my powers, more and more. My Seer powers are—

Inside.

We're inside.

A fire. Flames. The sound of the raging snowstorm outside.

Dominika stands over me. She's frowning, and the frown's etched deeply into her chest. "What the hell was that white light, girl?"

"You ain't a Seer," another voice says.

"That wasn't—" Viktoriya's voice, and they're her words—not mine. "That was Seven Sarr."

There's a moment of silence, when everyone stares at her—at me, at us—and then Taras stands.

"I'm glad you came back. I was beginning to wonder." And he looks into our eyes, but it's mine he sees. I just know it. "Just as well when you left your powers with my granddaughter."

"What?" Dominika splutters.

"No." Marina shakes her head, stamps her foot. "It is not right. This—" She shakes her hand at us. "Impossible."

"She just saved us. Blasted all the spirits, got us enough time to get in the chum. She saved us, and it's just as well."

I stare at Taras from the corner of Viktoriya's eyes. "I left my powers in her?" Viktoriya's voice sounds stranger when I use it.

The man nods. "You must've stayed too long. Couldn't sustain the connection—not on your first proper journey…and so far too. It jarred your Seer powers, lost them between you and your host. They sprang back to Viktoriya. And they've been calling

DIVIDED

to you. At last, you heard the call, and now you're getting them back. And you're sewing them into your soul now—they are yours, you'll know how to control them from now on."

Seven!

"Someone's calling you," Taras says. "Someone back in your part of the world."

I nod.

"Go."

My body tightens.

Something inside me snaps as I disconnect, as I shut my eyes, think about my body at New Kitembu... I'm lying on the bed...with the dog....

No, that's not right....

Something squeezes inside me, and then there's pain in my chest. My body? Where is it?

Floating. Floating. Floating.

The dog barks, and I hear him like he's next to me, like he's—

I gasp, spluttering—can't—

Water in my throat, burning...muscles squeezing together and—

Too much water...the lake, the black lake with Jed, and—

I move, splashing, thrashing my arms about. Something hard hits the back of my left hand, and I turn sharply, but I slip—I'm lying on something and—

Hands pull me up in one swift motion, and I yell out, try to get away from Jed, manage to turn and water flies everywhere. I cry out, and cold air rushes against my bare skin. Naked.

The bath—

"Seven! It's all right!"

And then—and then Jed's face changes, and it's not Jed.

It's Three.

My brother. He's—

He passes me a towel, then turns away, toward the open doorway. "Dry yourself and get changed. Don't do anything else—I mean it. I'll wait out there."

My heart pounds as I watch him pull the door shut after he leaves. I wrap the towel around me. I can see it's soft, fluffy, but it doesn't feel like it. It feels like ice, ice against my skin. Ice and—

A low roaring noise fills my ears, and I turn, heart pounding. See the bath, with the water draining out, and the whirlpool the suction makes. I take a step back, shaking. When did the plug get pulled?

But, as I stand here, my hearing gets better. I hear other sounds. My dog whining nearby. Three's lowered voice.

I dry myself quickly, change into the clothes I took off before, because they're all that's here, then I stare at the wall, and I...I see through it for a moment.

A storm gathers in front of me.

When I enter my room, Three's sitting on the bed and patting the terrier awkwardly. The dog's here again? The terrier keeps looking at him, starting to wag his tail. Then stops. He's confused and looks toward me.

My hair drips down my neck. I expect the terrier to run at me, happy. But he doesn't. He stays with Three, though he doesn't rub against my brother's legs, but keeps a short gap away.

Three jumps up the moment he sees me. "What the hell were you doing trying to drown yourself?"

I shrink back, eyes widening. Drown myself?

"*Seven*? Have you any idea how selfish that is—trying to—" He breaks off, shakes his head, then grabs the back of his neck, rubs the skin there hard. His whole body shakes with anger—anger that an Enhanced One shouldn't have. "Gods, if I hadn't been coming to find you—and if the dog hadn't been whining at that door, scratching it—look." He grips my arm and turns sharply. Pain shoots down my shoulder. "Look at the scratches! Thank the Gods the dog realized what you were trying to do and got help."

What I was trying to do....

"I—I wasn't!" I cry. Then I swallow quickly, realize

what he said.

Seven. Three called me *Seven*. Not Shania.

My brother—*still* in there?

No. I can't hope, can't believe that he is, not again.

And then I frown, frown so hard that my head feels heavy. When I was with Taras and Viktoriya, someone called my name. Was that his voice? Calling me *Seven*? Like he did before…just after I'd been bound to the Enhanced….

And then I feel it, the power within me—feel it in a way I've never felt it before. It's like a mountain inside me, growing and growing, the summit getting higher and higher. And I can feel every part of it. Every single part. The way the ground shakes with the power, how new earth forms, is pushed up, exposed from the earth's crust and…and I *know*.

They're back. Properly. The powers.

And they've grown. They're full-sized. They're—

Oh Gods!

A strong tingling starts off at the back of my scalp, then spreads.

I am a strong Seer.

I'm the one the augury speaks of.

And I *will* beat Raleigh.

"I will," I whisper, and my lips burr together.

"What?" Three grabs me by the shoulders, shakes his head hard. "I—I… Gods, I don't even know what to say—why would you want to do that?" He releases me, wipes the back of his hand across his mouth. Then he turns toward the door. "I need to get Raleigh—"

"No." My chest tightens, and I lunge for him, get his arm. "No. Three, you can't."

Because Raleigh will know.

As soon as he sees me, he'll *know* my powers are back and—

Shit.

I need to get out. Get far away.

I look at my brother carefully. Really try and see him, like I keep trying to. Would he help me? And it's confusing, because he's both like the other Enhanced and *not*. There's emotion when he speaks. And his fear—I can see it in his eyes, his *mirror* eyes. Fear over me. Brotherly fear.

Still Untamed?

I nearly scream. I just don't know. Too many mixed messages. I can't trust him to help me, can't rely on other people, on him.

And then I feel the guilt riding in, my guilt, guilt over what he is now. My fault. I gulp. Am I reading more into his behavior because I want part of him to be Untamed, not just because he's my brother, but because it will lessen my guilt too?

But what if part of him—part of the Untamed Three—*is* still there? Just a small part...and maybe it wasn't in control before...maybe it can't greatly control him... And I know. I can't bank on it. No, I need to get out, not waste time overthinking this.

"Just...why—tell me *why*, Seven," Three says.

I shake my head, my chest rising and falling quickly. "I wasn't—I..." I look around. Weapons. If I'm out there—*once* I'm out there—I need weapons. There's nothing in this room. I look back at Three, wonder if he's got anything on him, and he's still staring at me. "I fell asleep," I say. "I wasn't—"

"You fell asleep in the bath?" He exhales hard, then steps away from me. His shoulders droop. "Hell, I shouldn't have even come here—but thank the Gods I did...if I hadn't...if I hadn't stopped you from—"

"Three! Stop it! I *wasn't* trying to drown myself." I muster up as much strength into my voice as possible. "Now, have—"

"But you cut yourself before—Raleigh told me, and I read the reports and—"

"*Three*! Believe me. Just trust me—"

He swears under his breath. "It's not right. Not right that Raleigh's letting you suffer like this. There must be some augmenters you can—"

I cut him off quickly. "Three, why are you here? You

said you were looking for me when..." I start again. "*Why* are you here?"

My heart pounds frantically. Because...because he's going to help me?

A voice screams inside me, and I'm doing it again.

"My name is Tomas," he says.

"Fine. *Tomas*." I fold my arms. "*Why* are you here? To spy on me? Report back to Raleigh?" I breathe deeply, and I get that feeling again—of the strength in me. "Or..." Or something else?

He clasps his hands together tightly, turns his head toward the door. "Because...because I thought you should know...."

"Thought I should know what?" I swallow slowly and wait.

Know that there's a way out of here? Something I can use as an advantage?

Know for sure that my brother's on my side? That him locking me in the corridor and preventing my escape was a blip—a moment when the Enhanced part of him got more control? But that he can resist....

"What?"

"Eriksen." Three exhales loudly and his whole body jolts. "The men caught him before. He's been here a while, and I thought you should know, Seven. Corin Eriksen is here."

TWENTY-NINE

FOR A MOMENT, EVERYTHING AROUND me stops, and all I am aware of is myself: the way my heart beats…not fast, just forceful, as if it's telling everyone I'm alive, reminding me I'm here; how my breathing gets louder, as if each breath is fighting for its release, begging not to be dragged back into my lungs, back into the darkness; how my fingers are cold…cold like a dead man's fingers…stiff, cold….

But then Three's words creep in, and they echo over and over in my head. I look up. My brother's watching me. There's a slight line etched between his eyebrows—he always gets that line when he's worried.

"Are…are you all right?" he asks.

I stare at him, open my mouth. Shut it again. Something strange filters through my body. I try to clench my hands into fists, but it's like I haven't got control over them. Not properly. The best I can do is watch my fingers curl slightly. But it's not like Raleigh's controlling me. No. It's just….

"Corin? Corin's here?" The words are rusty, bad. He can't be.

Corin can't be here.

Three nods. "We caught him...before. A while ago. Raleigh didn't want you knowing."

He didn't? He didn't want to gloat, make me feel bad...let me continue to think that Corin was out there. He lied. Lied to me. False hope.

But hope nonetheless.

Because he wanted me to be happy?

Maybe the Enhanced aren't so bad. He was trying to protect you.

I swallow hard, with difficulty, and look at my brother. "How?" I shift my weight from one foot to the other "How was he caught?"

"A drone detected a human out there. It wasn't until the team went out that we knew for sure it was Eriksen." Behind his mirrors, I'm sure Three watches me carefully, and I wish I could reach up and pinch those mirrors, drag the films away from his eyes so we can all see clearly.

I shake my head slowly. "I don't believe you... Corin can't be here."

No.

No.

Corin has to be out there. He has to be free, Untamed. He can't be in here. He just...*can't.*

Three shifts his weight slightly. The floor creaks. "He's here, Sha—*Seven*. He's here."

I look at him carefully. "Why are you calling me *Seven*?" I take a step forward, but I'm shaking. "You keep doing it, Three. Why? I don't understand. *Are* you still one of us?"

He wrings his hands out in front of him—a gesture that might've shown that the Untamed Three was nervous. But is that Three still in him?

He clears his throat. "You can trust me. I'm your brother."

I hold myself carefully. "Are you Untamed though?"

He lifts his hands up higher. "Why are you questioning *this*? After what I've just told you? Look,

Seven—Raleigh didn't want you knowing about Eriksen, but I've let you know. Doesn't that tell you that I'm still *me*. I'm still thinking about you. Your feelings."

"Me? My feelings?" I shake my head. There's a bitter taste in my mouth, and I bite down on my bottom lip for a moment. My heart beats fast. "Corin's here? Really here… You're not lying?"

"No. Eriksen is here."

My shoulders drop.

Corin's caught.

Trapped.

Here.

Everything in my body tightens. I bring a hand to my chest, touch my collarbone. It feels more bony than usual, like it's sticking out farther. Then my hand finds my pendant.

"I'll take you to him," Three says, and he looks at my pendant.

My eyes widen, and I watch my brother carefully—very carefully. But Three doesn't give anything away. A master of disguise now. Even lets his hands fall to his side. Just looks at me, his face a blank slate.

"Why?" My voice is small. I hug myself. The terrier's by my legs—I'm acutely aware of the way his fur tickles my ankles—and his presence is reassuring. My vision darkens as I look at my brother once more. "Why would you let me see Corin? Put two Untamed together?"

Three sighs. "I know which cell he's in. I'll take you to him and I'll… I'll let you see him. Our dog will have to stay here though. It's too risky taking him out."

I watch him again, waiting for something more. But he doesn't answer my question.

"Look, I'm reaching out to you here, but I've got to be careful," Three says. "It's the middle of the night—we can't draw attention to ourselves. If you don't want to—" He starts toward the door.

"I didn't say that," I cut in quickly, and he turns

DIVIDED

back.

"You can trust me, Seven." There's a strange look on his face, and it's only accentuated by the metal plates obscuring a good deal of his face.

So it's *Seven* all the time now. I turn that thought over in my mind.

"I'm sorry," I blurt out. "For not rescuing you. I—I thought you were dead."

Three looks at me for a long moment, and I feel sick, like my heart is going to explode. Then he offers his hand to me.

"Come on. We'll have to be careful. Make sure no one sees us. But I'll take you to Eriksen now."

Three leads me down two levels, until we're far underground, and my heart beats frantically. Corin's here. He's actually here. He didn't get away far enough after all. Didn't escape….

And he's going to end up Enhanced too.

No.

No one is. I'm going to stop it. I don't know how—or what I'll do when Raleigh produces suitable augmenters—but I'll do something. Sort something. Contact those other Seers, and we can work together. Find a way. And I'm sure I can do that now—find the other Seers. Body-share.

Or maybe I won't even be in here. If Corin and I are together, our chances of escape are better.

And he's *here*. We can get everyone out, all the Untamed. We can all just go.

I feel sick as we walk; jittery, weak, like my legs aren't strong enough. Several times, I want to lean on Three as we walk, but I don't. Don't want to show that I need support, that I'm weak…even if he is my brother...even if he is on our side. And he is. Has to be. He's reuniting me with Corin.

Three keeps looking around, behind us, constantly checking. Enhanced Ones aren't supposed to feel nervous, but the emotion is radiating off Three in waves, blowing his cover, and I wonder if I should tell him.

But I don't make a move to, not with each step that takes me closer...closer to *Corin*. My lips tingle; the pent-up energy inside me fights for an escape.

Three stops outside a door, and I look at him.

"Is this where he is?" I survey the door quickly. It looks old, made of wood, and my eyes are drawn to the huge cast-iron hinges.

"Yes." Three takes out a key from his pocket. His hands shake, and he pauses for a moment. "I'm going to wait out here. Give you time to..." He swallows hard, and his throat makes a strange gulping noise. "I'll keep watch. And nothing more than talking, Seven—I'm still your brother, and I still don't like him that much. Understand?"

I nod, but I would've nodded to anything. "Just open the door." My breathing speeds up.

Three does. It seems to take him an age to turn the key, for whatever mechanism inside the door to click several times, and then—

And then the door opens.

And I see him.

He's here.

Corin really is here.

THIRTY

CORIN SITS ON A BENCH at the back of the small room, lit up by a flickering bulb on the ceiling. His feet are shoulder-width apart, and his head is in his hands, propped up with his elbows on his knees. A moment after the door opens, Corin looks up.

The instant our eyes catch each other's—our *Untamed* eyes—a thousand fireworks go off in my body.

"Sev?" Corin stands up, looks uncertain. He looks from me to Three, takes a step toward us.

Then he says my name again, and the sound of my name on his lips physically pulls me to him, and then I'm in his arms, breathing in his scent. Musk and sweat and—

No cigarette smoke.

But there wouldn't be. Not here. The Enhanced wouldn't give him cigarettes…they want us to all be perfect…and cigarettes are bad.

Yet they have packs of them in their shops…that's where Corin gets them, on raids…still, they're getting harder to find.

I shake my head slightly, moving against Corin's

chest. He shakes as he holds me, and his shirt rustles. He's not wearing the blue overalls. So all the Untamed are allowed actual clothes again?

"It's really you?" His voice sounds different. Weaker. Like he's got a cold. "Really you, Sev?"

"Ten minutes," Three says from behind us. "And nothing more than talking." And then the door closes with a soft thud, and a click follows.

My pulse quickens until I feel giddy, like my soul is dancing far, far away, and I can't catch up.

"It's really me." My words are breathy.

I pull back, look up at Corin, study his face. The left side is more sunburnt than the right, and there are fine pinpricks of red over the burns. Looks painful. A fair amount of stubble covers his chin and jaw, and his eyes are...there's something so true about them that it physically hurts me, makes my sides ache, makes me never want to leave him. And I'm engulfed by it all, this feeling, this feeling of being with Corin. Of knowing that he is okay, that he's with me, that we're together. That there's hope after all.

Corin moves his arm abruptly, and then his hand is against the side of my face. Warmth floods me. He exerts a little pressure with his fingertips, against my temple.

"Gods. Oh Gods..." he whispers, and his voice is so full of emotion, full of fear and relief. "You're... You're okay? *Gods*. Sev, what's going on? What's been happening?" His thumb brushes over my bottom lip, exerts the slightest bit of pressure. "Are you okay?"

I nod, keep my eyes on his. They're so beautiful, they drink me in. And then I'm drinking in the whole of his face, losing myself in him, and I feel silly—like I'm one of those girls Five was always talking about, and longing to be: a girl in love.

But the feeling's real.

This is *real*.

"Why haven't they converted me? Or you? They haven't even tried with me." Corin's words are a

DIVIDED

whisper, and his thumb rests against my chin as he holds my face, tilted slightly, so I can't look away from him.

"A problem with the augmenters." And I don't try to break our eye contact, don't want to be empty, don't want to lose anything.

"A problem?"

"We reacted to them—you must be the same...or they think you might be, don't want to take a chance yet."

His eyes narrow. "Did you cause the problem?"

"What?"

"Your Seer powers?"

I shake my head. "No."

Corin nods, then cups my face in both of his hands. He breathes deeply, shuts his eyes for a moment, and his whole being trembles. When he opens his eyes, his gaze is on me. For a moment, we stand like that, then he moves his hands away from my face and presses one against the small of my back. A deep noise sounds from the depths of his throat. His arms wrap around me, tighter though, more protective than before, and I press myself to him, overcome by the need to be as close to him as possible. Our bodies touch everywhere. His hand moves back up to my head, and he holds me against him firmly. Like he never wants to let go. Hotness and sparks. My breath hitches in my throat, and I lift my head up, look at his lips. Memories of before—in the Zharat's Fire Mountain, when I was desperate to be with him—burn through me, and I stare at his lips.

He looks down at me, as he holds me there, and I keep looking at him. A circle we can never break.

And I still want him....

"Remarkable," he murmurs.

"What?" I whisper.

"I never thought I'd see you again." His voice breaks as he speaks and the vulnerability in it—the rawness of his emotion—makes my throat constrict.

His emotions are getting to me, digging into my soul. But being surrounded for so long by the Enhanced, with their artificial emotions, was bound to do this—make Corin's realness stronger. He's *true*.

"It's… This makes being caught almost worth it," Corin says. "Just to see you again. Gods, I love you, Seven—and when I was out there…us being separated…it was… I didn't even know if you were…" His eyes glaze over with tears, and he quickly wipes them away.

"I missed you," I say, and then the words pour out, and I can't stop them. "Oh Gods. Corin, you've got no idea how much I've missed you, wanted you here, but didn't want you to be here, to be caught too."

"It's okay," he says, and he takes hold of my hands, lifts them up slightly, makes the gap between our bodies slightly bigger as he steps back. "It's *okay*."

I shake my head, concentrate on the way my hands feel, encased by his. "It's not—Corin, it's not okay. Raleigh can control me. He's made me kill a girl with my powers already and…and he's going to force me to wipe us all out. I can't stop him."

"But…but you're a Seer, Sev. Doesn't that mean anything?"

Yes, it does.

I think of my body-sharing powers, and—

And Jed appears behind Corin's shoulder.

I cry out, jerk back. Corin lets go of me, turns, and—and Jed points at him. At Corin.

"No!" Jed says.

I freeze.

"Seven?" Corin's voice is full of alarm.

"You cannot be with him, S'ven. What are you doing? Get away from him."

My breaths come in tiny, pointy fragments, and my throat feels like it's getting thicker, swelling up with abrasions.

"What is it?" Corin says. And he looks at Jed, but I know he's not seeing him, and he's not hearing him either—I just know. I point at Jed, but Corin shakes his head. "There's nothing there. There's nothing in the room with us."

No. There *is*. Jed is there. Jed is very much there. But he can't be—he can't be real—he's... And I'm screaming those words, screaming them inside, but I can't get them out; they tangle on each other—the words are getting stuck, ensnared in me, caught, trapped.

Jed steps closer. There's a sense of darkness around him, darkness that builds into waves, waves that thrash about, thrash over me, try to drag me toward him.

"S'ven," he hisses. "Get away from him. Come to me. Come to me, *now*."

"Jed." I point again, but my hand's shaking, and my finger wobbles, and I can't hold it still. Jed's glaring at me, and the darkness is growing. "It's him... He's right...right there."

"Jed? Jed's dead, Seven. He's not here—there's nothing, no one here."

"S'ven. Get away from him. I will not ask you again."

I stare at Jed, and his words play over in my mind. He's here...but he's...a ghost?

He's trapped.

Jed's trapped and he's still after me, still won't let me be with Corin.

Corin steps toward Jed, and Jed makes a growling sound.

I grab Corin's arm, yank him back. He turns and looks at me, his eyes narrowing. Concern whirls within them.

"Are...are you seeing Jed a lot?" he asks, but now's not the time to talk—doesn't he realize that?

I keep my eyes on Jed, don't answer Corin—can't concentrate on him. Not when Jed's here...and I don't know what he really is, what he's capable of in this form.

"Seven?" Corin takes my hands, and I jump at the

touch and—

"*Get away from him,*" Jed snarls, runs at me. His body hits mine, makes contact and—

I scream, stumble back. He's solid, solid like before. And he's in here with Corin, and Corin can't see him, and Jed hates Corin and—

"Don't hurt him," I shriek. "Please! You can't hurt him!"

Something clicks somewhere, but I can't concentrate.

"Seven! It's okay, it's…" Corin's shouting, but I tune him out—got to focus on Jed, especially when Corin can't see him, can't see the danger he's in, can't—

Jed disappears.

Gone.

Just like that.

I stare at the place where he was. Then I turn around—look all around me. He can't have just gone.

But he has.

Like before.

Disappeared.

Vanished.

As if he was never here.

"Sev?"

Corin's looking at me strangely when I turn back to him. And then, behind him, the door opens.

Three appears, and he looks between us. Worry crosses over his face when he sees me, how I'm shaking.

"What's going on?" He turns and looks toward Corin—suspicious. "What did you do?"

"I didn't do anything," Corin says.

"Seven?" Three prompts.

I shake my head. "Corin didn't." And, still, I'm staring at the space where Jed was.

"I think it's time to go now," Three says.

My chest tightens. No. Can't be—not when….

"You'll let me see her again?" Corin asks, his voice hard. There's a strange look in his eyes—a desperate look. "You have to."

DIVIDED

After a moment, Three nods. "If I can."

"You will," Corin says, and it sounds like he's instructing Three. "You *have* to let me see her again, like this."

And then everything's happening so quickly, and it's only later when my brother drops me off back at my room that I realize I didn't tell Corin about my body-sharing power. Because Jed stopped me. Stopped me from telling Corin the little hope I have.

I curse Jed—petty, even in his afterlife.

But Three will let me see Corin again, won't he?

I nod.

He has to.

And then we can concentrate on the important thing: escape.

Escape and winning. Winning the war. Uniting the Untamed.

And escaping is the first step.

I need to tell Esther. She needs to be ready, ready for when it happens.

I lie on my bed. The mountain of energy in me is moving still, but it fills me, fills my body, fits me perfectly. The earth is mine, the trees are mine, the shrubs are mine.

I turn my mind over, breathing shallowly. I reach out for my Seer powers, for the body-sharing, and I see doors and locks. Faces swirl toward me. I step toward one door, in my mind, and I think of Esther.

I think of her, so I *become* her.

And it's so easy. It's part of me, and the strength of it fills me.

Snap.

THIRTY-ONE

DARKNESS. THE HUM OF A machine.

My chest hitches. I lie silently within Esther, stretched out, horizontal. I can feel how wide her eyes are, how she's shaking. She clears her throat and then clenches her fists.

And I marvel at just how amazing this power is. I'm so connected to her body that it feels like she is me, and I know I could control her movements easily, just like I did with Viktoriya.

The humming gets louder.

Esther's in a machine—I'm in a machine, with her. In her.

She's in a machine in the middle of the night?

Then I feel the pain. The torment she is in. Her left hip, how it's throbbing. And her fear. How she thinks the walls are going to get closer and closer and squeeze her into nothingness.

"Stay still," a voice—an Enhanced voice—says, but the words are loud, so loud, and there's something over Esther's ears, over my ears, that makes them louder…but different too.

The humming softens, but then a moment later,

turns into a more cacophonous sound. Louder this time. I flinch, make Esther flinch. Or maybe she does that on her own. She takes a deep breath, filling her lungs up.

Stay calm. Stay calm. Stay calm. Think of calm water. Her thoughts are loud—she's saying them to herself, in the same way that Viktoriya and I said things to each other.

Esther blinks several times. I feel the movement of her lashes as they lap against the skin under her eyes. A muscle in her foot twitches, and she inhales sharply as the movement jolts her hip. I feel the pain it causes, and her heart beats irregularly, feels light, fluttery. Her nausea makes me feel sick. Nausea—because she's pregnant? How far gone is she? I try to think, but I don't know.

Esther! I reach out to her, send my voice to her, inside her. *Esther, it's okay.*

Her body jolts around me. Her fists shake.

Esther, it's okay. It's me. Seven. I'm using my Seer powers...to check on you, to—

"Get me out of here." Her voice is small, but it doesn't matter. I feel every part of her fear, every part of—

"Five more minutes, then this scan will be complete."

Tears slide over her eyes. Hot tears. Saliva pools in her mouth, seeps under her tongue, and she moves her head sideways.

"Help me, Seven," she whispers. "Help me."

Esther. Just stay calm. It's okay. We're going to escape. We're going to find a way. We're going to get out of here.

My own heart pounds—in my body, my own body? Or Esther's? I'm not sure, just feel it, my own reactions—I think they're my own. Jumpiness, nervousness.

Esther, what's happening?

The humming drops in pitch, lower. Unease fills me.

"Get me out of here," she says again, so quietly.

"We will take you out when the scan is complete,"

the woman's voice says again. Headphones, Esther's wearing headphones. "Now stay still, else we will have to restart it."

Stay calm. Stay calm. Stay calm. She shudders.

Esther, just talk to me, but don't say the words. Just think them. I can hear your thoughts.

Telepathy? She sounds confused.

Yes, I can hear you. What's happened?

She swallows hard, and a bead of saliva trickles down her throat. Her chest swells as she coughs, and I gasp at the pain it sends through her hip. The woman's voice starts again, but Esther's coughing is too loud, too labored, and it fills me up—all the sensations— and I can't hear the woman's words.

At last, the coughing subsides. I think, back in my own body, my eyes are watering. I'm vaguely aware of my *own* body this time.

Esther, are you okay?

She nods, the slightest of movements.

"Keep still. We have to restart the last scan."

Quick breaths. Her heart pounds faster, faster, faster. So fast, we're both dizzy.

Seven?

I'm still here. I feel like I'm holding my breath, like I'm going to burst.

I hurt my hip, badly. They said they need to scan me again…that I might need emergency surgery…proper surgery, no augmenters yet. They scanned me before and… and said they'd wait until the augmenters were okay and… but it's got worse.

I frown. Surgery? Shit. *Esther, is it broken?*

I don't know. She sucks in a shaky breath.

How did you do it?

When they caught me. They… I was running. Fell, fell on a rock.

Her breathing quickens again, and, in her mind, I see the jagged end of a rock as it zooms toward us, hear a sharp scream.

The baby's okay. They said the baby's okay.

DIVIDED

I stay as still as possible. *Good. But your hip could be broken?*

Oh Gods. That's not what we want...not if we're going to escape. A broken hip can take months to repair.

Seven, what are we going to do? I heard them say they'll convert us soon. Esther moves her lips slightly, then presses them together.

We'll get out, I tell her, but, even as I say the words, there's a darkness within me. How can she escape when she's injured like that? The only quick fix would be the medical augmenters, but they're out of the question.

I try to think, but nothing comes to mind, and we're both silent.

At last, I break it.

Corin's here as well—did you know? They caught him again.

No. She inhales sharply, and we both cringe, wait for the Enhanced One to speak. But she doesn't. Esther breathes deeply. *Is he all right? Did they hurt him?*

And I—I didn't ask Corin, did I? I didn't check that he was all right...didn't ask about his capture.

He's fine, I answer. *We're going to get out. Just...just tell me where you are, Esther. This place is huge.*

In my 'fun' days, I never once came across any rooms or areas of the compound that seemed to house other Untamed. Raleigh—and all the Enhanced—was still careful.

I don't know. A cell usually. Don't know where this scanner is. They blindfolded me.

I grimace. *Any windows in your cell?*

Yes.

I feel an emotion that's very nearly envy sweep over me, and I have to pause for a moment.

Can you see out? I ask.

Yes. There's sand out there. It's far below, I'm high up—oh Seven! I want to see you. I'm scared. They're not letting me see anyone. Please, come and get me!

Esther, calm down. I don't know if I can get to you. But I can use my Seer powers to check on you like this. If that's okay? Your body, I can feel what you're feeling, and hear what you're thinking.

You're here, *in me?*

Yes. I'm here.

Will you always be here?

Not all the time. Just when I...check in. There are other Untamed out there, I've been contacting them...as best as I can. And then I freeze. Oh Gods. I shouldn't have told her that. What if she tells the Enhanced—or they torture the information out of her? *But you can't tell anyone, Esther. Do you understand? Raleigh doesn't know I can do this.*

I understand.

The humming gets louder again, more abrasive. I wince, and the hold I've got on Esther's body makes her wince too.

Sorry. That was me.

She's quiet—so quiet. And I can't hear her thoughts anymore. Have I lost that part of the connection? My eyes widen—hers widen. I'm connected still, but....

Check on Clare, Seven. They shot her.

Her words are strong in my head, her head. I try not to react bodily, try not to make her move.

What? I ask.

When they found us, out there... Clare stabbed an Enhanced, and another shot her. She was so still, so quiet in the truck on the way back...and no one will tell me what's happening with her, or if she's okay.

I breathe deeply. Shit.

Can you check on her now? Connect with her, like you have with me. See if she's okay?

I'll have to leave you to do this, Esther. Do you understand? I can only body-share with one person at a time.

Okay. Yeah. Do it. Her thoughts get faster. *Just come back as soon as you know.*

I take a deep breath and disconnect from her. The transition isn't as smooth, and pain jars through me.

DIVIDED

I wince, sit up, stare around at my room. My vision takes a moment to adjust to the light. And—

A pair of eyes watches me.

I turn, heart pounding.

It's the dog. My dog. I breathe out hard. Tiredness tries to pull me over, and I touch my temples gently, listen to the rhythm of my breathing.

Right. I need to concentrate. Need to find Clare.

I rub my eyes and lie back down. I think of Clare, picture her that last time I saw her, when she tried to get me out. She was wearing the blue overalls, but her Zharat color, violet, looks better on her. I let the violet color fill my head now. Picture her. Her whole body, tall, her blond hair, the fierce look on her face. How she has knives all the time, how she was one of the only women who stood up to Manning and the Zharat.

Fierce. Independent. Secretly plotting.

Yes... I'll kill him... They'll think it's another man's doin'. They won't know it's me.

I let her voice fill my head—those same words, over and over again.

With my mind, I reach out, look for her. I picture doors, so many doors, all old and falling down, and I push through them, watch the wood splinter. My hands shake as I reach for the next door—then the next. Keys overflow from my pockets, and voices fill the air. So many voices, so many eyes—Untamed eyes—all looking at me, looking at me through the doors.

I search for Clare's cool blue eyes. The fierceness in them. How she glares at people with them, and it's as if the people wither under her gaze. I let her image fill my mind, and I'm drifting toward a door. A very old door. One that's covered in cobwebs.

I touch the door, and—

Pain zaps through me.

I cry out, but the door falls down.

And there's nothing.

My eyes bolt open, and I look up. Darkness.

For a second, I think I've found her after all. But then, as my eyes adjust, I recognize my ceiling. The dog whines. Exhaustion pulls at me, but I try again and again. Try to find Clare, but each time it's the same: nothing.

Every now and then, in my room, I glance at the clock; its screen is just visible. Hours pass. The numbers move too quickly.

And I can't find her.

At last, I reconnect to Esther. She's no longer in the machine, back in a cell. A small room. A thin, scratchy blanket covers her, and I look up at the ceiling through her bleary vision. Her hip still hurts, but it's not too bad now, kind of numb. Painkillers? Or surgery already? I don't know what it would feel like after surgery.

I'm silent within her for a while.

Then I speak into her mind.

Esther? I couldn't find her. I couldn't connect with Clare.

She sits up, and we both gasp as her hip sends out new pain. Tears fill her eyes, and she wipes them away, presses too hard. Her eyes sting, and I wince.

She's dead, isn't she?

I feel sick. *No. It doesn't mean she's dead. I'm—I haven't been body-sharing for long. I might just not have been able to find her. I'll keep trying, Esther. I will.*

But when I get back to my own body, I don't keep trying. It's getting too early now—Raleigh could be along any moment. And I can't risk him discovering my powers. I'll have to search for Clare when I've got more time.

I close my eyes, and it's like something stirs inside me, because I know what to do. And, this time, I don't need to imagine my father instructing me. I trust myself.

I concentrate, search within me for the energies—my Seer powers—and I see them as gold threads and silver threads, spinning round and round a mountain. Some lead to the body-sharing doors that dot the earth like stone steps. Some lead elsewhere.

There's a darkness behind them, and I reach up with my mind, twist the threads together, securing them, fastening them to one another, trapping the doors together, against the earth. And then I reach into the void beyond the mountain, pull it down, pull it hard, pull it over. Because I know what to do.

Coldness douses me.

Are you sure?

I'm sure.

And I'm doing it all. The knowledge is within me. It's strange, eerie. I know what to do—exactly what to do, and I'm doing it—as if I've been taught, as if I've been told before. As if it's old knowledge.

An image flashes into my mind. I'm at a table, sitting under some trees. Old trees. And a woman—a woman who looks like my mother but is different as well—sits opposite me. She smiles widely.

Collect them soon.

I mark the space in the void with an energy only I know.

And when I'm back—when I open my eyes—I know they're no longer there. Like before, except it's my choice now.

I've sealed my powers away.

And I know Raleigh won't find them, but I still vow not to sleep for what's left of the night…just in case Raleigh comes back. Just in case he hooks me up to his machine again, just in case he gets a different reading.

THIRTY-TWO

THE NEXT MORNING, WHEN RALEIGH discovers I'm 'still' powerless, he's a picture of calmness. I stare at him, uncertain. We're in his office again, and he only exerts the smallest amount of control over me—an encouragement to sit quietly and eat the breakfast he gives me: tea and four mandazi. I have no doubts however that if I try to get up, he'll push me down much more forcefully.

"Still no powers then." He shakes his head, but his lips twitch in an odd manner that doesn't go with his voice. "Remarkable."

"No," I say, around a mouthful of rich mandazi. "Still no powers."

"Not to worry," Raleigh says, his voice strangely cheerful.

My eyes narrow, and I watch him carefully for any signs. My vision blurs with my lack of sleep and the huge amount of energy I used yesterday: visiting Viktoriya and Esther, trying to find Clare. And the shock of seeing Corin again. I am exhausted. But the food is helping.

"You were angry before—you said I'd better

have them back this morning," I say. "Now you're smiling...."

"Anger is a negative emotion. I wasn't angry. Just eager."

Eager?

He steps nearer, then stands over me. "Anyway, it isn't *your* fault, is it, Shania? It's this evil in you. But I have some good news."

My back cricks slightly. Painfully. I wait. And Raleigh obviously enjoys keeping me in suspense. He walks around his office twice, inspecting the dust on the windowsill and then rearranging the books on the shelf behind his desk.

"I never know how to organize them," he says, picking up a paperback and turning it slowly over. "Alphabetical by the author's last name or grouped by genre—alphabetical still, of course. But then what about my poetry... What do you think?"

"Just tell me what this good news is."

"Certainly. And there are two lots. Isn't that good, Shania?"

I wait as he places the paperback carefully on top of the bookshelf, stretching up high to do so. Then he turns back and beams at me.

"Firstly, my labs have created a prototype augmenter base that appears to be successful under the conditions stimulated by our tests. Adding the individual emotions also seems to be successful. We shall begin testing it on the Zharat under controlled conditions. If all goes to plan, we can convert you in no more than forty-eight hours."

He's smiling.

"Two days?" My voice comes out a little weaker than I would've liked.

"No more than forty-eight hours." His smile gets wider, so much wider, until it looks like he can't possibly be comfortable. "Isn't that great news? And today, my darling, the Section are here, and they want to meet you."

"The Section?"

"The other world leaders." He sighs. "Do you not remember that map? Come on, Shania. You have to do better than this. The leaders of the other six sections are all in this compound. Our meeting will start in half an hour. And we have just enough time to get ready."

He walks quickly to the cupboard in the corner of his office and opens the door. A moment later, when he turns back, he's holding some folded-up garments and a small white container.

"Hold out your hand," he says as he places the clothes on his desk, then opens the container.

My hand holds itself out, just as I knew it would as soon as he'd said the words. He didn't even need to say them.

Raleigh shakes out several white tablets into my palm.

"What are these?"

"They'll help you recover. From your grief," he says. "Prevent any hallucinations, any wild thoughts."

"I'm not grieving."

"You are." He gives me a stern look. "Dr. Andy has confirmed it—he wrote your case notes up last night, and we have agreed that this is the best course of action. You need them. We are still trying to secure the counselor. And I want you to take your first dosage now. Maria has kindly volunteered to see that you continue taking them."

Raleigh directs me to put the tablets in my mouth, and then hands me a glass of water. I try not to take it, try to drop it—try to spit the tablets out—but pain flickers through me. I wince as I swallow them, as he makes me swallow them, as if he's individually controlling all the necessary muscles in my mouth, my throat, my body. He probably is because I'm powerless against it.

"Good girl," Raleigh says. "Now, change into these clothes." He points at the folded garments on his desk. "And then we will be ready to greet the other section leaders."

There are eight of us at the table. Six unfamiliar Enhanced, Raleigh, and me. We're in a huge hall, and chandeliers hang from the ceiling. Their glass beads catch the light and refract it in multiple directions. It is disorientating, but spectacular.

Around the room, other Enhanced are standing. One is behind a podium, and he scribbles down everything that's said. The displaced leader of New Kitembu, Zahlia, smiles at me whenever I catch her eye, and each time I feel uncomfortable.

"So, this is the girl whom the augury speaks of? The one who will save us all—ensure that the Chosen Ones are victorious?" It is the man opposite me who speaks. He introduced himself as Karl, the leader of Section Six.

Next to me, Raleigh nods. "This is Shania Sarr. The seventh child born of Light. The Seer chosen by Death and given the divine powers that make her so special and powerful."

All the section leaders look at me, except for Raleigh. He just grins. Looks smug.

There's only one female world leader, and she wears a crisp red dress; her eyes narrow as she assesses me. Amber jewelry drips off her, from every available piercing and place. She said her name was Sophie, and she's from Section Four.

"She hasn't got a very good dress sense," Sophie says. "Poor child."

My lips twitch at the assessment of the tweed suit Raleigh picked out for me. What a shame she can't see the leather boots with stars and moons engraved on them.

"And what is the order of proceedings to be?" the man on the other side of me says. His voice booms. "Raleigh, I assume you have a plan and have made some process since you sent word that this girl was yours?"

Raleigh smiles. "Yes, significant progress."

Liar. My eyes narrow. Part of me wants to call him out, make sure the others know he's not in control. He can't even access my powers. But just as I'm about to speak, something jabs the side of my thigh.

I look down. Raleigh has a fire-poker.

And I know for sure he doesn't want the others knowing he can't access my powers anymore. A smile tugs at my lips, and I check that my powers are still hidden. They are. And he doesn't know that I got them back.

"And I hear you've caught many of Section Three's elusive Untamed from the Noir Lands," Karl says. "That's impressive. Or it would be if they'd actually been saved. It is my understanding that you're keeping them prisoner, allowing them to suffer?"

"We had a problem with our augmenters, which you are very well aware of, Karl." Raleigh's voice is smooth. "My captured Untamed were reacting to them. Severe reactions. We lost many of them because of it, so it is kinder to temporarily allow the Untamed evil to take hold while we sort out the situation."

"I've had no problem with mine." Sophie adjusts several of her amber bangles, and...and the way she does it, there's something about it that reminds me of Elia, and I stiffen. Just... I don't even know what it is, why I think of the girl. The dead girl. "My teams caught seven Untamed in the last week from the large islands, and they have not reacted. What about you, Akim?"

I freeze. Untamed, caught.

"I have only caught one, a woman," Akim says. "The spirits are wild in the Frozen Lands at this time of year, and it is harder to save those poor people.

DIVIDED

But the one I did save was fine. She's an astonishing mathematician and has a photographic memory."

The Frozen Lands. I try not to react. It doesn't mean the Untamed woman is from my group—Taras's group.

"So it would appear only *your* Untamed are reacting to augmenters?" Karl gives Raleigh a pointed look. "And it is only *your* section that is not saving anyone."

Raleigh clears his throat. "Perhaps my Untamed were exposed to something, in the Noir Lands, maybe. Spirit interaction—"

"There is plenty of spirit interaction in Section Five, is there not, Akim?" Sophie says. "And there are spirits in my section too. And Section One."

"Not as many," Raleigh counters. "Sections Three and Five have the most spirits, as you know, but Section Five's are contained in a larger area. The Noir Lands are the most concentrated area of both spirits and Untamed. Nonetheless, I have Shania, and she will save everyone—convert all the Untamed out there, from my section *as well* as Four, Five, and One. She will rid us of them all."

"And how is she going to do this? You mentioned significant progress earlier, but you failed to give details." It is another man who speaks. I think he said he was from Section Seven. Or Two. I can't remember. But he's from one of the sections that has no Untamed left in it. "I assume, Raleigh, that you have coded her powers and worked out specifics, created a few potential plans, assessed methodology?"

"I am working on that, and tonight we will discuss it further. We don't want to bore our savior, do we, with this talk?" Raleigh glances at me quickly, tight-lipped. Then he raises his hands, gesticulates widely. "Shania is very powerful, my friends."

Sophie leans forward. "What are her specific powers? Raleigh, we need details *now*. We need a timeline."

"Yes," Karl says, and he looks to the right, exchanges

a glance with Zahlia—a glance that I know Raleigh's noticed. Karl smiles. "We need to know that you're competent enough to lead your section and command Shania. Effectively, you would be in control of the entire population. Both of Untamed and us Chosen Ones. An overall leader. An important, but crucial, position."

"I can assure you I am competent," Raleigh says, glancing at me. "Like I said before, we have made significant progress, which I will update you on tonight."

I frown. That's twice he's talked about another meeting tonight—one I won't be at... My frown gets a little heavier. Logic tells me he can't have any plans he's keeping from me but wants to tell the Section, as he doesn't know my powers have returned. So, he must be trying to buy time, hoping that, by later today, I will have got my powers again, and that he can then give the Section concrete information.

I shudder, envision another torture session after this meeting.

Raleigh clears his throat. "For now, I will say that soon—*very soon*, mark my words—we will make a huge jump in such progress."

"Raleigh, I am assuming that—given your reluctance to answer my question and give us information regarding Shania Sarr's specific powers, that you do not yet know this information." Sophie raises her eyebrows, and the jewels pierced there sparkle like the chandeliers. "Am I right?"

Raleigh folds his hands carefully in front of him, on the table. "It takes time. Things like this cannot be rushed."

"But how much progress has been made?"

He glances at me, sideway. "We are on the verge of great progress, like I already said. I assure you this is true, and I will have impressive results to report to you, *very soon*." Raleigh smiles widely. "It *will* happen, I can guarantee that."

DIVIDED

"How can you say that without knowing her powers?" It is Zahlia who speaks, stepping forward on heels that clip-clop.

Raleigh visibly bristles. "I can assure you—all of you—that very soon I *will* know her powers. Very soon. Remember, I command Shania's soul—that is proof of how powerful I am."

"Your power isn't being questioned. Your competence is," Karl snaps. "If Shania had been in my section—not that I would've left any Untamed roaming free—"

"You do not have any spirits in your section though, Karl," Raleigh says. "Drones cannot easily or accurately detect life-signs if there are too many spirits about. Therefore, there are areas of my section that I cannot scan to locate the Untamed."

"Nonetheless, if Shania was in my section, I would already have found out what her powers are. And we would already be saving everyone. You're too lenient."

Raleigh laughs, a deep rumbling sound. "I assure you I am not too lenient."

"Have you had any sessions with her?"

"Of course. I can show you the results of her defensive powers. She can kill. She is a very proficient killer, as naturally she would be."

"Every Seer can do that," Karl says. "We're interested in what every Seer can't do. *Her* abilities. Raleigh, perhaps when it comes to the Renewal, a new leader for Section Three should be—"

"A new leader wouldn't command Shania's soul," Raleigh fires back. "And may I suggest that you take some Calmness? Your aggressive tone is not helping in the slightest."

I look to the side, see Zahlia smile.

"May I suggest that you remember what the priority is? To *save* the Untamed. You're stalling, and you're letting them suffer. You need to be firmer with Shania. You also need to get your augmenters fixed." Karl peers at me. "Dear, you know this is the right thing, don't you?"

I wrinkle my nose, start to open my mouth to say something—but the strangest feeling crosses over me. It's as if there are thousands of tiny fireworks in my body, going off. But they're so small, I can barely feel them.

One of the other men leans forward. "You'll be saving everyone, but you have to work with us."

"I am managing perfectly fine," Raleigh says. "Shania is under my control. And, believe me, when I make great progress with Shania's powers, you will regret having questioned me."

And then—then I feel it.

Something is wrong.

My powers. My Seer powers, they're pushing through the seal—the seal I made and—

Oh Gods?

Was I too exhausted? Didn't I seal them off properly?

Of course you didn't! You don't even know how, you haven't done it before! You didn't even know you could. And you haven't slept. How can you expect your seal to work? Why did you trust yourself to know?

But it felt like I knew, almost like I'd done it before—like I knew what to do. Old territory.

I breathe deeply, close my eyes for a second, try to hold the seal in place, keep it all together—and away. Away from me.

But the threads are unraveling, and earth's rising.

I open my eyes, my breathing heavy, and I see a door. A door, suspended in front of me. on the table, with the section leaders around it.

And they're still talking, they haven't noticed it.

It's just me who can see it.

Just like how I'm the only one who can see Jed.

Help me.

A lone voice. familiar, but...a woman...a woman I know. A woman who's in trouble. A woman who needs me.

My Seer pendant flashes hot, then cold, against my

skin where it's hidden.

And then there's darkness everywhere, a darkness that clutches at me, and I know I need my Seer powers—just *know*.

Save her!

The seal breaks.

Immediately, I'm pulled, tugged. Not me, but—my hands...someone's *pulling* me.

I look down at them, dizzy, disorientated. My hands are in my lap, still but....

This way!

The voice makes me jump, and—

Shit.

No.

I shake my head—and I'm pulled into another person's body.

And I know—just know—that Raleigh, or one of the Section, is going to notice, going to realize, going to know what I can do.

THIRTY-THREE

A LAKE STRETCHES OUT BEFORE me, frozen. The surface looks like marble, and white lines streak it, mark the turquoise mass below. To the right, the ice is broken—broken into a jagged mess, and the water moves. Behind, there's a bank—a bank opposite to the one I'm standing on—and I see people there. Viktoriya and Taras, others too. Men—more men I haven't seen before. All wrapped up, bundled. One carries a harpoon.

And the land is different—more trees, more wooded. A different part of the peninsula? I look to the right, and I see the reindeer. See them moving backward, their noses pointing up in the air, see others frozen to the spot, and some racing away, lichens still in their mouths.

I suddenly realize Viktoriya and Taras are screaming.

They're *all* screaming.

Chaos. Shouting. Everyone's shouting, and there's someone behind me. It's cold. Fur tickles my face, and the person I'm in takes a step forward. Don't know who it is—not Viktoriya, not….

"No!" someone screams. A man's scream. "She's

under the ice! Dominika's under the ice! She's fallen—"

I turn—take control, make whomever I'm in, turn. See Marina crying, screaming—her face red.

"Get her out!"

And then the person I'm in—the man, it's a man—he's running. He gets to the edge of the hole in the ice—and he kneels down. Cold ice grabs me, and I wince. A strange heat seeps through his knees.

He looks into the water—strangely blue, compelling—and it's so dark. So deep. Yet gray too. Sludgy, with ice crystals in it. He dips a hand in, and I feel the iciness of the water as if it's my own hand. I wince—make him wince. Or maybe he does it anyway.

He leans farther forward—leans right over. Oh Gods, he's going to fall in if he leans anymore... I get ready to exert control, to pull him back, but then he does so himself, turns.

"I can't see her!" he yells, and his voice reverberates through me.

And I can't see her either—I look as hard as I can through the man's eyes, trying to see Dominika, and—

I have to get her out.

That's why I'm body-sharing. Part of me knew this was happening? Because I'm connected to Viktoriya? And I made this new connection, so I could help, because this man's closer to Dominika than Viktoriya is, on the other bank... My eyes widen and—

"I can't swim!" the man I'm in yells. "Someone has to get her out!"

He can't swim?

I go cold.

The man I'm in *can't swim*.

Shit. If I can't take over his body properly and squash him out, and he gets control and panics and fights me—oh Gods. My heart pounds.

And his body's bigger than mine, heavier—heavier than what I'm used to, and Dominika is heavy too—how can I make this man swim *and* try and bring her up to the surface, to the—

"She's been under there too long! Her heart!"
Something clicks in me.
Dominika.

"Rope!" someone shouts, but I disconnect from the man, feel myself pulled back to my own body—*tug, tug, tug*—but I fight it, push off, and—

Cold water, ice, all around me.
Take control! Full control!

Pressure against my head, my body—my throat, it's being squashed, and pain, pain around my jaw, my neck, my chest. Dominika's body is heavy—we're sinking... And—and I can't feel her, she's not moving.

Her heart is....
Take full control!

Something buckles through me and—

I can't breathe, taste something sour. I thrash my arms and legs, but they're hers, and she's heavy. Short limbs, and—

And then her heart is my heart and it's beating and her lungs are burning, and I fight against the water, turn my head, look up. Pain nuzzles down my spine and back—lots of backache and—

The water's dark, hazy. I turn again, turning in the water, then I see a spot of dim light. But it's like a halo.

I push toward it, swim, swim as hard as I can.

But Dominika's body is heavier, cumbersome. I put all my effort in, barely make it any distance, and my head—dizziness pulls at me. Can't breathe—but I'm aware I should be, wherever my body is, I'm breathing, aren't I? Or if I die here, will I die completely? My death...my death's supposed to be important.

I'm sinking. My head pounds. Fabric floats around me, pulling away from the roundness of the body.

I look down. Heavy snow boots with metal and—
Shit.

I fight to pull them off, strain against the round stomach to reach my feet, to reach the boots, and—

I manage it, my lungs burning, burning, burning.

I shove all my energy into swimming—swimming

DIVIDED

with this body, this body that—

My head pounds harder. Lightness and—

Keep swimming.

I've got to get out. Got to get her out. And I know I shouldn't still be alive—that Dominika shouldn't be… not in this icy water…but Seer powers, it has to be.

I fight the water, and I'm getting closer, closer to that pool of light, the entrance to the world and—

A snake slaps down in front of me.

I freeze, suck in water, and—

A kavalah.

No. No. No.

Spluttering, choking, a bad, bad taste. Shut my mouth and—

My eyes are on fire and—

It's a rope, not a snake.

I grab the rope and kick out with my short legs, curse internally. Somehow, I manage to hold onto it, and—

My head bursts through the hole in the ice. Blurry figures, faces, hands reaching for me, hands that wrap around my short arms, hands that heave and pull me out. Shards of ice catch onto me, scratch me, and then…then I'm on the ice, lying there, grunting, shivering, and—

I fall back into my body. My own body. Pain and grunting. Cold, so cold, freezing, shivering and—

I look up, see Raleigh's face hovering above me. With other faces. So many other people—the Section, Zahlia, more Enhanced. And hands—Raleigh's hands are on my head.

I sit up, feel sick. Raleigh doesn't let go of me. I'm on the table, at the edge, and they're all looking at me. And—and there are wires attached to me. I look at my arm, see the wires sticking into my veins. I follow the wires to the machine. A similar machine as before, with a screen, except there's no chair, there's… No, I'm sitting on something on the table. A padded mat with sensors on and—

People are cheering.

Raleigh beams at me, then turns that beam to everyone else. "Did I not say that we were on the verge of new progress? Did I not say that I had a significant update for you that I would share at our meeting later today, where *only* section leaders would've been present?" His eyes narrow at Zahlia for the smallest of seconds.

Then Raleigh smiles—smiles like he knew this would happen. But we both know it's a lie. He was trying to buy time—avoid admitting in this meeting that he didn't know a thing.

And now this has happened. Now he knows I can body-share.

Shit.

Raleigh lifts his arms above me; I've never seen him so happy. "And how wonderful of Shania to demonstrate it now for you," he shouts. "So here we have it. Shania Sarr is a body-sharer who, remarkably, has the potential for *unlimited* universal connections. And that, my fellow Chosen Ones—*that* is how she will win the war and wipe out the Untamed."

THIRTY-FOUR

FOR A MOMENT, THERE'S SILENCE.

"Unlimited universal connections?" Zahlia peers at me. "An infinite body-sharer?"

"Yes," Raleigh says, and he points at the machine's screen.

"That's impossible. Body-sharing bonds can be made to a maximum of two hosts. No more than two."

"But she is the key to the Untamed. A master body-sharer who fits them all. The reading indicates it—that is the code for *unlimited*. Shania hasn't just got the capacity to forge bonds with one or two. She can connect to *all* of them."

I squirm, try to move off the mat with the sensors, but Raleigh holds me in place. So I try to seal my powers off, stop them from monitoring them—only I can't.

I can't do it.

It doesn't work. Shit. Why? I look down, my hands are shaking. I'm too jumpy, too much adrenaline in me. Need to be calmer to do it.

Sophie points at Raleigh. "Who did she go to? An Untamed, I assume? But which?"

"I—I…" Raleigh turns, looks at me. "Who did you go to?"

My eyes widen. He doesn't know. He's supposed to have my soul—have my eyes—yet he doesn't know. Couldn't see? Can't see through my eyes when I'm body-sharing…because they're not my eyes. They belong to other Untamed.

And the machine didn't tell them who it was?

"*You* didn't go with her," Karl says, and he says it triumphantly, points at Raleigh, a vicious look taking over his face. "Nor do you know who she went to. You're supposed to be in charge of her soul. Is body-sharing too powerful an ability for you to follow her when she goes off? Are you too weak for this, Raleigh?"

"I *tried*," Raleigh says. He casts a withering glance at me. "But it was shut off to me. I could tell *what* was happening—but not *where* she was going, or *who* was hosting her."

"But body-sharing, that is a rare talent," Akim says, and the section leaders either side of him nod. "It is not unlike your command over Shania, Raleigh—except that you had to have her soul bound to you. Yet it seems that Shania can connect with anyone, anywhere, regardless of whether she has *their* soul. She just has to make the connection to the individual."

"Such a great power," Sophie says. "And it will save us."

"Bring up all the information we have on body-sharing," Raleigh says, and then a virtual display appears in the air next to me, and tiny text fills it. All the Enhanced lean toward it, toward me, automatically, and silence descends as they read.

I try to look too, but my eyes don't feel right, and I keep thinking the text is moving. And the font's too small for me.

The next few minutes pass in a blur of talking as information is processed. They're all making plans with Raleigh, with each other. Plans for me, working

DIVIDED

out how I'm going to use this power.

"If she shares their bodies, then she *becomes* them. For the time when the power is active, their body becomes her body."

"What about the mind?"

"A body-sharer forges a connection with their host mind's too. A permanent channel, if you like. One that does not rely on soul control, so it does not take too much energy. Shania will house hundreds of channels within her, once she's dug the initial route to each Untamed who is still out there."

"It means keeping her Untamed though—even once the augmenter problem is solved," Zahlia says. She points to the screen. "Marta's Lore indicates that body-sharing is a Seer power that cannot maintain a viable connection between an Untamed and a Chosen One. If an Untamed body-sharer is converted, he or she can no longer connect sufficiently or at all to their Untamed hosts as those pathways would fall in, a restriction placed on the Seer by the spirits and Gods and Goddesses. The only way for the bond to work again, would be for the host to also be converted."

I chew on my bottom lip. Was that why the first few times when I body-shared it didn't last for long? Wasn't a sustainable connection, because I was being converted...and trying to connect to the Untamed?

"So, Shania will remain Untamed, breeding evil?" Karl asks.

"Shania will be under my control. And soon, it will all be over." Raleigh smiles. "And this is the progress I knew was coming. My new augmenters are nearly ready. I can convert the Untamed prisoners we have here—with the exception of Shania, now we know she must remain Untamed for her to connect with the hideaways out there." He raises his hands. "And now we know her amazing power, we know how the Untamed will end. Shania will forge connections with *all* the Untamed we've not been able to catch. I will use my powers to *ensure* this happens. She will then body-share with all the Untamed, dominate all of them, and during it we shall convert her—both with augmenters and the *most* powerful mind-conversion, and I shall also use my powers on her mind—and the connection will mean she converts everyone she is controlling at that moment."

I feel everything inside me freeze.

"I haven't got any control over it, or who I connect to," I say. "I can't connect to *everyone*."

"Nonsense," Raleigh says. "You'll learn."

Karl clears his throat. "But connecting with so many Untamed would destabilize her, fracture Shania into too many pieces. She would lose control of one individual as soon as she entered another. You cannot body-share with more than one person at the same time. Marta's Lore reports that a body-sharer tried to connect to both of his hosts at the same time and it divided him, destroyed his mind before he even connected. Shania will *not* be able to connect to all the Untamed at the *same* time *and* have them all converted through her."

"But she will," Zahlia says. "Shania Sarr will be able to connect to multiple Untamed if she has a Seer to anchor her—a Seer she is related to whom is also of great power."

Raleigh smiles. "And I have one."

At that moment, my mother enters the hall.

THIRTY-FIVE

RALEIGH CANNOT STOP SMILING. "MOTHER and daughter. And you're both mine. Two very powerful Seers. Go on, Shania. Hug your mother. I do so love reunions."

I start to get up, at last able to move from the sensor-mat, but my mother shakes her head. She sits at the side of the room. Raleigh still tries to make me climb off the table, but I resist, my eyes on my mother. At last, after what seems like several minutes, he gives up.

The room around is silent.

"Glad you could join us, Katya," Raleigh says, then he turns back to the Section. "Allow me to introduce Katya Sarr, Shania Sarr's mother. As soon as I knew the augury, I believed Shania would need an anchor, whatever her conversion powers turned out to be. Upon learning that her mother also had Seer powers, I guessed the anchor would be Katya Sarr…a familial connection is always best. And it was just my luck when she gave herself up to us, that I did not have to pursue her too. Then, I knew it was only a matter of time until I had the two of them. And we have been training Katya's mind, creating an even stronger anchor. Additionally, Katya herself is useful. A Seer of Light sees far, and she has unfulfilled visions from her time as an Untamed individual. My men report that we are close to learning what those Seer visions were of." He smiles widely. "And so you see, we have all the necessary components to save the Untamed. An unlimited body-sharing powerful Seer and an anchor Seer to stabilize her and prevent fracturing."

There's a slight cheer.

"We really are close to succeeding," Raleigh says. "Just as I promised earlier." He looks at me. "I wanted to tell you without Shania present, given the darkness in her. Didn't want her getting distressed. But after that demonstration, how could we not talk about it?"

I grit my teeth. He's lying. He hadn't a clue—and I'm sure it's evident to the others in the way he was lapping up the information about body-sharing and constructing a plan *with* the Section for the end of the Untamed, not sharing one he'd already made.

"I think we're forgetting one thing," Karl says. "Harnessing that amount of power, and dividing herself so many times to body-share with such a vast number of Untamed—let's not forget that we believe there to be around four hundred in the wild—would have negative effects on Shania. Katya may be able to anchor her daughter and pull each piece of her back during the process, thus completing the initial conversions of so many Untamed—"

"Of course she will," Raleigh says, "Katya is a Seer of Light. Very powerful."

"But Katya could not hold her daughter together forever. A few hours at most, until the first stages of the conversions are done, and then Katya would have to let go, else *she* would die. And letting go would mean her daughter would fracture. It would kill Shania," Karl says, and his mirrors show the world how scared I look. "She would be too unstable after harnessing such great power, and her body would no longer take it."

Raleigh shrugs. "We know, though, that Shania will die. It is the only way the war will end." He nods, turns, looks at me. "Before you die, you'd need to direct all the Untamed to the nearest compounds, we don't want them wandering around for days, lost, trying to find us, possibly getting eaten by predators."

I look toward my mother for help, but she's not looking at me. And I don't understand why she's here. She hasn't said anything.

I strain my neck, trying to see her. Is she being controlled? Are the augmenters stopping her from wanting to look at me?

"How soon can we start?" one woman asks.

Raleigh turns to me. "As soon as Shania has developed a connection with *each* Untamed individual out there."

"So they're all to be converted in one go? Wouldn't it be easier to do it in stages? Or one-by-one, less dangerous for Shania if simultaneous body-shares will destroy her?"

Raleigh shakes his head. "No. Marta's Lore. If we did that, we'd have to wait a long time after each conversion until Shania was completely Untamed again before she could connect with the next one to save them—and there's no guarantee that she would even become Untamed again, that the darkness *would* return. Certainly not for over three hundred times. It's too big a risk. It has to be every Untamed in one go. And we have to make sure it's *all* the Untamed at once, none left behind, because yielding that amount of power would kill Shania in the end—even with her anchor. Were you not listening? We have one shot with this, and we have to wait until she's connected to *everyone*. We have to do it in one go."

It's going to kill me. Raleigh's going to kill me.

And you'll return to Death, just like you're supposed to. Just like you knew you would.

I gulp.

"How long will that take?" another voice asks.

My head spins, and I miss the answer.

"I've got DNA models and photos. Even belongings of some who are in my section," Sophie says, and then several others say they have extensive records too.

"Perfect. Shania and I will go over them shortly." Raleigh stands up. "And I think, my people, that you will agree that this has been a very successful meeting." His head turns to Karl. "You cannot declare me incompetent."

My eyes narrow. It wasn't Raleigh who made this progress. It was me. Me knowing I had to save Dominika's life. But for how much longer?

Once I've changed out of the tweed suit and leather boots, Raleigh has two women strap me up to the chair with the wires again and take more readings of my Seer powers. I try to lock them away again—but my head hurts too much. I'm just too tired, and I still can't do it. I should've slept before, after I'd disconnected from Esther. I was on my own then. Raleigh didn't come for me until the morning.

I should've slept.

I curse.

Or—or what if I can never seal them off again?

The women reel off several numbers, and one of them clicks away at a computer.

"Most are uncoded," the woman says. "No obvious pattern. Except for the unlimited body-sharing. But there are other patterns repeating—ones that haven't come up before, not with such clarity and vigor. She's strong, and these other powers are unknown."

Behind the women, Raleigh stands with his legs crossed at the ankles, and his arms limp by his sides.

DIVIDED

He's smiling.

"I'll have Tomas check the results for any previously identified patterns and codes," he says. His voice drips. "Your brother is very good with numbers."

I ignore him. "I want to see my mother."

"Katya is only visiting, Shania."

"I *want* to see her."

"If you are a good girl, you can see her before she returns to New Kimearo."

I grit my teeth, speak through them. "I want to see her now."

"Careful, Shania. You're sounding like a whiny child. You don't want to sound like that, do you?"

One of the women steps forward and unstraps me from the chair, pulling the wires back with ease—the wires that had held me in place and refused to move for me.

The moment I get out the chair though, Raleigh exerts control over my body. I start to fight him, then stop. I need to save my energy.

Raleigh beams at me, then he straightens out my shirt. It's one I chose, a fitted button-up one that's dark green. I grit my teeth as he pulls at the hem, tries to pull the creases out.

"Come on," he says, cheerfully.

I follow him out the room and to a large conference room. There's a big table in the center, and photographs have been neatly stacked in several piles around the edge of the polished wooden top.

Raleigh instructs me to sit, and I do.

"We know the names of these individuals, but not those." He points at several piles of photographs on the table, moving his hand quickly, as he stands over me. "Those ones are more elusive. Properly wild. And we're guessing that there are probably more women and children with these men than the ones we know about. But, as soon as you're connected to one in that group, you can give us the updated numbers."

My neck clicks, and I fold one leg over the other,

stare at my skin. A gold splash peeks out from under my beige shorts. I lift that leg up, stretch it out, see another gold splash around my ankle that disappears under my white and gray tennis shoe.

"And we've got DNA models for approximately two-thirds of these Untamed. Now, we don't know how quickly you'll naturally make new body-sharing connections, and we cannot let these people suffer for long, so stimulating a connection between your mind and the minds of others is vital to speed up the process. There are two groups of people I believe you'll connect to more easily—those you're close to and those who are Seers. Now, that first group, well, you don't need to connect to them. I've already got them, and they'll be converted as soon as the augmenters are ready." Raleigh points at a third pile of photographs. Underneath each photo, someone has written *Seer* in bold letters. "So, you need to connect to the other Untamed, the ones we haven't got. And I want to start with the Seers. Go on, have a look and see if you can find them, forge the connections."

No. I can't! Can't make any more connections—not to any of them. Any who I connect to, I'm signing their death warrant. Not death but....

Oh Gods.

Raleigh encourages my hand to move forward, and I splay the photos out on the table, looking from one to another. Unfamiliar Untamed faces. Then I see Taras.

I inhale sharply, look up at Raleigh.

"Where'd you get these photos?"

"Security cameras and CCTV in our towns and cities."

My eyes linger on Taras's face.

"You know him?" Raleigh peers at me.

I shake my head, but my ears feel hot.

"You're lying. Lying is bad. Come on, Shania. You may be Untamed for now but you have to at least try." He sits down next to me, leans in too close. He picks up the photo of Taras and looks at it for a long few

DIVIDED

moments. "Have you already body-shared with this Seer? He's in the Frozen Lands, Section Five. There's no way you could've met him in person."

I press my lips firmly together, keep them sealed.

"Was he the one you were body-sharing with earlier, during the meeting? Come on, Shania. You can tell me."

I ignore him, look at the other photos.

"It was him, wasn't it?" Raleigh says. "Excellent. We can cross him off the list. You've already got a connection with him."

Raleigh takes out a pen and puts a giant red tick next on the border of Taras's photograph. "Are there any others you've already joined with?"

I glare at him, don't even look at the card. "No."

"Or any non-Seers?"

"No."

"Very well," he says, and I don't know whether he believes me. Then he picks up five of the other Seer cards and pushes the others away. His clothes rustle as he spreads out the new cards in front of me. "Pick a card."

He makes me turn my head toward them, and my eyes scan the images briefly. Three women and two men. All Seers. And the men—Zharat. I recognize them instantly. The ones who are still out there—must be.

"Pick one, Shania."

I look away from them, up at the wall, where the clock is. Manage to hold my gaze there for a few seconds before Raleigh takes control.

He scoots his chair closer to me. "How about this one?" It's the photograph of the oldest female Seer. "Yes. We've got a DNA model for Eberly Nicholson and information pertaining to the frequency of her Seer powers. Now, we have a machine that'll help your Seer powers search for specific energies given off, yet it will take time to calibrate successfully. But, I don't think you need that. I think it's all inside you.

You're powerful. So, let's try this now."

He stares at me expectantly.

"Connect with her."

"I can't *control* the body-sharing," I tell Raleigh, hope that my voice doesn't sound too high-pitched. "I can't just do it like that. It just happens. I haven't got control over it." The lie feels like it's burning me.

Raleigh's face is pensive for a moment. "Nonsense. You can learn to control it. It's like anything. Riding a bike. It takes time to learn. And what better way is there to learn, than to practice?"

"It's not like riding a bike—you don't suddenly find yourself doing that with no warning. I told you, it's unpredictable." My face flushes, and I'm sure he knows I'm lying: it's only unpredictable *at times*.

"But once you learn, you'll never forget it." Raleigh smiles. "You have to believe in your powers."

But I *mustn't* body-share with anyone else. I'd thought it was my advantage—a clue as to how I was going to unite the Untamed, just like what Taras said—but, if each time I body-share, a new connection is formed that Raleigh will later make me use to destroy my people, then I'm paving the way to the end of the Untamed.

"So," he says. "Are you going to willingly try and connect, or am I going to make you do it? Make sure that you're trying."

My eyes narrow. "*You* can't body-share."

"I can't. No. That is a fact."

I fold my arms, and he makes me unfold them. I glare at him. "So, you can't control my body-sharing powers."

And I'm onto something—I'm sure of it.

Raleigh laughs. "I am a powerful Seer. Adaptable. I may not have the power myself, but I can use someone else's if needed."

I fold my arms again. "But they said at the meeting that an Enhanced can't body-share to an Untamed."

"A Chosen One apparently can't. But I wouldn't

DIVIDED

be using *my* Seer powers to body-share. I'd be using yours. And there'd be no problem. You're Untamed."

"Well I can't just do it. And neither can you."

"Let me have a look," Raleigh says.

"No!" I cry, but he seizes my head with his hands, and then I feel him there.

He probes around, digs deeper. I flinch. Oh Gods. Oh Gods. *Oh Gods.* I start to reach up, to seal the powers away, but then stop—what if he finds them because of me trying to do that? What if I show him where they are, give him exactly what he needs?

"Don't close up the channels, Shania. Let me have free access." His voice is soft, strangely melodic. "Let me explore, find the right power. Just relax, my darling."

I take a stuttered breath, then feel my shoulders soften a little, less tension. Because of Raleigh—because he's making me do it.

"Close your eyes," he whispers.

No. I force them open wider, despite the sudden pain in them—but only manage it for a second.

My eyes close. Darkness.

"Good girl."

"*No, S'ven. Don't—*"

My eyes spring open, and there's a fresh wave of pain. I flinch and try to move forward—

Something clicks in my head.

"No," Raleigh shouts.

Then something hits my chest, and I fall back against the chair and—

Jed.

Jed's right in front of me, crouched on the table's edge, his hands stretching forward, touching me.

Not Raleigh.

I scream, pull back—pull back from Jed's hands—and manage to stand up, kick the chair between Jed and me.

"Get off! Get off me!"

"Shania!" Raleigh's voice—but I can't see him.

"*S'ven, stop it!*" Jed yells and his voice is different. Echoing and hissing at the same time—and it twists around me. And—and it can't be real. Just can't. He can't be, but....

His hands fly toward me.

I scream again, turn, and run—

Raleigh grabs me—he's here too. Shit. Father and son.

I cry out, and Raleigh shakes me. My vision blurs and I try to turn.

"Get him away from me!" I cry, pointing at Jed.

"*S'ven, stop it. Stop behaving like a child. I am trying to help you.*"

"Who?" Raleigh demands.

"Jed!"

Raleigh makes a deep sound in his throat as he looks around. As he looks right at Jed.

But he doesn't see him.

How doesn't he see him? My heart pounds.

"You're not well," Raleigh says.

"Not well?" I cry. "You're the one who can't see Jed!"

"This has been too much for you. I should've realized. You've body-shared once today. You're tired. Worn out. We will wait until you are well again to use your Seer powers. Give them time to strengthen again too. That will be best."

My vision wavers again, darkness creeping at the corners.

Dizziness tugs at me, and I stumble, fall, and—

Elia rises up, laughing. And it's her too—she's here as well.

"I'm sorry," I whisper.

And then there's no more.

THIRTY-SIX

I OPEN MY EYES, GROGGY, disorientated.

Dr. Andy peers down at me. "She has revived. The Untamed are prone to faints. It's all the negativity within them, gets them too worked up."

"She says she saw my son." Raleigh's voice is cold, and I see him watching me from the other side of the room. He turns toward Dr. Andy. "I want your best psychiatrist to assess her as soon as possible. I know I referred her before—but she needs to be seen quickly. These hallucinations are not good. They are bad. Negative. *Some* Seers are prone to psychosis. And I cannot have Shania developing any…anything that would slow down our progress." He paces the room for a few moments, then stops, his hand on the door handle. "I have work to do. I will have her brother come here. Stay with her until Tomas arrives."

And then he's gone.

So quickly.

Dr. Andy and I watch each other for a long, long time. He makes *humph* noises at the back of his throat every so often, and gets me some toast and water from a side-kitchen. The main room we're in isn't his office. It's a big room, with a locked door. No friendly, welcoming vibes here.

And, when my brother arrives, a couple of hours later, Dr. Andy leaves as quickly as he can.

"Are you okay?" Three asks. "You've had a stressful day, and your Seer powers exhausted you."

I shrug.

"Raleigh believes you're having a…a breakdown. He mentioned you've been hallucinating."

I shake my head. "No. Jed was there. I know what I saw. I've seen him before."

"Raleigh's son?" Three looks uncertain.

"Yes," I snap, then rub at my head. There's slight pain in my temples, nothing too bad though. "Raleigh's son. My fiancé. Whatever you want to call him."

Three's eyes get wider.

"What?" I look him up and down when he doesn't look away.

"*Fiancé?*" Three stares at me, aghast.

"You didn't know?"

"I thought you were with Eriksen." Three says the words carefully, but there's a hardness to his words.

"I wasn't with Jed *by choice*," I say. "It was the Zharat—their rules. Oh Gods. How can you not know this? It was Jed. All Jed. All of this—he gave me to Raleigh."

But it wasn't his fault.

Three lets out a strange breath. Not shaky, but not calm either. "Fiancé…" He shakes his head. "Not with him *by choice*… Did he hurt you?" He leans closer. "*Seven?*"

"No," I say. "Not like that."

"Like what then?" Three moves a little closer.

I grimace. Jed hit me before—because I tried to save Kyla, the little girl they killed for being a Seer. He manipulated me, scared me, controlled me. And then he bound me to the Enhanced, giving my soul to Raleigh.

I wrinkle my nose, look around for a moment, and

DIVIDED

then get up, ignoring Three's question. "Where's Mum?" I ask.

Three watches me carefully. "She'll be at New Kimearo, where she's stationed. Look, Seven, if this man hurt you in any way—"

I cut him off, my shoulders sagging. "She's gone back there already?"

My mother's left...gone without even seeing me properly...that fleeting glance, all that I had of her. And she's just gone.

Your mother's gone....

Three's eyes get bigger. "Gone *back* there?"

I let out a frustrated exclamation. "She was here, Three—Mum was here...earlier, the end of the meeting with the Section, she was there." I march toward the door. It's locked, but Three will have a key. "I need to see her. Come on."

And it's the one thing I know for certain now: I need to see her, talk with her. And she has to still be here. She wouldn't leave without seeing me. And... I pause. I can *sense* her... I frown, concentrating. My Seer powers? But, suddenly, I'm sure she's still nearby. Not gone back to New Kimearo yet.

And my mother will know what to do.

But she's one of them too.

No. She's not. Not really.

Three grabs my arm. I turn and look up at him.

"She didn't tell me...and Raleigh didn't tell me Mum's here either," he says, his voice loaded. "Why wouldn't they tell me?" He shifts his weight slightly, then looks conflicted.

"Doesn't matter." I shake my head. "We can go and find her now."

"Oh." Three looks at me, then down at his feet. His grip on my arm begins to feel sweaty.

"What?"

"I was going to let you see Eriksen again...now... Raleigh's busy for the rest of today. It's a good opportunity. And...and I know you both miss each other."

My chest tightens a little. *Corin*.

"Okay," I say. "But I need to see Mum first."

Three's grip on my arm tightens. "We don't know where she is."

My eyes narrow. "We'll find her. This compound can't be *that* big."

Three breathes out heavily. "It is big. And I—wouldn't it be easier to see Mum another time? *If* she is here. You don't have to see her in secret. But you do with Eriksen. And now is the perfect time to see him. There aren't many opportunities, you know."

I rock back onto my heels and look at my brother, my eyes narrowing even more. "You *want* me to see Corin?"

"He wants to see you," Three says. "He made it very clear what he'd do if I didn't arrange another meeting for the two of you."

Corin *wants* to see me. A jolt of hotness runs through my body. And, if we're together, we can sort out this mess.

Three lets go of me, folds his arms. "Look. You're not due any other checks from Dr. Andy just yet. If I take you to Eriksen, you can stay there, with him." He breathes deeply, makes a strange gulping noise. "And I'll find out where Mum is. Then when I collect you, we'll know where to go."

"What if she's not staying that long?" I shake my head, watch my brother carefully. Very carefully. "It would be easier if we found her first and you took me to Corin after."

He looks conflicted, and the expression doesn't sit well on him. After a second or so, he straightens up and looks me straight in the eye. I try not to look at myself in the mirrors.

"There's no point in wasting time," he says. "It'll take me a while to track Mum down here—she could be in any of the regions now. And I need to do it subtly. Raleigh hasn't told me she's here for a reason. I don't want him to get suspicious. I'll find her, while you're with Eriksen, and then I'll come and get you. No arguments, Seven."

No arguments. His words ring in my ears.

I eye my brother carefully. Something's not right. The Enhanced part of him's taking more control? But no—he's going to take me to Corin, put two Untamed together.

"Okay," I say slowly. "Unlock the door."

Corin hugs me tightly, and I lean in closer to him. I'm shaking now, but Corin's arms are an unshakable cage. After a moment, he pulls back slightly from me, looks at Three. His Adam's apple bobs a little.

"You're *sure* Raleigh doesn't know about this?" Corin asks.

Three nods, curt. "I'm sure."

"I don't want her being punished." There's a hardness to Corin's voice that makes me gulp. "Not for this. Not for us being together."

"She won't be," Three says. He grips his hands together tightly in front of his stomach, and a strange look passes over his face as he assesses Corin. Corin and me together.

It makes me feel peculiar, standing so close with Corin, while my brother's watching. But it was what Three wanted. He was insistent. And it was how insistent he was that makes me squirm. Something's really not right.

Three shifts his weight. "*But,*" he says, looking at Corin. "I'm not exactly happy with this arrangement. So you better look after her, *Eriksen*. If I hear anything from Seven—anything at all that she's not happy with—I'll come after you. Understand?"

I pull back to see Corin nod, looking strangely amused.

"I mean it," Three warns, his voice low.

And I stare at him, try to fathom him out.

"I understand," Corin says. "You can go now."

Three glares at him for a long time, but then he leaves. Leaves me and Corin alone. In here. Again.

"What's been happening?" Corin says, drawing me closer again. He tucks my head in, against his chest, and his stubble grazes my forehead. His arms lock around me.

I let out a long breath. "Did Three seem different to you?"

"Well, he's...Enhanced. He's not going to be the same as he was when he was Untamed."

I shake my head against him. "No. I mean today. Just now. Different to before. There's something... He's acting strangely."

Corin shrugs. "Seems like the same old annoying Three Sarr to me. Overly protective as well. Did you hear him threaten me?" But he says the words in a way that makes his voice dark, almost sexy.

I frown, try to think. I pull back a bit. My eyes fall on a bottle of water by the wall. They give Corin bottles of water when he's locked up? "My mother's here," I say, "and I wanted to see her, but Three was insistent I came here instead."

"I'm glad." Corin's voice is breathy, hot air against my ear. Then his lips press against my ear lobe. He kisses me there. "Very glad. I've missed you, Sev."

My heart stutters, then I pull back again. "But Raleigh didn't tell Three that our mother's here. Three didn't know." I stare up at Corin.

His expression slowly changes, gets more serious. "What are you thinking?"

"What if..." I shudder. "What if Raleigh's onto us?"

"You and me?" Corin's eyebrows shoot up. "No. He can't be. He would never let two Untamed be together."

DIVIDED

"No, *all* of us. Three, included. I think he's still Untamed. At least partly... He's letting us see each other when that's not allowed." More than letting, more like instigating it. "And he gave my pendant back." I mull it over. Could I have been right about that the first time—that it was a sign of resistance? I pull the crystal out from under my shirt, then let it hang freely. The dark green of my top gives the crystal a darker glow. Corin's eyes widen, but I continue. "What if Raleigh suspects that Three's still Untamed, or partly Untamed...and he might suspect the same thing with my mother too, and that's why he didn't want him knowing she was here. In case they came together and made a plan or something."

Corin frowns. "A plan to get us out?" But then he shakes his head. "But if Raleigh suspects Three, then he wouldn't let him see you, or any Untamed. He could just as easily make plans with *you* to escape."

I process his words. "So why else wouldn't he tell Three that our mother's here?"

Corin's arms tighten around me, and then his fingers exert pressure against my back. "Who knows what that man thinks? He's one of them, Sev. They're not rational. Maybe he likes the power of it, knowing he's keeping people in the dark."

I nod slowly, then breathe in Corin's scent. He smells different, though, without the cigarette smoke. I lean my head against his chest again, wonder how long it'll take Three to find our mother. But when he does come back, we've got to get out of here, I know that. Me, Corin, Three, my mother, and Esther—somehow. If Raleigh *does* suspect Three, then my brother's in danger.

But Three's not Untamed, he won't come willingly.

But he's not fully Enhanced either. He can't be. I'm sure of that. He's my brother. Sarr blood.

But not a Seer.

I look up at Corin. "We need to make a plan, have it ready. We need to get out of here."

"Get out?" He looks surprised. "Sev, I don't know if you've noticed, but we're locked in here."

"My brother will help...and if we're right, he could be in danger. Plus, the augmenters will be ready soon. We've got to get out before that happens."

And we've got to get out *before* Raleigh makes me connect to all the Untamed out there. If I've got the pathways dug, then all it takes is for him to make me use the bonds and convert me.

Corin nods, and a muscle in his jawline pulses. His hands find mine, and our fingers entwine.

"He can't make me find the others who are out there," I whisper.

"Make you find the others?" Corin's head jolts a little. "You can find others?"

"I think so." I take a deep breath, realize he doesn't know. And so I tell him about my body-sharing abilities, how I can share with more than two people, and how the Section knows and wants to use me. I don't tell Corin about body-sharing with *him* though—something stops me; he wouldn't like it. I know that.

Corin lets go of my hands and touches the base of his neck slowly, then rubs the skin there. It looks redder than normal, rougher. Like he's reacted to something. "Okay. So you can *choose* to go in other people's bodies?"

I shrug, stepping back slightly. "I don't know how it works. At first, it was by accident. But now? Now I know how to do it. It just sort of clicked, and it feels familiar. Like I instinctively know how to do it. But the last time was a surprise too—unexpected, like I got pulled there. But it was a life and death situation."

I breathe deeply, and I feel the powers within me. They're there, but they're worn out. Exhausted. I used a lot of energy earlier to save Dominika—more than ever before? And I try again now, to seal them off, but it's still the same. I can't do it. Need to replenish them first?

"So you've got control over it?" Corin leans in closer.

DIVIDED

I nod, fold my arms, but then stretch them out. My elbows feel strange. "I suppose so. Yeah." I exhale hard. "That's why we've got to escape. Raleigh thinks I can't control it, but it's only a matter of time before he knows, before he makes me form more connections and send the Untamed into a grave."

Corin nods, then walks to the door. He tries the handle, but of course it's locked.

"When Three comes back," I say. "That's when we've got to get out."

"And you think Three's Untamed too?" His voice sounds strange. "He'll help us?"

"I'm certain of it." I breathe deeply, hope I'm right. "He's not like the others. I mean, he's my brother, but...but I resisted. I know my mother can, so it could be familial." Only, as soon as I say those words, I think of what my father said. No, what my mind made me think my father said. I think hard. "And Three wanted us together—what if it was his way of telling us to make a plan—the exact thing Raleigh doesn't want?" I nod, and I know I'm right. "So, when Three arrives and opens the door, we'll escape."

Corin runs his hands through his hair. "But what if that's not what he meant? What if he *is* Enhanced and was just being kind to you?"

The Enhanced aren't kind. I want to say that, but I don't. Instead, I say: "Then we'll run past him, get out somehow. Corin, I've got to escape. Raleigh can't have me. And you need to get out before the augmenters are ready. They don't need me to convert you—they've already got you, and they'll do it as soon as they can. They're just using me for everyone they haven't got."

Corin presses his lips together for a moment. "Okay. I know the way out. The gate I used last time. But I'm not sure where we are now. They blindfolded me, leading me here, once they got me, thanks to the drone."

"We're deep down," I say. "Underground. Dungeons."

"Dungeons?" He snorts, but then he sees the look on my face. "Don't worry, we'll make it out. We will, Sev."

His arms encircle me again, and I lean in closer. My hands rest on his chest, feeling the hard muscles there through his tight, white T-shirt. He's in top condition. Even after being out there, on his own—foraging, hunting, scavenging for, what? Days? But how long was he really out there? They could've had him here most of the time….

"We've got some time together before the big escape," Corin whispers. "We don't know how long Three will be. And it's late…."

I nod. "Good. We need time to make plans."

"Plans? No, Sev. We need to sleep. We need to be in good form for tomorrow, or later today, tonight—whenever Three comes back—"

"He'll be back soon. We had ten minutes last time." I look up at Corin, and part of me expects him to have a different idea of what we can do. Unless he doesn't really mean to sleep… A smile brushes my lips.

"But he's going to look for Katya," Corin says, his arms around me tightening. "He could be a while. At least an hour, I'd say. We should…rest. We don't want to be sleep-deprived. It's then that you make mistakes."

My jaw tenses. I don't want to sleep. The last time I slept, Raleigh got to me. Drugged me and my dog.

"My dog's back," I say.

"Oh."

"We've got to get him out too… I think he's still in my room." I sigh, but I feel keyed up. So many people, as well as my dog—and what about the Zharat? Do I leave them here?

"Sev, you can't save everyone," Corin says. "Stop worrying. We don't know how it's going to work, whether we really will have help or not. There are too many variables to make a proper plan. We'll have to play it by ear when the time comes. But you and I *will* get out, I promise. And we'll be together. I'm not losing you this time."

I turn in his arms. "But what about our families? Three and Esther and my mother?" I shake my head. "We need to get Esther out at least before they get the augmenters sorted."

Though the augmenters would fix her hip, wouldn't they? Without them, she'd have to be carried.

I squirm a little, look at Corin.

"We'll do what we can," he says, and I'm not sure whether he knows about her injury or not, but his words ring in my ears for the next few moments.

Corin takes me by the shoulders, looks into my eyes. He doesn't say anything, just stares at me. And I stare back, allow myself to be swallowed by his eyes, to get lost in them.

For minutes, we stand like this. And then he bends his head slightly, kisses my forehead.

The contact sends jolts through me, and I lift my head up, pull him toward me.

I kiss him, hard, surprise myself by the ferocity of it. Because, if we do get caught when we try and escape, this could be the last time.

And then his hands are all over me—and it's like before, like in the Zharat cave, before Jed interrupted us. My heart pounds and everything inside me dances. My hands are in Corin's hair, and then his lips dip down, cover my neck in tiny kisses that try to flutter away.

I breathe deeply, and he pushes my head back, exposing more of my neck for him. A thousand feelings pull through me as I press myself into him. His hands get rougher, pulling at the thin material of my shirt, harder and harder. His lips press against my collarbone, and he kisses me there, repeatedly. His hands knead the fleshy parts of my upper arms, exerting more pressure. A moan escapes him, and I pull back a little, see his eyes, see how they're burning.

"I've missed you," he whispers, and then I kiss his

lips again, but kiss them softly, slowly.

The full force of my feelings hits me. I've really missed him. More than I ever thought it would be possible to miss someone. I just—I *need* to be close to him. To feel close.

Corin's the one thing I've got left. I've lost everyone else. But not him.

He's still here.

With me.

Together.

I press myself closer to him still as we kiss again. His hands find their way under my shirt and then he's exploring every inch of my skin, until his touches slide onto the cups of my bra. He squeezes my right breast, firmly, and I gasp, then his other hand's on my wrist.

Next, he directs me to touch him, makes my fingers slide over his skin just above the waistband of his shorts. He makes a deep sound in his throat, and then his hands move around to my back, and then down to my bottom. He pulls me against him again, and I feel his body respond against mine, respond in a way that's—

Corin steps away from me abruptly, breathing hard. His lips curl with a smile, and I've never seen his face so flushed.

"I've missed you too," he says in a voice so ragged, so labored, that my heart nearly breaks into a thousand pieces. "Gods, Seven, I really want you...need you... but your brother said..." He shakes his head. "Shit. Not now, okay? Now we need to sleep."

I stare at him, my mouth dropping open. "Sleep?"

But I don't want to sleep. What if Raleigh comes in and uses me again? But Corin's here...and the cell door is creaky. At least one of us would wake up, I'm sure.

"We *need* to rest," Corin says firmly and sits down, gestures for me to sit next to him. His hands shake. "We need to be ready for when that door opens...not getting distracted." His lips twitch, and he reaches for the bottle of water, and, somehow, he reaches it with ease despite the distance. He takes a small sip, then licks his lips. "And then, and then when we're out there—together, free—we'll have all the time in the world. Time to do whatever we want..." He lets his words trail off, his voice so deep, so suggestive.

My chest hitches. He smiles at me—a smile that is so sexy, so inviting—and I want to press myself against him again.

I sit next to him, willing my body to calm down, and he offers me the water. I take a small gulp, but he tells me I can have it all. I drink greedily, and then he puts an arm around me, draws me in. I rest my head against his shoulder, trying to control myself, when all I want to do is kiss him again, climb onto his lap.

Corin reaches over, pulls a blanket toward us. He drapes it over both of us as we lie down. I think about taking my tennis shoes off, but it's best to keep them on in case of a quick escape.

Then Corin sits up. He takes his T-shirt off.

I stare at his chest, as he stays sitting up for a moment, looking down at me. How...how chiseled it is. I've seen his bare chest once before, when we showered in the Fire Mountain, but my memory doesn't serve it justice. Corin smiles the kind of smile that says he knows he's attractive.

He lies down again. A small gap—the tiniest—runs the length of our bodies. No physical contact, but I want to reach across, slide my hand across, know what his muscles feel like beneath my hand.

My heart pounds. I tell myself to stop it, but energy buzzes through me. Electricity tries to set every part of my body on fire.

After a moment, Corin turns his head fully toward me. So close. His face is the picture of calmness. "Just sleep, okay? But we'd better not touch," he says, and he scoots over a little more—even though we weren't touching. "Temptation and all that. Gods, this could be difficult."

I start to laugh. "But we've slept before, like this... where we haven't actually done anything... At the Spirit temple. In the Zharat's lorry. Even in their den, that first night."

"But you didn't look as irresistible as you do now. And I didn't have your brother's warning ringing in my head." He chuckles, but it sounds forced. Then he looks at me. "We'll be together soon. Now, Sev. Get some sleep. Rest. We don't know how much time we've got."

I nod, but I don't go to sleep. I start thinking. Thinking about everything. The events of today whirl back and forth in my mind, blending with one another, like colors mixing to create new shades. I start to wonder what will happen if Three opens the door and sees us lying together under the blanket. The blanket's not covering Corin's shoulders and I wonder if it'll look like he's completely naked beneath the cover.

Naked.

And that makes me actually think about him... naked. About what he'll look like and... Heat rushes to my face. I wonder if he's thinking the same thing about me.

After a while, Corin asks if I'm asleep, then he breaks his *no contact* rule and takes my hand, looks into my eyes.

"Have you thought about trying to connect to those other Untamed?" He pauses. "I know it's what Raleigh wants. But it's also a lifeline. An advantage... You could tell one of them what's going on. See if they can help on the outside, be waiting for us."

I shrug and breathe deeply. There's a seam of my shorts digging into me, and I shift around a little. "I don't know."

I start to nestle into him before I even realize what I'm doing. Corin's body tenses at first, but then he relaxes. His arm goes around me, and I rest my head against his chest, listen to his heart. He moves one of his legs, then the side of his knee presses against mine.

DIVIDED

Skin against skin.

"We need all the help we can get," he says. "Now, try and get some sleep, Sev. I'm here. You're safe with me. I won't let anything happen to you."

Safe. Safe with Corin. He'd protect me if Raleigh came in here. I know that.

And so I sleep.

We do. We sleep like this, together, safe.

THIRTY-SEVEN

I'M NOT SURE WHAT TIME it is when I awake, because there's no window in here. Corin's hand feels heavy over my side. My back is against his chest, and my skin is hot, sticky. He's warm, very warm, and I'm sure the back of my shirt is damp with sweat.

I slide out from the blanket as quietly as I can, careful not to disturb him, and—

I catch a glimpse of his face as I turn.

My blood turns to ice.

No.

No.

No.

It's not Corin.

Oh—oh Gods.

It's—

No.

No.

No.

The man opens his eyes. He smiles at me.

I stare at him, at his eyes, at the—

Every part of my body recoils, every part of me feels sick, every part of me screams.

DIVIDED

I propel myself away from him, grab hold of the blanket, wrench it from him, to cover myself. Even though I'm fully dressed. Never took any clothes off. Thank the Gods. But my heart's still pounding.

"What..." But I can't speak properly, my words, they're tangled and sticky. My heart pounds. I look around, then back at him. "Where's Corin, where's—what the *hell* are you doing? What've you done to Corin?"

Raleigh sits up. "What's the matter?"

And he speaks in Corin's voice.

Corin's voice.

I go cold. Completely cold. No. No. *No.*

Raleigh looks down at his hands, then curses. And the way he curses....

And—and... Oh Gods. Why didn't I check?

Stupid. Stupid. *Stupid*.

I can body-share. I'm connected with Corin, and I didn't even check it was him. I just assumed, and—

Oh Gods.

And it's *him*. Not Corin. Oh Gods.

I hold my own hands up slowly, flex my fingers, then clench them into fists. My heart pounds. My legs start shaking.

"*What* are you doing?" My voice trembles, and thousands of things fly round and round in my head, try and make me feel sick.

Raleigh doesn't even blink. "I was getting to know you better. But *someone* thought they'd sabotage my plan. Switched my concoction. Different grade. Not long-lasting." He swears again. But he must see the look on my face, because he laughs. "You really are good at kissing, aren't you? Extraordinary, for such an Untamed individual... Such sensual lips."

I feel sick.

My heart pounds as I stare at him.

It isn't Corin.

It was never Corin.

Can't have been....

It was Raleigh. All the time. The augmenters...the augmenters can do *anything*.

And Three—Three *knew*. He must've. Oh Gods. He's with them. My own brother—he set me up. Played me. Pretended and—

No wonder he was so desperate for me to see Corin. Because it wasn't him. He and Raleigh must've planned it—to trick me.

Oh Gods.

Three's with Raleigh. Not one of us after all.

But someone sabotaged it...changed the augmenters, made them last fewer hours?

My mother.

It has to be her.

Raleigh stands up and looks at me. "The channels to your mind were practically wide open when you were unconscious—such easy access. And sleep renewed your powers remarkably quickly."

Dread fills me as I look at him. My powers. They weren't sealed off. He....

Oh Gods.

Raleigh leers. "Oh, yes. I've connected you to eighteen Untamed, individually, of course—for now."

THIRTY-EIGHT

EIGHTEEN UNTAMED.

I'm connected to eighteen Untamed. And he must've felt my connections to the others…to Taras. To Corin.

The *real* Corin.

I clap a hand to my mouth, stare at Raleigh.

"Don't look so alarmed, my butterfly."

Nausea pulls through me. I kissed him. I *kissed* him. I pressed my body against him, I slept cradled into his chest, I listened to his heart beat. I thought about him naked.

Oh Gods.

And for how long? How long has it been? How long was I asleep in there with him?

The door creaks open. Harsh light. I blink. A silhouette in the doorway. Three's silhouette.

Three.

My brother.

I see red.

The traitor.

Fire charges through my bones.

I catapult myself upright, turn, fire in my blood. And I run, manage to skid past Three before either of them realizes.

Shit.

Shit.

Shit.

I look up. The corridor. Which way?

And I'm out—Gods, I'm out, running free and—

Oh Gods. It was all lies. Lies!

My head pounds.

I've got to get out.

Before Raleigh uses me again.

"Shania!"

But what about Three?

The traitor!

And Esther? Your mother? Your dog?

Oh Gods. I start to slow, then realize I can't. I can't save them. Don't know where Esther and my mother are, and I wouldn't be able to get Esther out. Not with her injury. And my dog—is he still in my room? But I can't go back. I *have* to get out. I can't do anything that might compromise my escape. Because the Enhanced can't have me…not now…now when the next time I'm asleep, or drugged, Raleigh will use my powers, if he has me. Even if I seal them off, something tells me he'll find them somehow, break the seal. Or he'll trick me again… He'll make more connections and—

Shit. *Escape.* What am I even thinking? I'm not going to escape—hell, Raleigh won't let me.

And, as if on cue, I feel him trying to take over my body, trying to control me, and—

I turn back, as he wants, but I scream, and I—I break the control. Somehow, I do it. Pain snakes from my head, down my neck, my spine, *and* I lift my hand up at the two of them—Raleigh and Three.

My powers surge within me—fueled with their anger at being exploited—and I send the white light at Raleigh.

It hits him.

He grunts, loses his grip on my soul, and—

And I don't stop to watch.

DIVIDED

I run.

I run as fast as I can.

An alarm blares down the hallway, the red light chasing me. I dive to the left, skid into the next corridor. There's no one about. It's empty. Just me. Me running, and I'm like a mouse, trying to escape, knowing the cat will be just around the corner.

I keep running, get to some stairs, ascend them so quickly my legs feel like they're moving too fast, and I'm going to fall over.

And then there's another flight.

My lungs are going to burst. The red flashing lights are disorientating, dizzy, and—

Voices.

Behind me.

I spin around, my heart pounding even harder. See men coming. Enhanced. Mirror eyes flashing.

Shit.

I turn and run again. Got to keep running. Have to keep running. Need to breathe properly—not breathing right, I'm going to crash, using up all my energy.

I pump my arms faster, try to think what to do—but can't. My head—there's too much going on. Just got to run. Need to run. Must get away.

But they'll catch you. You know they'll catch you.

No.

They can't.

They won't.

Eighteen Untamed are connected to me. No—shit, there're more... Corin, Viktoriya, Esther, Dominika, the man who leant over the ice, the person I shared with when I saw the blue-eyed Seer, the Zharat man with the hairy arms. Oh Gods. What's that? Twenty-five. Twenty-five people who can get converted if the Enhanced have me. Twenty-five people I have to keep Untamed.

I plow ahead, reach more stairs. My heart thuds against my ribs. Waves of dizziness wash over me—

tightness spreads across my scalp. My chest feels like it's going to cave in.

"Shania!"

My head turns, like there's a string attached to it, and jagged pain darts down my spine. I see shadows and men. Mirror eyes, but not Raleigh.

He's injured? My white light hurt him? And he's not controlling me.... It's just the other Enhanced here.

"Stop running! You cannot escape!"

I don't stop running. Somehow, I manage to go faster. I pass a window—a blur of sky and—

I'm higher up now than I thought.

Shit.

Shit.

Shit!

Too high—there's no escape up here. I need to be on ground level. I curse, feel my momentum slipping away. How have I got so high up? But Esther's high up too, isn't she? For a moment, my mind backtracks. Could I get her out? What about my Seer powers? Raleigh said about super human strength. I could carry her....

But there's no time. And I don't know if she's in this part of the compound.

My breath comes in rapid bursts, and—

Stairs.

I see the sign to my left, and then I skid wildly. My hands grab for something—anything to stop me falling as I turn, and I knock hundreds of tiny things off a counter before I even realize what it is, what they were.

Augmenters.

But there's no tug in me now. Just nausea. Conditioned to make me feel sick looking at them.

Shouts fill the air.

I keep running, and the soles of my shoes *slap slap slap*, then—

Shit.

I've missed a turning?

DIVIDED

Because there are no stairs. There's nowhere to go. A dead end. Just a big window ahead, several feet wide, square. One huge pane of glass.

I try to turn, but I'm going too fast and—

They're right behind me. An army of Enhanced Ones.

I can't get around them.

I can't stop.

I skid, reach out for something, but my body's speeding up. I can't stop. My legs are—they're not mine. I'm not in control. Raleigh? But no—it doesn't feel like—

It's me.

I'm doing it.

I know what to do.

I run at the window.

My shoulder hits the glass first. Pain shoots down my spine.

Glass smashes.

People scream.

I shriek.

And then I'm falling through the air, outside. Free.

THIRTY-NINE

I FALL, SCREAM, AND—

Cold, ice-cold water. Around me, over me—my head and—

Gulp a mouthful down, splutter. My limbs lock, and I try to move them—need to move them but—

Pain in my head; a lightning bolt with a tongue of iron.

Raleigh.

I can't move. Falling. Sinking. Lower. Lower. Lower. In the water, the ice-cold water and—

No.

No.

No.

Drowning.

Shit.

Again, I try to move, but—

Oh Gods!

My lungs—pressure in my chest.

And my feet—my shoes are getting heavier, filling with water, and I kick out, kick wildly. Need to get them off—like with Dominika and—

Pain, sharp, and—and then my body's mine again.

DIVIDED

I thrash my arms, my head pounding, my heart pounding, everything *pounding pounding pounding*. Manage to turn. Murky blueness all around me and—

Something clasps my ankle.

I jerk back, splashing, try to turn, but my head—I'm dragged down, deeper, deeper. Its fingers—whatever it is—clamped around my ankle. Long, splayed out, dark fingers.

I kick at the arm—can't see past it, the water's too dark.

I kick again, make contact. But my shoe feels too heavy, and my foot numb. My chest tightens and—

Thud.

I'm free, kick up to the surface, somehow manage it despite my stone-heavy shoes. My head breaks the water. Light and—coldness and—

Enhanced Ones. On the bank, the bank of the moat. Their eyes glisten like new stars. And then I realize I'm *in* the moat, and they're coming for me. There's a *moat*?

And they're heading for me.

Dread fills me, my shoulders try to stiffen, but I force myself to keep moving. Look left, then right—my chunks of short hair spray surprisingly large watery worms across my arms as I turn, splashing. Right. Got to go that way. Less Enhanced there.

"Get out," one of the mirror-eyed men yells. "Shania, get out of there."

I try to tread water, reach down to pull my shoes off, and my balance goes. My shoulder ducks under the water, and the coldness invades me. I splutter, choke, eyes streaming. See the Enhanced coming—nearer and nearer—

Shit.

I forget about the shoes, just swim as fast as I can, trying not to think about the creature—the spirit?—underwater. A kavalah? Oh Gods. Energy fizzes through me, I kick harder and harder. My legs wail. My teeth start to chatter.

There's a bridge up ahead—but there's not enough room for me to go under it and keep my head above water. It's too low. Shit. But on the bank, either side of the bridge, there's a wall, a wall perpendicular to the moat, one that cuts across it, across and over the water. People can only get onto the bridge from the compound buildings either side. There's no door for people walking alongside the moat, it's just a brick wall that turns into a bridge. The Enhanced on this side won't be able to get over that wall quickly...and on the other side I'll be free....

Unless there are more Enhanced there.

It's my only chance, I know that. They're closing in. And, for the moment, I've still got power over my body. I have to do it.

My head pounds harder as I swim to the bridge. The water's getting warmer. Or I'm numbing...can't feel it as much.

I duck my head under, my eyes open, try to see as I swim down. The bridge—how deep do I need to go to avoid it? For a second, I feel sick—what if it isn't a bridge? What if it's just a wall? What if I can't get under it? Or what if it's a dam? But there's no current yet; I'm not being sucked under—does that mean anything?

Dizziness clutches at me. Lightheaded, I plow on. No choice. Got to. Force my arms to keep moving, my legs to keep kicking. Nausea unfurls its hands, tries to drag me deeper and deeper.

Drown. Drown. Drown.

The word pummels through me.

Spirits...they're here, around me, in the water.

My left foot spasms as I try to kick harder. My head jerks up—my eyes stinging, I try to see... Where am I? Have to be under the wall now—the bridge, it must be a bridge—surely? But how wide is it?

Can't breathe—need air....

And then my body's propelling itself up to the surface, and I break into air, away from water,

DIVIDED

spluttering, choking, eyes streaming. Turn—see the brick wall a few feet behind me. I made it. Made it past it and—

I look up onto the bank. And he's there. Jed's there.

For a moment, I freeze. Then I kick out, tread water, and stare.

Jed points behind him.

That way. There's a car... S'ven, get out now!

He shouts the words, but his shout isn't out loud, it's...it's different, makes my head hurt. For a moment, I don't do anything, just stare at him, feel the shape of his words—how did he do it? That was...like it was in my head, but out loud too...wasn't like normal speech...and somewhere, I remember other words spoken like it, but I can't think, not now.

Then I hear the Enhanced Ones' shouts, and my body kicks to life.

I swim to the side, try to get a handhold on the bank, try to—

But it's too slippery, the sides are too steep, and I can't—

Jed reaches his hand out. *Take it*, he says, and his accent nearly swallows his words—if they're words at all. If they're....

I grab his hand before I can think any more. Solid. Substantial.

He pulls me out. I scrape my shins on the bank—brief pain. And then I'm standing up, soaked, shivering, and he's pressing something into my right hand. I look down—see what's in my hand: a car key.

That way! Go! Jed screams, pointing.

And I run, clenching the key to me so hard I know it's indenting its shape into my palm, writing itself onto me. But I don't care. I skid, slip—my grip wet—throw my arms wide, and look up. Don't lose my balance though. There are more buildings ahead, with trees—surprisingly thick foliage—between them. My wet shoes slam the ground, and my feet slip about inside them, squelching.

"Shania!"

I turn at my name—unsure whether I choose to or not—and I see them.

Those same Enhanced. A couple of hundred yards behind me. And they're running toward me. Jed? He's gone. Nowhere to be seen.

But he—he was here? Wasn't he?

I look down. The key is still in my hand.

Keep going.

I run harder. My chest feels like it's going to explode with adrenaline.

I skid around the nearest brick building. The ground turns into pale gray tarmac with bright yellow markings painted on. Warm tarmac, from the sun. I look around—the Enhanced Ones' steps and shouts come closer…closer…closer.

I go left, pump my arms. My wet hair drips everywhere, and—

Two women step out in front of me, mirror eyes flashing. One holds a baby, the other a canvas bag, and they both stop, stare at me. The canvas bag hits the floor.

I skid, change direction, sprint away.

More buildings. I go between them, running as fast as I can, faster than I ever have before. The wind whips through what's left of my hair, kisses my wet clothes. My shoes slam against the ground. *Bang. Bang. Bang.*

"Shania! Stop this instant!"

My lungs seem to get bigger, allow me to go faster, faster, faster. So fast. And I try to look everywhere at once.

Another alarm goes off, drives through me. I jolt to the left, before I even realize I'm turning and—

Enhanced. There.

I skid, change direction, wrestle control of my body back, run faster, harder, better. Turn a corner, and I see vehicles. Vehicles inside an open-ended, shabbier building on the right. I run for the vehicles, look down. The key's in my hand. It's got to be for one of these, surely? I pray to whatever Gods and Goddesses are there, are listening, are on my side.

I fumble with the key, turn it the right way, point it at the vehicles—the four-by-fours. But there's no button to press. It's just a key, a key that has to go into the door's lock and—

Shit.

I run for the nearest vehicle, try to jab the key into it and—it doesn't fit. The next one, I turn to it. My hand shakes, and I whip my head around. Shit. The Enhanced—

"Come on!" I shout, fumbling with the key, and then my heart pounds even harder.

I try the third vehicle, run straight past the fourth one—it's too new, would have a remote button—and the same with the next ones, and—

"Shania!"

That leaves one. One vehicle. A silver Mark 1 Pajero, right at the back of the barn.

I fly toward it, shove the key into the lock, the driver's side. It turns. The locking pin behind the window lifts up. I yank the door open and—

Barking fills my ears.

It's the dog. My dog.

I look around.

No, get in the vehicle, S'ven. Jed's words again—he's back?

But I can't see him, can't—

The terrier flies out of nowhere, and then he's barking and running and jumping, throwing himself into the Pajero.

My heart pounds.

"Shania!"

My head jolts up. They're in the building too. Oh Gods—no.

I pull myself into the vehicle, slam the door, push the locking pin down—expecting all the locks to move, but they don't. No central locking. I lunge for the pin on the passenger side, partly crashing into my dog, and try to press it. But it won't go down any further—it's already locked? What about the tailgate? I twist around.

There is a switch on the dashboard for it.

Jed's voice makes me jump.

My heart pounds as I turn back, look, and then I see it: a rocker switch, marked with *GATE LOCK* and *UN-LOCK*, on the instrument binnacle behind the left side of the steering wheel. I push the top part of the switch, hear the clunk as it locks, then force the key into the ignition, turn it. The engine roars, louder than expected, and I look around, shedding more water. The terrier's sitting on the passenger seat, ears alert, watching as the Enhanced run over.

Shit.

I look down at the controls and throw the Pajero into reverse, pump down on the accelerator as I yank the wheel, move backward. Something clinks. I turn my head, check where the Enhanced are: too close.

The tires squeal, and there's a dull, heavy sound as I move the vehicle. And then a stutter. My heart pounds, and my chest shudders.

"Don't you dare," I hiss, glancing at the fuel gauge, and then up and—

Their faces are against my window.

I shift into first gear. The Enhanced rattle the door handle, and they're shouting. My hands tighten around the wheel, my knuckles click. I press down on the accelerator, moving over bumpy ground and up the gears, and then I'm really going, flying, careening around the corner.

The Mark 1 picks up speed.

More Enhanced appear out of nowhere, and I veer to the left, floor the accelerator, get out of the building. Something screeches. The windscreen's grimy under sudden bright sunlight, and the dog jump up, going for the controls, and cold air blasts out the vents, onto me. My wet clothes feel like icy stone.

My eyes stream, and I try to push the dog back onto

DIVIDED

the seat as I turn onto the road—the road ahead. The escape?

The engine's noisy, and there's a rattling noise, but I can hear the Enhanced Ones shouting still. My heart pounds; I drive faster and faster, past buildings, more buildings, so many buildings. All of them part of the conversion compound? Or the parts of the city, the other regions where the Enhanced live, their shops, their—

I hit the curb as I take a corner too sharply, and everything jolts. I let out a cry, but then—then it's okay. Still going, and I'm just driving and—and it's so big. This city! So many buildings on the sandy ground, and low-creeping olive-colored vegetation, and a few trees nested together by the side of a white building with so many windows. I peer ahead, think the buildings are thinning out to the left, and I turn down the next road. Bumpy tarmac. Get jolted about. Change into the highest gear, put my foot down. Pass parked cars and—

Pain erupts in my head—*Raleigh*—no, shit.

I struggle to breathe, feel him try to take my arms, my legs. A sudden stoniness to them, but I push it back, resist his control. Think I hear his voice: *Stop it, Shania.*

But I don't stop it. I fight. I have to fight. My breaths get more ragged as the pain intensifies. But Raleigh's not controlling me. Why? Can't he do it now? Why not? Am I getting too far away? Or did my white light injure him too much? And again, I think of him—of us, nestled together for the night—because it must've been the night, because the sun's over there now so it's morning and—

I jolt up in the air as I steer over potholes. My dog barks again.

And then—then I see the edge of the city. The edge of the buildings. So soon. Too soon. Freedom.

At last!

But so soon… I've lost time? I glance in the mirror,

see a big blue building—tall—that I don't recognize. Yet I drove past it? A strange feeling fills my chest.

Concentrate.

Yes. Need to concentrate. I'm getting away! I feel the excitement build, and I fight to stay in control. Need to stay calm, not get overwhelmed, excited.

My eyes narrow, and I see the greenery far ahead, lushness that fades to a fawn color in some places. And trees. Clumps of foliage, lower-lying stuff. In the distance, pale hills that change from mauve to beige, shadowed and misted.

I follow the road, driving as hard as I can. Check the fuel level again.

"Shit," I mutter. It's below a quarter now. So soon. Too soon? It's leaking…a leak. Got to be? Or a faulty reading. I sniff the air. But I can't smell anything. No fuel. But would I smell a leak from inside the vehicle? And how far can I get without a full tank, with a tank that's possibly leaking?

The road I'm on branches into two. I narrow my eyes. Both roads appear to lead out of the city, into the wild land beyond.

I glance at the terrier.

"Which way?" I mutter. "One bark for left, two for right."

He barks twice—two sharp, short barks—and right it is.

I put my foot down. The engine hums. In the mirror, I see the dust I'm churning up, and—and it's exhilarating. A smile graces my lips, and, suddenly, I never want to leave this vehicle. It's mine, it's freedom.

I'm escaping. I'm actually escaping.

Raleigh has my soul, and I'm *escaping*. No one's following me.

I drive as fast as I can—faster than I've ever driven before. Keep one eye on the rear-view mirror, the other in front of me. Still no one's tailing me. Yet. No one's on the road at all. The Enhanced rarely use their vehicles. And they rarely leave their towns and cities,

DIVIDED

rarely want to be surrounded by wilderness.

And no one's coming after me.

Too easy.

My body hums with energy.

Five minutes later—driving at break-neck speed—my dog and I make it out of the city. Onto a dust track—a sandy-orange color that throws dust everywhere. The verges are covered in greenery, but it's not a thick cover. The arenaceous ground shows in numerous patches. The sky is blue, filled with small fluffy clouds. Looks idyllic.

On the passenger seat, the dog shifts around a little, then settles down, lies on the velour, watching me. I try to sit up straighter, pull my sopping clothes away from my body, but they cling to me like watery cobwebs, holding me in place, like wires…wires that will never let go.

No. I shake my head. Need to concentrate on now. Stay in the present.

I drive on—wonder at what point I should slow my speed, try and preserve the fuel. But not yet—can't do that now. I look in the mirror, adjust it quickly so I can see out the back more easily. The city's still in sight.

But no one's followed me.

No one at all.

And…and they should've. I know it's better for me, but they *should've* come after me. They shouldn't be letting me get away. Nervous energy fizzles through me. They've no reason to let me escape—not like before, when they let me go so I could become the Seer the augury speaks of before they recaptured me.

Ahead, the land levels out a little—the verges aren't as high, and the trees become thinner. I steer the four-by-four up to the left, over the small verge, and then we're lurching through low vegetation, off-road.

I steer around what I can, the best I can, but I hit several holes and clumps—whack my head against the driver's window twice. There's a copse far ahead, and I aim for it. Imagine the trees as people. Six tall people.

The land gets sandier. Dustier.

And then it's all blowing up, the sand, everywhere. The wind howls. I hunker down in my seat, try to see. And then sand and dust somehow get inside the vehicle, and the air conditioning throws it around, at me.

I curse, fumble with the switches, wincing—but I can't turn it off. Slide several levers across and back again. No difference.

Go south! Jed yells, and I jolt, look around for him. But I can't see him. And it's his voice...but that different voice. Like it's in my head but also out loud—like a... *Go south until the city's completely out of sight. Keep going, then east, veer around the city else you'll get to the coast, stay off-road.*

I wipe the back of my arm across my forehead, and—

Raleigh gets control of my arm, makes me grab the steering wheel, yank it—and I sense him, so strong now. In my head, spreading his control, trying to take my body.

No. *Taking* my body.

Taking it from me. Powerful and—

I shriek.

One of us wrenches the vehicle to the left—I can't tell who, but—

The Pajero crashes against something. I cry out as the movement rebounds through me, manage to press the accelerator down—my own decision—but can't do much else. Stinging sweat drips into my eyes.

I press my foot down again.

The vehicle hits something else, and I turn it to the left sharply. The dog stands up, looks out the window, barks and—

And then—then I see Corin...no, *Raleigh*.

He's crouching to the side, behind rocks. His eyes meet mine and—

I inhale sharply.

How the hell is he here? So soon and... I curse and—

DIVIDED

No wonder they weren't chasing...not when...but how'd they know where I'd drive? How did Raleigh know? How—

Oh Gods. I swear loudly. Raleigh's got my soul. He must have suggested the route to me without me knowing... Then I frown. No. He can't have—my dog chose the—

The trees jump up ahead of me. I try to yank the wheel to the left—try, but I can't. My arms won't move and—

Raleigh.

He's doing it. He won't let me and—

The trees get closer.

Shit.

No.

No.

No.

But I can't change direction, and I'm going too fast. I look down. My foot's on the accelerator, the pedal's on the ground. Try to move my foot, and I can't and—

"Stop it!" I scream, and I fight for control, try to resist him, and he's out there and—

The dog yelps.

The trees get closer, closer, closer.

More power surges through me—his and mine and—

"Raleigh! Stop!"

But it's going to happen. He's not giving me my body back and—

I shriek, try to brace myself for the impact. Try to move my arms up to shield my head.

Try to—

FORTY

GLASS SHATTERS AROUND ME.

I scream.

The world tips on its side, and I fall, try to hold onto the wheel, but can't.

My head smacks against something—hard—and pain rebounds through my legs. Something grainy, sharp, abrasive, rubs against my face, eats me. The engine whirs, seems to get louder.

I try to turn—can't. Pain. My legs are higher up than my head, my body all twisted, jilted, and I feel blood rushing to my head. But my neck's all, all bent… feels….

A lone bark…somewhere.

My breathing, heavy and thick.

The dog.

My terrier.

No…no, not the dog, *not him*.

I try to turn, try to—manage to move my head, but then sharp batons of pain grip my neck. I let out a cry. My vision blurs, murky—like I'm underwater.

Underwater….

A soft whimper brings me back, and then something

DIVIDED

shifts inside me. A heavy click, and my vision gets sharper, stronger. Colors swirl toward me, start spinning. I clamp my eyes shut as the nausea takes hold, as it....

Let go.

The voice in my head startles me. My eyes spring open. I see things in glimpses. The orange dust, the trees looming up and...a snap so big it echoes in my ears, my body, my soul.

A snap as if something's irreparably broken.

And I *see* the snap. *See* it.

It is a ceramic rod in front of me. And it snaps cleanly in two. One perfect line, separating its two halves.

Cold air whistles past me.

I try to move my arms and—

My left one—can't feel it—think it's twisted around behind my back... My right one's in front of me, but it looks strange, floppy. And my ribs; jaggedness, darkness. It takes me a moment to realize the vehicle's on its side; the left side of my face is against the beaded glass of the passenger window, inches above the ground. The rest of my body is caught above me, my knees somehow wedged around the gearstick, my feet stuck in the driver's footwell, up in the air. My body is strewn across the two seats, angled down, and the engine's making a strange noise that reverberates through me.

Pain in my head, sharp, sudden. I wince, taste blood. And feel it. My face, the left side, my temple to my chin, wet, sticky.

My lungs strain, my chest makes a wheezing sound and—

Raleigh.

He's out there, nearby—I saw him. He was right there. He's going to come over, and I won't be able to fight him, won't be able to stop him from taking me back.

My heart speeds up. My head's going to burst, too much pressure. And then the car creaks—the frame?

And there's something slipping over me with soft fingers…liquid….

A sour smell fills my nostrils, strong and tangy and—

Get out, S'ven!

Something jolts in me, and I try to move, try to lift my head, but nothing happens.

Not my body.

Not connected.

But I'm here, and—

Can't move.

Trapped.

Fear builds in me, and I feel the way it makes my head pound harder and harder, feel my breathing get faster, until I'm breathing too fast, and I can't get enough oxygen. And then the smell changes. It grows, the intensity grows and—

The dog whines. And I see him now, don't need to lift my head. He's…he's right there, in front of me, in the passenger footwell: a mass of matted brown fur, shaking, trembling. He moves a little, whines. Then he emits a shrill sound that breaks my ears, and I'm gasping.

Get out.

Don't know whose thought it is. Mine or Jed's….

No. That's not right… Jed's not in my head. I'm the only one in my head, the only one who owns the thoughts in my head….

Get out. Get out. Get out.

But I can't.

Heat washes over me.

Then I feel a tingling—as if fine feathers of steel are brushing over me. My spine? My legs? I can't—

Another ceramic rod breaks in my mind, and I look up, to my right—able to move my head a little—see the spiderweb-shatter across the top edge of the windscreen.

Feeling shoots into my right arm, and more blood rushes to my head. My arm—I get my arm to lift up,

DIVIDED

slightly. Feel…feel something strange in it.

Then I hear the footsteps. The footsteps I knew would come, and every part of me darkens, darkens like a black beetle scurrying along.

Raleigh.

A thousand thoughts fly through me. And I reach for the dog, twisting forward, something digging into my stomach and chest. I press my right hand over him, feel his damp fur, use every ounce of my willpower to do it. More pain flares over me, but I ignore it. What is pain? And it all numbs in a matter of seconds, far too soon and—

A shift of energy. A new balance. My hand tingles faster, harder.

I don't know what's—

The dog moves.

A doleful eye looks at me. I stare at him, and he's close. So close. That eye is inches from my own. Staring into me.

Eyes are the route to the soul.

"Seven!"

Raleigh's voice. No. *His* voice. Corin's. No. Torturing me, even when….

"Go!" I whisper to the terrier, as he lifts his head, as life—the full spectrum of it—floods back into his eyes, as he—

As he twists into darkness.

Thick, black darkness. darker than the darkest parts of the night sky.

Hot breath over my face.

Thank you.

My eyes close.

"No!" Raleigh screams in Corin's voice.

And it's the last thing I hear, the last sound from the world of the living, because his scream goes on and on; and everything else that once was the world— my labored breathing, the whimpers, the Pajero's engine—melts away. There's only his scream as the teardrop of ice silently smashes the petal, the last

petal, and strangled life swallows me.
   And then—then….
   Then there is nothing.

FORTY-ONE

I AM A THOUSAND FRAGMENTS, fallen.

A man is screaming,
another cries,
and my mother feels my death;
She knows, she feels it—the chasm inside, raging—
because she feels all her children's deaths.
It should've ended in fire.

Life.
Death.
Always in opposition, always fighting.
Each is jealous of the other.
Life and death, and death and life.
And the seconds after the snap, once the door has clanged shut,
and the last of the tolling bells has struck.

Long ago, I sprinted through the sands.
The wind kissed my face,
and my mother ran behind me, with Five and Three.
And my father peeled his hand from paper,
and ridges of paint marked his life.

We were happy.
In life.

But you can't choose
between life and death, when your earth-energy has gone.
When it's taken.
When the branches finally meet.

When you step from one world to the other,
you mustn't look back.

And I never told Corin I loved him.
My Corin.
In life.
I love you.
Hope and the long sleep.
I failed.

Seven, says the voice.

FORTY-TWO

I AM IN A CAVE. A beautiful cave.

The air is a shimmering turquoise, and thousands of beads of light dance across the rocky ceiling. Everything looks blue, green, turquoise, that magnificent shade. It warms my heart. And the water glistens with the color, the beauty. The water by my feet.

The cave is long and thin, magical, and water flows through it, around my ankles.

I am wearing a short, turquoise dress—because everything is turquoise, and it's the most beautiful color ever.

Wind chimes play in the distance, caress my soul.

"Seven," says the voice, again.

I look up, and a woman is coming toward me. An old woman, but she looks familiar. Familiar, yet forgotten.

The light gets darker. A tunnel of turquoise darkness, but there's light somewhere at the end of it. I know that.

The woman holds her hands up as she nears me, splashing in the pool.

"Don't come this way yet, Seven. Stop. You mustn't complete the journey." Her voice echoes, and her tones are soft, so smooth.

She looks like my mother. But she's got Five's eyebrows. And—and she's tall, tall like me. Very tall.

"My name is Vala Sarr. I am the first Sarr Seer," she says. "The *original* Seer. The first trusted by the Gods and Goddesses to change things. My line has built its power, getting stronger with each generation, a collection of power that is waiting for you, soon to be unlocked… But you were not supposed to die now, Seven. Find Waskabe. Leave the path you are on, and find him. Find him before you reach the end of this path. Don't let him collect you. Find him before he comes for you. You have time, your soul is lingering. But be quick. For only Death can save us all now."

FORTY-THREE

THE LIGHT IS BRIGHT, HORRIBLY bright—and, everywhere I look, there's just whiteness. Whiteness that burns. Whiteness that eats me.

Too hot… My skin, it burns and screams. And—

And there's a table. A table a hundred feet in front of me.

Death sits at it.

One chair is vacant.

My skin stops burning as he turns to me—his full, cloaked figure—swiveling around on the chair. Instinctively, I try to look away—mustn't see his face.

"Look at me."

My breath hitches in my throat.

"Look at me."

I look at him. I look Death in the eye. Only he hasn't got an eye—hasn't got either of his eyes. There are just two dark pits there, and the skin's all papery. Looks thin, like it's showing the blood underneath. Dark blood.

And his face. It's—the shape, it's…it's narrow, so narrow.

"You should not be here." His words are quiet,

almost neutral. Not angry at all. Death stands slowly, points at me. His finger reminds me of Rahn's. Skeletal. I stare at the joint of the finger. At the space where the two bones nearly meet, but don't. The gap. The end part of his finger is just hovering. "But you *are* here."

It gets colder. A lot colder.

"Do you like it?" Death asks.

He stares at me pointedly—somehow manages, even though his eyes are just pits—and I know he's waiting for an answer.

"Like it?" My voice wobbles.

"The peace." He gestures around us, and the white light intensifies. I wince, narrow my eyes. "Death's plane is very peaceful at the moment, is it not?"

I frown, feel pressure start to build in my head.

"And you'll belong to Death very, very shortly," Waskabe says. "Your screams will fill this void, rewrite the music, as torture rises and rots you… A new kind of peace, made of your screams."

I'm dead. I'm here…and…this is where I'll be when he collects me? This is his realm? I look around, but there's nothing here. It's just the whiteness that's too bright, and Death and his table.

The mask of betrayal hangs over your aura, like gold cobwebs, rusting. Your body will rot under Death's command, long before your soul is allowed an escape from the decaying flesh of your ribs.

"Death does not like traitors." His voice is too relaxed—too casual—makes my chest go all jumpy.

I turn and look around me, look for something—anything but the white light. But there isn't anything. It's just nothingness.

Nothingness and Death, sitting at his table.

"Sit down," Waskabe says. A command. Not a suggestion.

I sit. The wooden seat is hard.

Death looks at me. Something deep inside me starts to burn. The burning gets stronger, stronger until I'm sure there must be something visible on my arms,

DIVIDED

some external sign of the pain I'm in.

I look down.

"Do you feel it?" He leans forward, then touches my arm. Coldness zaps through me. I flinch. He laughs. "This isn't your real body. You want to see your real body? Your real body is down there."

He looks at the top of the table, and, instantly, it's no longer wood; it's an image. I blink, and then the colors and shapes make sense to me.

A vehicle on its side, trees twisting around it, the driver's door open, sticking up.

A dog—my dog—barking.

And—

And a man cradling a girl's body, next to the Pajero.

My body.

Raleigh.

A bitter taste fills my mouth as I watch.

"I've locked your soul's roots there. You're divided. Both here and there. Soon, when I have officially collected you, you'll feel the full pain of your broken body down there—as it lies bleeding, as it rots, as it swells—and here, you'll feel Death, Waskabe, *me*." Pain flickers through me. "Because that's what happens to traitors. Double pain."

A pause.

"This is a bit of a disappointment, Seven Sarr. An anti-climax, you dying early. And Death is not happy with this. Did Death not tell you that you must die at the *end* of the war? Once the suffering is over? That it is a set point in time and that *that* is the only way this war can end? And did Death not give you the chance to prove yourself after your traitorous actions aligned you to the enemy? Yet you did not make sure the Untamed were victorious, did you? Instead, you bound yourself to them and then thought you would take your own life to save yourself."

Take my own life?

"No," I say. "I *didn't*," I say, but he raises his hand, and I stop speaking.

"You, Seven Sarr, by dying, chose to condemn your people to endless suffering—because the War of Humanity will *not* end now. The war will *never* end now. You were born to end it, and you have been selfish. You have failed. You may not have saved the Enhanced and given Death a reason to torture you for infinity, but you *have* written an infinity of misery—a worthless existence—into the future for your people. Always hiding, being hunted, on the run. Predator and prey. Eternal suffering… Death does not like suffering. Suffering is just as bad as extinction. And your selfishness has caused all this."

"No." I manage to speak, but it's difficult. "No—listen. You're supposed to know everything, but you *don't*. I didn't crash the car—that was Raleigh! He was trying to get control of my body…and I was fighting him…and I never even chose the Enhanced! My soul was given to them, it was beyond my control! You have to believe me—it's what happened!"

Somewhere, far away, thunder rolls across hills I cannot see.

"Actions speak louder than words, Seven Sarr. And you have died before it was time for your death. And you think you can rewrite the future, make the Untamed suffer forever. You think you can play with their lives, watch their pitiful existence and be happy with that—with your choice. Well, no. You can't." He slams his hands down onto the table. "You are *not* in control here. Not like you thought you were. This is Death's world, and in Death's world, Death presides. He is in charge here for ever—even when Death is longer here, this realm will still be his. And you belong to Death, but Death will *not* have you here now. Death will not let people suffer."

Pain snaps at my Achilles tendon.

Death watches me, and then the papery skin peels from his face—great sheaves of it—and the wind catches it, lifts it toward me. I hold my breath, feel his skin against my face.

DIVIDED

Death laughs, and, through the translucent film, I see black blood pouring out of his eye sockets.

"Death cannot return a Seer of his to the world of the mortal planes once the Seer has expired. He can only *exchange* a Seer of his for a similar person. A life for a life. So, tell me now, Seven Sarr. Whose life should Death exchange you for? Which of those closest to you will die for you?"

FORTY-FOUR

I GASP AWAKE, AND—
No.
No.
No.
Death's laughter fills me, and I breathe in air—actual air—into my lungs.
And someone is dead. Will be dead? Is dead now?
Dead because of me.
"Sev!" Corin screams and…and he's holding me—his head so close to mine—and he's crying and—
Crying.
It's not him.
Raleigh. He was here…he made me crash the car…the Mark 1—my Mark 1, my freedom, my escape.
My body jolts, and then Raleigh reacts, wipes a hand across his face, and—
His eyes widen as he sees me. As he sees me looking at him.
"You're alive?"
Alive.
Alive.
Alive.

DIVIDED

The word pounds through me.
Get away. Get away now.
I try to lift my head, but pain wracks through me, my chest, my ribs. I move my head down a fraction, see the blood. I'm soaked, and covered in blood. So is Raleigh.
Somewhere to my right, a dog barks.
My dog.
My terrier.
Get away from Raleigh.
I brace myself for the pain as I lift my arm, as I plant my hand squarely on Raleigh's chest and push. I expect him to stop me, but he doesn't. Doesn't push me back, physically or mentally. Doesn't—
I feel lighter. Freer.
Freer.
I stop and then I really feel it: the difference.
Raleigh's control over me. I hadn't realized it was so heavy, not until now, not until it has gone. Because it *has*. Gone when I died... Raleigh was only going to have access to my soul until my death, because he didn't want the connection sustained, didn't want Death accessing *him* after my life? Or because he can't command a dead soul...like Jed.
And it has gone—the connection. I stare at my arms. The fitted shirt has long sleeves, but one of them is ripped and the fabric falls away. I can see my skin. Pure, beautiful. No gold marks. The Promise Marks have gone. *Gone.*
I died.
And I'm back.
And Raleigh can't control me. Raleigh no longer has my soul. I feel like screaming.
Now Raleigh looks at me. "You—your heart stopped beating—I heard it... I tried to..." And then, "Sev?" And he buries his face in my chest, and he's shaking, shuddering with emotion that can't be true....
But I sense his emotions, the waves of them, like they're tangible, wrapping around me, trying to fool

me.

"Get away from me." My voice is weak, and it sounds strained, raspy. I blink hard as light-headedness swarms within me. But I can feel my powers are there, my Seer powers, and they make me feel stronger, internally. Not as vulnerable.

I push at him again, but, physically, I'm weak. So weak. Do I use my powers to get him away from me?

Raleigh lifts his head and stares at me with Corin's eyes. Why is he using Corin's appearance? Again? Still? *Why?*

To torment me.

"Get away from me," I say again. "Leave me alone. And at least have the decency to use your own image."

"My own image?"

"I know it's you," I growl.

"What?" Raleigh says, pushing his sleeves up. His shirt's blue: brighter in some places, faded in others. He's changed his shirt—his whole outfit. I look at his torn jeans, heavily scuffed. But...but they look familiar... "Sev, it's me. Corin."

"Don't lie." I shake my head then gasp as pain engulfs me, sends sparks down my spine. "Don't lie, *Raleigh*."

"Sev?" He shakes his head. "Look, it's... It is me. I'm not...not Raleigh."

He shakes his head harder, and then the faint smell of cigarette smoke teases my nostrils.

Smoke. Corin? My breath catches in my throat. It—

"We need to move," he says. "They could be out here any minute. Where's Esther? Is she still in there?"

Esther. He's asking about Esther.

Raleigh didn't ask about Esther before, when he was pretending to be Corin. My chest twists.

This is Corin? The *real* Corin?

A strange taste takes over my mouth, and I wince.

The man in front of me looks grim for a moment, and I don't know who he is. Corin or not-Corin. Because he can't be Corin—not *my* Corin—because he'll be

DIVIDED

long gone. He won't have hung about. The Enhanced Ones' drones would've found him, wouldn't they? And it can't be Corin—coincidences like this don't just happen.

Yet he's asking about Esther.

A knot in my stomach hardens and twists.

"Sev?"

Corin grabs hold of me, turns me away from him, just as I throw up. My vomit is watery, dark in color, and has even darker bits floating in it. The sight of it makes my stomach flip again.

I lift a hand to my head, breathing hard. "What...."

I wait for the next bout of nausea to pass before I look at him. My dog trots into view. He's not growling at the man. At *Corin*? The man I love? The man who doesn't know I love him?

"How do I know it's you? Really you?" I whisper.

He grimaces. "Because it's *me*. And we're—we're a team, Sev. You and me." He holds my hand gently, then presses my fingers against his heart.

We're a team.

Something in me stutters.

I shake my head and pull my hand back, ignore the hurt on his face. "I need to be sure... Tell me something about Nbutai."

His eyes crinkle. "After Finn emptied the toilet pot over you—years and years ago—I caught a scorpion and threw it at him."

"A scorpion?" I stare at him. "That didn't happen."

He nods. "It did. Rahn found out. Went mad at me. But he told me and Finn never to say a word about it."

I frown, feel the lines on my forehead. "No. Tell me something else, something that proves it to me."

"That wasn't good enough?"

My breathing gets shallower. I look down at my once-beige shorts; they're covered in stains, and there's a rip across the fabric on my upper thigh. I can see more of my skin through it, skin with no gold marks. "It's got to be something I know too...something I can verify. The details." I wince as more pain snakes around me. It's on my left side mainly. My ribs, my chest, my shoulder. My hip, my leg.

He's quiet for a moment. I stare at the sky behind him. Is it darkening already? Or is that my vision? Got to be my vision...it was morning wasn't it, when I escaped? Or...how long was I dead for?

"I broke the decent radios, before. At Nbutai. I was angry, and I trashed them. Gave your brother a load of extra work. And Esther told me off about that. Made me feel like a piece of shit. I was just so angry, and I didn't even mean to break them—I just. I wanted to break something. That good enough?"

"Why were you angry?" I ask.

"Does it matter?"

I nod.

He exhales hard. "I heard Finn talking about you."

Cold air pushes against my teeth.

"He was saying some stuff. Stuff he shouldn't have been. Stuff about you. And Nico and Yani were laughing with him. But I wasn't." His hand tightens into a fist. "Gods, I wanted to punch him—to break him, because of what he was saying. Not just because it was about you—I didn't... That sort of stuff shouldn't be said about any girl. But Rahn was watching, and I knew..." He shakes his head, then looks at me. "And...and I love you, Sev. Maybe I loved you even then, I just didn't know it... But now. Gods. What the hell were you thinking? I saw you drive at those trees and...and you weren't breathing when I got you out, and I tried to resuscitate you, but you were just...."

Resuscitate.

Mouth-to-mouth. I flinch.

I kissed Raleigh, because I thought he was Corin. And I don't know why I think of that—why I let it consume me—when Corin's here. The real Corin?

My Seer pendant flashes cold against my skin. I want to reach up and touch it, but I don't.

Corin takes my hand again, and his fingers around

mine *should* send jolts through me, I know that. But they don't.

"Can't you feel it?" he asks. "It's me. It's really me."

I swallow hard, my eyes smart with the effort. And then—then I know I can verify that it's him for sure. Dying didn't take my powers away—I can feel them—and Death wouldn't have thrown me back to life if it had. I need them to end the war. And I'm connected to Corin—all my connections to the Untamed, they're still there. Suddenly, I can feel them, sense each one individually.

And the thrill of it fills me, the thrill of body-sharing, of becoming someone else.

You're just like Raleigh. He loved controlling you.

No. I'm not like Raleigh. And I won't be controlling Corin. I'm just doing it to confirm that this man really is him. Not another imposter.

I breathe deeply. I connected with Corin before—when he was outside, running—and it's easy to follow the route to him now, to climb the mountain, find the key, to put it in the lock, to turn it. And before I've really thought about it, I'm in him. A quick snap and—

Emotion hits me. Waves and waves of it—the most turbulent sea.

I look through his eyes, see myself. See myself looking so...so different. Gaunt. Broken. They're the only words I can think of. My cheeks have sunk, and my eyes—they're haunted. So much pain in them. Cuts and bruises cover me.

Shit. She looks awful. Scared. Something's happened to her, when she was in there. Must've, if she tried to—

I snap back into my body.

"Sev, it's me." His voice cracks, and I know he didn't even sense me. I was careful. I hid.

"I know," I say. Because I'm connected to the real Corin. And this is him.

So why do I feel empty?

Corin carries me across the sand, weaving between rocks and low-creeping foliage. My head is against his chest, jolting against him with the momentum of his walk. The texture of his shirt is scratchy, and some of the buttons catch against my face. After a while, his arms—under my shoulders and knees—start to feel like rock.

The dog walks at his feet, and, every now and again, I catch a glimpse of him. I tried to walk at one point, but my injuries were too much.

Now, though, Corin stops for a short rest and sets me gently on the ground, helping me to sit up. I grimace as pain wracks through me, but I manage to support my posture myself.

We're by two small trees—some cover, at least.

I swallow hard. I know we need to talk.

"I don't think you know everything that's happened," I say. "All of it. And you need to."

He's sitting opposite me—so, between us, we've got eyes on most of the land around us—and his gaze snaps onto me. The look in them reminds me of lightning.

I look down at my arms. At where the Promise Marks were. Where that scar is now, from where I tried to cut one off. I run my thumb over it, wince. When I look up again, I see Corin's watching my movements. He's noticed the scar. He doesn't question it though, just waits for me.

So, I start at the beginning. The very beginning of what he doesn't know: the first time I saw Death, saw Waskabe. And I keep talking. I tell him about how the steam eruption in the Zharat den got me, how I lost consciousness, how I found myself in the Dream Land. And how it was my banishment. How

DIVIDED

the Gods and Goddesses were furious that I'd ignored multiple warnings and let people be converted. And how I didn't understand because I'd only had one dream that could've been a warning—the nightmare of Three—and I'd decided it wasn't as I hadn't seen the bison. But I hadn't had any other Seeing dreams. And I tried to tell Death that, but he didn't believe me, insisted I'd let multiple conversion attacks happen—and Death thinks he sees all, but he doesn't.

Then I tell Corin of the augury—why I'm so special, how I'm expected to end the war. His eyes never leave mine.

I tell him how Jed must've got me out of the Zharat cave, and what he did at the top of the Fire Mountain, how he bound my soul to Raleigh, how he was taking orders from him the whole time. And how I found out it was Jed who orchestrated it all—how he used kavalah spirits to block my Seeing dreams. Supposedly to ensure I wasn't killed for being a Seer.

"He knew, Corin." I grab a handful of sand, watch it run through my fingers. "All that time, he knew I was a Seer—and he was...he was trying to protect me." My eyes widen.

"*Protect* you?" Corin shakes his head. "That man has caused all of this and—" He breaks off, then swears. "You think he was *protecting* you?"

"He kept me alive in the Zharat cave... The other men couldn't kill me for being a Seer if I had no dreams." My voice is low.

Corin shakes his head harder. "That is a twisted way to look at things, Sev. Jed is evil."

Then he groans as he stretches his legs out, and I stare at the rips and scuffed marks on his jeans, see how the sole of one of his shoes is coming away.

"He was following his father's instructions. He wanted—I don't know what he wanted. Raleigh to like him?"

"Raleigh?"

"He's his father. And Raleigh killed Jed, just like

that. His own son." It still makes me feel *wrong*.

Corin swallows hard. His hands close into fists, get tighter and tighter. A muscle pulses in his jaw. Then he shakes his head, and I continue.

I tell him what happened in the compound. How Raleigh had control of me, tortured me, how the Untamed were strangely allergic to the augmenters, how Raleigh activated my Seer powers, how he used them—made me kill Elia Jackson. When I talk of how I can body-share, my voice lightens a little—though I notice how Corin tries to hide his unease, his shock at this revelation. Then I tell him that Raleigh made me connect to other Untamed. And how he plans to end the Untamed with me.

Corin groans.

But I don't tell him about Raleigh pretending to *be* Corin. How he tricked me. Even though, I suspect, Corin has probably guessed something along those lines, given how I was convinced he was Raleigh when I…when I came back to life. But I can't tell Corin how we slept—me and Raleigh—curled up together. How I kissed him. How I pressed myself against him. How I was desperate to touch his bare chest, how I wondered what he'd look like naked. The memory makes me feel sick. Bad and sick. I shudder. A cold wind blows across my back.

I finish the story with how I escaped and how Raleigh made me crash the vehicle.

Corin exhales hard, then he looks at me, and I see tears glistening in his eyes. I watch as they spill over, make tracks down his face. "I'm sorry I left you. Both times."

"Both?"

He nods, and his posture almost seems to get smaller. "In the compound, New Kitembu…and before…in the Zharat den."

The skin around his eyes creases as he looks at me, holds my gaze for a second. When he looks away, I feel like I've been stabbed, and I reach for his hand, cling

DIVIDED

to it, feel something at last—even if it's not the same.

"I left you there, Sev. In the Zharat cave. When the eruption..." He looks past me, but I see more tears in his eyes—the rawness. "Shit. I'm so sorry, Sev. It was—it was chaos. And we got separated, and then I saw you—on the ground—but I couldn't get to you. Jed was nearer, and he shouted that he'd get you, and I had to get his daughter."

"Jeena?"

"Yeah. I shouldn't have agreed, but it was... I should've gone for *you*. And I didn't even reach Jeena in time, her screams were... And then—then I saw Jed carrying you away, and I thought you were safe. Sev, I really did. I didn't know he was going to bind you to the Enhanced. Make you do all—"

He meets my eyes again, and the watery layer does something to me. Makes something inside me twist uncomfortably.

Corin breathes deeply, like he's struggling with everything. "I just had to get out after that eruption started. I didn't—shit. *I* should've been the one to get you out. Not him. Not that bastard. If it had been me, none of this would've happened, and Raleigh wouldn't be...."

"It's all right." I grip his hand harder, so hard I think I feel his heartbeat. The strong beat of life, thrumming into me.

"It's not all right! It's not f—" He takes a deep breath. "It's *not* all right." His nostrils flare, and he pulls his hand back from me—as if he can't bear to touch me. "We've lost—"

"No," I say. "We haven't. Not yet—and we won't."

"But Raleigh can control you—he made you kill a girl. We've got no chance, and the Gods and Goddesses have turned their backs on you thanks to Jed and—"

"Stop," I say. "I—he can't control me now. Raleigh hasn't got my soul. Not after I..." *Died* doesn't seem like the right word, not when saying it out loud.

But that's what happened.

And then Death took my death from me, threw me back to life with the promise of taking someone who was close to me. Who? Has it happened? What if it's... what if he's going to take Corin?

I gulp, suddenly filled with images of Corin dropping dead in front of me.

Corin sniffs loudly. "Does he still have your eyes?"

"What?" Then I frown, press my lips together, think hard. I lean back a little. "I don't think so. Not after all that... The soul-commanding connection broke. The tracker must've too. All connections must've broken."

But you don't know that.

Corin's silent for a long time. When he finally speaks, his voice sounds strange—a low murmur that's angry and harsh.

"I should've protected you, and I didn't." A new film slides over his eyes, but he wipes the tears away with the back of his hand, won't let these ones fall. "I *didn't*, Sev. And I'm so sorry."

His words are so angry, yet his face is so sad.

"You couldn't have stopped any of that," I say. "And it's not your job to protect me. But we're together now."

And I love you.

I want to say the words. But...but I don't, and I don't know why I don't because they're burning a savage hole in me.

Corin turns his head, and I think he's wiping his eyes again. When he turns back, his face is even redder. "Well, at least it's sorted now. Jed's mistake—everything he did—it's been corrected. We're back to where we were, as if we never went to the Zharat den. You and me."

Except we're not, and we both know it. I'm probably still banished from the Dream Land. Still a useless Seer? Or will Death be able to persuade the others now we've spoken, now that the Promise Marks have gone? But it wasn't Death who undid them. It was *my* death. And did Waskabe even believe me, that I

DIVIDED

had no say in being bound to the Enhanced, nor in ignoring the dreams that Jed blocked?

But you have your powers now. Your Seer powers.

I try not to think of the girl I killed. The way Elia's eyes followed me. How I dream of her in the moments I forget upon waking. How the guilt eats me.

How it felt, having Raleigh controlling me. How I couldn't do anything.

How my brother's one of them, fully, completely. And it's my fault.

How it's just me and Corin now, and the dog. No Esther. Just the two of us.

Nothing has been corrected. Just undone. Jed's mistake has been undone. But, as Keelie would have said, a load more shit has happened.

But you know more too now. More about the augury. And you can connect to them all now as well. Good stuff's happened too.

Like my Seer powers: unlocked. It seems crazy.

Corin moves and then pulls me close, carefully, gently. "You're free, Sev. Free of them, free of it all."

Free. I am not free.

He turns my face up to his, his thumb on my jaw. I barely register the brush of his lips against mine. And I don't feel anything. Not like before. There are no sparks within me. I'm empty. A shell. A shell of—

Raleigh. His lips.

I pull away from Corin, breathing hard. My hands shake.

"Sev?" His voice is low. "What is it?"

And I want to tell him, but I don't. And I tell myself I'm thinking of him, because I know how jealousy eats him up. How it burns and burns and burns and burns.

Jealousy? How can it be jealousy? Raleigh tricked you. You thought he was Corin.

But it still burns me. Fire inside me. And Corin's eyes are trying to put it out.

"Nothing," I tell him. The lie makes me feel sick, but I don't want him to know. I should have realized it wasn't Corin. Corin, who I loved. No—*love*. And I didn't even recognize when it wasn't him.

Corin gives me a dubious look, and then we set off again, him carrying me.

"I tried to get into the compound twice, to get you and Esther out," he says after a long time.

"How close did you get?"

"Not that close." He jolts me up a little in his arms. "There were too many Enhanced about. It's a bloody big city that one."

"No one spotted you, did they?"

"No."

"What about the drones? Three said they use drones to scan this area, to find Untamed."

My chest tightens. Three said Corin had been detected by a drone. Liar!

"Yeah, they're monsters," Corin says.

"They haven't detected you though?"

He shrugs. "I'm still here. Still Untamed."

And the way he says it sends warning shivers down my spine. As if it's a clue that he's not really who he says it is. Because he's been conveniently undetected… because he's Enhanced? Because I'm no freer out here with him than I was inside, under Raleigh's control?

My body tenses. But I body-shared with him. I know it *is* Corin this time.

"What is it?" Corin asks, and his pace slows.

He holds me tighter, more firmly, and I look up, see him twisting his head to look behind us. He turns back a moment later; when his eyes meet mine, they bore into me. Bore into me in a way they haven't done before—with a burning intensity. Flames that grab me, flames that promise to engulf me, never let me go.

It's supposed to end in fire.

I flinch. Don't know where that thought came from.

But there's something…somewhere, digging away. Only I can't remember.

"Nothing," I say.

Corin carries me a long, long way—his pace getting

slower and slower, and his breathing heavier, more ragged—and then he sets me down. We're in the middle of a copse of low trees. There aren't many leaves on them, but there are some strange-looking large nuts hanging from a couple of the lower branches.

"I've been staying here," Corin says, gestures around. The dog is nose-to-the-ground a few feet away. "On the other side of the trees, there's an old vehicle. I checked it for a GPS tracker before I dug out the sand under it, made a cave. It holds enough heat there at night. I've been sleeping there."

He sits down next to me, and I can't help but think how awful he looks. And that makes me feel better—even though I *know* it is him. No Enhanced would choose to look that bad. Sweat stains have dripped around his collar, under his arms. His hair's greasy, looks matted at the left side with something dark. Blood.

Corin stares at me. He rubs the back of his neck. "You look different without your hair long."

My shoulders tighten, and I grimace, don't know how I'd forgotten and—

And he doesn't like it. Corin doesn't like it. I can tell instantly, and a sadness builds in the pit of my stomach, even though I know his opinion shouldn't make me feel like I do. But I prefer my longer hair too. I wrap my arms around my body as tightly as I can, ignoring the pain across my ribs.

"Did Raleigh make you do that too?" His voice is low.

I nod. Raleigh *did* it.

Corin looks grim. "Made you cut your hair *and* made you kill children." He shakes his head. "And made you make connections to other Untamed." Then he looks at me sharply. "Are you connected to me?"

And I know it's the question he wanted to ask earlier, when I was telling him. And the answer makes my body flush with heat.

"It happened...yes," I say at last. "Not with Raleigh

doing it though."

He inhales sharply, and the look on his face changes, like he hadn't expected that to really be the answer. Like he was certain I wouldn't have shared with him. Like he thought he knew me, and that asking the question was just for his own peace of mind.

I watch as he swallows—with some difficulty—then wipes his hand across the back of his mouth, hard, so his lips drain of color for a moment.

"You were one of the first..." I quickly say. "I—I didn't know what was happening at that time though—it was before I knew what body-sharing was. It just happened—I had no control."

But the last time you knew exactly what you were doing.

I try not to breathe. Even though my shirt and shorts are nearly dry now, they feel a lot heavier, as if they're weighing me down, trapping me.

"You were inside my head?" Corin's tone changes.

I nod. "Your body too." And I don't know why I even say the words, why I try to make it worse than it already is.

"You were in my *body*?"

"I didn't control you," I say quickly. "I was just... there. Didn't even hear your thoughts."

Except for the ones, earlier. About how awful I look, and how he's sure something bad happened to me in the city. But I can't bring myself to say that, and I need to reassure him.

Corin's eyes narrow. "You can hear thoughts in some people? It's not just sharing bodies?" A vein in his neck pulses.

Slowly, I nod. "But it's different each time I do it—even with the same person sometimes. It's like... sometimes I *become* the person, but they're still there. We're moving together—and communicating, talking. All in our heads. Or *their* head—I don't know. Other times, I'm hiding, just witnessing stuff. And everything the person does, I'm aware of it. But it's like I'm watching, and I know it's not happening to *me*.

DIVIDED

I feel it...but I don't. It's hard to explain. And then...a few times I've taken control completely, squashed the person."

"You've taken control?" He doesn't hide the anger in his voice.

"Yes." I lift my eyes up to meet his. "I saved an Untamed woman who fell through ice. She'd gone into shock, couldn't swim to the hole in the ice." Or maybe she was already dead? I think of how her heart felt. And I brought her back to life with my powers? "I took over her body, became her. Got her out the ice. And she survived. She shouldn't have—not under icy water like that. But she did."

Corin swears under his breath, looks at me, then looks away. "No privacy around here, is there?"

And I know what he's feeling—how it's made him feel. How, every time, he's going to wonder if I'm in his head. If I'm going to control him, if I'm listening to his thoughts.

Invasion of privacy.

My mouth dries.

I know all about that.

"What've you been doing then?" I ask. "Since you escaped? Beside trying to get us out."

He folds his arms and groans. "But that was all I was trying to do, really. Kept circling back to the compound. Tried to break in. Hunting, gathering food. Got some kindling in, but there's not exactly a lot of good wood, and I didn't want to take much of what there is in case a drone noticed."

"What are the drones like?"

"Noisy. I'm sure you'll see one for yourself. They come over often enough. Every eight hours or so. And through the night."

I inhale sharply. They'll be looking for me.

Except—except they won't.

Raleigh will think I'm dead, won't he? And he'll know I'm dead because he's lost his command over my soul. Unless he has got my eyes—no, he can't have. And I know I'm right about it, I feel it.

Still, I can't risk being found. Being 'dead' is my advantage. My weapon.

"How far out do they go?" I ask Corin. "The drones?"

The terrier comes back over to us and lies down next to me. He's panting. I frown as I look at him. Not a scratch on him. Not hurt at all.

Corin points far to the left. "They've disappeared over that horizon before. Gone right over my head. If they're supposed to detect us then they're doing a cracking job, aren't they?"

"But one caught Esther and Clare."

The look on Corin's face changes so quickly it's as if a switch has been flicked. "What?" His eyes widen. "Esther? She got out too?"

I nod and look down at my hands. "The Zharat organized an escape. Clare shot Raleigh, and she got me out of the room—but I got separated and caught again." By Three. I try to keep breathing evenly. "But Esther did…she got out, and then…" And then my brother went out to bring her back. "They got her again… And she's injured. Her hip. Might be broken. I don't know. Must be horrible for her," I say. "With the baby. Knowing it's going to be an Enhanced if it's born there. And her too—Raleigh said they'll have augmenters perfected within a couple of days or something…but that was before—might be sooner now. Oh Gods, I've lost track of time. But I can't save all the Untamed, bring us all together, before she's converted. Before we've lost her."

I breathe out slowly and look up at the sky. So blue. So peaceful.

Something clicks next to me. The kind of click a joint makes.

I turn my head.

Corin stares at me, his eyes wider than ever and his face a strange color. He opens his mouth, then shuts it. His brows knit together a little, and he squints at me. "*What* did you say?" His words are heavy and clumsy, as if they're catching on rocks and getting thrown back and forth, crashing from side to side. "A baby?"

I freeze, go completely cold.

"Sev?" He clenches his fists.

I wring my hands together. "Esther's pregnant, Corin. She—she found out there. At the compound." Or, at least, I assume she did.

Corin's nostrils flare, and he jumps up, tension snapping through his body. "Whose is it?" He points at me as if I'll say the answer on command.

I lean back a little. "Manning's, I guess."

Corin swears, then makes a deep growl at the back of his throat. Then he takes a step from me, shakes his head. The light in his eyes makes him look savage.

He looks at the dog. Points at him in the same way he just pointed at me. "Look after Sev, okay? You understand? I'll be back soon."

"Corin?" I stare at him as he breaks into a run—a run away from me.

A run back to the compound.

FORTY-FIVE

I CALL AFTER CORIN, BUT it's no use. Either he's ignoring me, or he doesn't hear me. And then he's gone—disappeared into the pale orange landscape.

I take several deep breaths, and then I try to get up. After a moment, I manage it, and I take a few shaky steps. My legs seem to be okay—I'm just weak. The pain is mainly in and around my torso. I hold my arms up, see the bruising on them and marvel again at the lack of gold marks. They've really gone.

A strange sensation fills me. I look at the dog, and the dog looks back at me. He steps closer. I lift a hand to my eyes—ignore my protesting shoulder—and shield my face as a ray of the sun brightens. I try to see the way Corin's gone—as if by looking hard enough, my eyes will pick out his figure.

But I can't see him.

He's gone from sight.

Gone to the compound, to get Esther out.

But he can't go there! Not on his own—especially after I've just escaped. There's a good chance the compound will be on high alert, even if they think I'm dead—and they should think that. Raleigh *must've* felt my death when he lost my soul. And how's Corin even going to get Esther out? I doubt she can walk.

I grit my teeth. Then I muster up what little energy I have and follow Corin. The dog whines at me, but he follows, sticks close by. I breathe heavily as I walk, feel sweat break out across the back of my neck. I touch the skin there gently, but when my hand comes away, blood glistens from my fingers. For a moment, I stare at the redness. How much damage did I do when I crashed?

Not just damage. You died. Actually died.

The thought makes me shudder, and I try to think, try to remember that time *after* my death, but before the cave with the woman, Vala Sarr, before Waskabe... And it comes back, fragments float back: my mother...a connection to her, so strong and I know she felt my death...memories, my family...and a man screaming and another crying... Corin and Raleigh? One screaming, one crying?

And Raleigh knows. *Knows* I died. Confirmation.

But the whole memory feels different...not like other memories...not like anything I've experienced. Just...just different.

And my mother—does she still think I'm dead? Or is our connection enough to tell her I'm alive again?

I gulp as I walk. Two minutes later, my legs give way. I crash onto the earth. My head pounds, and the roof of my mouth tastes strange and furry. I breathe hard, my nostrils flaring, and stare at my splayed out fingers on the sand, at the bits of grit around them.

I'm not going to be able to follow Corin.

He's going to be on his own.

And if he never makes it back, I won't even know what happens to him. And I never told him I love him. *Still.*

The realization pulls through me, makes my chest ache. Corin—who I've only just got back. Corin—who I've lost again.

The dog pushes his nose against my arm, looks into

my eyes. My own eyes water. My dog came back. Corin will too, won't he?

Except he'll get caught, a drone will find him. And he'll be converted. And I won't even know. Won't even know when it happens.

Except you can know. You can know exactly what happens to him, if you choose to.

My back clicks.

No.

Not that. Corin made it clear he wasn't comfortable with me body-sharing with him. Invasion of privacy. Spying.

I stroke the dog slowly. His fur is a little matted on one side. And I stare at the dog, think of Corin. Think of how easy it would be to body-share, to stay hidden. And he wouldn't even know. Not if I was just there, just an observer. And I know I can do it.

No. I shake my head firmly, as if the action will inscribe the thought in me forever. I can't do that.

I look at the sky, then around me. I haven't gone far, but I'm more out in the open now. More exposed. More detectable? I press my lips together as I think of the drones, try to work out what I should do when one comes over. My throat feels raw, and there's a humming in my head. Three said they used thermal imaging, but Corin wasn't detected. My eyes narrow as I think. The question of *why* burns through me. And would I be the same? Esther wasn't…she was detected, they got her.

I narrow my eyes at the horizon. Corin said the drones come over every eight hours or so. I don't know when the last one was or when the next is due.

The terrier lies down next to me, leans against me. His body feels warm and solid. I look around, know that I should walk back to the copse, but I can't. My muscles are screaming, and, now I'm concentrating on my body, I feel all the pain.

As if I could have ever gone after Corin! And to do what? To stop him? Or help him get Esther out?

DIVIDED

Esther.

Something whirs in my head, makes me think of a slow-turning wheel. I *can* help.

I breathe out slowly, then make the transition to Esther's body quickly, easily. She's sitting up, and, at first, I don't realize who she's with, because he blends into the background so well. But then I see the movement as he turns his head, as the reflection in his eyes changes.

Raleigh's hand touches Esther's thigh—her good one—and she pulls her leg away sharply—or maybe I do it for her. Pain ricochets through to her bad hip, but the pain is lesser now. Not broken then?

"Stop it," she whispers, but her voice hitches, and then I feel the dampness on her face. Tears. Her body shudders, and she wraps her arms around her good leg as she brings that knee up to her chest.

"I am deeply sorry for your loss," Raleigh says, his voice like liquid chocolate. Too sticky, too sweet. "Death is such a sad thing, a terrible thing for Untamed creatures to experience. But it's not for the Chosen Ones, and you have to concentrate on that."

I go cold, feel what little warmth there is in the world freeze over, and I want to run, to hide, to never be found again. Get as far away as possible.

Someone's died.

Three.

It's Three. He's dead. Raleigh killed him, because I told him that Three was on our side and—and I was wrong and—

Oh Gods. Death wanted someone close to me.

My head pounds, everything's spinning across it too fast. Raleigh must know that Esther and my brother were close, and now he's telling her...and Three's dead.

My brother's dead. Because of me, because of what I said, what I told him, how Three was helping me and—

But he wasn't! He was on Raleigh's side—completely

converted. Didn't help me. Three knew that 'Corin' wasn't really Corin, that he was Raleigh...and he was desperate to get me to see him, so Raleigh could use *my* powers. Something close to hatred burns in me, but it can't be hatred because he's my brother...no, *was* my brother.

And he's dead.

Raleigh smiles and looks at Esther—looks at me. And, for a moment, he stares right at me inside her. At me. As if he can see me.

My breathing gets faster—Esther's gets faster.

"She's dead?" she whispers, and her voice catches. "Seven's dead?"

Every part of me jolts.

Me? Talking about me? Not Three. And I don't even know whether to feel relief.

My head pounds, and then I'm reaching for her.

No. Esther, it's okay. I'm here.

She jumps, and I jump.

"What?" she says, looks around. Her neck clicks. "Sev—"

Talk to me in your head, I cut in quickly. *Raleigh can't know I'm alive.*

Esther breathes in deeply, and her breath whistles. Then she rubs the back of her neck. Pain flares up in her hip, and I try to ignore how it feels like it's happening to me—because her body is mine now, while I'm here.

"What happened?" Esther says.

Raleigh folds his arms slowly, then unfolds them. He's got a gold ring on his finger, and he twists it around. "Shania escaped and chose to kill herself."

Esther's eyes widen.

No, I tell her. *I escaped and Raleigh got control of my body. He made me crash. I... I did die, but I came back. Death saved me, Esther. But, listen—Corin's coming to get you out.*

Esther bites her bottom lip, hard. We wince. She looks down at her hip.

I'm not sure I can get away.

DIVIDED

"Shania's death is a tragedy," Raleigh says, still twisting his gold ring. "She has died at the wrong time and the augury will be a lie now." He clears his throat. "Shania's loss means the augury cannot be fulfilled. It means the Gods will write a new augury, or they may not. Perhaps the war will never end. Shania may have caused eternal suffering, though I will, of course, do my best to end it myself."

I stare at him, stare at him through Esther's eyes, feel the anger rising within me—my own body, back in the open—feel it threatening to tip, and then Esther gulps, and I feel the hot rush of her tears as they run down her face, feel her body shudder, her nose prickle, and—

But I am alive! Esther, Raleigh doesn't know. We have the advantage. Us, the Untamed.

Briefly, I wonder whether I can get a message to my mother via Esther, a message telling her I'm definitely alive. In case she doesn't know, in case she's grieving... But, if my mother knows, could Raleigh extract the information from her?

A radio blares out, and Esther and I both jump. I turn her head, look to the left.

Raleigh pulls the device from his pocket, speaks into it. I try to hear what he's saying, but he's talking quietly, secretively, and Esther's breathing is too loud, and she's still hiccupping and crying.

Raleigh smiles widely at Esther as he puts the radio away. I feel the goosebumps rise on Esther's arms. Her heart speeds up, matches my own, far away in my body. She takes a deep breath, and her gulp stutters.

"I have good news," Raleigh says. "Very good news—and this will make it much easier for you to cope with Shania's death. You're feeling too much, and it is destroying you. The badness and the pain. But the augmenters are ready now. The new ones. We've been using your friend Soraya to test them, and she has shown no reaction to these ones, even after multiple administrations of the different grades."

I feel the blood drain from my face—Esther's face—and I grip my hands together, clench them hard—realize I've made Esther do it.

Oh Gods.

"Oh Gods," Esther whispers.

And then Raleigh grips her, grips me. His fingers, bruising around her arm, and—

And I fight back.

Esther cries out as I take over her body, every part; somehow, I stand up, wobbling, my body wracking with pain. Esther's leg on the injured side seems shorter, makes me feel off-balance. I look Raleigh in the eye.

Then I punch him.

The movement twists through my body, but my left hip—Esther's left hip—won't turn, and jarring pain fills my spine. I gasp and—

Someone grabs me, hands around my throat. Big hands with gnarly fingers, fingers that dig into my skin, my throat.

My own one.

I'm thrown back into my body, lose the connection, lose Esther. Leave her with Raleigh and—

I scream, try to turn, try to see, kick out as I'm dragged backward by someone. Sand and dust fly up, create a cloud. I try to flip my body over, try to see my attacker—but pain kicks through me. My ribs. Something moves and—

I see my dog running away, running as fast as he can, yapping and—

My head's yanked back.

I see him, my attacker.

I see him, and everything stops.

No.

No.

No.

It can't be.

Dead. He—

But he's not dead. He's here. Right here and—

DIVIDED

This keeps happening. How can it keep happening?

His lips peel back as he smiles, delivers the most aggressive smile I've ever seen. He drags me to my feet, then lets go of me, and my body locks up. I can't breathe; it feels like there's ice in my veins.

I stare at him. "*Rahn?*"

FORTY-SIX

HE LOOKS THE SAME.

Rahn Eriksen looks the same. Messy dark hair, sunglasses, that hooked nose. The lean body that makes him look weaker than he is.

I stare at him. My breath catches on the lumps in my throat. Nausea squeezes me with its fine fingers.

I stare at him, continue to stare—it's all I can do. He's here. *Here*. Really here.

But he's dead.

Three killed him. Shot him. I saw him die.

He *died*.

But he's here, back. And he's real? Substantial—unless….

My hand goes to my neck, and I feel where his hands were only moments before. I swallow hard, my throat feels thick. Bruised? He's real. Whatever he is, he's real.

He steps forward. *You're goin' to help me, Seven. And you're goin' to help me now.*

It's—he's like Jed, speaking the same way Jed did that last time and—

But they're real. They're both real. Jed got the key

DIVIDED

for me, so I could drive out of the city.

Real. But not?

Do it! Rahn yells, and I step back, feel the wind pick up around me. Warm fingers.

I look around for the dog, can't see him—where did he go? A whimper builds in my throat.

"Rahn," I say, but my voice is weak. I sound pathetic. "Rahn…" And I shouldn't even be saying his name. He shouldn't *be* here.

But Jed shouldn't have been here either.

"Rahn!" I throw my arms up in the air. "I don't know what you mean. I don't understand!" Oh Gods. How can it be him?

The sun glints off his dark glasses, and I think of the eyes underneath. My stomach drops a little. Then Rahn moves his arm—his hand goes to his pocket. He pulls something out, points it at me.

A gun. A Fort-17. A semi-automatic pistol. A *real* semi-automatic pistol.

My breath bursts from me in short, sharp bursts. I stare at the gun as he points it at me, lines it up with my face. The light glints off it.

How about now? Rahn's hand shakes wildly, and the Fort-17 jumps about. *Do you understand now?*

I try to see if the safety is on, but I can't. My eyes won't focus properly. I'm panicking. My head pounds—not enough oxygen, and my mind's going wild, trying to work out what he is…like Jed? Disappearing and reappearing whenever they want? But the gun's real… and the vehicle's key was real and….

Neither made it to the New World. They can't have. They're both trapped here, their souls.

I take a step back and—

Rahn pulls the trigger.

I scream, throw myself down. Taste grit and sand. The sound of the bullet ricochets through me. I scream again, my voice breaking, lift my head up, look at my arms. There's no pain—no new pain, no—

Something clicks in front of me, and I turn my head,

see Rahn coming for me again, the gun leading him, as if it's in control. Adrenaline pours through me, and I shriek loudly—a high-pitched squeak that hurts a part of me, some part, far, far away. I roll over. My foot hits something as I pull myself up, and I leap forward, but at an angle.

It's your fault! Rahn roars at me, and he's waving the Fort-17 like a mad man.

My heart pounds, and I look behind me, quick. Then I lift my hands up, show my palms, the surrender gesture. "Rahn…put it down. Just…just put the gun down."

But he doesn't. He leaps forward, bounding toward me like a gazelle, and I twist out of his way, pain snaking through me.

It's your fault I never made it there, he screams, and then he points a finger at me. A gnarled, twisted finger. *And you have to fix it. You have to do it now. You didn't send me off! And I'm trapped—but you! You claim to be a Seer. So do it. Open the channel for me. Do it now!*

Do it now? I stare at him, feel my eyes go all glassy.

"Rahn, I… I can't. I—"

He lunges for me, and I jolt backward, feel something shift in my chest—a movement that makes me feel sicker than ever.

Do it! Do it now! I know you can! And you don't understand….

He throws his arms into the air wildly—the pistol still in his right hand—and then he's knocked his glasses from his face. And—

And his eyes aren't Enhanced.

But they're not Untamed either.

Fire pours through me as I stare at him. They're not there. His eyes *aren't* there.

Just dark sockets. Like Death's, but…but different.

And the more I stare at his face. The more I see it. See *him*. See the layers dropping away. How his skin isn't an intact sheet but is in tatters, falling away in shreds, revealing muscles and sinews and tissues that have a

DIVIDED

ghostly sheen. The light around us flashes and in that second, I see a skull.

His skull.

Rahn's skull.

He lifts his arm up—and the wind wraps around him, tries to drag his shirt away, but it just exposes his form. The thin arms. Arms that are bones with chunks of flesh hanging onto them.

Pressure builds in my chest, and then I can't breathe. I turn, choking, but he's there—on the other side of me, moved too quickly. And he's leaning in closer. I see every grotesque feature of his face.

I'm disintegratin', Rahn whispers, and that whisper wraps around me, squeezes me, and his words are abrasive, like sandpaper, dragging against my skin.

I try to lean away but the tendrils of those words encase me, force me closer to him. And the smell—I gag. Putrid, rotting flesh.

I'm disintegratin' and it's only goin' to get worse. My voice was the first to change...and now my body's shatterin'... I'm lost between worlds, floating in the void, yet trapped here... Pain is everywhere, Seven! Make it stop! Send me to the New World. Do it!

I try to step back, but he grabs me. That skeletal hand and—and it burns.

Burns me.

Like flames. And then I see fire—see it for a second before I blink: huge, orange flames dancing.

Rahn hisses. *It gets worse, every day, every hour. My shell is unwrappin' more, and it* hurts. *You've no idea how much it bloody hurts. Send me to the New World—do it now! I ain't becomin' one of them. Send me there now!*

His words echo through me.

"One of who?"

One of the spirits! What's left of Rahn's top lip quivers and curls.

My body jolts. A spirit? He's—I yank my arm from him, breathing hard, try to turn. Need to get away.

He's wrong. He's not going to become one. He's a

spirit already.

Oh Gods.

How didn't I realize? He's dangerous. He'll hurt me, eat me.

Evil spirits want to kill people—and Rahn's one of them...not a good one, is he? But even the good ones can be bad.

I look at him, my jaw slackening. He's a spirit. *Rahn's a spirit.*

He opens his mouth, and I see a lone tooth, but it's different—not human. Too pointy, a big fang.

It's everywhere! he screams. *My anger, everywhere. Anger at you, at me, at everyone—and the hunger. It's killing me! I want to eat you, Seven! But I can resist now because I am still only just transformin'. It can take years for some. Days for others—there are no rules—I've watched it! But save me! I've seen what they're like. How desperate they are, the spirits. The anger that fills them, that consumes them. Anger because of the pain. An eternity of sufferin' that their family and friends didn't save them from.*

You should've sent me to the New World. You should've done that—when your brother killed me, you should've done it! Do it now. You owe me that. Do it now, because I'm hungry.

The sky cracks, and I see colors. Dark blues and oranges. Purples and reds. All swirling together.

My mouth dries, and my tongue's all scratchy. My heart pounds.

No. No. No. It's happened too quickly—no warning. None at all.

The Turning.

Shit. He's made it happen. Rahn's brought on the Turning.

Now's the time to do it, Rahn whispers, but his whisper is a snake, a snake weaving toward me. *Now's the time when I'm strong enough. Send me to the New World!*

I turn and run—somehow manage to run, despite the pain and my broken body.

The sky hisses—everything around me hisses—and

DIVIDED

then Rahn's hissing. He's right here. But it's just his face. His face floating along next to me, keeping up. Trails of wispiness fly out behind him, and he's just like the spirits in the Noir Lands, the ones that tried to eat me, the ones that ate the Zharat man and—

I scream as something hits me, and I fall forward. Turn in the sand, panting, see something dark, a mass of it behind me, quivering. Another spirit? Another person who never made it to the New World? My heart pounds. Is that what they really are?

My head pounds with images, with flashes, with words. I can't think. Got to run. And I scrabble up, and I'm running—I died earlier, yet I'm running.

But not fast though.

Seven! Rahn yells, and—

My foot hits something, and I fall again. Fall heavily, this time, most of my weight going through my right wrist. Feel a heavy crunch, and the wind's knocked out of me. I gasp, look to my left, see Rahn—

Rahn and the other spirits.

I swallow twice, quickly, my throat raw. My chest rises and falls too quickly as I stare at them, stare at the skulls and bones, the dancing eyes, the masses of color. They all look different. Different and—

A spirit shrieks, and the sound haunts me. Pain in my head and—

And I'm out in the Turning. Shit! The most dangerous time. Oh Gods—

Save me! Rahn screams.

I whirl around as I try to get up, stumble and put a foot wrong, onto something cold and—

My body jerks, and then I'm upright. But I can't see him, Rahn, not now and—

Oh Gods. My chest tightens. The spirits…so many of them…and they're all here and….

And what if they're all like Rahn? What if they all want me to save them? What if that's why they come after us in the Turnings? What if that's their main reason, but they're hungry too—and they can't help it…but they first come because they want help…they want to be saved…and we didn't know.

My head pounds, my lungs feel like they're going to explode. I can't save Rahn, can't save any of them. I can't open a path to the New World for them—it's too late. People have to be sent off as soon as they die to help their chances of getting there, to the New World… we all know that! And these people didn't make it.

But Five got there, and she wasn't sent off.

But she was Untamed.

She'd have a better chance of getting to the New World anyway. And Rahn…was Enhanced—the Gods and Goddesses would've stopped him from getting there. I go cold, look around. Were most of these spirits Enhanced in their lives? And that's why they didn't make it to the New World, why they're here now… and that's why there are more sprits now? More spirits than before, than years ago…because the number can only grow when the Enhanced are increasing, and dying when even their augmenters can't save their far-aged bodies or when we kill them….

My head pounds. dizzy, I'm dizzy. Disorientated.

Do it now!

Suddenly, Rahn's right in front of me, and he looks more human again. But then his image wavers, wavers like it's a projection—a projection, except he's solid, solid because he grabs me again, screeches into my ear, and pain—so much pain and—

I throw white light at him, but he dodges it, and it hits a spirit behind him. A mesh of snarling and hissing and—

Come here!
Save me!
Help me!
Let me eat you!

The voices jolt through me—and I hear them as people now—and it does something to me, makes me feel sick.

Lightning forks through the sky, and I scream—

scream as thunder encases me, scream as more spirits come for me.

I start running again, running blindly. Don't know where I am. It's just desert, sand and desert, and I'm so disorientated, and I've covered ground. The copse with the old vehicle should be somewhere about, but it's not and—

I throw more white light as a spirit gets too close. How are there so many *here*? I thought the land around New Kimearo had few spirits…but there are loads—they're all coming, coming for me? Because Rahn's called them? Because it's the Turning. Oh Gods. I turn my head, try to see where Rahn is, but can't. It's just the others. The skulls, the bones, the ones with thousands of eyes. And they're shouting at me, and my ears are roaring with blood and their words, and I'm running as hard as I can, as fast as I can. Feel more energy flood into me. My chest numbs a little, the pain eases. Against my skin, my mother's Seer pendant burns, and I think of Corin. He's out there in this—the Turning—and he's not a Seer. He can't defend himself against spirits.

Neither can you.

The words swoop at me, and I shriek and—

Something bites me.

She can save us all, get us to the New World!

I kick out, feel a splattering of liquid across the back of my head, my neck, turn and—

A skull, in front of me.

And everything goes white.

FORTY-SEVEN

I OPEN MY EYES, GROGGY, confused, but certain that some time has passed. Pain dances over me, and I blink—the light's too bright, but it's only in slivers. A strip of it, on either side of me. Above and below is darkness, but the light itself is too white. I squint, feel my head get heavier. My neck creaks.

I sit up and bang my head on something, hunker back down, groan and—

It is over, S'ven.

I turn sharply, my chest feels like it's going to explode. Jed's eyes are in the narrow strip of white light on my left.

Come out, he says. And his voice is soft. Softer than it's ever been.

I move slowly, cautiously. Reach my hand up. Metal, covered in dirt. Mud? I crawl out from under the metal thing, blinking in the daylight. So bright. I squint. The sun's so strong. Is it still the same day? Or the next? I can't tell, my head just feels...strange.

I stand up, look around. It's just Jed and me. Standing next to an abandoned car, among a few trees and—

I recognize the trees to the left. That's where Corin

carried me, where he left me. We're back here?

I breathe out slowly.

Jed moves closer to me, and I flinch, pull away from him, feel my heart speed up.

It is all right, he says. *They have gone. That one who was after you has gone.*

I stare at him for a few moments. "Where's he gone? Where have they all gone?" And why is Jed still here? He's one of them too, isn't he?

He points upward, and I stare at his arm.

To the skies, he says. *The void. Already, in these two weeks, I have seen it: the longer they are spirits, the Lost Souls, the harder it becomes for them to stay here. Some manage it, the strong ones. And the ones who feed regularly. But most only appear to take their physical form during times of great power.*

Like the Turnings. So it was going to happen anyway? It wasn't Rahn's doing?

I breathe slowly, then look at Jed. "You didn't make it to the New World either. You're one of them too?" And I don't know why I phrase it as a question, when I know the answer.

Jed nods. *It is too late for me now. I have tried, but we only have one chance to get there. We are the Lost Ones, and we degenerate fast.*

My bottom lip feels strange. "That's going to happen to you?"

That is going to happen to me. I was a Seer, so I am strong. Maybe that is how I can walk these lands at times when it is not the Turning. But soon I will become like them. Already, there are times I am not in control enough for anyone to see me. But I can feel my strength—I hid my image from my father. I do not want him knowing I am suffering.

"You don't want Raleigh knowing? But he deserves to! He did this to you."

Not yet. I want to surprise him. I want to plan it. Jed shakes his head. *There is only so long I can experience this pain before it too drives me mad, before I deteriorate. When I am fully a Lost One, I will seek my revenge on him. Make him feel my pain.*

I stare at him. "You're in pain?" My voice is soft, and part of me can't believe I'm having this conversation, that I'm feeling sorry for Jed.

Like nothing you have ever imagined.

I press my lips together, feel sick.

I moved you here, and I protected you from them, he says. *They're already Lost. They wouldn't hurt you if they still had their minds.*

Part of me feels like I should thank him, but I don't. And then—

"Corin!" My eyes widen.

He was out there and—

It is all right, Jed says. *I got Corin to safety first. Before I came for you. You could defend yourself. He could not.*

I stare at him. "You saved Corin?" My eyes widen further...this, this can't be real, can't be happening. "But you *hate* Corin."

I would rather you were with that arrogant boy than my father.

"Your father?" I take a step back. "Raleigh? Gods! I would never...."

Jed turns on me. *You have already kissed my father. You, my fiancée. And my father. It is disgusting. And I saw you sleeping, wrapped up in his arms. No, Corin is a welcome successor.*

Successor? My gaze hardens. I'm not an object.

I hold my hands up, heat flooding through me. Heat, and the memories of Raleigh, and it's all I can think about: the way his lips felt against mine. *Raleigh's* lips.

My stomach hardens.

"I didn't know." I spit the words out, aware of how defensive I sound.

You did not check. You did not even look.

I turn on him. "But he looked like Corin. He looked—"

And appearance is enough now, is it? There is fire in his eyes that I don't like, don't like at all. Not in a spirit. *You need to be careful, S'ven.*

DIVIDED

Careful.

The word pulls through me.

"Why didn't you tell me?" I freeze. "You saw me *sleeping in his arms,* and you didn't say?"

It was one of the times I was not strong enough for you to see me.

Great.

So, Jed could by spying on me at any moment. I feel heat rush to my face, and breathe deeply, stare at the trees.

At last, when I look at Jed, my words aren't as angry. "Is he okay? Is Corin okay?"

He is fine. He doesn't look at me.

"You got him to safety? Where is he?"

He is on his way back now. I pushed him to a cave, so he could take cover during the Turning. I stayed invisible; he would not have been happy to see me and likely would not have trusted me had he seen me. But he will be back soon.

I digest the information quickly, part of me glad that Corin hasn't seen Jed.

"Had he got as far as the compound?" I ask. "Did he get Esther out?"

Jed shakes his head. *No. I told him you needed him. He did not appear to recognize my voice, must have assumed it was just one of the spirits of the Turning advising him. Not me. Nonetheless, he listened.* He pauses. *There was a dog with him. A horrible little thing.*

My pulse quickens. "A terrier? Small-ish? Brown hair, a bit matted? Huge eyes?"

Yes.

My head spins. "Wait—a horrible little thing?"

I do not like dogs.

Jed advances slowly, holding his hands up. I stare at his palms, expecting the skin to peel off at any moment. But it doesn't.

S'ven, you have to believe I am sorry for everything that happened. But you are free of my father now. And so am I. You cannot let yourself be caught again by him, by them. I know the true augury now, and we can win. You must win.

His words float over me, but there's something insistent about the tone of that last sentence that grips me.

Jed is right. I must win.

"I will," I say, swallow hard. There's a low buzzing in my ears. Very faint, but it's there. "Somehow."

You're a body-sharer, Jed says.

"I am."

My father thinks you're dead.

I nod.

Then use that to your advantage, Jed says. *Bring the Untamed together and lead them when he does not suspect your involvement. My father is going to send more teams out to try and find the Untamed who are out there.*

But you can see through all the Untamed Ones' eyes. It is the gift of supreme body-sharing, an ancient power. Mazel, one of our old Seers, had it in the lesser version—one host. But he died when his host was killed. The poison dart got him too. You must be careful. Nonetheless, you can be everyone's eyes. Warn them of attacks. If the Enhanced get one group while you are watching, then you must warn the others who live close by. And bring everyone together. Rise up. There are still Seers out there. Put your powers together, and you will find a way to make the augury come true. That is what I believe you need to do. You must lead it, S'ven. You're the most powerful one, born to end the war.

I can't help but snort. "So you do believe women and girls can be Seers?"

It was my culture that did not, and it is the rules and the culture that control people's actions first and foremost in most instances. We do what we need to do in order to fit in.

The humming in the air is getting louder, and—

Esther.

I swear, look at Jed. How the hell had I forgotten?

Because of Rahn, because of the Turning, because of....

Shit.

I punched Raleigh when I was in her body, and she's—

DIVIDED

He was going to convert her.

The augmenters.

I flush hot then cold. I lie down and open up my Seer powers. I find her door, and I step toward it. Somewhere far away, I hear Jed's voice—the strange voice that speaks on a different level—out loud, but in my head too. I push thoughts of Jed away, step through the door to Esther.

Coldness and light and—

"It's all right." Three's words. "They can't find us here."

Esther turns and looks up at him, my brother with his mirror eyes. The little light glints off the metal plate in his face. They're in a small place, very small. A cupboard; lines of light mark the doorway.

I stare at Three, feel anger in my veins. There's a cut on his face. But he's alive.

"Are you sure?" Esther whispers, stepping closer, and I step closer with her, feel the pain of her hip—so it's not been fixed—no augmenters? Yet it can't be broken, can it? Not if she's standing up—and she must've walked here, and she's moving and—

She presses her hands lightly to Three's chest, tiptoes up, and—

Oh Gods.

Esther, what's happening? I cut in before she kisses my brother.

She jolts, pulls away from Three.

"Seven?" she says, shock filling her voice.

"What?" Three looks startled, turning and—

No, don't tell him, Esther. He's one of them. But saying the words to her, they still don't feel right—even though I know they are. He's the enemy. He locked me in with Raleigh. Twice. Let me think that Raleigh was Corin. And he knew.

I feel the confusion in Esther in the way she narrows her eyes and how her vision darkens, how she rubs at her chin, and the rising temperature of her body.

But, Seven, Three's on our side, she says to me.

No. He's Enhanced. Even in our heads, my words are brisk, sharp.

But he got me away from Raleigh, stopped me from being converted. He has to be Untamed. You resisted it, so has he.

What? I breathe hard—make her breathe hard too. *Oh Gods. I don't know anymore. Things aren't black and white. And his actions are too conflicting. He saved you from them? Just...just don't tell him I'm alive. Not yet. Not until I've thought about this.* I pause. Three's looking at her strangely, makes me squirm inside, because it's like he's looking at me. I am Esther. I gather my resolve. *But you're okay? Esther?*

Yeah. We're hiding out. Waiting until the guards switch over. Three said he'll get me out of here.

Get you out of here? Not both of you then. And I don't know how I feel about that. Because Three is predominantly Enhanced—more Enhanced than he is Untamed, and he doesn't want to leave?

Where's Corin? she counters, and her tone is different now. More forceful. *You said Corin was coming, but he didn't arrive. Has he been caught?*

No. Not according to Jed, anyway.

Where are you?

Outside. I keep my answer vague. She's still in the compound. Anything I tell her, they could find out. *I'll keep checking in on you. And when you're out, I'll direct you to me. Okay?*

"Okay."

"Okay what?" Three says.

"Nothing," Esther says.

I breathe deeply. *I'm going now. Talk later.*

I don't wait for her answer, just disconnect, shut her door.

Jed's looking down at me strangely, asks if I'm okay.

I nod slowly, push Three from my mind—because I can't work this new Three out—then rub at my ears. The humming's louder now, louder and louder. I look up and—and then I see it.

It's low in the sky, just above the horizon.

DIVIDED

And I know it is a drone.

A drone searching.

A drone that will find me.

I jump up.

Jed swears. Then he starts to move, away from me and—

For a moment, my thoughts freeze, but then, just as quickly, the ice breaks and the water crashes through.

"Jed!" I cry, and my head's all over the place, but there's something, something there—somewhere—telling me something. Something important. And I listen. "Don't go! Cover me!"

What? He turns back, looks at me. And he looks worried.

The humming gets louder, and I look up—the drone, it's getting closer, closer and closer—so quickly. How can it move so quickly?

"Cover me!" I yell at him, and Three's words veer over and over in my mind: *The Chosen Ones use thermal imaging to scan the lands as relatively few spirits inhabit these regions when it's not the Turning, so few spirits can interfere with the imaging.*

But Jed is here. He's a spirit, he can interfere with it—can't he?

I yell at Jed, try to tell him what my brother said, but the drone is so loud.

I dive back toward the vehicle, yank on the door handle—need to get inside, need cover—but it doesn't budge. I swear, look up and—

Shit. No time.

I drop to the ground, roll under the vehicle—that same space. The metal above me—will that be hot? Hot enough to mask my signature thanks to the sun? Was that how Corin avoided it? By hiding here? Or was it Rahn? Was he about too, affecting the drone's detecting ability and protecting Corin? Has Corin seen his uncle again?

I hold my breath, feel tears pierce the corners of my eyes—what about Corin, out there? Jed said he was coming back...what if he's been detected? He must've already seen the drone and—

I suck in gritty air sharply, know I need to stop overthinking, I'm too close to panicking. But the sounds of the drone are getting louder, louder, louder. I clench my hands over my stomach, over the knot of muscles pulsing in time with my heartbeat, and I'm shaking, shaking so much.

Jed rolls under the vehicle too. The dug out space isn't big, and he crashes into me—his *solid* body. I try to pull myself away from him. But he could be my only chance if the vehicle isn't enough—and the Enhanced can't know I'm alive. They can't, *can't*.

I hold myself carefully, tensing my muscles until they feel heavy, aware of every part of my body that touches Jed, and how it feels; a fiery rill that runs from our shoulders, down to our feet. Scorching heat fills the gaps between us, where my body curves away from his for a moment before joining back up.

And I don't know why the air is burning around us, or why my breathing is so ragged.

The drone gets louder. Louder and louder. I try to breathe evenly. Need to remain calm. Have to. Need a clear head in case I'm detected, in case I have to run.

Do the Enhanced monitor their drones in New Kitembu in real time? Would they immediately know there's an Untamed human out here? And what about Corin? Do we even have a chance?

I try to remember what Three said when he told me how a drone had detected where Esther and the Zharat were...when they sent a team out soon after.

Oh Gods.

I freeze. But that's good. That means there'll be some time between detection and capture—time I can get away in?

Only I won't know if I've been detected.

I press my lips together. As soon as Corin's back, and the drone's gone—gone for now—we'll have to leave. I try to picture the map with the spirit allocation. We

DIVIDED

need to go to a place where there are more spirits... spirits all the time—a place where Rahn could be now, in less-than-human form? I grimace. But the spirits are the key. The Untamed only survive where the spirits congregate. The world map proved it. And we need to be in a place where the Enhanced don't send their drones, a place they can't use them, if we're going to have the smallest chance of survival. The smallest chance of winning the war.

I take a deep breath and turn my head. Look at Jed, so close to me. Even his beard looks real, so detailed, each scratchy hair. He'll have to come with us. His presence could deter our detection.

Corin's going to love that.

But then I frown. What was it Jed said before? That he can't stay visible for long...we'd be unprotected some of the time... And how long before Jed *does* start to degenerate, become one of the wild, bad ones? Rahn said he had a burning desire in him to feed. Jed's a 'good' spirit at the moment, but how soon before he reverts, attacks us? Even if it's just temporary?

Spirits aren't safe. Too unpredictable, even the ones who are benevolent can turn.

Spirits are dangerous.

Spirits kill people.

The whirring gets even louder, fills my ears, my brain, every part of me. So loud. My ears feel hot, like they're burning and warm blood is sloshing through my ear canals.

It's all right, S'ven. Jed moves his hand a fraction, and his searing skin brushes against my leg.

My heart pounds, and I feel sick. Has the drone already passed over where Corin is—detected him? Or maybe Corin's immune...no, that wouldn't work. It uses thermal imaging. I let out a shaky breath. It must've been Rahn protecting him. Must've been. Rahn's his uncle. And family matters. Matters very much.

I pray that Corin's safe.

The humming gets louder still. The land starts to shake.

And Jed and I wait for the drone to pass, pressed up against one another.

FORTY-EIGHT

TWENTY MINUTES LATER, WHEN THE drone's gone over and the hum's faded to a distant thrum, Jed and I move from our hiding place. I'm still breathing hard, feel jumpy.

"We need to get going," I mutter, then look around. "Where is he?" I peer through the trees, out at the sand, looking for any sign of Corin, then I turn back to where Jed was and—

He's not there.

I get a strange feeling in my chest, and I crouch down, look under the vehicle. Just the burrowed-out space. The wind whistles through the trees, sounds eerie. I search for Jed, throughout the copse, groaning as each step pulls on my damaged ribs. They're hurting again now, the adrenaline's wearing off.

But Jed's not here.

He's gone.

I'm alone. All alone. And what if Corin isn't coming back? What if he's hurt? Or what if this was a different type of drone, and it picked him up there and then? Tingles crawl down my spine. I grip my hands together, squeeze them. My breathing gets faster. I've got to stay calm, I know that. I lean against the vehicle. The sun is low in the sky, like it's going to get dark soon.

But how long do I wait? I can't stay here. I'm too close to the compound, and I need to go—find somewhere safe.

But Corin waited in the area for me. And he didn't know I was still alive or Untamed. Or that I'd ever escape.

I've got to wait. I know that. And Esther—if she gets out, it's better if I'm nearby, not hundreds of miles away. Even if her hip's not broken, she's still injured.

"Just hurry up," I mutter, gripping my hands together. My fingers click as I scrunch them up.

After a moment, I try to busy myself, clearing fallen leaves, arranging them in patterns. Then I scan every part of the land I can see. I even look at the old vehicle, work out how to get the seized-up door open and go through the contents in the glove compartment: an old, stained map; a compass with a broken screen, but, as far as I can tell, a working needle; two pamphlets written in a different language, and a packet of wipes. I pocket the compass, take out a wipe and clean a cut on my arm—though the wipe itself smells odd—then look at the map, spreading it out on the sandy floor.

I've never been great at reading maps, and this one's old, stained, and faded. I squint, barely able to see the marks on it, and, as much as I try, I can't match up anything on the map to anything here. The map shows lots of trees and forests and there are many contour lines close together. But there are no heavily wooded areas around here that I know of, let alone steep wooded ones. And maps aren't reliable anyway, not when the spirits can change the land. I wonder if Raleigh's world map somehow updates automatically or whether it's not that accurate anymore. Or never was?

Frustrated, I fold up the map and put it back. My wrist twinges with pain, and my stomach rumbles, but there's no food here. There's a small wooden branch not far away and a small chunk of gray stone. It looks like Corin's been crudely sharping the end of it—or at least someone has. To make a weapon? Or a hunting spear?

I pick up the stone and the stick—it's not that thick, and there's a twist of a knot halfway through that weakens the strength—but I sit down, continue the work that Corin must've started.

The sky gets darker, and the world gets colder. I give up on the stick and put it to one side, bring my hands up to my face, breathe on my fingers for warmth. I touch my Seer pendant for a moment.

Corin's still not back.

Because he got to the compound? Because he got caught?

I lean back, then open my mind, connect with Esther and—

I find her door…but I can't open it. Not this time. Can't get the connection.

I curse, open my eyes, look around me again. Images of her being force-fed augmenters and converted fill my head, and I blench. Three lied—even to her? Trapped her in the cupboard, so she could be caught? Like he did with me in the corridor? Or—or it wasn't Three's fault, but she still got caught?

My stomach roils. Esther—my friend.

Gone?

And I can't ask her if Corin's been caught…because she's been converted now?

And I can't get a connection to an Enhanced One.

Oh Gods.

Oh Gods.

Oh Gods.

Esther.

Nausea rises, and I slap a hand to my mouth.

But it doesn't have to mean that, I tell myself. It doesn't. Maybe…maybe I can't body-share with everyone all the time. Maybe she's busy…with Three?

I swallow hard, feel even sicker. I wouldn't want to witness that. Maybe it's just my mind protecting itself...or I'm too worn out to use the power? No, I got to the door—found the connection just couldn't complete it. It felt like the door was locked.

The jittery feelings I've been trying to suppress rise in me, like an army of winged creatures, each one flapping against the other. I breathe deeply, press my lips together. I think of Corin. If I can't connect to Esther, I could try and connect to him.

But it's a violation of his privacy. He made that clear.

I look at the darkening sky—can barely see it against the trees now. I take another deep breath, then I nod. I have to try. And I curse myself. I should've done it earlier.

I lie back down, try to tell myself I'm calm even though I'm far from it, and I open my mind. Find my Seer powers, feel the familiar energy of them. The pulse and ebb of the flow. I picture Corin, really *see* him: the recent hard edges of his face that make him look a lot older than twenty, the warm darkness in his eyes that tingles through to my core, the scars and imperfections of his skin.

And nothing happens.

I breathe deeper, feel panic rising. I'm trying too hard. Or maybe I really am worn out?

Connect with him.

I try again. I think of everything I love about him—the way a vein pulses in his jaw when he's thinking hard, how his arms feel around me, the intonation of his voice when he's concerned. I picture him again, see him walking through the desert. His stride is big and powerful, and he pumps his arms ever so slightly as he walks. The dog will be with him, walking close by his feet, but keeping a slight distance. They'll be coming back and—

I find his door. It opens easily.

I slip into him. A fizzle of energy, a snap of white light, and I'm jolted forward, and—

DIVIDED

He's walking, breathing hard.

I try to be as silent as possible, passive. An observer.

The sky is dark, and the land is dark. A jolt runs through me, and Corin reacts, looks behind him, eyes searching. Darkness. A boulder. Where's the dog? I want to keep looking, but he stops—looks up at the sky, then down. Not left to right.

But I could make him look from side to side.

No.

He turns slowly, and I hold my breath, still looking. His breathing is ragged, heavy. I can feel sweat on his forehead—feels like it's on me. After a second, he lifts an arm, wipes it off quickly. His sleeve is tickly against his skin, my skin. He flexes his fingers—they're cold, like ice, and I feel the joints crack as they move.

"Shit."

His voice. Corin's voice. I feel his lips buzz as if they're my own, and I feel my own power. Know that I could take control of him so easily, squash his presence, take his body, just as I took Viktoriya's—even when I didn't mean to.

But it would be easy to flatten Corin too. Take control of him.

The realization fills me with something. A sense of power. I'm not sure I like it. But all the same, it's there, and I recognize it. And I don't push it away. I don't know why. But I don't. Because everyone's programmed to like power. Even when they think they don't. Even when they think they can resist it. There's still a part of them that believes they can control everything better than someone else can. And I'm no different. That part is there, deep down.

And that's why I stay hidden. I know what it was like to have someone controlling me. And, for a moment, I see Raleigh, wrapped up in his desire for power, to control. It's like a disease. He let it take him.

I will not let it take me.

I will remain hidden in Corin. I'm just checking on him, seeing where he is. Seeing what's happening. An update, that's all I'm getting.

Corin looks straight ahead again, and I recognize the landscape—two angular rocks, rising up in the darkness. Corin and I passed them before, when he was carrying me.

Relief pours through me.

He'll be back soon. Unharmed.

I break the connection with Corin, return to my own body. The transition is the smoothest it's ever been, and I look around, smile. It's dark, but I can feel it now. Corin is close. Close and safe.

And that's all that matters.

Is it?

FORTY-NINE

CORIN AND THE TERRIER RETURN an hour later. Corin hugs me briefly, then sits down. It's dark, but a sliver of moon hangs in the sky, and I can just about see enough. Corin sits with his head in his hands for several moments, then he looks up at me.

I can't see his face too well, but my mind fills in the detail. I see the ragged look in his eyes, the dark shadows under them, and the way he's tensing his jaw.

"I couldn't get her out," he whispers. "I couldn't even get in the conversion unit's grounds. It was the same as before. Too many Enhanced."

I lean forward. "You went back to the compound, right back?"

He gives me a look. "My pregnant sister is still there."

The words hang in the air, make what I need to say harder. I grit my teeth for a long moment. My stomach rumbles, and I can't remember when I last ate. But there's no food here.

"Corin, we need to go." I hate saying the words. But it's too risky staying here, where there are drones, when either of us could've been detected. And there's no point in staying. Not when Esther could have been converted... When she *has* been. I felt the door, it wouldn't open.

"No," he says. "*You're* not going back there. Just me. You're injured. I'll try again tomorrow to get her out."

I reach for his hand. It's cold. I cover his hand with mine, then draw his arm closer to me. Pain flushes through me. "No, I mean we have to leave here. Now. We need to get as far away from here as we can. A drone went over here earlier. It could've detected me. And we need to be somewhere they don't use drones—places where there are a lot of spirits. Somewhere safe."

A place where Rahn could be.

I try to keep breathing evenly.

Corin lifts his head slowly. His eyes bore into mine, but there's a fierceness in them. "I'm *not* leaving Esther there." He shakes his head. "How can you even say that?"

"She might not ever get out of there. Not with her hip," I whisper. Darkness swarms my gut. "And...and she could be Enhanced soon."

I can't bring myself to say the actual words, that she's most likely Enhanced already—she has to be. That's why I couldn't body-share with her. But I can't tell Corin that. It would destroy him.

"So you think I should just give up on her?" His voice is dark, and something flashes in his eyes. Anger. He stands up, points at me. "You should've got her out when you escaped. It's your fault she's still in there. If you'd just done that—looked out for her, she's your friend too—then we could be far away now, the three of us. But instead, she's in there, trapped. And it's your fault. *You* left her. And now you're giving up on her."

I stare at him, feel the muscles in my face slacken. "Corin, that's not fair."

"No, I'll tell you what isn't fair," he yells. "It isn't

bloody fair that all you care about is yourself and saving yourself."

"Stop it! It's not like that." I stand up, refuse to wince at the pain. I point at Corin, and my finger shakes. "If I'd looked for Esther, I wouldn't have escaped at all. I'd still be there—"

"Yeah, and at least you'd be together!" Corin shouts. "She's on her own now, scared, hurt and—"

"She's *not* on her own—I've been body-sharing with her." Except I can't now. My stomach twists. "I've been talking to her, Corin, and—"

He stops short, then he lifts a hand up slowly, points at me. "You've been taking over my sister's body? Invading her?"

"It's not like that." I hold my hands up, grit my teeth for a moment. "It's just talking. I wouldn't control her—not like what Raleigh did with me."

Except I made her punch Raleigh.

"But body-sharing isn't natural." Corin shakes his head, then spits at the ground. "It's wrong. Seers are all wrong. Freaks."

I feel my face drain. Feel every part of me shrivel, crumple.

"No, you should be relying on proper human stuff, Sev. You know, stuff that's *normal*. And you shouldn't have left without her. You should've stuck together."

"You left without us!" I yell. "And it's the right thing to do—we can only get out individually, you know that!" I grit my teeth, then throw my hands in the air. "If I hadn't left, I'd still be under Raleigh's control. He'd still have my soul, be able to control me—and he'd have made me forge more body-sharing connections, and he'd be making me use them. I told you his plans, didn't I?" I feel my face heat up, until it's burning. The dog barks. "He'd make me connect with everyone and then convert me when I was body-sharing with everyone—*including* you. The Untamed would be wiped out in the blink of an eye. And you want that to happen, because you want me to be back there still? Is that what you want?"

Corin steps closer. His body shakes with emotion. "I wanted you to *try*. To try and get my sister out, to save her. She's all I've got."

His words get to me. *She's all I've got*. He doesn't count me.

My breaths are noisy. "I did try!" I yell back.

"No, you didn't," he snaps. "As soon as you got free from Raleigh you ran. You didn't try and find my sister. You didn't try and save her."

I grit my teeth, exasperated. "I *couldn't*. Are you not listening? Her hip's—"

"Of course I'm bloody listening! And that's how I know it's your fault. And because of you, I've got to put myself in danger tomorrow too, trying to do what you should've done. Untamed are supposed to look out for each other. Work together. But you don't know the meaning of that, do you, Sev? No, it's all about you. *You* getting out of there. *You* going somewhere safe where there are no drones."

My temper rises; heat floods my hands, and I clench them tightly. "*I'm* the key to the Untamed. I'm important—I can't pretend I'm not! I've got to protect myself if I'm going to protect all of you."

"Don't let your importance get to your head, will you?" he mutters, darkly.

I shake my head, exhale hard. "You're not going to get Esther out. You *know* that. And she's—" I bite my words, refuse to tell him I couldn't connect—and what that probably means. "We've got to trust that she can get herself out. Or Three or one of the Zharat will help," I say, but I know it's a lie. "We have to trust them. We can't save her ourselves. As soon as she's out, I'll tell her where we are. But you can't go back, Corin. You'll get yourself caught too. And converted. And they'll find out from you that I'm still alive and come after me. If I'm still here, their drones *will* find me. I can't rely on Jed all the time. Not when he disappeared without even warning me—and he's only going to get more unstable."

Corin's body jolts. He stares at me. "*Jed?*" His eyes narrow, then he looks from side to side. "You told me Raleigh killed him."

Oh Gods.

I swallow hard and straighten my dark green shirt. It doesn't feel as fitted now. "He didn't make it to the New World. He's still here... They become the spirits, the ones who don't make it. The Lost Souls."

For a moment, Corin's quiet. "*Spirits,*" he mutters. "Well, isn't this bloody brilliant?" He turns away from me. "That man is still here. Let me guess. You've been meeting up? Having secret liaisons? Or maybe it's not been secret at all? What's been going on then, Sev? Back at the compound, was Jed with you in your cell all the time? You been getting it on with him? With a bloody ghost—because that's what he is. A glorified, physical ghost. Bet you've been loving it."

My eyes narrow as I glare at him. "How *dare* you."

"How dare *I*?" He shakes his head, a dark smile on his face. "You know what, Sev? You're welcome to Jed. I don't care. You go and pair off with him, travel to some safe land together. I'll get my sister out. I don't need you anyway."

Something pulses inside me. "*Fine,*" I say, and I put as much force into the word as I can. "I'll leave now. *Bye*, Corin."

I call the dog to me, and I walk away, through the darkness, the terrier at my heel.

Anger boils inside me. I roll my sleeves up, ignore the pain. It's not my fault I couldn't get Esther out. And how dare Corin say that stuff about me and Jed. How *dare* he.

I kick up the sand, feel it stick against my ankles and lower legs. Sounds crackle around me. The sound of the night. I don't even look back. Why would I even want to see Corin now? I don't need him. I don't need him or Jed.

"It's just me and you," I say to the dog. He whines

a little, and, in the moonlight, I see the way his eyes look uncertain. He turns his head, looks behind us. "We're not going back." I snort. When I said goodbye to Corin, I meant it.

My chest tightens, and I ignore it, furiously blink the hot tears from my eyes. I sniff loudly, then dig out the compass with the broken screen from my pocket. There's just enough moonlight to see the needle and markings—the ones that aren't obscured by the two-inch crack across the plastic.

I take a deep breath and try to clear my head. Raleigh showed me a map. I try to put the information together, work out which way I need to go. I'm not entirely sure, but I believe a southwest direction will take me back toward the Noir Lands.

I pray that I'm right. As soon as I've walked farther, and I'm out of the drone-scanning area, I'll stop and use my Seer powers, find the Zharat who are still out there, join back up with them. Being part of the Zharat again doesn't exactly fill me with confidence, but it's a start. And they know how to survive. They'll have weapons—or will have made new ones. I breathe deeply. Yes, it's a start. And they'll have to accept who I am—that I'm a powerful Seer. *The* powerful Seer. And then we can find the others. The others nearby and in the other sections.

Unite the Untamed.

I'll bring everyone together, just like Taras and Jed said.

But what about Corin?

No. I refuse to think of him. The corners of my eyes start to burn again. I curse loudly.

I walk faster and faster, check the dog's still with me every twenty seconds or so. When I've walked a long, long way, and my body's aching, and my ribs are protesting, I lessen my speed a little. The night's still dark, and I've no idea what time it is now. It's cold, but my body's numbing itself to the air now.

I keep walking, keep checking the compass. Hours

pass. Hours and hours, until the sky's lightening again. The dog whines. He's tired. I don't feel tired. I just feel…strange.

I shake my head, rather violently, and my neck cracks. I wince, then massage the area. But my fingers are locking up with the coldness. I wish I had a coat or something.

After another hour of walking, my head pounds. Tiredness, now. I need to sleep, but then I think of how Raleigh tricked me, lay with me all night. My stomach twists, nausea floods me. I bend over and gag, watch my watery vomit hit the dry ground.

I wipe the back of my hand across my mouth. The terrier looks at me and barks. A loud, shrill bark.

I turn, my head foggy, and—

There's a figure.

A figure following me.

He's in the distance, but—

Corin.

I'd recognize him anywhere.

You thought that before though. You pressed yourself against Raleigh and you thought about—

My stomach turns over, and I'm sick again, and my eyes smart, sting. I take a deep breath, check behind me. Corin's gaining on me now. Fresh anger flares in me. What's he even doing, following me? He made it perfectly clear he didn't want to leave with me.

I shift my weight from foot to foot, wonder if I should wait for him or not. I look down at the dog. He looks exhausted. Well, I suppose it will give him a rest if I wait for Corin.

I kick up some of the sand, use it to cover my vomit on the ground. Then I sit down slowly, several feet away and find myself staring at my arms. I just stare at my skin. It's smooth, unblemished, bar the knife scar. I examine more of my skin—it's the same. Even the kavalah spirit scars have gone. And the bruises, the cuts. When did they go? A strange feeling fills me.

My dog sidles over to me, lies down, panting. His

eyes look a little duller, and he rests his head on his paws.

It takes Corin twenty minutes to reach me. And he doesn't look happy.

"You were sick," he says. "Tell me you're not pregnant too."

I glare at him. "You really need to ask that?"

"I didn't think it would be a possibility with my sister and Manning, but it is. So you're having Jed's ghost-baby?" His tone is blunt, harsh.

I swear at him, stand up, and turn away, feel my insides start to crumble. But I won't let him see me cry.

I walk fast.

"Sev!" he calls after me a few minutes later, and I hear his footsteps speed up behind me. "Sev!"

He grabs my arm and pulls me back. I whirl around, anger driving through me.

"Sev. I'm sorry."

His words catch me off guard.

"Sorry?" I repeat. "Sorry for what? Accusing me of being with Jed? Or accusing me of being pregnant? Or for saying it's my fault Esther's still in there? Which one is it?"

He presses his lips together. I try not to look at him, because I know that just looking at him is going to do something to me.

"All of them," he says at last.

I snort.

He lets his fingers fall down my arm, then takes my hand. "You're cold."

So is he.

I pull my hand away, and I don't miss the hurt look that appears in his eyes.

"Sev, talk to me."

"What is there to talk about?" I stare back at him. "You've already said everything."

He shakes his head. "Just...just anything, please."

"There's nothing to say." I fold my arms and wince at the pain that dives through me. "You made your views perfectly clear."

Corin steps closer. "You're badly hurt. And I've been an idiot, saying all that stuff. And I thought I'd lost you earlier—you stopped breathing, you died, and now that you're back, and I've just been…."

"Yeah, you're an idiot," I say, my voice dark.

The faintest of smiles touches Corin's lips, and I realize I'm staring right at him—at his mouth. I look away quickly, glance at the terrier.

"You've no idea what it was like in there," I whisper, and I don't know why I even say it. "What Raleigh made me do."

How Raleigh made you kiss him.

I bring a hand to my mouth as the nausea starts again, and I turn away.

"Torture?" Corin asks, and he says the word so lightly, as if he can't possibly understand the severity of it.

I shrug. The recent conversion seems a lifetime ago. But Corin will never understand it. And that's a good thing. I don't want him to know what it was like—to feel it.

But Esther…what if she's being tortured too, in her mind-conversion now? And I hurt her. Raleigh made me hurt her. And she screamed. And even when I made her punch Raleigh, I felt the pain it sent through her hip. I shouldn't have done that.

I shut my eyes briefly.

"It's all right, Sev. You're not there now."

I turn back. "But Esther is. You were right. And—and Corin, I should've told you. I tried to connect with her. But I couldn't. And I can't body-share with Enhanced. You can only do it with your own people."

The look on his face hardens. He swallows, and I watch his Adam's apple move. "Conversions can take days," he says. "We don't give up. She's not lost yet." But then the light in his eyes changes. "How bad is her hip? Or would they have fixed that before converting her? Do you think we can get her out? Or rather—me.

Can *I* get her out? Because you're right, Sev. We can't risk them catching you again."

I shrug and immediately regret the movement as it hurts more this time. "My mother and Three are in there too. You're not the only one with family there."

"One person for a multi-rescue mission." Corin shakes his head, then lets out a bitter laugh. "That's stupid. Utterly ridiculous. It would never work. Even the two of us wouldn't stand much chance."

I bite my bottom lip. "Well, there are two other people who could help."

"What?" His eyes narrow.

He's not going to like it, and for that reason, I almost want to shout the words at him, to make him hurt like he hurt me with his words.

"*Jed*. No, Corin, just listen. He's a spirit. He can do stuff. And he's not at the wild, unpredictable stage yet. He says he'll degenerate soon—or I think he said *soon*—but he helped me escape, got me the key for the Pajero. And I think he stopped the drone from detecting my heat signature."

Corin exhales hard. "Fine. Who's the other person?"

I pause for a moment. "Rahn."

"*Rahn?*" His eyes widen until they're the biggest I've ever seen them, and he takes a step back, as if I've pushed hm. "He's a spirit too?"

"Yes. Degenerating fast now, it seems." I nod and remember the gun, the Fort-17. Then I frown. What happened to it? When Rahn relapsed into angry spirit mode—or whatever it was that happened—did he drop it? Why didn't I look for it? I curse myself. "He was pretty angry with me."

"With you? You've seen him?" Corin looks around, then steps closer to me.

His hand hovers above my shoulder for a moment, before he makes contact. Lightly though. But I step away.

A line appears between Corin's eyes as he looks at me and then at his hand in the air.

DIVIDED

"Did he hurt you?" he asks after a moment.

I shake my head and stare at his hand as he returns it to his side. Why did I step away? It's him—it's really him this time. Corin, who I *love*. Or did I just think that when I'd died—because I thought it was over then? Thought there was no chance….

No… I *do* love him.

But I don't want to get hurt, and maybe that's why I haven't said it, haven't made it real. Because then I'd be exposed, raw, vulnerable. And if something *did* happen to Corin, then my pain would be so much worse if I'd made my love for him concrete, made it a certainty.

I don't want to be vulnerable, don't want to get hurt.

"Rahn was just angry," I say. "It was the Turning, that's why he was stronger then. But he wanted me to send him to the New World. Said he was in pain."

"No one wants to *not* reach the New World," Corin says. He exhales hard. "Do you think we're going to see him again?"

I shrug. "I don't know. Jed's the only one I've seen regularly." I wince when I realize how that sounds. "And Rahn's been dead for a while. This is the first time I've seen him in his spirit form."

Corin just nods. "Well, if either turns up we can ask for their help to get Esther out." But he doesn't sound as though he likes this plan.

And Three. And my mother… We need to get them out too.

"But you think we need to get away, somewhere safe?" Corin's voice is low.

I nod. "A drone's going to detect us sooner or later, if it hasn't already. And I can't go back there, not to Raleigh."

"You won't." His voice is dark. "I won't let him get you again, Sev. I mean that. I really mean that."

His eyes brim with emotion, then they lock onto me. His face flushes, and my hands feel moist as I look at him. I wipe them on my shorts, feel my heart speed up.

"Can I—" Corin starts, but then he swallows hard, and he looks so...so different. Vulnerable. Nervous. He steps a little nearer to me. "Can I hold you, Sev?"

Hold me.

And I think of Raleigh. I shudder. But it's Corin. I know it's him. If anything, his outburst earlier proved it.

"I'm sorry. I am," he says.

I nod slightly as I lean into him. His arms go around me. My cage. My cage against the world.

I tip my head up, look at him. His eyes. Those dark pools. Untamed life. We stare at each other for a long time.

Then I stretch up and kiss him. Kiss him lightly. The slightest of kisses. Our lips barely brush, and I want it that way, because with Raleigh it was desperate. No. When I *thought* he was Corin, it was desperate, us pressing our bodies against each other. Him kissing my lips, my neck, my collarbone. His hands all over me.

And now Corin's lips match mine, small touches, gentle. He's letting me lead, following my pace, and I like that. I like it a lot, because I'm in control now.

He's a better kisser than Raleigh.

I don't know where that thought comes from, but it startles me, and I jolt back.

"Are you okay?" Corin looks at me. And I know he can sense that something's wrong.

A thousand emotions swirl through me. I just nod.

Corin leans back further, looks at me properly. He offers me his hands, and the look in his eyes—it makes me want to cry. Because I don't want to talk about it, not with him. And now, just looking at Corin is painful. And there's a battle inside me, because I want to kiss him again. I really do.

I take his hands slowly, then look down at them, at us, joined. But I don't want his hands all over me. Not yet. Not so soon. And maybe I'm being silly. It was nothing really. But I think of how rough Raleigh was, how he pulled at my shirt, how his fingers kneaded my arms as we kissed, how he squeezed one of my breasts, and I feel sick. Betrayed. Violated. And I don't want to feel like that when I'm with Corin.

So, we stand here, holding hands instead.

"What is it?" Corin's voice is low, his eyes on me. Dark pools of hope that I want to reach up and fall into; I'm obsessed with his eyes now. "Are *we* okay, Sev?"

"What?"

"You and me… Us?" His voice wobbles—actually wobbles. "It's just so much has happened—at the Zharat cave too. Made it all happen…quickly. And… and I understand if…if you don't know what you want now." He looks at the ground between our feet. "Or if you don't want me. Just—just let me know. Because I love you…because I don't want you feeling trapped or like we have to be together because we were before. And we don't—not if you don't want it. I'll still look out for you—I won't abandon you, not unless you want me to and—"

"Corin." I say his name slowly, the slowest I've ever said it, and I'm not sure why. But it sticks to my tongue, and then I lean closer. "I want to be with you."

He lets out a heavy breath, relief on his face, and I stretch up and press my forehead against his—I just manage it. I breathe deeply. His hands, in mine, shake. The distant smell of smoke clings to him, and it's comforting. Makes me realize that it is really him here—as if I've constantly got to be reassured.

But Raleigh never smelled of smoke when he pretended to be Corin—because he wouldn't want to risk his health. Even though he drinks.

Then I scold myself. Mustn't think of Raleigh.

I slouch as I relax. My eyes find Corin's again. My mouth tingles, and I stare at his lips, transfixed. Then I look into his eyes. *Those* eyes. And there's so much in them. So much that speaks to me. That connects me.

That draws us together, unites us, makes me sure that, together, we can do anything.

And I know. I *know*. The doubts that were in me evaporate. I *have* to tell him, have to tell myself.

"I love you, Corin."

His smile captures me, and everything inside me swells, threatens to burst.

"I think that's the first time you've said that," he whispers, and he squeezes my hands a little. "And *I* love you, Sev. You're…you're everything to me. Gods, I shouldn't have said what I did. I know it's not your fault. And…and it was knowing that you've seen Jed—that you've had *his* company, even though he's dead, when I wasn't there… It just…" Hurt fills his eyes for a second, but he blinks it away. "I was such a…."

"Corin." His name is a whisper.

But I can see him now. The real him. Under all his confidence, arrogance, and his bristly exterior, there's insecurity about his relationships with those he trusts, those he values most. And I know it's been there since his parents were killed, and maybe it got bigger when he found that Rahn was secretly Enhanced for years. Because he's scared. I can see it. And stressed. We both are.

I squeeze his hands this time. "I *only* want you, okay?"

He nods. His bottom lip shakes. "But you *were* engaged to him. You were around him all the time—"

"I was engaged to you too," I remind him. "For what? A minute?" My smile gets sadder, even though I try to hold it up. "But, Corin, Jed sold me to Raleigh—I haven't got any feelings for him. You have to trust me."

Corin frowns. "You said he didn't know though—that it wasn't really Jed's fault. That Raleigh tricked him. It sounded like you were making excuses for him. And the way you said it, your voice was soft."

"Corin. Stop. It's you—*you*. I want you. Just you. Not

Jed. Not anyone else. *You.*" I kiss him again, holding his hands down by my sides, but I keep the kiss soft, sweet, short.

Short, because—

My vision blurs.

"Sev? What is it?" Corin's voice sounds strange, echoing and—

And then he swims away. Everything swims away.

Access granted.

FIFTY

I AM IN THE DREAM Land.

Somehow, I am in the Dream Land.

The bison is here. I recognize him immediately.

The Dream Land.

Oh Gods—I'm back, I'm—they let me back. And Death knows the truth—all the truth? He believes me? And now they all know. And I'm no longer exiled and—

And I'm in the Dream Land.

Oh Gods.

This is a warning. It has to be. That's how the Dream Land works.

But it's not quite right. Seeing dreams are supposed to start from the moment the Seer is in in real life. But I'm not this close to the city, I know that. And Corin and the dog aren't in this vision.

I frown. Little details aren't always right. Is this a little detail?

I turn slowly. There's no one here. It's just me, me in the desert, with the city in the distance.

I'm within sight of New Kitembu.

There are some rocks nearby, and I creep toward

DIVIDED

them, trying to keep low and—

And I see the men coming. Loads of them. Enhanced Ones. They are an army, hundreds of individuals moving as one. And they're coming. They're coming for me and Corin, I just know it.

One of us was detected.

And then they're right by me. Too soon, too quickly, and—

"There's one!"

The shout is loud, shrill, and it fills my ears.

Run.

I run.

My heart pounds, adrenaline fires through me. I run as fast as I can, snake between rocks, in and out. My feet throw sand up.

Their shouts are behind me, filling the sky, filling everything—reaching for me with their tendrils, trying to lasso me and yank me back.

My foot catches something hard, and I'm thrown off balance. My arms jerk out, and I change direction, risk a glance behind me. Angry faces, running toward me.

I force myself to run faster, try to look ahead, glad that my body's not hurting as much here. But I need cover, need something. A weapon? But there's nothing—nothing visible. Just the rocks on the sandy land. Nothing else.

The bison in the sky catches my eye, and I beg him to tell me something.

But he doesn't.

I run harder, feel my breathing get more even. A runner's breaths. The Enhanced shout more and more.

I look ahead, see Corin.

He's by the copse—we're at the copse already, and then the dog…the dog's barking, going mad and—

A gunshot fills the sky.

Run, the bison says. *Do not let them catch you.*

FIFTY-ONE

I GASP AS I OPEN my eyes, feel my breath flood into me. Corin's face hovers above me for a few moments—apparently on its own, just his head—before I see the rest of him.

"What is it? Was that—"

"Dream Land," I say, panting. Out of breath. Can't breathe. My head, my chest.

Corin frowns. "I thought you were exiled."

I struggle to sit up. My head it's—something's not right. So much pain. It's not normally like this after a Seeing dream, is it? I breathe hard, look at Corin. "They…let me back… Death must've believed me… We've got to…got to go…they're coming…."

"What?" And then Corin jumps up, pulls me up, and I nearly fall over with the momentum.

"The drones must've detected one of us! They're coming out here…the Enhanced got to the copse we were in!" I picture the trees, start to feel sick.

The branches are like jagged knives, cutting the sky. Cutting lives.

And everyone falls down dead.

Destroyed.

DIVIDED

I startle, don't know where that thought came from. I touch my head.

"Do they know you're alive?" Corin asks.

I try to remember the dream. "I don't know." I don't see how the Enhanced can realistically know it's *me*. I mean, they can't…unless they interrogated my mother, if she knew? Or Esther? "But they know there's at least one person out here. They have to know that."

"Which way do we go?" Corin asks.

"Away from the compound." I frown; my eyes feel old, tired. I pull the compass out my pocket. "We still need to get to where some spirits are—they could help us…" I turn and point. "That way! And we've got to be quick."

Corin stares at me. "Where the hell did you get that?"

"What?"

"The compass."

"It was in the car. The one you were sheltering under." I shake my head. "Come on, we've got to go… uh, that way."

I snatch his hand, and then we're both running. My terrier bounds next to me, on my other side. My heart hammers and pain forks around my body. White light flashes into my left eye a couple of times, and I wince.

Oh Gods. It really *was* a Seeing dream.

I'm back—un-exiled. Forgiven? *Access granted*. I heard those words, didn't I? The Gods and Goddesses realize now that I didn't choose to bind myself to the Enhanced? They must do. I've got access to the Dream Land again.

I'm a proper Untamed Seer again.

A smile breaks across my face, and—

A figure. A figure's running toward us, in the distance. My eyes narrow, and the land behind the person shimmers. But it's definitely a person. I tense, look around for a weapon, but can't see one. But I've got my powers. My stomach twists; using the white light on a person again will make me like Raleigh, and

I don't want to kill anyone, but—oh Gods, the figure's coming straight for us.

"Shit!" Corin yells, then he pulls me into a run fast, and we're going back the way we came—I think.

No. New rocks rise up. I look around, confused, try to remain calm as I run. There are trees far, far ahead, but they're the small, thin, wiggly kind. The kind that won't give us cover. And the land between them and us is flat—suddenly so flat—and we're too out in the open, exposed. But where's the copse, the copse we were in? Do we go there?

Oh Gods.

My heart pounds as I run, and the dog's speeding ahead. Sand sprays around us; for a moment, I think there are spirits about—invisible ones in the air, sending the sand up and—

My foot catches something, and I trip, start to fall. Corin yanks me up but the movement sends a spasm of pain through my ribs. I gasp, eyes watering. And he's pulling me along, trying to look behind us too.

I flick my head around again, need to know how long we've got. The person's nearer now. So much nearer. Gaining on us too quickly. Shit.

We scramble forward again.

"There's only one of them." My breathing's irregular, my words sound strange. "There were loads in the Dream Land warning."

Corin pants, and I see the wild look in his eyes. "But details can be wrong."

He trips a little, but recovers. The wind races around us.

"No, there've got to be more," I shout. They work in packs. Always. We know that.

Corin's hand tightens around mine and he's trying to pull me along faster—shit, I'm slowing. Didn't realize it.

The dog barks, and I look up, try to see him and—

A streak of dark fur races past me. Going behind me, back the way we've come and—no!

DIVIDED

I turn, crying out, and Corin yells something but the wind carries his words away, and—

"Sev!" Corin yells, and then he's turning and—

I see her. The person pursuing us. See her eyes, the lack of mirrors. She stops as my dog reaches her, and the terrier's yapping and jumping up at her, wagging his tail.

My mouth dries. The wind howls.

No. No. *No.*

It can't be.

Corin's hand in mine slackens. He looks at me, his eyes spacy.

"It's not her!" I yell at him, but the wind's so loud, and it steals my words, and it's laughing, because it knows, and it wants us to lose. "Corin! It's not her!"

But Corin takes a step toward the woman. His eyes narrow a little. "Esther?"

And then he's trying to move nearer to her, like he's compelled, not in control, and I grab his hand harder, grab it with both of mine, try to haul him back, but he pulls free, and then he's running toward her.

The muscles in my legs tighten. No. No. *No.*

"It's a trap!" I shout, my heart pounding. Oh Gods. "Corin! It's not her! Her hip—she can't be running!"

And it can't be her. It just can't. She can't be Untamed *and* have a fixed hip.

"Corin!"

But he's nearing her. My gut clenches. No. I'm going to lose him. Can't lose him and—

Body-share. Take control.

I freeze. But Corin—

The woman grabs him. I scream as her arms wrap around him, hugging him, and—

And she looks at me, thirty feet away. My breath catches in my throat. I flex my fingers, heart pounding, as I look at the relief in her Untamed eyes as she hugs Corin.

The door opens effortlessly and I enter her mind, her body. I feel Corin's arms around her, around me.

No pain at all. And the shock of it throws me out, back into my own body and—

How?

How? She was...her door before...it...she was Enhanced and...? Wasn't she?

I stumble backward, and the ground feels too soft. My knees start to bend, and I throw my arms out, wobble and the dusty ground meets me. I land awkwardly, pain everywhere. So much pain. Grit gets in my eyes, and I rub them, look up and—

They're coming toward me.

Esther and Corin. And the dog.

And it *is* her.

I shake my head, again and again, tiny, tiny movements. And then they're in front of me. Corin pulls me up and—

I frown. Try to see her hip. But it's—it's healed? I didn't feel it, in her body, did I?

Esther's smiling. Looking happy. Happier than I've ever seen her. Radiant. She grins widely, and then she's fussing over the terrier, and he's happy too. And Corin's happy and everyone's happy.

Then Esther looks at me. Her face changes.

The wind gets colder.

"Seven, listen," she says, but the way she says the words, it's as if they're daggers. Daggers that dig into me. I start to wobble, and I wait, feel strange.

"It's—it's Three," she says.

I feel a weight fall on me. I start to move my lips, but no sound comes out. I clear my throat, try again, and, at last, I make a sound—but it's no word. Nothing sensical. My heart pounds too fast, but too light. Dread fills me, weighs me down.

And it's like before...like when she....

"Three—we got caught." Her face is flushed. "I couldn't get him out too. I'm sorry. Raleigh was...."

And I don't know why I feel like I do. Because my brother's the enemy. When an Untamed is converted—*fully* converted—they're lost to us. You can't save

DIVIDED

them.

I shake my head firmly, force myself to say something. "He's Enhanced anyway, he's gone. Not the same person."

Somewhere deep inside me, a chasm rips open.

Esther wobbles as she looks at me. "No. Seven, he—he... I saw Katya. She told me she was making him resist...like projecting to him or something? I don't understand it, but she was giving him instructions at times, trying to get him to help us. We—Seven, he's still in there. *He* stopped them from converting me—and that was his decision. Not Katya's."

I stare at her. She wobbles. Corin looks at me, a hard stare in his eyes.

"And then Katya came for me, and she was a mess," Esther says. "Thought she was too late to save them from getting me, and she was so proud when I told her Three had saved me. She said maybe the Enhanced could resist if a Seer was helping? Ah, I can't remember! But—but Three had already gone back to his quarters, only a minute before. And Katya told me to get him out while she distracted Raleigh—but I couldn't do it. Raleigh turned up and—and I ran. I'm sorry." She gulps. "Raleigh was angry, and I left Three with him. And Katya was there and...and she said I had to get out."

I stare at her. At first, I can't take it in.

My mother was helping him? Three was... My head pounds. He gave me my pendant back, and I remember the words he said: something about my mother saying it had to stay in our line. He only gave it back to me because she made him? And when he stopped me escaping, that was really him. The Enhanced him: Tomas.

But then *Three* helped Esther. His first truly Untamed action?

"How did you get out? And how'd you find us?" Corin asks.

Esther exhales. "It was the weirdest thing—Katya

just…she said I had to get out, and then…then it was like she threw me here, and I saw you in the distance. Seer powers." She shakes her head in bewilderment.

"What about your hip?" I ask, and I know I'm partly trying to distract myself, trying not to think about Three—because it's too complicated.

Esther touches it. "Katya fixed it."

Seer powers? Could I have done that? Healed her?

Corin grunts.

I breathe out hard. "Right, well, we still need to be moving." I tell Esther about the Seeing dream and how we need to find a place with high spirit activity.

"But what about Three?" she whispers. "Seven—he's on our side! He's been resisting the whole time!"

I shake my head. It was my mother's doing, wasn't it? It was down to her. My mother helping a desire that was already there? Or creating it?

Does it matter which it is?

But what about now? And there's a voice inside me screaming. Three saved Esther. His own decision. Not my mother's.

I press my lips into a thin line.

"We can't go back there," I say at last, and the bison's warning rings in my ears: *Run. Do not let them catch you.* I breathe out, fast. "My mother's still there, right? Then…then she'll get him out."

It can't all be down to me.

We set off. The air feels strange. Like something's physically not right with it. Or maybe it's just me with this news about my brother… Three—resisting, because of our mother?

I sniff loudly. But the air doesn't get any better. It's—there's something wrong. Something big.

It's…it's something *huge*.

Something I can't put my finger on.

"There's some cover over there," Corin says, pointing to some vegetation that looks about four feet high. "I think we should go over. We're too out in the open here. And we don't know which way the

Enhanced will come."

I nod and—

And—and my mother appears in front of us.

Shock plasters her face, and then she's reaching out and touching me. Actually touching me, like she's really here and—

"Run!" she screams, and her hand is cold on my face. But she presses harder, presses her fingers into my cheek—checking I'm real, that I'm here? "Oh, my baby!" Her voice hiccups. "But run! Raleigh knows you're alive—he's found you! Run!"

He's found you.

Raleigh will always be able to find you.

I go cold.

My mother's hair whips around in front of her face, obscures her eyes. "Run!" she yells again. "Just run and find somewhere, and hide! Wait for me! I'm coming for you—on my way now! Together, we're stronger—but he's going to reach you first. Run!"

Corin swears and grabs my hand. The dog jumps up, hackles rising.

My mother's hand drops to my shoulder. My good one. "Seven, if he has you again, he'll use you to end the war. He'll control you—find a way to make you do it—and it will *all* happen. So run and hide!"

And then—then she's gone and—

And we see them.

The Enhanced. Rising out of the land like ghosts.

FIFTY-TWO

A DEADLY ARMY, FAR TO our right—not the right place? Doesn't match with what the Dream Land showed me. My breath catches in my throat.

"Run!" my mother screams, and I turn and look at her—as she disappears. Her mirror eyes go first, and then the rest of her and—

They're here already.

Oh Gods.

"Come on!" I shout.

I yank Corin to the left, and we're running. My feet skid on the sand, and the dog crashes into me. I stumble, but Corin grabs me. His eyes are wild.

"Which way now?" he yells, and, behind him, Esther looks scared. She reaches out, clasps his other arm.

But there's only one way we can go. Away from them.

I drag more air into my lungs, feel dizziness enter my body again.

Keep breathing. Got to keep breathing. But I'm breathing all wrong.

"Stop!" a voice yells.

The hairs on the back of my neck rise. Sweat breaks

DIVIDED

out across my forehead.

Lesson one: You can never outrun the Enhanced Ones. They are better, faster, and stronger than you.

I grit my teeth, grip Corin's hand tighter. The terrier streaks ahead. He's fast, very fast. I look around; where's Esther gone? She was right here a moment ago.

"Shit," Corin gasps. "They're—"

I turn, I look, and—

Guns. The metal of the guns, flashing under the bright light. The flashes scar my vision, leave murky streaks behind, and—

It's happening too quickly. It's just like the Seeing dream.

Run. Do not let them catch you.

My lungs burn and burn, they're going to burst. I can't get enough air. Not quickly enough. My Seer pendant slams into my chest with every step, harder and harder.

"Surrender at once, Untamed Ones!"

The voice is loud, so close and—

Hot breath on the back of my neck.

I turn.

Face to face with—with *Raleigh*. Super Enhanced and smiling. And so quick.

A jolt runs through me, and then Corin's hand's gone from mine. My hand…empty and—

Do not let them catch you.

A hot hand lands on me and—and it's Raleigh's.

Of course it's him.

"So, it's true. You tricked me." His voice is slow. "You broke my command on your soul. You died. But you came back."

I fight him, kick out, land a foot against his shin, but he shakes me, doesn't seem to feel it at all. Somewhere behind me, my terrier yaps—high-pitched and scared. I try to turn; has an Enhanced got him? But Raleigh's grip on my arm tightens.

I turn back and see his eyes narrow.

"You *tricked* me." He spits the words at me. "And you thought you could get away with this. You thought you could beat me. Do you want to know what happens to people who think they can beat me at my own game? Who think they can play me?"

Sudden pain sears through my head.

"You want to know, yes? I think you should know." His words drip darkness into me, and then the darkness changes. Shapes emerge. A man appears, in my head, and—

Three screams a guttural scream that comes from every ounce of his being. A scream of pain and fear. Proper fear.

I scream. "No!" And I'm trying to see Three, but the room he's in is dark. So dark, and I can just make him out—his body, as he writhes in pain.

Three turns and tries to move, but two Enhanced men unfold from the darkness and grab him. They hold him upright, between them, and my brother kicks out and screams, but he doesn't get away.

Bright light floods the room. Three's eyes fill with terror, terror that pushes the mirrors away.

I gasp, and I try to look away. But I can't.

"You need to see this." Raleigh's voice crawls over me like a thousand hairy insects. "You need to know what happens to those who trick me."

No. No. *No.*

Sweat pours in huge rivers from Three; his screams get louder. He turns and the metal on his face flashes under the brightness and—

One of the Enhanced grabs his head, holds him still.

"No! No! No!" *Three bellows, kicking out, screaming, crying.* "I didn't mean—"

The second Enhanced man steps up to him. His fingers go to the metal plate in Three's face, his metal cheek. The Enhanced One's fingers slide over the plate, down to Three's jaw. Then he sticks his nails into Three's flesh—the edge of the flesh, by the edge of the plate.

Three screeches.

The Enhanced gouges deeper. Blood spurts. Three writhes,

DIVIDED

but the other Enhanced holds him still—superhuman strength.

I scream as I watch the Enhanced rip the metal plate from my brother's face.

Raleigh chuckles.

"You don't play me and win." Raleigh's voice, low, dangerous, creeping over Three. "You never play me and win."

White light shoots toward Three. It hits him in the chest, square. And—

Three doesn't scream.

He just falls.

Raleigh's laughter fills the air, blocks out the sounds of Three's last breaths.

His last breaths....

My body jolts.

And I wait for more. Wait to see the image of Three getting up. But it doesn't come.

I stare at Raleigh, my eyes wide, fear pulsing through me. My breathing's too noisy, and there's something crackling in my ears. I shake my head.

"You killed him? You—" I clutch at my chest, feel sick, wrong, bad. And I feel it. He's dead. My brother's *dead*. My eyes water. "Why? He wasn't playing you, he was..." And I don't even know what I'm saying. Because he was playing him, wasn't he? He was becoming Untamed. He helped Esther get away.

And Raleigh killed him for it.

My muscles quiver. Heat flushes through me.

Raleigh licks his lips. "Oh, he was playing me all right. Your darling brother thought he could help you. Thought he'd be clever. He switched the grade of my physical alteration augmenters so you'd know it was me. He exposed me, and he thought he could get away with it."

I stare at him. I hear Corin shout something, and the dog's growling, and the wind's howling. My lips flatten against each other. Something pulses in my forehead.

He did that. Three did that?

No. My mother must've made him...she was getting him to do things and—

But if my mother knew it was really Raleigh, she'd have told me directly that it wasn't Corin, projected to me. Found a way. My eyes widen. She didn't know, can't have. It was...it was Three. The Untamed part of him. Trying to help me. Finding a way to show me the truth.

And killed—killed because of it.

Raleigh shakes his head savagely. "He thought he could play me. Pretended to be on our side, when, really, he was helping you. And he let you get away. He unlocked the compound doors that day as well. He left them unlocked. He made it easy for you to escape, even if you wanted a more dramatic exit."

My breath slows. And I left him there.

I should've taken him with me when I escaped. Should've realized he was on my side.

Raleigh looks up at me, and a sly smile spreads across his face. His top lip flares, shows me his teeth. "*I'm* still in control, Shania, regardless of what you think. I chose to have your brother saved before, when he was on the brink of death. But *my* killing powers are final. *This* is final. That memory I showed you—your brother is dead." His voice is too calm. Atrociously calm, and it wraps around me like toffee. Sticky. "See, Shania, I am a Seer of Life, and I can end life in a heartbeat. You'd do well to remember that."

I stare at him. He's still in control. He did that—killed my brother—to prove his control over me.

He killed my brother to make a point.

Something clicks in my head. A latch. Loud. Certain.

A door opens.

No! My voice.

No! Taras's voice.

No! My mother's voice.

No! Other voices.

"Do you understand?" Raleigh whispers. "I am

DIVIDED

going to win, and I'm going to make sure my people survive, that we live. That six billion people live. You're a Seer of Death. You're Untamed. Don't you see? That means your race *has* to die out. Unless, of course, you become a mass-murderer, and kill the majority of people in this world. Innocent people. But, then again, you are bad. Even Death himself chose you." He laughs. "Don't you see, really? You're misguided. You can't see it clearly. I can. And it's my responsibility—as a logical and rational thinker—to do the right thing. You're coming back with me, Shania. And you're going to connect to the other Untamed. I may not have command of your soul now, but I'll still make you do it. I know the frequency of your powers. It will be harder without owning you—but possible. And we're *going* to save everyone."

Raleigh grabs me and…and—

Three's body lies lifeless on the floor.

I scream as it sets in—as it really sets in. Something in me buckles, and then there's only heat. Heat that soars.

And things happen.

So many things, all at once.

Corin screams.

My mother screams.

Taras screams.

The blue-eyed Seer screams.

My terrier screams.

Everyone screams.

Raleigh yanks me toward him, and something burns the side of my face, eating me and—

Mirror. Mirror. Mirror. Corin. Esther. My mother. Mirror. Mirror. Mirror.

No.

The well of darkness inside me opens.

It is a volcano.

I am a volcano.

And I am erupting.

Red tongues lick and orange flames—they fly out

from me, from my hands, hot and—

Energy floods me. So much. Too much. It fills my body, pushes at everything, until it flies out of me. A continuous stream and—

Power.

Power.

Power.

I see faces. Faces all around me. Glimpses. Viktoriya. Dominika. Marina. Elf. Other Untamed I don't know.

Snap.

"Seven!"

That voice—my mother's voice, and then—

Then I see her. She's here.

"Stop it!" she yells.

But I can't stop. I *can't*. The flames are getting bigger, bigger, they're pushing out and—

He's *dead*! Raleigh killed my brother. Killed him.

I shriek. Sparks fly across the sky. Orange tears and yellow tears and—

The ground rumbles, shakes. Sand flies up—abrasive sand that hits me, scratches me, claws me and—

He's dead.

Raleigh *killed* him.

Red fills my vision.

I look for Raleigh.

He has to die.

He has to die *now*.

And I see him. I see Raleigh.

Nothing else matters. Not what Corin's screaming at me. Not what my mother is. Nothing.

I'm a Seer of Death.

And Raleigh knows that.

I know that.

We all know that.

And he *is* going to die.

I lunge for him, screaming. Send fire toward him—send it along the ground, and it does what I want it to do because it's mine. It's all mine, and it makes a circle around him. Flames shoot up in the sky. A wall

DIVIDED

he cannot pass.

The ground's shaking gets stronger, stronger. Rocks are moving, far to my left, rolling and—

"*Sev!*"

I let the fire grow. The sky above shimmers. Voices fill the land. Hundreds and hundreds of voices. A piercing wail pulls through me.

Something snatches at me, and I turn.

I am in the heart of the fire.

I stare at the flames. An orange basket around me, friendly, enticing.

Burn with us!

Burn with us!

"Stop it!" My mother's voice is louder, louder than the others. "Seven, stop it! Look what's happening!"

And she grabs me, pushes me back.

I trip, fall into the fire, but it doesn't burn me. It's my fire. It can't hurt me.

"Stop it! Stop the fire!" she yells. "It's tearing the—"

Something snaps—something loud.

I look up, my shoulders tighten painfully.

And I'm so small.

I am a speck of dirt in a universe so wide, a collection of worlds and planes and lands, and they're coming together around me, spinning and pulling, tugging and pushing.

I turn—a hand on my shoulder.

Ice and—

"No!" My mother screams, and everything crashes.

I step up, into the magic.

It shimmers around me.

The bison roars.

Glass shatters.

I reach it—I get there. My decision for the first time.

And Raleigh grins as he follows me into the one place no Enhanced is allowed to go: the Dream Land.

FIFTY-THREE

RALEIGH MARCHES INTO THE DREAM Land, and, for a second, he looks shocked. He takes a step back, looks around. Then his eyes get bigger and a wide grin unfurls across his face.

"Destroy it!" he commands. "Come in! Destroy it all!"

And there's fire and flames—but it's not my fire, it's—

I scream as the edge of a flaming cone passes over me, singes me—

They crawl in, the Enhanced Seers. They crawl in like ants. So many of them. So many Enhanced Seers. Ones I've never seen, and they're from all over the world. All these Seers—all these Seers who used to be Untamed.

The ones we lost.

The ones who turned against us.

My mother yells at me, and she's here too, following Raleigh and his army of Enhanced Seers—following them, but then she breaks off, runs toward me, and her lips are pulling as she shouts, looking too thin, far too thin, like they're going to stretch to breaking point.

DIVIDED

She reaches me, and—

And then the Untamed Seers are pulled here. Flashes of light, screeches, avenging figures. Power. So much power.

Five…ten…twenty….

And the Enhanced Seers—so many!

"Get them out!" a shrill voice cries. "They'll destroy the Dream Land, destroy our only advantage…there'll be no more Seers, no more—"

A Zharat Seer—the one who was part of mine and Corin's welcoming ceremonies—pushes past me. He screams, and he runs toward the Gods and Goddesses as they group together, far to the right—the Gods and Goddesses are *here, shrieking, shouting, fuming*—but they're shouting at him too. At the Zharat Seer.

"Get back!"

"Traitor!"

And then—and then every Seer—every single Seer, Enhanced and Untamed—is in the Dream Land. It all just…happens.

Seers.

Hundreds of us. A tide of energy, of power, of will.

The hot and angry air pulses around me. And there's tearing—something's still tearing, tearing because the walls are melting…melting because…because of me. And—

I feel the click as I shift into Esther's body—*Esther's*—down far, far below.

She screams a reverberating scream that draws a knife through the world—as she's….

I lose the connection, and then I'm in Dominika, in Elf, in an unfamiliar Untamed woman—one after another. Snap. Snap. Snap.

Elf? Alive?

"Seven!"

My mother's cry anchors me to the Dream Land, pulls me back, and I look and—

The land is bleeding. The sky is bleeding. Everything is—

A sickening crack.

White light shoots over me, in an arc. My mother pulls me to the ground. I taste the blood, the blood oozing from the land, and—

"I told you to run, to hide!" my mother screams.

"Seven!"

I look up at Taras's shout, duck just as a streak of white light hurtles toward me. I turn, follow it with my eyes and—

I see the Goddess at the last second. See her step into the comet's path, blocking it from an Untamed Seer. I see the look on the Goddess's face as the white comet hits her. See the way her body fractures into thousands of fragments, like a rock exploding, hear her shrieks and—

I scream as the pain takes over me, as—

Can't see.

I fall, can't breathe.

My lungs.

Out of the corner of my eye, I see my mother on the ground too—shaking, writhing, and everyone I can see is….

Another Goddess is dying…and the pain, it's too….

I turn my head, breathing hard. Feel saliva pooling in my mouth. But it's like syrup, thick syrup and—

"Come here!" Raleigh thunders.

And I see him. See him standing—he's shaking, the pain is etched on his face, the pain from the Goddess's death—but his arms are spread wide and then—then there's blackness behind him. And it emphasizes him. Makes him look bigger, and he's all there is.

"A Seer of Life versus a Seer of Death!" Raleigh throws a bolt of white light at me. I duck, and it flies over my shoulder. "But we've always known which of us—which of our people—is going to survive! And this is it!" he roars. "Come on, Shania—draw all your people here, call back up—make it more of a fair fight at least. Give yourself a chance! Bring all the Untamed here!"

DIVIDED

My people....

"No!" my mother roars. "Don't connect to anyone!"

White light flashes in front of me, and the blackness behind Raleigh deepens. And it can't have been blackness before, because it is now. Because there's nothing there.

A hole in the Dream Land and—

Raleigh screams.

Fear washes over me, a blanket.

And I see them. The Enhanced. *His* people. Loads of them. An army, all coming for us and—

And they're here. They're just *pulled* here. By Raleigh. They're not Seers, but they're here. The Dream Land and—

Oh Gods.

He's strong.

So strong.

Hundreds of them. Thousands.

Mirror eyes, everywhere.

"Destroy the Dream Land!" he cries. "Destroy this Untamed abomination!"

I struggle to my feet, manage it. My heart pounds, my body feels like it's on fire, like something's eating me. I cry out, raise my hand. Send white light toward Raleigh.

It misses him, but it reaches one of the Enhanced. One of the Enhanced who isn't a Seer and—

"They outnumber us!" an Untamed Seer yells. And she's by my side in an instant, reddish-blond hair catching me, wrapping around me as she pulls me back. And—

Blue eyes. *She's* the blue-eyed seer. Younger than I thought.

She seizes my hand, then we're running.

"We need more of us—more of us to fight them!" the blue-eyed Seer yells, and people race past us, around us, behind us. Deafening sounds echo through the land, and we blanch.

"But the Gods are on our side!" another voice yells,

and then another Untamed Seer joins us. A middle-aged man with a pot belly.

To my far right, I see Taras wielding white light, shooting it at a group of Enhanced as they near him.

The land shakes and dust flies up.

I turn, skidding to a stop and—

Dust whirls tightly around, giving substance to a figure.

Death has arrived.

He pushes back his hood.

Blinding light bites the world.

I scream as heat burns me, as I fall to the ground. The blue-eyed Seer falls with me, but the middle-aged man grabs us, hauls us up.

"Run!"

A gun goes off. And then several more shots follow.

I turn, heart pounding even faster. What the hell? They've brought their guns into the Dream Land? And they're—

"Destroy it! Destroy it! Destroy it!"

Something splinters. I scream, turning—see…see something fall. A mass of darkness. It crashes down, down onto the people, the Enhanced and the Untamed and the—

I feel the death of another God or Goddess. Or several. I don't know. But I feel the holes it makes in me. The man next to me gasps, and I turn, see the fear on his face and—

I don't see the gun, don't see the Enhanced. Don't even hear the actual gunshot or see the bullet hurtling toward him.

Just see him fall. See the blood appearing, the way it spurts in slow motion from his chest. How it rises in an arc, and splatters down in a pattern, like beautiful red raindrops.

I grab the blue-eyed Seer and run.

"We need more people!" she cries. "They've bringing more and more—we can't let them destroy the Dream Land!"

DIVIDED

And she's right. They're everywhere. Millions and millions of them. Closing in... The Enhanced are *everywhere*.

A wave of Enhanced rises in front of us. They move in unison, as if they're one body.

We scream, hold onto each other as we turn, and—

But we're surrounded by them.

White light bolts from my hands, and then the blue-eyed Seer's doing it too. We hit as many as we can, but there are so many of them. The pounding in my head gets louder. War cries fill the air.

Another Goddess is hit—I see her fall in my peripheral vision—and brace myself for the pain. More pain than ever, and I'm out of breath. Can't breathe. Everything's...rugged.

"We need to bring the Untamed here, even up the numbers!" the blue-eyed Seer pants.

"But it won't even it up!" I cry, my mother's words in my head. She told me not to connect to anyone. "There are too many of them, only a few hundred of us—"

"But—"

"Don't bring any here!" Taras yells at me, and he's running for us, running with speed and strength. "That's what they want! They're destroying the Dream Land! You're the only one who can bring the rest of our people here, and, if you do, they'll trap us, destroy us all. We'd *all* die. The war would end today. No, *we've* got to get out before they destroy the Dream Land—we can't leave our groups without Seers!"

Without Seers?

My mind reels.

Get out. Get out. Get out.

I turn and—but I don't know how to get out.

The blue-eyed Seer shoots a bolt of white light from her hands at another gang of Enhanced. Frazzling and sizzling sounds fill my ears.

Somewhere, my mother screams.

Her scream turns my blood into ice. It eats me.

I let go of the blue-eyed Seer's hand, yank away from her, and then I'm running, ducking under bullets and bolts of white light, skidding and slipping on the blood and—

Something splashes over me. My vision fogs red and—

Blisters rise on my skin. Fire.

I'm on fire.

I yell, throw myself down, try to—

Raleigh looms over me, smiling.

I send white light at him, but he sends his at me. I roll over, hear fizzling, somehow see my light hitting his, and his hitting mine, and they burst together, spray out over us. Over us both. Darkness and pain, but only for a second. I look up, see his eyes. His on mine. Mine on his.

Two feet exists between us.

"Come on, Shania. Bring your people here! Bring all of them here! Connect to them all now! Make it a fairer fight!"

"So you can kill us all, trap us all here as you destroy the Dream Land?" My ears pound, and I raise my hands, get another bolt of white light out. But it misses him, and I curse. "You'd die too! You and your people."

Raleigh grins. "It would still end the war. We'd be heroes, ridding the mortal world of evil and suffering. Leaving the world pure for the Chosen Ones still in it. Just bring them all here, bring the Untamed here, Shania!"

The land rumbles, and I can't move. My body's locking up—fresh pain and—

Raleigh screams.

I scream.

All the Seers scream.

Another God is dead.

And—

"No!" my mother screams.

Hands grab me, wrench me back. My mother. I

DIVIDED

know it's her, even though I can't see her. She drags me backward. And everything goes on around me.

It's like I'm frozen.

Like it can't happen to me.

I'm just...here.

And I watch.

Watch, transfixed as the army of Enhanced—so many of them—shoot the Gods and Goddesses. And they shouldn't be dying. They shouldn't be. They're *Gods and Goddesses*. But the bullets are killing them, and the Dream Land isn't strong enough, not now it's tearing, torn open—gaping black holes. And the Seers are reacting, in pain, can't breathe—

Like me. I can't breathe.

And as the Seers are falling, the Enhanced are killing more and more Gods and Goddesses, and they're shooting the walls of the Dream Land, the very fabric and—

It's my fault.

I let Raleigh in here. He followed *me*. He brought his army.

I ripped the worlds, broke into the Dream Land, and they—they all followed me and—

Traitor.

And the voice is right. I've ruined it. Without the Dream Land and the Gods and Goddesses, there'll be no more new Seers, no more warnings, no more—

Death's face looms in front of me, and he's screaming at me, but I can't make the words out. Not properly. Something about the augury and solitary confinement.

Then...then something tears.

A sickening tear.

"Seal it, Seven Sarr!"

Bang.

I look up. It's caving in. the Dream Land is caving in, falling in on itself and—

"Get out!" Raleigh yells and his voice is so loud. "She's not summoning them! We're going to die for nothing!" And then his army is disappearing. He's throwing them out of the world, and they're just disappearing and—

And then there's a black hole, a black hole that grows. A black hole that gets bigger and bigger. It reaches the edge where two Untamed Seers are, and then the Seers...they just disappear. They're sucked into the darkness in the blink of an eye and then the black hole is heading for a group of Gods and Goddesses. They're ripped away, and pain rips inside me, jagged, broken. Their deaths are quick and—

Run!

And I'm running, trying to outrun the darkness because I know if the hole takes me, then I'm gone. And I can't go. I've got to end the war, got to save my people, got to try, and—

Got to get out. The Untamed Seers, we need to get out—we're the *only* Untamed Seers, the Dream Land can't survive this—

Icy water lashes across my back. I turn, see the edge of the hole right behind me and—

Screams fill my ears.

How do we get out?

A flash of blinding light.

Two Gods left. Only two. Death and—and Life, I know it's him. Instantly, I know. He's small, very small. Blond hair. A kind face.

And they're coming for me, Life and Death, but they're struggling. I see the effort, the pain—feel the pain...and they're dying... Huge great holes appearing in them, holes as black as the external one.

They reach me, and Death is dying.

I feel it immediately. They both are. Pain emitting from tiny, tiny holes, like grains of salt, dissolving, spreading, contaminating water and purity.

Fine gold whispers of thread twist from Death's mouth. They form shapes, loosely at first, but they get stronger, bigger. Leathery lumps that twist and twist, yet they look graceful against the backdrop of the Dream Land ripping. And the shapes are words,

DIVIDED

Death's words, and they fly away, escape the black hole, and they're slipping between a seam and—

And they've gone.

"The augury will stand even without any Gods or Goddesses alive," Life yells, gasping.

The augury?

But Death's in the augury? I look at him. The augury can't complete without him. He can't call me back if he's not there. And that's the only way the war ends—he's told me enough times.

"Death has sent his words forward to call you back to his realm, even though Death will no longer be there." Waskabe's voice rasps into every part of my soul, spreading pain, and I think of those twisting shapes—his words? "The augury will still stand, even when we've fallen, and you will go to Death's harrowing realm—his cage for you—and reside there alone. Death owns you now, and Death will still own you. Death's commands are waiting."

A blast resounds through the land.

I flinch, cry out, and the Gods both scream. Their pain fills me.

"Seven Sarr, make sure the Untamed win, for Death's realm will know if they don't, and your suffering in his solitary realm will be greater if you fail."

Blinding light bursts forth, and every part of me burns, and Death's words resound through me. I twist and—and my body, it's....

Darkness and light.

Hissing fills my ears and—

And I see it all as if I'm not part of it myself, but I am. I'm divided, and I'm one. And I see it.

See it...and it's too much, watching Life and Death get ripped apart as they're sucked into the raging, storming cavity. My eyes shut. I can't—

Can't take it in.

"The augury will still stand, even when we've fallen!"

Hissing fills the air, and I'm suspended in it all, the last one here.

Everything rushes around me, leaving only blackness behind, marked with a pinpoint of light for each God or Goddess's grave. Life and Death burn the brightest, in the center.

And there's no one left.

The Gods and Goddesses—they've gone. All of them.

The bison screams—and I can't see him, just hear his screams. Shrill, loud, pain. And it's gone.

The Dream Land has gone.

FIFTY-FOUR

I STARE AT THE WORLD as I fall. Far away, I sense two Seers, and I reach out, pull them closer. They were getting too far away, and we need to be together—we have to be together. When we're together, the hope in the world gets bigger.

Divided, we are nothing.

And so I hold them close, these two Seers, and our powers recognize each other, and there's a moment of understanding, of—

The augury will still stand.

And then I see my body. Far, far below. And I fall toward it. Hurtling. Crashing down and—

My real body?

Corin's leaning over me, down there.

And I can't look away. Not from him. Not from me. From us.

Two people, together.

Silver strands around us. Tightly binding him to me.

I crash back into my body, land heavily, and—

Corin's breathing hard, saying something. He's covered in blisters, and I reach out, cup my hands around his face, watch the blisters heal and disappear.

His eyes widen.

And I stare at him.

He stares back. The silver strands have gone.

My lips burn and buzz. I look past him, toward the fire. Raise my hand, to make it go out, to make the land return to normal.

But it doesn't.

The fire gets bigger. And it burns, and the screams—the lost screams—fill me, lacerating and slashing.

"What's happening?" Corin's eyes remain wide.

Then he looks to the sky, where there's darkness swirling about, but, as we watch, the darkness gets lumpier. Somewhere, far away, there's a deafening crash. We flinch.

"The..." Pain resounds through me. *It's gone.* Gone. Gone. "The Dream Land's gone... They're dead...the Gods and Goddesses are dead."

All of them. And...and they're all *dead*. Gone. The Gods and—

But the augury will still stand. Death sent his words to his realm, to call me there...to command his plane.

Your body will rot under Death's command, long before your soul is allowed an escape from the decaying flesh of your ribs.

"What?" Corin stares at me. "Sev? The Dream Land's *gone*? It can't just go... It's..." Then he turns his face back to the sky, shakes his head.

The hairs on the back of my neck rise.

Behind Corin, I see movement. And it's like the world expands because I immediately see them, become aware of them: Esther and Taras and the blue-eyed Seer. They're all here. Taras stands slowly, rubbing his side. Scratches cover his face. The blue-eyed Seer is looking around, uncertainty and shock on her face. I stare at them, the two Seers, remember how I pulled them to me. Everything in me goes cold. Are we the only Seers left on our side? Did the others get out?

Then I see my dog. My little terrier. My heart nearly

DIVIDED

stops. He's cowering, cowering by some rocks, his back curving sharply up and down, all four legs pressed together. Trying to make himself smaller. His fur looks darker—darker with soot—and he's emitting a strange high-pitched noise that whines and wobbles. The fear in his eyes arrests me. He's looking down, but toward me at the same time.

I rush toward him, and he flinches. My dog. My own dog. Tears pierce the corners of my eyes, and I gulp, swallow, start shaking. I crouch down, space between us, and call to him. hold my hand out.

"It's okay," I whisper, and I stare at him, trembling.

"Sev," Corin says, but I ignore him.

To my right, I'm aware of the blue-eyed Seer stepping toward Esther, asking her who she is and where we are. And I detect their words even though the fire—my fire—is roaring and hissing and crackling and—

The fire.

It's still around us. I feel the heat promptly.

My dog whines. The flames are licking toward him, and—

My eyes catch movement behind him. In the flames.

My chest tightens.

My mother.

Another Seer here too. But she's Enhanced—thrown from the Dream Land by Raleigh? And, oh Gods. I didn't pull my Seers out the land...was I supposed to? I flinch, imagine their deaths. I didn't save them.

Or maybe they got away... Because Taras and the blue-eyed Seer were already out of it, traveling back, when I found them.

My mother stands in the flames, not far away, and she's trying to move, but I see the pain and the way it grabs her. And it's like a net, a net holding her down. And I need to reach her.

I surge forward, yell at Corin to get my dog, that I have to get my mother, but the fire burns my arm, and I scream—it's burning me now... Shit. I've lost control and—

"We need to get out of here!" Corin yells. "It's going to burn us—"

But everywhere we look, there's fire. So much fire. A ring of it, around us. No, it's everywhere. The world is on fire, burning everything and—

A deafening crack splits the sky, and six figures appear.

Rahn. Jed. Clare. Two men I don't know.

And Three.

The world stops.

My brother. He's here.

I see him, standing there, looking alive and Untamed and—

His gaze locks onto mine. A deafening boom resounds through the land. We both flinch, as if we're on the same string and that string has been tugged. A tug that pulls away a layer, that reveals the soul that's been fighting to be seen, but has been hidden for so long. The soul in his eyes. The *pain* in his eyes, like the cracked desert floor.

His hands are shaking.

"Sorry," he says. And the word breaks inside me, swims toward my heart. Sorry, sorry, sorry. A sound for each beat.

And I whisper the word back.

And then the spirits race toward us, and they shriek and shriek as the fire burns them and—

Rahn seizes Corin, who's struggling with the dog in his arms. I've never seen my dog so scared, so terrified.

Three looks toward me—the *sorry* and the pain still in his eyes—but he grabs Esther, and I see that pain turn to tenderness.

Clare gets me, grinning wildly.

The two unfamiliar spirits lift Taras and the blue-eyed Seer.

Jed goes for my mother. Or he tries to.

But he doesn't. He doesn't get to her in time.

I see it all.

DIVIDED

A woman falls in flames. She screams, and long, dark hair whips around in front of her face, obscures her features. Orange tongues rise around her. They eat her.

Her scream goes on and on, cuts the night.

And then it's over.

My mother.

Her vision of the far future. It was her.

Her death?

No! She can't die—she can't!

I scream, and then I'm fighting Clare's grip, and I'm breaking free, and I'm running for my mother again, running through the flames, and they grab me, burn me, eat me, and—

"Seven!" My mother's shout goes on and on and—

She's alive? What?

Blinding gold light wraps around me, knocks all the wind from me. Clare screams, and then her arms are like steel and she's lifting me up...flying and....

"No!" I look down see my mother, try to fight Clare, need to get to her and—

"You can't!" Clare yells at me, and she's shaking, shaking violently... Unstable—she's unstable. *"We've got to—"*

"Get my mother!" I yell at Jed, and he's just... floating there. "Get her!"

He dives into the flames and—

Colors fly past me. Shapes bolt and fly. Everything inside me twists. Rushing sounds fill my ears. I look down: the land is a blur and—

We're moving. Moving too fast.

To my right, I see Three and Esther—and—

My brother. He's...he's a spirit too. The Spirit Releasing Words weren't said and—and he's trapped.

Oh Gods.

Pain. Pain. Pain. And then—then, for a moment, I see something else. An embrace. Him and Waskabe. Not here, but...but *there*.

And Death's cloak covers Three.

Which of those closest to you will die for you?

The exchange.

But Three's here? Thrown back from Death's plane when Waskabe died? Thrown back here to help us and—

A blinding flash of gold. Esther shrieks.

I hear Corin shout and—

I feel Clare weaken; we plummet several feet. I scream, twist around in her arms and see her eye sockets getting bigger and bigger, too big for her eyeballs. And then one of them falls out. I follow it with my eyes, breathing hard, as it drops far, far below and—

And we're slowing, and the flames, they're still here and—

Heat washes over my feet and I look up, see how much higher the others are…how Clare and I are still falling. And she's shaking, weak, and—

Flames lick my feet.

I scream.

"Feed from me!" I yell, and she starts to protest. "Clare! You need energy! Just—just don't kill me."

For a moment, nothing happens and then…then my eyelids droop, and the world darkens until there's no light left.

FIFTY-FIVE

IT'S QUIET. SO QUIET. A faint hum in my ears. but even that is quiet. It's like the world's asleep.

I sit up slowly. Pain pulses through the left side of my head. I stare at the land around me…at the water lapping against the sand a few feet away. At the *sea*. We're…we're at the coast.

And there's…there are no flames here. The spirits moved us to safety.

"Where are we?" Corin's voice.

I jump, turn my head. He's just behind me, looks dazed. Esther's just to his right and—

And I stare at her. At her *heavily pregnant stomach*. She's….

"What the hell?" My voice comes out about ten times louder than expected, and, behind Esther, Taras and the blue-eyed Seer turn to me quickly. My dog's crouching next to the blue-eyed Seer, and he watches me warily. My heart squeezes.

Esther touches the…the bump, tentatively. Her face is pale. She's shaking. "It happened when Three… when he touched me. When his spirit… His spirit's Untamed. That's—that's amazing…if all the spirits are…even the ones who were Enhanced in life…."

Three. I look around. But he's not here. None of the spirits are. Just me and Esther and Corin and Taras and the blue-eyed Seer and—

And my mother.

She's lying a few feet away.

A strangled sob escapes me, then I'm running toward her—and…she's still breathing.

Still.

That vision. It was—it was wrong? My mother doesn't die?

I reach her, and then I'm trying to lift her up. We've got to go—I don't know how I know—but I do. We've got to get out of here. I don't know what's happened to Raleigh, but I know—I can feel it—he's not dead. He got out of the Dream Land in time, so did his people. And they're going to be after me, still.

Raleigh will always be able to find you.

I reach my mother, and everything inside me rips open.

"Come on!" I yell at her, and I try to lift her up again, trying to get her to stand, try to—

"Leave me. I'm dying." Her voice is sharp, like a short bark.

I shake my head. "No, you're not—"

But she nods. "I'm dying, Seven, and, even if I wasn't, I'm still Enhanced. I'm addicted to augmenters. There may be a small part that is Untamed inside me—a part that gets control when it can—but it is suffocating. It will not survive. I am Enhanced, Seven. And I have to die now…."

"No, you don't," I cry. "And you're not Enhanced. You can resist it! Overcome it. You did before."

But my mother shakes her head again.

"No, you *can*!" I yell. "I managed it, and you're my mum—I get it from you, my powers are from *you*. I am from you! We're the same—if I can do it, so can you!"

"I *can't* resist it. Not anymore. I will be a liability. You have to go. And I am dying—"

DIVIDED

Tears blind me. "But you must be able to resist, if I can—"

I sense Corin stepping closer, and his hand lands on my shoulder.

I flinch.

"Sev." His voice is soft. "I don't think it's about resisting, about being Enhanced or Untamed. Not for her, not now. She's…" He pulls me away, and I don't want to be pulled away, because I need to be by her side. But he holds me a few feet away from her. "Look at her, Sev. She's hurt badly. I'm sorry, but I don't think she's going to…."

I stare at him. And then Taras and the other Seer are looking at me. And Esther too. They're all looking at me, and I know what's on their faces. What they're thinking. But….

The terrier's doleful eyes watch me, and then he scurries over to her other side and pushes his nose into my mother's hand.

I shake my head. "No. She's not. She's going to survive." And they're stupid! Stupid for saying that!

"Look at her, Sev. Look at her *properly*."

Corin's words wash over me, and it's as if his words make all the burns appear, all of them on her face, her arms, her chest, her legs. The skin's broken and raw, shiny in places, sooted in others. Her throat makes a wheezy sound as she inhales. The dog licks her hand now, licks it once, twice, three times, keeps going, over and over again.

"I can heal her," I say, and I pull away from Corin, reach my mother. My terrier recoils a few feet.

I touch my mother's chest, I'm drawn to do it, and….

And I wait for her to heal as I pull on my powers and….

But nothing happens. But it should—I healed Corin. The blisters on his face: I did that, I healed them!

"It's too late, baby." My mother's voice is hoarse, croaky, doesn't sound like her. Can't be her. "And I know now. They told me I have to die."

"What? Who?"

"They told me, baby...and it...it makes sense... For you, my baby. And...and I couldn't live, not after this...not as an Untamed... I took too much."

I stare at her. My bottom lip wobbles. "The augmenters? No. Mum. You *can* resist them."

"No, baby." She reaches out and somehow manages to move her arm. She removes my hand from her chest, then grasps my fingers. "I took too much of it... I took part of Three's addiction so he could resist at times, and, baby, I poisoned the augmenters, used my Seer powers to do it...when I was strong enough. It was hard—doing it from afar. Some were more effective than others, especially at first...but all were bad for Untamed souls. I did it for you, so you could all resist. Even those without *your* soul. But doing it made me more addicted... I took your addiction—and theirs... all the addiction they should've felt, it came to me... and it's filled me up.

"I pushed it down, ignored it, pretended I was the same, but it has been eating me, making it harder and harder to...and I want them. So I *need* to go. It's time."

"What?" I stare at her, feel everything inside me crumble. "No! Mum, no—"

"You don't need me—not as I will be. And this is right... I feel it. This is what's supposed to happen. Seers of Light see far, and I've seen far, far ahead, beyond what is my life, because that vision... This—this is supposed to happen. I realize it now: I end in fire. You live on, baby..." She inhales sharply, closes her eyes, and her whole body convulses.

"Mum?" I squeeze her hand, but she doesn't squeeze it back.

For a moment, I freeze. No—no... But then her eyes flutter open again.

"Listen, Seven: bad things are going to happen to you..." Her voice croaks. "Be brave. My visions, they always happen, and these haven't yet... Stay strong. You can get through this. And I know you can win.

DIVIDED

You're a Sarr." She blinks, and a tear squeezes from her left eye. "I won't be *here*. But I'll still be with you, in your heart. And you end this war, yes? Then you can join me, just as the...."

I gulp, hold her hand tighter. "No—no, Mum, you're not dying, you'll be *here*." I try to smile, but I can't.

"It's too late to stop this from happening... And there are some things that have to happen, that are written into the fabric of the world. And I *have* to die for you to win. And we are shown some things, not so we can stop or change them, but so we can prepare. So we are not in the dark. And my death is the stepping stone to the last night... Let me go, baby. You have to let me go."

My eyes glass over. "Mum, no, don't... You're... you're all I have left now...our family, Mum. It's just you and me. You can't go, Mum. I can't... *I love you*." I'm shaking my head and hot, furious tears spill.

"Power divided is no power at all, Seven. You need this. They told me as I burned. Part of me has already gone. Don't let my soul get sundered."

She lifts her arm. It shakes. Her fingers are dry and hot, the skin peeling. She touches my face, and I see through her eyes, see through them like they're a portal to another place. A gateway.

A gateway that is a mirror, that reflects what is but shouldn't be. The inner truth that only a few see.

People.

People inside me.

The Sarrs.

All of the Sarr Seers.

And the first, the original, the first chosen by the Gods and Goddesses and spirits. Vala Sarr. I see and sense her, and, below her, is her daughter. I follow the line, find all the Sarr Seers in a blink of an eye, so quickly, all the generations, all of them created in the last two hundred and fifty years. And there's at least one new Sarr Seer for each generation, sometimes more; and later, other families were chosen too, but that doesn't matter. Because our lineage is the strongest. We have the original magic. We stand together.

And now there's just me.

And the people I see, the Sarrs inside me—I am connected to them all, I stem from her, from Vala, the original Seer. Direct lineage.

I see it all—know it all.

And it's…they're all in me…the previous Sarr Seers…they're here and in the New World… connections and…and so much power. I feel it.

Feel it inside me.

It is an angry tide crashing against the shore, throwing stones in high arcs. Driftwood arms try to reach the sky, but they can't. They fall, forgotten.

It is the roar of an engine, power under foot. Acceleration, fast, furious, angry.

It is the sinewy muscles of a silverback gorilla.

It is the savage canine of a long-lost saber-toothed tiger, the point of mammoth's tusk, the chiseled edge of an axe-head that bleeds.

It is the rush of blood from a wound.

And it is me.

It fills me, and I blink and it's mine—the power, the people… and the image of my ancestors has gone. Like everything I just saw is far, far away. A glimpse from another world. Hundreds of worlds and—

My mother.

The last blink.

No.

I stroke her face. My tears mark an army across her skin and her last breath tangles in a net of words that bloom in me, words that scorch into my soul. Words that write themselves into me. Words that become me.

You won't be alone, Seven. We are always with you, wherever we are, all with you. Ya Saba Moja. We are woven together, in you. And you are strong. You can resist because of your strength, because you are the accumulation, the pinnacle. And now, you will be the strongest Seer, the last Sarr, the goblet that collects us all together, that unites us.

DIVIDED

Send me off, baby, release me, and correct what mankind has done. We have been in the darkness for so long—the longest time with no daylight. Even when we think it is light, it is not. There is so much evil. Make the sun rise, make it rise properly. Make everything right again, because you have all our power now. You are ready now. End this war, drink from our goblet, embrace your rightful power, and end it with you.

Her last breath tangles in me. Her eyes shut. And….

And then it's over.

She's gone.

I feel it. And…and I should've tried harder… should've used my powers, should've healed her and….

The power in the Sarr bank boosts. I feel her power there, her…her presence?

Emotion wells up inside me. I grip her hand harder. No. No. *No*.

Corin touches my shoulder, and then he pulls me against him. I start to crumble. And then I'm screaming into his chest, and his arms are around me, and darkness lashes across the world.

I scream and I scream.

And I don't think I can ever stop screaming.

FIFTY-SIX

WE SEND MY MOTHER'S BODY off. I say the Spirit Releasing Words. I make the signs of the Journeying Gods and Goddesses, even though they're gone. I wonder if my mother will get to the New World without them all.

I wonder if I'll see her. If she'll join the Lost. If it's not really goodbye.

But I know it is, in that sense.

I feel it.

And I know.

She's a powerful Seer. She'll get to the New World. I just know it. Two did and...and I must've seen him... seen him in the gateway and didn't recognize him. But can I sense his power in the line too? After a moment, I think I can. Though I never really met him; he died when I was five. What I feel could be anyone's.

And so I say goodbye to my mother, and I feel her power in me, and I watch her body float away. Inside, I'm raw and screaming. It is a scream that can only stop when I stop. And stopping is what I want to do. But I mustn't.

Corin holds my left hand. Esther, my right. The

DIVIDED

dog's not far away, but he won't come near me.

Taras and the blue-eyed-Seer watch. She said her name is Jana, I think… I don't know. Time has passed. Too much time. And not enough. Conversations have happened—Jana's spoken of her people, and Taras has worried about his, now left unprotected—but I didn't really listen. It was when I was preparing my mother's body for the send-off. And I tried to make her look as beautiful as her soul is.

I tried but…but she was too burnt. And, realistically, a part of me doesn't know how she survived as long as she did.

Now, we walk away, just when her body's out of sight, claimed by the sea with the sparkling lights. The wind kisses the tears on my face. Dullness throbs through me, pulls me along.

The augury will still stand.

We keep walking.

I think of Three's face. The last time I saw him. My brother, a spirit. The pain in his eyes as he looked at me. *Sorry.* And the raw shame under that one word, layered over and over again. How his fingers shook. How he wasn't strong enough to resist by himself, not at first. How our mother couldn't make him resist all the time, only in glimpses. But how those glimpses must've got stronger. Because he then acted on his own. Twice.

And the first time was for me.

And now he's dead.

The only way I've got him back is through his death.

But he's free now.

Free, but still suffering.

Suffering. Suffering. Everyone's suffering.

But maybe my mother isn't.

"What do we do now?" Corin asks, his voice low. The terrier's walking on his other side, about three feet away, and he's limping slightly.

A hardness creeps into me. It fills my body. Turns me to stone, stone that shatters into fragments. Fragments that scratch and tear me up.

"We beat the Enhanced," I say. "And we unite the Untamed." I look across at Esther, then Taras and Jana. It's already happening. I know it is. Our numbers are growing. "We unite the Untamed. We all come together, and we find out if there are any more of our Seers out there, others who got escaped the Dream Land in time. And we get stronger. We get stronger, and we end the war."

And it's going to end soon. The augury said I was the strongest Seer, and now—with my mother's powers boosting the Sarr legacy inside me—I *am*. I feel it. The power is mine.

And I don't know how exactly I'll win the war for the Untamed, but I know I *will*.

And I'll do it soon.

I look up into the sky.

The darkest night—*the last night*—is starting.

END OF BOOK THREE

ACKNOWLEDGEMENTS

In many ways, *Divided* is probably the hardest book I've written, and I'm so grateful to all the wonderful people who have helped me with this manuscript and given me encouragement when I most needed it.

To Rachael Bundy and S.E. Anderson, my wonderful critique partners: thank you. Your enthusiasm for this series is so uplifting, and the detailed feedback you've given me is incredible. I'm so grateful to both of you for the time you took to read countless drafts and passages of this book—as well as the *hours and hours and hours* you've spent workshopping different parts with me, even fitting these sessions into your already-busy days. You rock! I also love how we talk about my Untamed characters like they're real people (and how, in public once, Rachael and I probably left those around us wondering what kind of people we associate with, when we spoke about how creepy Raleigh can be—using plenty of examples).

I also need to thank T.A. Maclagan and Katlyn Duncan, my wonderful beta-readers—your comments helped greatly. And Kiersi Burkhart, my accountability partner, thank you for keeping me on track with everything and for regularly checking in with me to see how it was all going and that I was meeting my daily word count goals. It was great talking to you on those days when I was stuck in the writing/editing cave with no idea of what was going to happen next for Seven—and your reassurance meant a lot. I did *finally* finish those revisions that I thought would beat me!

My writing groups have also been thoroughly amazing, not just in the technical advice they've offered, but in just being there and supporting me and my books. So, my heartfelt thanks must go to everyone in the YA Story Sisters, the Dry Spell Writers, and the YA Writers' Critique Group HQ. Other authors I wish to thank for their on-going support are Stephanie Burgis, Deva Fagan, Megan Crewe, Tara Kelly, Dana Mele, Tiffany Schmidt, Catrina Burgess, Clara Kensie, Kimberly Sabatini, Tracy Clark, Jennifer Brody, Pintip Dunn, E. Mitchell, Lizzie Colt, and Kari Trenten. And additional thanks must also go to S.E. Anderson and Tracy Clark for blurbing *Divided*.

I'd like to thank Stephan Dudeck for the insight his blog (https://stephandudeck.wordpress.com/) gave me into indigenous groups of reindeer herders from his fieldwork in the Arctic. It was fascinating learning about the cultures of these different groups, and the information gave me a good grounding upon which I was able to build my own fictitious group of reindeer herders.

Next up in the list of people I must thank is my awesome editor, Michelle Dunbar. THANK YOU! Seriously, you've helped in so many different ways, and I can't thank you enough for all you've done. I can't wait to work with you again.

Molly Phipps: with your stunning cover art and interior designs, you've really made *Divided* come alive. Thank you. I'm so proud of the book that *Divided* has become, and I can't wait to see the designs you create for the final book in the Untamed series!

To my friends: thank you for being so supportive of my writing, even if it means I don't always reply to your messages as quickly as I should, and, that when we meet up, I'm often talking about the characters in whichever manuscript I'm currently working on… Your support honestly means a lot.

Huge thanks must also go to my parents, my brother, and the rest of my family; as usual, you have been great and your support never-ending. I'm very lucky to have you all.

And finally, to my readers: thank you. Your support means the world to me.

ABOUT THE AUTHOR

MADELINE DYER lives on a farm in the southwest of England, where she hangs out with her Shetland ponies and writes young adult books—sometimes, at the same time. She holds a BA Honors degree in English from the University of Exeter, and several presses have published her fiction. Madeline has a strong love for anything dystopian, ghostly, or paranormal, and she can frequently be found exploring wild places. At least one notebook is known to follow her wherever she goes.

Find Madeline online:
Twitter: @MadelineDyerUK
Instagram: @MadelineDyerUK
Facebook: MadelineDyerAuthor
Website: www.MadelineDyer.co.uk

Sign up to Madeline's Newsletter:
http://madelinedyer.co.uk/newsletter/

THE STORY CONCLUDES IN . . .

LOVE. DEATH. SACRIFICE.
THE LAST NIGHT HAS BEGUN.

Seven Sarr, the most powerful human in the world, is alive—and she's on the run from her enemy. With the Dream Land gone, the Gods and Goddesses dead, and the Untamed's number of Seers at a record low, Seven knows her people must attempt to work with the Lost Souls—including the most volatile and dangerous spirits—if they're to have a chance of beating the Enhanced Ones once and for all.

But when the Enhanced impose a new threat and Corin's life is at stake, Seven must make her hardest choice: save the man she loves and let her people perish, or allow Corin's death so the Untamed can survive.

Locked into a tight countdown to her own demise and solitary entrapment within a torturous realm, Seven must make her decision quickly. Her Seer powers are the strongest, and her death will end the War of Humanity once and for all. When the new morning dawns, the world as she knew it will be gone. What—and who—will be left behind is up to Seven.

Will her love shape the future of the world?

COMING SPRING 2018

Made in the USA
Columbia, SC
09 July 2017